Acknowledgements

As always, my thanks go to my mother, Mary Redmond, for being the first person who encouraged me to write.

Secondly, my thanks go to my cousin, Anthony Webb, and to my friends who all offered encouragement, advice and patient good humour whilst suffering heavy doses of my so-called creative angst. A big thank you to David Bullen, Emile Farhi, Paula Hardgrave, Simon Howitt, Iandra MacCallum, Rebecca Owen, Lesley Sims, Gillian Sproul, Russell Vallance and last but not least, Gerard Hopkins, for serving an exceedingly good curry.

Thirdly, my thanks to my agent, Patrick Walsh for all his efforts on my behalf, and to my editor, Kate Lyall Grant for her ongoing faith in my work.

Finally, my thanks to Ian Chapman, Suzanne Baboneau and all the team at Simon & Schuster.

Apple of My Eye

Apple of My Eye

Patrick Redmond

SIMON &
SCHUSTER

London · New York · Sydney · Tokyo · Singapore · Toronto

First published in Great Britain by Simon & Schuster UK Ltd, 2003
A Viacom company

1 3 5 7 9 10 8 6 4 2

Simon & Schuster UK Ltd
Africa House
64–78 Kingsway
London WC2B 6AH

www.simonsays.co.uk

Simon & Schuster Australia
Sydney

A CIP catalogue record for this book is available from the British Library

ISBN 0 7432 1993 7 (HB)
ISBN 0 7432 1994 5 (TPB)

Typeset by SX Composing DTP, Rayleigh, Essex
Printed and bound in Great Britain by
The Bath Press Ltd, Bath

To Mike

Prologue
Hepton, Greater London: 1945

A late afternoon in June. In the stuffy office with grey walls the doctor cleared his throat and prepared to act out the scene he knew by heart.

'There's no doubt. You are pregnant. About five months, I'd say.'

The girl made no answer. But then it could hardly have come as a surprise.

'So no more starving yourself. You need to keep your strength up. After all, you're eating for two.'

Still no answer. He sat back in his chair and studied her. She was a pretty thing; strawberry blonde hair, delicate features, pale blue eyes and no wedding ring. A small hand rubbed at a lower lip. The white blouse and knee-length skirt made her look like the child she still was. Her name was Anna Sidney and she was three months short of her seventeenth birthday. He had read that in her file. And he had read some other stuff too.

'Is the father a soldier?'

A nod.

'Is he still here?'

'No.'

'Do you know where he is?'

A pause. The hand continued to rub at the lip. 'No.'

He shook his head, having seen it all before. Naive, romance-starved girl meets libidinous, silver tongued soldier and is charmed into losing her virginity and much else besides. Someone had told him once that a woman learned to desire the man she loved while a man learned to love the woman he desired. Only some men were very bad learners.

But that was just the way of the world. He was old and tired and there was nothing he could do about it.

He picked up his pen. 'You need more vitamins. I'll give you a prescription.' His tone was brusque and businesslike. 'And you'll have . . .'

'He will come back.' Her voice was soft as a whisper. 'I know he will.'

'No he won't. They never do. Not in real life. Only in films.' He carried on writing, trying to be quick. Longing to get home to his supper and bed. In the street outside a man walked by, singing loudly. It was only a month since VE Day and the sense of euphoria was everywhere. Peace after six long years.

The nib of his pen scratched on the paper. A drop of ink fell on to his desk. He looked up, searching for some blotting paper, and saw that she was crying. He remembered her file. What he had read.

And felt suddenly ashamed.

He put down his pen. She was wiping her eyes with her fingers. There was a clean handkerchief in his drawer. 'Here,' he said gently. 'Use this.'

'Thank you. I'm sorry.'

'Don't be. Forgive me if I sounded harsh. I didn't mean to. Life should be like the pictures, only most of the time it's not.'

'He told me that he loved me. That he'd send for me. That we'd be married.'

Of course. That was what they all said. But perhaps the words had been meant.

'Do you like the pictures, Anna?'

'Yes.'

'Who's your idol? Clark Gable? Errol Flynn?'

'Ronald Colman.'

'My wife and I enjoy his films. The characters he plays. Kind and honourable. There isn't enough of that in the world.'

'He looks like my father.'

Again he thought of her file. Thought of the hard road she had travelled and the harder one that lay ahead. There was little comfort he could offer but still he felt the need to try.

'Anna, people are going to try and make you feel ashamed. Don't let them. A new life is growing inside you and that is a wonderful thing. My wife and I wanted a child of our own more than anything but we were never blessed. And that's what it is, Anna. A blessing. No matter what anyone says to you, never lose sight of that.'

She looked up. Her tears were slowing. 'I won't,' she said, and suddenly there was a world of dignity in her voice. 'Because he meant what he said. He loves me and now the war is over we will be together.'

'I hope so.'

'I know it.'

That evening, after supper, Anna told Stan and Vera.

The three of them sat at the kitchen table of the house in Baxter Road. The window was open, looking out on to the tiny back yard that Vera insisted on referring to as a garden. The breeze, tinged with the scent of a hundred meals being cooked in neighbouring houses, never quite dispelled the smell of stale chip fat that hung in the air like invisible fog.

'I knew it,' Vera announced. 'I said something was up.'

Stan nodded. He was a cousin of Anna's father. A tall, thin man with receding hair, slack chin and asthma, who worked in a can factory two streets away.

'I'm sorry, Stan,' Anna whispered.

A sigh. 'Well, I suppose these things do happen.' His expression was sympathetic. Though a weak man, he tried to be a good one.

But it was not his reaction which mattered.

'Not in my house they don't.' Vera's small mouth was set in an ominous line. She was tall, like her husband, but twice as wide. 'How could you do this to us after all we've done for you?'

Anna stared down at the tablecloth. From the living room came excited squeals as four-year-old Thomas and two-year-old Peter raced toy cars across the floor.

'You had nothing. We took you in. We gave you a home and family and you repay us by acting like some tart.'

'It wasn't like that.'

'How did it happen, then? An immaculate conception?'

'We love each other.' Emotion rose up in her. She fought against it, not wanting to seem weak. Not now.

3

'So where is he? This knight in shining armour.'

'I don't know.'

A snort. 'You don't know anything about him!'

But that wasn't true. She knew his name was Edward. That he was twenty-five and nearly six foot tall. That he was not classically handsome but had beautiful grey-green eyes and a smile that could release a million butterflies in her stomach. That he had a small birthmark on his neck which he called his little map of England. That he spoke with the faintest trace of a lisp. That he was clever, funny and kind. And that they loved each other.

'You fool! You don't have the brains you were born with.'

'Don't be too hard on her,' said Stan suddenly. 'She hasn't had it easy.'

'None of us have had it easy, Stan Finnegan, but we don't all spread our legs the first time some squaddie gives us a smile. We've done everything for this girl and this is how she repays us. We gave her a home . . .'

And so it went on. The anger, the contempt and the constant reminders of all she owed them. She sat in silence, feeling as empty and afraid as she had on the day three years earlier when she had returned home after spending the night with a friend and discovered that a German bomb had destroyed her house and the lives of her parents and younger brother.

Stan and Vera had taken her in. Given her somewhere to live. But it was not a home and they were not her family. She was an outsider. Tolerated but unwanted. And sometimes at night, in her bed in the tiny room at the back of the house, she felt so alone that she wished the bomb had killed her too.

'Well, you can forget about keeping the baby. You're having it adopted and that's that. The last thing we need is another mouth to feed. Particularly not some squaddie's bastard.'

A lump was forming in her throat. She swallowed it down, determined to be strong. Not to let Vera win. To hold on to some last vestige of pride. Closing her eyes, she strained to hear the voice in her head that had once been as loud as thunder but now grew fainter with each passing day.

He loves me. He will take me away from this and we will be happy for ever.

He loves me and he will come and save me. I know he will come. He has to come . . .

October.

Nurse Jane Smith looked about the maternity ward. Visiting hour was well under way and combinations of proud parents, happy husbands and curious children sat around every bed, clucking over the screaming bundle that the tired mother held in her arms.

Every bed except the one that contained the pretty girl with the strawberry-blonde hair.

The crib at the foot of the bed was empty. The baby had been born the previous day after a hard labour. It had been a boy. Seven pounds, nine ounces and perfect in every way. A baby of whom any mother would be proud. A baby who would be loved by his adoptive parents as soon as he was handed over to them.

He was being kept in a separate room. The adoption papers were being signed the following day. Then it would be final. Signed, sealed and delivered. Those whom the legal profession has joined let no natural mother set asunder.

The table beside the bed was bare of flowers and cards. Just as the left hand was bare of a wedding ring. There had been no visitors. No telephone calls. No sign of anyone who cared.

The girl sat staring into space. Her skin was ashen; her expression numb. On the wall behind her head faded bunting still hung. A remnant of the celebrations that had greeted VE Day. In this atmosphere of joy and rejoicing she looked completely out of place. A small, broken creature, totally alone.

Jane knew that it was none of her concern. Decisions had been made, forces set in motion. She had no right to interfere.

But she was a mother herself. One who had lost her husband on a French battlefield four years earlier, and with him her will to live. Until that day, three months later, when their newborn daughter had given it back to her.

And that gave her every right.

Five minutes later she approached the bed, walking through air that was thick with laughter and the smell of excrement and warm milk. In her arms was a crying baby boy. Seven pounds, nine ounces. Perfect in every way.

'Anna.'

No answer. The eyes remained focused on the far wall.

'Look, Anna. Please.'

Still no response. The arms hung limply by the sides. Gently, Jane placed the baby in them, bending the elbows, massaging them into a makeshift cradle. Then she stood back and waited.

The baby wriggled, clearly not comfortable. The mother's face remained impassive.

Then, suddenly, the baby quietened and lay still.

'He knows you, Anna. He knows who you are.'

Slowly the eyes turned downwards. The baby began to gurgle, stretching up one arm.

'He's saying hello. He wants you to like him.'

More gurgles. The tiny face formed itself into a smile. The doctors would have dismissed it as a contortion of the features. Perhaps they were right. But every new mother in the world would have known different.

'He's perfect, Anna. Perfect in every way. And he needs you. You need each other.'

The eyes remained focused on the baby. The numbness was fading, replaced by wonder, together with the first traces of a reciprocal smile.

'But if you want him adopted that's your choice. No one can stop you. Give him to me now. Let me take him back.'

She waited for the protest. None came. But no relinquishment either.

'Is that what you want, Anna? For me to take him away? To never see him again?'

Silence. A single moment that seemed to last an age.

Then a soft whisper. 'No.'

The smile remained. One finger slid around the outstretched arm.

'He's yours, Anna. No one can take him from you. Not if you don't let them. Fight for him. He is worth it.'

She slipped away, back into the bustle of the ward, leaving mother and son to become acquainted.

*

Midnight.

The ward was quieter now. One baby cried; an exhuasted mother snored. All else was still.

Anna Sidney gazed down at her newborn son.

He was sleeping. Earlier she had fed him for the first time. In spite of her anxiety it had gone better than she had dared hope. As if he had sensed her nervousness and wanted to make it easy for her.

His forehead was covered in lines. Nurse Smith had told her that all newborn babies looked like old men for the first few days. Then the skin smoothed out and they became beautiful.

But he was beautiful now.

She traced the lines with her finger, remembering a similar pattern on the forehead of her father. His name had been Ronald. Like her idol Ronald Colman. It was a name she had always loved.

The baby stirred and half opened his eyes. The corners of the mouth stretched upwards. A weary smile.

'Hello, my darling. My angel.'

Hello, Ronnie.

Rocking him in her arms, she began to sing:

> *You are my sunshine, my only sunshine.*
> *You make me happy when skies are grey.*
> *You'll never know, dear, how much I love you.*
> *Please don't take my sunshine away.*

The eyes closed again. He drifted back into sleep. A crinkled Buddha, wrapped in a blanket, lost in a world of dreams.

She wondered whether his father would ever see him. It had been five months since the declaration of peace in Europe and still she had heard nothing. Perhaps he was dead. Perhaps he had just forgotten her, his declarations of love as hollow as a drum.

But it didn't matter. Not now.

Who will you look like, little Ronnie? Your father? My parents or my brother John? The only four people in this world I've ever loved.

All were lost to her now. But when she gazed down at her child she felt as if she had found them again.

No one would take him from her. She would kill anyone who tried. Vera would be furious; perhaps try to order her from the house. But she would stand her ground and fight back. And she would win. A strength was building inside her. One she had never known before. She had Ronnie to take care of and she would die for him if necessary.

There was movement near by. The woman four beds along had risen and was checking on her daughter, Clara. Clara was a foul-tempered baby with a face like a bulldog who did nothing but feed, scream and vomit. Clara wasn't beautiful. Clara wasn't perfect.

Clara wasn't Ronnie.

He stirred in sleep but did not wake. Safe within her arms. The two of them bound together for ever.

Sleep well, my darling. My angel. My little ray of sunshine. My little Ronnie.

Little Ronald Sidney.

Little Ronnie Sunshine.

Part 1

Hepton: 1950

A slow Saturday in May. At the counter of the Moreton Street corner shop, Mabel Cooper read a magazine article about Elizabeth Taylor's recent wedding. Nicky Hilton looked very handsome, and the writer of the article was sure that Elizabeth had found a love that would last for ever. Mabel was sure of it too.

Footsteps signalled the presence of customers. Her forced smile became genuine when she saw the pretty young woman who led a little boy by the hand.

'Hello, Anna.'

'Hello, Mrs Cooper. How are you?'

'All the happier for seeing you and Ronnie.'

'Is your sister feeling better?'

'She is, dear. Bless you for asking. And how are you today, Ronnie?'

Ronnie looked thoughtful. 'I am very well today, Mrs Cooper,' he said, speaking slowly and deliberately, as if considering each word before it was uttered. Though not yet five, he had an old-fashioned dignity of manner that Mabel found enchanting. He was the image of his mother. The only difference was in the colour of the eyes. Hers were blue, his grey-green.

Mabel folded her arms and pretended to frown. 'Ronnie, what are you to call me?'

The solemn expression became a smile. 'Auntie Mabel.'

'That's right.' Mabel smiled too. 'And what can I get you today, Anna?'

A special look passed between Anna and Ronnie, just as it did every Saturday. Mabel reached under the counter and produced a small notepad and a new pencil. Ronnie's smile became radiant.

'He's already filled the last one,' said Anna, her voice swelling with pride. 'A different picture on every page and all of them wonderful.'

'Next time you must bring some to show me. Will you do that, Ronnie?'

'Yes, Auntie Mabel.'

Mabel's husband Bill appeared from the back room, crumpled after his nap and bringing with him the rich scent of pipe tobacco. 'Hello, Anna. Hello, Ronnie.'

'Hello, Mr Cooper.'

'Ronnie, what are you to call me?'

'Uncle Bill.'

Bill handed Ronnie a chocolate bar. Anna looked anxious. 'I don't have any coupons.'

'That can be our secret.' Bill gave Ronnie a conspiratorial wink which he returned.

'You start school next year, Ronnie. Are you excited?'

'Yes, Auntie Mabel.'

'Are you going to work hard and make your mother proud?'

'Yes, Uncle Bill.'

'Good boy.'

Anna paid for the notepad and pencil. 'Thank you for the chocolate. You're both so kind.'

'A pleasure,' Mabel told her. 'Take care, dear. Look after your mother, Ronnie.'

'I will, Auntie Mabel. Goodbye, Uncle Bill.'

'Goodbye, Ronnie.'

'Poor girl,' said Bill once Anna and Ronnie had left. 'Can't be easy for her.'

'Especially living with that awful Vera Finnegan.' Mabel shook her head. 'I'm just thankful the father wasn't a Negro. Imagine if Ronnie had been coloured like Elsie Baxter's friend's baby. Yesterday Elsie was telling me . . .'

'You spend too much time gossiping with Elsie Baxter.'

'That's because it's more fun than gossiping with you, Mr Keep-your-nose-out-of-other-people's-business.' Mabel's expression became thoughtful. 'I don't think Anna would change anything, though. She absolutely adores that boy.'

'He's a good lad. Mark my words, he'll make her proud one day.'

Friday evening. Anna followed the other secretaries out of the typing pool and into the yard of Hodgsons can factory.

It was full of men, smoking, laughing and radiating the good cheer that came with the end of the working week. Some wolf-whistled as the more attractive secretaries approached. Judy Bates, a lively blonde of eighteen, blew them a kiss. Ellen Hayes, an older secretary, shook her head disapprovingly. Ellen thought Judy the sort of girl who would land herself in trouble. She had once said this to Anna over a cup of tea before realizing to whom she was talking and hastily changing the subject.

Anna walked with Kate Brennan, a cheerful girl the same age as herself. As they crossed the yard Kate was hailed by Mickey Lee, a machine operator. Kate touched Anna's arm. 'Have a nice weekend. Give Ronnie a kiss from me.'

'I will. You have a nice weekend too.'

Kate hurried towards Mickey, her slim figure giving no indication of the baby she had borne five years ago. An illegitimate girl, fathered by a soldier just as Ronnie had been. The child had been adopted and Kate never talked about her now. Acted as if she had never existed. But sometimes Kate would stare at the tiny picture of Ronnie that Anna kept on her desk and a troubled look would come into her eyes. There for a moment and then gone, replaced by a smile and a joke about nothing in particular.

As they approached the gate, Anna saw Harry Hopkins, a small, serious man of about thirty. Three years earlier Harry had started taking her out, and after six months had asked her to marry him. Though not in love, she had been fond of Harry and willing to build a future with him. Until that moment when he had said, very gently, that it wasn't too late to have Ronnie adopted . . .

Their eyes met as she passed. Each smiled, then looked quickly away.

Stan stood at the gate, wearing the suit that hung much less comfortably than the overalls he had once worn. He had a minor managerial role now and sat behind a desk all day. Anna knew that he would be happier back on the factory floor but neither hell nor high water could have persuaded Vera to renounce her new status as a manager's wife.

Together they passed through the gates and up the road towards Hesketh junction. To the right was Baxter Road and the other narrow streets full of tiny houses with outside toilets, packed in together like sardines. Until last year that would have been their route. Now they turned left, towards Moreton Street and the more prosperous area occupied by the aspiring middle classes of the town.

Stan told her about the events of his day, trying to make them amusing. He was no comedian but she laughed to make him happy. Five years ago it had been Stan who had supported her decision to keep Ronnie, refusing to throw her out of the house in spite of Vera's demands. It was the one time she had seen him stand up to his wife.

They entered Moreton Street: a nondescript road of semi-detached houses, built in the 1930s. Their house was on the right-hand side, backing on to the railway line that carried trains from London to East Anglia. At the corner of the street was a tiny park where a group of boys played football. Nine-year-old Thomas stood by a makeshift goal, talking to Johnny Scott, whose elder brother Jimmy had already been in court for theft. Vera did not approve of the Scotts and Thomas was forbidden to associate with Johnny, but Stan hadn't noticed them together and Anna was not one to tell tales.

Half a dozen smaller boys played football in the street. Seven-year-old Peter scored a goal and was congratulated by his teammates. Mabel Cooper stood outside her shop, talking to Emily Hopkins. Mabel gave Anna a cheerful wave. Emily did not. She was Harry's sister and had opposed his involvement with Anna from the start.

As she walked on, Anna thought of Kate and Mickey spending their evening watching a Robert Mitchum picture before eating fish and chips on the way home. Hers would be spent making the supper and doing whatever chores Vera decreed.

But that was how things were. She had made her bed. It could not be unmade now.

A cry disturbed her thoughts. Ronnie was running down the street, his feet moving so fast they barely touched the ground. His shorts, handed down from Peter, were still too big for him. His socks hung around his ankles. Flinging his arms around her, he began to tell her about his day; words pouring out of him like a torrent so that she could barely make sense of them while Stan stood by, watching them both with a smile.

As she gazed down at him love consumed her, burning away regret like a blast furnace devouring a sheet of paper.

On Saturday evening Ronnie knew it was his turn to have a bath.

Each member of the household had an allocated bath night. Auntie Vera bathed on Monday, Uncle Stan on Tuesday, Thomas on Wednesday, Peter on Thursday, Ronnie's mother on Friday and Ronnie on Saturday. On Sunday the bath remained empty because even though the house in Moreton Street was bigger than the one they had left in Baxter Road and Uncle Stan was earning more now, Auntie Vera didn't believe in wasting money on hot water if it wasn't absolutely necessary.

There was a red line drawn on the side of the bath. A limit on the level to which it could be filled. Ronnie wished he could fill his bath right to the top but on this, as with everything else in 41 Moreton Street, Auntie Vera's word was law.

His mother knelt by the side of the bath, measuring out shampoo. Only half a lidful per head. Yet another rule. 'Shut your eyes, darling,' she told him before massaging it into his hair. He lay back in the water while she washed it out, then sat up again.

'Did Ophelia have dirty hair?' he asked.

'Ophelia?'

'In the picture book.' One that she had borrowed from the library about famous painters. A man called Millais had painted a girl called Ophelia lying in the water with her hair spread out like a halo. That was the picture he had liked best.

'Probably, but not as dirty as yours.'

He climbed out of the tub. 'Who's a clean boy now?' she asked, while drying him with a towel.

'I am,' he replied. Her hands were soft and gentle.

After he had cleaned his teeth, using the ordained amount of toothpaste, she led him across the hallway to the back bedroom they shared. From downstairs came the sound of Thomas and Peter arguing while Auntie Vera shouted for quiet so she could hear her big band programme on the wireless.

It was the smallest bedroom in the house, though bigger than the one they had shared in Baxter Road. His mother had a single bed by the door while he had a camp bed by the window that looked out on to the back garden and the ridge that led up to the railway line. Kneeling beside it, he said the prayer she had taught him.

'God bless Mum and Auntie Vera, Uncle Stan, Thomas and Peter. God bless Granny Mary, Grandpa Ronald and Uncle John in heaven. God bless my dad and keep him safe wherever he is. Thank you for my lovely day. Amen.'

He climbed into bed. She plumped up his pillow. 'Tell me about our house,' he said.

'One day, when I've saved enough money, I'll buy us a lovely house of our own. You'll have a big room and can cover all the walls with your pictures. We'll have a garden so huge it will take a man a whole day to cut the grass. And you'll have a dog and . . .'

He watched her face. Though she was smiling, her eyes were sad. She worked as a secretary at Uncle Stan's factory but wasn't very good. That was what Uncle Stan told Auntie Vera. Sometimes Mrs Tanner, who ran the typing pool, shouted at his mother. Auntie Vera said that his mother was lazy but that wasn't true. She did her best and one day he would go and shout at Mrs Tanner and see how she liked it.

'When I'm bigger,' he told her, 'I'm going to help you with your work.'

She stroked his cheek. 'Of course you will.'

'And then, when we've got our house, my dad can come and live with us.'

Momentarily her smile faded. 'Perhaps. But if he can't we'll still be happy, won't we.'

'Yes.'

'What shall we do tomorrow? Go to the park and play on the swings?'

'I'm going to draw you another picture.'

'I'll take it to work and hang it on the wall and when people ask who did it I'll say that it was my son Ronald Sidney and one day he's going to be a famous artist and everyone in the world will know his name.'

She bent down to hug him. Her skin smelled of soap and flowers. He hugged her back as hard as he could. Once Peter had twisted his arm to make him say that he wished Auntie Vera was his mother. He had said it but his fingers had been crossed. He wouldn't change his mother for a hundred Auntie Veras.

When she had gone he opened the curtains and stared out at the summer evening. It was still light and in the next door garden Mr Jackson sat in a chair, reading the paper. Auntie Vera said Mr Jackson gambled on horses. Auntie Vera thought gambling was bad.

Soon it would be dark and the moon would slide across the sky. It was just a thin sliver but in time it would grow as fat and round as the apples Mrs Cooper sold in her shop. His mother had taught him about moons and the constellations of stars. Auntie Vera probably thought moons and constellations were bad too.

A train rattled past, pumping clouds of steam into the air as it left London for the country. It was full of people. A woman saw him at the window and waved. He waved back.

One day he and his mother would be on that train. His father would come and take them away to a beautiful house of their own, and Auntie Vera and her rules would be left far, far behind.

April 1951.

'Bastard,' whispered Peter.

Ronnie shook his head. The two of them were sitting under the kitchen table playing with Peter's toy soldiers. Ronnie thought soldiers were boring but none of Peter's friends was around so he had been dragooned into taking their place.

'It's true,' continued Peter. 'Everyone knows.'

Ronnie wasn't sure what a bastard was but he knew it was something bad. More importantly he knew that it meant something bad about his mother, so he stuck out his chin and said, 'It's not true.'

Peter grinned. He had his mother's heavy build and bad temper. 'Where's your father, then?'

'He's been fighting the war in his plane but he'll be here soon.' Ronnie was sure this was true. His mother had told him his father

might be in heaven but he didn't believe that. At Sunday school he
had been taught that God was kind and generous. Granny Mary,
Grandpa Ronald and Uncle John were already in heaven and Ronnie
was sure that a kind and generous God wouldn't be so greedy.

'The war finished years ago, stupid.' Peter began to chant under
his breath. 'Stupid bastard Ronnie. Stupid bastard Ronnie.'

It was five o'clock. Uncle Stan and his mother were still at work.
Thomas was upstairs doing his homework and Auntie Vera was in
the living room talking to her friend Mrs Brown. When they had
lived in Baxter Road they had been allowed to play in the living room
because the floor was covered only in a rug. But the new room was
carpeted and Auntie Vera was terrified of marks and stains.

'Stupid little cry-baby bastard,' continued Peter, punching Ronnie
on the arm. Peter liked making Ronnie cry. A year ago it had been
easy to do but Ronnie was five and a half now and learning to fight
back.

'What's seven times four?'

Peter looked blank. Ronnie smiled. His mother was teaching him
his tables. They had actually gone as far as the six times table but he
was keeping that in reserve.

'Maths is for girls,' Peter told him. Peter who hated school and
whose reports made Uncle Stan sigh and Auntie Vera shout.

'It's twenty-eight. I'm younger than you so who's stupid now?'
Ronnie began to mimic Peter's chant. 'Stupid ugly Peter. Stupid ugly
Peter.'

Peter punched Ronnie even harder than before. 'Least I'm not a
bastard,' he hissed before sliding from under the table and going out
into the garden, inadvertently treading on some of his soldiers as he
did so.

Ronnie remained where he was, rubbing his arm, while in the
living room Auntie Vera laughed at something Mrs Brown had said.
The soldiers lay scattered. They were kept in a tin box. Auntie Vera
did not allow toys to be left lying out so he began to put them away.

Peter's favourite soldier was a Napoleonic grenadier. It was lucky
for Peter that it had not been broken in the scuffle. But Peter didn't
know that so Ronnie snapped it in two before closing the lid.

*

Auntie Vera's hobby was reading. 'I love Dickens and those wonderful Brontë sisters,' she announced to her new friends in Moreton Street. Perhaps she did, but Ronnie's mother told him that Auntie Vera much preferred the cheap romance novels with shiny covers that Uncle Stan brought her from Boots and which she hid in a kitchen drawer when any of her new friends came to visit.

But Auntie Vera's real hobby was shouting. When in a bad mood, which was most of the time, any family member was fair game, but because Ronnie was alone with Auntie Vera when the others were at work or school he was the one she shouted at most.

It wasn't easy being alone with Auntie Vera. Of all the rules he had to live by, the most important was that when in Auntie Vera's care he was not to bother her with anything. Instead he was to play silently in his room or in the garden. At noon she would leave him a sandwich and a glass of milk on the kitchen table and he had to eat and drink in silence too before washing his plate and cup in the sink and returning to his solitary games.

When Auntie Vera had guests Ronnie was under strict instructions to stay in his room, but on this particular afternoon thirst drove him downstairs. The kitchen could only be reached through the living room. Auntie Vera was sitting on the sofa, drinking tea with Mrs Brown. She was wearing a short sleeved blouse, revealing arms that were fleshy and covered in freckles. 'What is it, Ronnie?' she asked, adopting an exaggerated smile and speaking in the careful, clipped voice she always used when one of her new friends was visiting.

'Please may I have a drink of water?'

'Of course you may.' Auntie Vera gestured towards the kitchen.

Mrs Brown put down her teacup. 'How are you, Ronnie?'

'Very well, thank you, Mrs Brown.'

She offered him her cheek. He brushed it with his lips, holding his breath to avoid the smell of stale perfume. She was older than Auntie Vera and buried her wrinkles beneath heavy make-up. Her husband was a deputy bank manager and she lived on the other side of the street where the houses were bigger and the noise of the trains less intrusive. Auntie Vera was proud to have a deputy bank manager's wife as a friend.

As he filled his cup, he heard them discuss him.

'Nice manners,' said Mrs Brown.

'I insist on them. After all, manners maketh man.'

'Nice looking too. Takes after his mother.'

'As long as he doesn't take after her in brains and morals.'

He gulped down his water. Mrs Brown was smoking a cigarette. Auntie Vera did not like the smell of cigarettes and Uncle Stan had to smoke in the garden even if it was raining. But Uncle Stan was not the wife of a deputy bank manager.

'She's lucky to have relatives as understanding as you and Stan. My cousin's daughter fell pregnant to a soldier and he threw her out of the house.'

'Stan wanted to do the same but I wouldn't let him. After all, she is family.'

'You're a good woman, Vera Finnegan.'

'I try to be.'

'Perhaps she'll get married one day.'

'I doubt it. There aren't many men who'd want to raise another man's bastard.'

Ronnie rinsed his mug and put it back in the cupboard. Mrs Brown said that she had to leave. Auntie Vera said that she was going to treat herself to another chapter of a book by someone called Jane Austen.

Back in his room he opened the drawer of his mother's bedside table and took out the photograph she kept there. A tiny black-and-white snapshot of a man in a pilot's uniform. A man with a strong jaw, a handsome face and a birthmark on his neck. His father.

His mother told him that he was her sunshine. Her little Ronnie Sunshine who made her happy when skies were grey. He wanted her to be happy always but sometimes, in spite of her smiles, he knew that she was sad. He wished his father were here to help make her happy. He hated it when she was sad.

The front door closed with a bang. Mrs Brown had left and Auntie Vera was summoning him downstairs. The clipped tone was gone now. Her voice was harsh and angry.

Before obeying, he stared out of the window. Above the railway line the sky was a beautiful blue. In his head he saw his father, sitting in a shining plane, carrying bombs to drop on Auntie Vera's head.

*

September. In a crowded classroom, Miss Sims studied the rows of five-year-olds and indulged in the game she played at the start of each school year.

In time these children would face an eleven-plus examination that would determine whether they finished their schooling in the grammar or secondary modern system. The former offered a bright child the chance of qualifications, university entrance and exciting new horizons. The latter gave the less academically gifted vocational training and a more modest career path. Though she knew little of each child's aptitude, still Miss Sims liked to look into their faces and try to predict the route each would follow.

Pretty Catherine Meadows in the front row was discounted. Catherine's father was a stockbroker and could afford a private education for his daughter.

Alan Deakins whispered to his neighbour in the back row, his eyes alive with mischief. An intelligent but impish face. The class trouble-maker who might have grammar school potential but not the requisite application.

Margaret Fisher in the third row stifled a yawn. A round, vacuous face that showed no interest in her new surroundings. Secondary school material without doubt.

In the second row Ronald Sidney stared solemnly at her. An attractive boy with lovely wide-spaced eyes. A contrast to his unprepossessing Finnegan cousins, who had both passed through her class. Peter, like Alan, had been a troublemaker, and Thomas, due to sit the examination this year, fitted squarely in the Margaret mould, as his results would likely prove.

Ronald responded to her gaze with a smile that lit up his whole face. His eyes were shining, as if excited at the prospect of learning.

Oh yes, a future grammar school boy for sure.

Smiling back, she thought, *I'm going to enjoy teaching you.*

She posed an arithmetic problem. Most of the class looked blank but a few hands rose into the air. One of them belonged to Ronald Sidney.

Each Friday Anna paid part of her salary into a savings account.

It was a very small part. Most of her money went to Vera for rent and keep, and what was left barely covered necessities and the occasional treat for Ronnie.

The girl behind the desk stared at her post office book. 'Sidney,' she said, pointing to the name on the front page. 'Are you Ronnie's mother?'

'Yes.'

'He's in my aunt's class. Miss Sims. She's always talking about him. Says he's bright as a button.'

'Thank you.' Anna smiled. 'Ronnie talks about your aunt all the time too.'

Actually that wasn't true. Ronnie rarely talked about his teacher or the other children in his class. Not that he was unhappy at school. It was just that the people he met there seemed to make little impression on him.

He was learning so quickly. Each day his knowledge grew. Rarely did he need her help when reading and his mental arithmetic was almost better than her own. Having little in the way of brains herself, it was wonderful to have a child who was so obviously intelligent.

The girl returned her book. She looked at the new balance. Still paltry. Not enough to buy a carriage clock, let alone a big house. Perhaps it never would be.

But she couldn't afford to think like that. Not even for a moment.

She walked out into the High Street. The drab centre of a drab town. A wind was rising so she fastened her coat. The sky was heavy and grey. Everything around her was grey in this soulless outpost in a constantly expanding London.

She wanted to escape from here. Get away from Vera and her contempt and all the others who judged her even if they didn't mean to. Go somewhere new. Somewhere green and beautiful where she and Ronnie could start again. Where Ronnie would have everything she had always promised him.

One day she would make it happen. But how?

December 1951. Ronnie's first report.

'. . . a joy to teach! An exceptionally bright boy who is also hard working and beautifully mannered. A perfect little gentleman, in fact, and a huge credit to his family.'

*

Christmas Day. Ronnie sat with his family in the living room. A tiny Christmas tree stood in the corner, covered with the decorations Auntie Vera kept in a box in the attic. Auntie Vera had decorated the tree herself. Ronnie had offered to help but she had told him he would only break something and sent him away.

It was early afternoon. They had just finished a meal of turkey with roast potatoes, peas, carrots and stuffing balls, all cooked by his mother. Last year they could only afford beef. Auntie Vera had made a point of telling all her new friends that they were having turkey.

Ronnie sat on the floor, next to his mother's chair, looking at the present she had bought him. A box of paints and two small brushes. 'Do you like it?' she asked anxiously. He allowed his smile to answer for him.

'He'd better not make a mess with those,' said Auntie Vera from the sofa by the fire. Auntie Vera and Uncle Stan had given Ronnie a scarf.

'He won't.'

'He'd better not.' Auntie Vera's tone was belligerent. She and Uncle Stan had been drinking beer since their return from church that morning. Uncle Stan snored beside her on the sofa. Thomas lay in front of the fire, absorbed in his new comic book, while outside Peter struggled to master new roller skates.

Ronnie reached behind the bookcase for the envelope he had hidden there. A card he had made at school, decorated with a drawing of a beautiful house coloured like a rainbow. Inside was written 'Merry Xmas Mum. Love from Ronnie Sunshine'. All his class had made cards for their mothers. Miss Sims had told him that his was the best and he had told her that it was because he had the best mother.

Now it was her turn to smile. 'It's the loveliest present I've ever had.'

He pointed to the front of the card. 'That's our house. The one you're going to buy.'

'What house?' demanded Auntie Vera.

'Mum's going to buy us a big house.'

'And how is she going to do that?'

'By saving lots of money. And when she's bought the house my dad is going to come and live with us.'

Auntie Vera took a sip of beer then put it back on the table, next to a bottle of expensive perfume that Uncle Stan had given her. The same perfume Mrs Brown wore. The shape of the bottle reminded Ronnie of something but he couldn't think what.

'You're a clever boy, aren't you, Ronnie? That's what your report said, isn't it?'

'Yes, Auntie Vera.'

'Then here's a lesson for you. Your mother's an idiot who's never going to buy you anything. Do yourself a favour and learn it well.'

'My mum's not an idiot.'

'Then let's write a letter to your daddy. Come on, Anna. What's his address?'

'Don't, Vera . . .' began Ronnie's mother.

'Or what? What will you do? Leave? Why don't you? Let's see how long you and Ronnie survive without us.'

'My mum's not an idiot!'

Auntie Vera began to laugh. Ronnie's mother put her hand on his shoulder. 'Auntie Vera's just teasing you.'

A lump of coal fell from the fire, waking Uncle Stan. Thomas looked up from his comic book. 'You snore like a hog, Dad.' Uncle Stan shrugged, then returned to sleep. Auntie Vera drank more beer. As he watched her, Ronnie realized that the perfume resembled a potion bottle he had seen in a book at school. A wicked witch had given the potion to a beautiful woman, who thought it would keep her young for ever. Instead it had turned to fire inside her stomach and burned her to ash.

He imagined Auntie Vera drinking from the perfume bottle by mistake. Just one sip. Then a scream as she clawed at her throat.

Auntie Vera was still laughing. He began to do the same. A look of confusion came into his mother's face. 'Hush, Ronnie,' she said quickly.

Biting his lip, he smothered the sound.

January 1952.

Anna sat on Ronnie's bed, listening to him read from a library book about a little girl whose magic ring gave her seven wishes. She had worried that it might be too difficult for him but he was managing it effortlessly. The previous evening he had been totally absorbed in the story but now he seemed distracted.

'What is it, Ronnie?'

'When is Dad coming?'

She felt a dull ache. The residue of a pain that had once been intolerable. 'I told you, darling, he may not come. You mustn't expect him.'

'I want him to come.'

'I know you do but we don't know where he is. He might be in heaven.'

The little jaw was set. 'He's not in heaven. He's going to come and help me.'

'Help you what?'

'Look after you.'

Outside it was raining. A stormy winter's night. Though the room was cold his words were like a gust of warm air. She took his hand and pressed it against her cheek. 'You don't need any help, Ronnie. You do a perfect job on your own. Now let's finish the story. Jemima's only got one wish left. What would you wish for if you were her?'

'That Auntie Vera was in heaven.'

She released his hand. 'Ronnie, that's a wicked thing to say!'

He stared down at the page while water pounded the window.

'You mustn't say things like that. Not ever. I know Auntie Vera gets angry sometimes but that's just her way. She and Uncle Stan have been good to us. They've given us a home.'

Silence. His pyjamas were striped and too big for him. Handed down from Peter, as so many of his clothes were. A train raced past in the darkness. Even though the window was closed the sound still filled the room.

'Ronnie?'

He looked up. 'We'll have our own house soon. You're going to buy it. Then it won't matter if Auntie Vera's in heaven.'

Troubled, she shook her head. 'Ronnie, it's wrong to talk like that. You mustn't do it anymore. You'll upset me if you do.'

Another silence. He stared at her with eyes that seemed suddenly like those of a stranger.

Then he smiled. The little Ronnie Sunshine smile that could lift her darkest mood.

'I'm sorry, Mum. I love you.' He continued to read.

Lunchtime. In the shadow of the grim Victorian school building the playground swarmed with life. Boys chased footballs or each other. Girls twirled skipping ropes, jumped hopscotch squares or played little mother over dolls.

Catherine Meadows, bored with skipping, watched Ronnie Sidney sitting by himself.

He was drawing. Just as he always was. Miss Sims said that he was very talented. Miss Sims liked Ronnie. When Miss Sims wasn't there, Alan Deakins called Ronnie and Archie Clark teacher's pets and Archie cried and everyone laughed, but Ronnie just shrugged and carried on with whatever he was doing until Alan grew bored and started teasing someone else.

She walked over. 'What are you drawing?'

Ronnie didn't answer. She leaned over to see but he pressed the paper to his chest and hid the image.

'Are you drawing me?'

'No.'

Catherine sighed. Her friends Phyllis and Jean thought Alan was the best-looking boy in class but Ronnie was Catherine's favourite. Sometimes she tried to talk to him but he never seemed interested, which was strange because she was pretty and her father was important and everyone else wanted to be her friend.

She stood, waiting, but Ronnie just ignored her. Catherine wasn't used to being ignored so she stuck out her tongue then went to rejoin the skipping game.

Ten minutes later the lesson bell rang. A groan echoed around the playground. Ronnie stood up, looking at the picture he had drawn, his expression thoughtful. Crushing the paper into a ball, he dropped it into the bin and followed the other children indoors.

Catherine walked over to the bin and removed the paper, hoping to see an image of herself. Instead she saw two separate drawings of a fat woman with an angry face standing in a garden behind a railway line. In the first drawing the woman was shouting at a small boy, unaware of the bomber plane flying overhead. In the second drawing a bomb had blown the woman into pieces and the little boy was waving to the pilot while twirling her severed head by the hair.

Disappointed, Catherine put the drawing back in the bin.

Summer 1952.
'. . . *an excellent year. The sky's the limit for a boy with Ronnie's brains and application. I predict great things for him.*'

November. Ronnie sat at the kitchen table with Peter. Though the living-room door was closed it could not block out the sound of Auntie Vera's voice.

'Stan had to plead for you! He might have lost his job, and why? Because you're too stupid to do your own!'

Silence. Ronnie willed his mother to shout back but she said nothing.

'But stupid's your middle name, isn't it?'

Ronnie struggled to understand what had happened. His mother had made some mistake at work. Something about a lost order. She had nearly lost her job over it.

'Look at Ronnie. Anyone with a brain would have had him adopted. Given him a decent start in life. You still could but you won't because you're too stupid!'

A chill ran through Ronnie. Beside him Peter began to giggle. Thomas was away, visiting a friend from his new secondary school.

At last his mother spoke. 'Leave Ronnie out of this.'

'Why? It's true. Not content with ruining your own life, you want to ruin his too!'

Peter kicked Ronnie under the table. 'No one would adopt you. They'll put you in an orphanage with all the other bastards.'

'That's enough, Vera.' Uncle Stan entered the fray.

'Why? It's what everyone around here thinks. And why are you sticking up for her? Just for once give me some bloody support!'

Peter prodded Ronnie with his finger. 'You're going to the orphanage, bastard.'

The arguing continued. Then there was the sound of foosteps. Ronnie's mother running upstairs. Auntie Vera appeared in the kitchen, her face flushed and angry. 'Looks like I'm making supper then. You two make yourselves useful. Peter, peel the potatoes. Ronnie, lay the table. And what are those roller skates doing on the floor? Put them outside.'

Peter jumped to his feet. Ronnie did too but made for the kitchen door, where a troubled-looking Uncle Stan was standing.

'And where do you think you're going?' demanded Auntie Vera.

'To see my mum.'

'Do what you're told. Lay the table.'

'I want to see my mum.'

'Let him go, Vera.' Another weak interjection from Uncle Stan.

Auntie Vera folded her arms. 'Lay the table, Ronnie.'

Ronnie shook his head.

'Now!'

For a moment he stood his ground. His hands were clenched into fists. In the background Peter was giggling again.

Then his hands relaxed. He smiled. A soft, sweet gesture of submission.

'Yes, Auntie Vera. Sorry, Auntie Vera.'

Meekly he went about his task.

Anna sat on her bed, staring down at the silver band she wore on her finger.

It had been a thirteenth birthday present from her parents. The last birthday she had celebrated with them before the fatal air raid. She had nothing else to remember them by. No photographs. No other mementoes or keepsakes. Everything of emotional value had been destroyed by the bomb.

All except her memories. Her father's voice. Her mother's smile. Her brother's laugh as he told her a joke or teased her about a film-star crush. Faint echoes of a time when she had not been frightened of the future. When she had known what it was to feel secure and safe.

She had to leave here. Take Ronnie and move away. But where would she go? What would she do? She had no brains or talent. She could not earn enough to keep them both. Not without Stan and Vera's help.

She heard footsteps. Ronnie stood in the doorway, watching her with anxious eyes. In his hand was a piece of bread and jam. As she looked at him she knew Vera was right. She should have had him adopted. Given him a decent start in life. Not kept him with her because she was too weak to go on being alone.

Self-disgust overwhelmed her. She burst into tears.

He ran towards her. Threw his arms around her neck. 'Don't cry, Mum. Please.'

'Oh, Ronnie . . .'

They stayed like that for some time. Not saying anything. Rocking backwards and forwards with him sitting on her knee so that to an outside observer it might seem that she was the one offering comfort.

Her tears slowed. She wiped her eyes. 'Don't mind me. I'm just being silly.'

He touched her ring. 'You were thinking about Granny Mary, weren't you?'

'Yes.'

'You miss her. And Grandpa Ronald and Uncle John. You wish they were here.'

She nodded.

'I don't want to be adopted, Mum. Don't make me be adopted.'

'Never.'

'Promise?'

'Promise.'

'Cross your heart and hope to die?'

'Cross my heart and hope to die.'

He rested his head against her chest. She stroked his hair. 'I'm sorry, Ronnie.'

'For what?'

'That you only have me.'

'My dad will come soon and then I'll have him too.'

'He isn't going to come, Ronnie.'

'Yes he is, and then . . .'

She cupped his face in her hands. Stared down at him. 'Ronnie, you must listen to me. Your father isn't going to come. Not ever. I'd give anything for that not to be true, but it is. We only have each other.'

His eyes became troubled. He looked much older suddenly; like the little man he tried so hard to be. She felt ashamed. Wished she had allowed him to hang on to his dream.

'Don't worry, Mum,' he said eventually. 'We'll be all right. I'll look after you. I promise.'

Then he began to sing. 'You are my sunshine, my only sunshine. You make me happy when skies are grey.' His voice was high and off key. A wave of love swept over her. So powerful she thought her heart would burst.

'Shall I tell you a secret, Ronnie? Whenever I feel sad I tell myself that I'm the luckiest person in the world because I have the best son in the world. Handsome, clever and good. And I promise that one day I'll make you as proud of me as I am of you.'

The piece of bread lay next to them on the bed. He offered it to her. Though not hungry, she ate to make him happy.

Tuesday evening. Anna walked along Moreton Street.

It was half past seven. She had been working late. An attempt to make amends for the disaster of the previous week.

Stan walked beside her. He had been for a pint with a couple of friends from the factory, though judging by his unsteady gait he had drunk considerably more than that. Though Vera was no mean drinker herself, she could be very moralistic when confronted with an intoxicated Stan. Anna considered taking him to the café on the High Street for a coffee but decided against it. Vera was making supper that night and their lives would not be worth living if they were late.

It was dark. The street was empty except for Vera's friend Mrs Brown, walking arm in arm with her deputy bank manager husband, wearing fake pearls and high heels that threatened to buckle under her ample frame. Out to dinner perhaps, at that new restaurant in the High Street. The Browns ate out regularly. Vera was always on at Stan to take her to restaurants and he would complain that it cost too much.

They exchanged brief pleasantries on passing. Mrs Brown, registering Stan's drunken state, gave a smile that merged amusement with contempt. Anna felt Mr Brown's eyes crawl all over her. The previous December, at Stan and Vera's Christmas party, he had cornered her in the kitchen and suggested that he take her out for a ride in his new car as she was a girl who clearly liked a bit of fun. She had declined and he had never mentioned it again, but even now she couldn't see him without feeling the need to go and wash.

They moved on towards number 41. The lights were on. Thomas sat in his bedroom window, struggling with his homework. He gave them a wave. She waved back while Stan reached for his key. He unlocked the door. She entered first.

And heard the scream.

It came from the kitchen. High and shrill. A mixture of fear and terrible pain.

She ran, followed by Stan. Vera lay on the floor, the chip pan beside her. Boiling fat oozed across the floor. The air was full of the sickly smell of burnt flesh.

Stan, befuddled with drink, looked too shocked to act. Anna took charge. 'Go to the Jacksons. Use their phone to call an ambulance. Now!' He turned and ran while she crouched down, pulling Vera to safety.

Thomas appeared, followed by Peter and Ronnie. 'Keep away,' Anna told them. Vera, already whimpering, was starting to tremble. Shock was setting in. 'One of you fetch me a blanket. Quickly!'

As she waited she comforted Vera, making soothing noises and trying not to look at the damaged flesh on the left arm. Instead her eyes settled on Peter's roller skate, partly covered by the pan as if attempting to hide its guilt.

Anna sat on Vera's bed, changing the dressing on her arm.

She tugged a little harder than she had intended. Vera winced. 'Careful!'

'Sorry.'

'You're not as bad as that bloody nurse. Where did they train you? I asked her. Belsen?' Vera laughed at her own joke but it did little to lift the grey pallor of her face. The painkillers didn't seem to be helping. Stan had told Anna that she regularly woke in the night in pain.

Peter appeared in the doorway. 'Are you all right, Mum?' he asked anxiously.

'Yes.' Vera's tone was curt.

'Are you really? Do you promise?'

'I've said so, haven't I? Now go away.'

Peter did as he was told. Anna finished. 'All done. Sorry if I hurt you.'

'You didn't mean to. Anyway, better you than Stan.' Another laugh. 'If he were doing this I'd be screaming the whole street down. Useless bloody man.'

'Peter didn't mean to hurt you either.'

Vera's mouth tightened. 'I'm always telling him to put his things away. If only he'd listened . . .'

'But he was so upset, and . . .'

'His being upset doesn't do me much good, does it?'

'I know, but . . .'

'When I was at school there was a girl in my class with burn scars. They were on the side of her head so the hair didn't grow properly. We used to call her Scarecrow. We made her cry and she'd tell us that one day the scars would fade and her hair would grow and she'd be more beautiful than any of us. Poor little cow.'

During the nine years they had lived together, Anna had seen many emotions reflected in Vera's eyes. But never, until this moment, had she seen fear. As she saw it she experienced a feeling that was just as new. Pity.

'It will fade, Vera. Give it time.'

'I was lucky, really. It's only my arm. Imagine if it had been my face, like Scarecrow.'

Silence. In the street outside two young men laughed as they walked by.

'I will forgive him,' said Vera eventually. 'What else can I do? He won't be mine for ever. What was it my mother used to say? A son is a son till he takes a wife. One day some girl will take him away from me just as another will take Thomas, and then all I'll have is Stan, God help me.'

'I'll always have Ronnie.'

'Will you?'

Anna pictured Ronnie as an adult. Handsome and clever. Talented and charming. Someone countless girls would love. Someone who would no longer have any need for her.

Suddenly she was thirteen again. Standing in front of the wreckage of her home. Tasting the dust in her mouth. Feeling the emptiness inside.

They stared at each other. Old enmities temporarily forgotten in a moment of shared dread.

'Perhaps you will. Ronnie's a good boy.' A trace of bitterness crept into Vera's voice. 'One thing's certain. He'll make you prouder than my two will make me.'

'I'd better start supper. The others will be getting hungry.'

Vera nodded. Anna made her way downstairs.

Sometimes, as a treat, Anna took Ronnie to the Amalfi café on the High Street.

The café was owned by the Luca family, who had emigrated to England from Naples. Mrs Luca made wonderful cakes that were displayed in a big cabinet on the counter, but in spite of Anna's urgings to be adventurous Ronnie always chose a jam tart washed down by a bottle of lemonade.

They sat at a table by the window. Ronnie ate the pastry, leaving the jam until last. 'Wouldn't it be nicer to eat them together?' Anna suggested. He didn't bother to answer. She remembered her parents once giving her brother and herself the same advice and receiving an identical response.

'Queen Elizabeth is going to be crowned, isn't she?' he asked between mouthfuls.

She nodded. The papers had been discussing preparations for the following year's coronation. Stan had been talking about it at breakfast.

'When she's crowned will she be called the Virgin Queen?'

She thought of Prince Charles and Princess Anne. 'I don't think so, darling.'

'Why not?'

She felt herself blush. 'Finish your tart,' she told him. A man at the next table overheard the exchange and gave her an amused smile.

The café was crowded. At a nearby table a girl of about Ronnie's age devoured an ice cream sundae, watched by a well-dressed couple who were presumably her parents. The girl waved to Ronnie. 'Do you know her?' Anna asked.

'That's Catherine Meadows.'

'Is she in your class?'

'Yes.'

'Is she your friend?'

'S'pose so.'

'As good a friend as Archie?'

A shrug. Ronnie carried on eating. His new form teacher had told her that Ronnie was popular enough with his classmates but he had yet to make any close friends. He had been for tea at Archie Clark's house but shown no particular desire to return the favour. In a way that was a blessing. Vera was always complaining about Peter and Thomas's friends, and to suggest entertaining some of Ronnie's would be like showing a red rag to a bull.

As she sipped her tea she thought of Peter. Stan had given him a thrashing and Vera had been very cold towards him, though she was warming now.

But it could have been so much worse. A scarred arm was better than a scarred face.

She shivered. Ronnie frowned. 'What is it?'

'I was thinking of Auntie Vera.'

'You feel sorry for her, don't you?'

She nodded. Her friend Kate walked past outside, arm in arm with Mickey Lee. Kate was marrying Mickey in two weeks' time. Both gave her a wave.

'Why?'

For a moment she didn't register what he'd said. When she did she put down her cup.

'*Why?* Ronnie, what a question.'

He stared at her, his eyes solemn.

'Don't you feel sorry for her?'

Silence. The eyes, unblinking, bored into hers as if searching for something.

'Ronnie?'

34

'She's horrid to you. She made you cry.'

'No she didn't. I was just being silly. I told you.'

'She wanted me to be adopted.'

'She was just angry. She didn't mean it.'

'Yes she did.'

Again she thought of Peter. In the aftermath of the accident he had insisted that he *had* put his roller skates away. That someone else must have left them there. Thomas perhaps. Or Ronnie.

But that was ridiculous. Ronnie had no interest in roller skating. He would never have left them lying around in such a dangerous place.

Unless he had done so deliberately.

Something stirred in her head. Threads of a memory buried deep in the dark side of her mind. A conversation betweeen Ronnie and herself over a story book.

'Jemima's only got one wish left. What would you wish for if you were her?'

'That Auntie Vera was in heaven.'

An image crept into her brain. Ronnie standing by the kitchen door. Watching Vera. Waiting for her back to be turned. Carefully picking his moment . . .

She pushed it away as if it were diseased, erecting mental barriers to prevent it from ever entering again. How could she think that of her own child? Her darling. Her little Ronnie Sunshine.

The only person in the world she had to love.

Someone called Ronnie's name. Catherine Meadows was leaving. She gave Ronnie another wave. This time he responded. Catherine smiled. She was a pretty girl who promised to be an even prettier woman. The sort of woman who might one day steal Ronnie away.

'You're teasing me, aren't you, Ronnie. You're sorry for Auntie Vera really, aren't you.' Her tone was declamatory rather than questioning.

He blinked. For a moment his eyes were troubled. Shame, perhaps. 'Yes, Mum.'

And he meant it. Of course he did. She knew it.

He took another sip of his drink. Bubbles went up his nose and he began to splutter. Everyone looked over. 'Hey, Ronnie, you wan' everyone think I poison you?' cried Mr Luca from behind the corner. She wiped his mouth with her handkerchief and both began to laugh.

Midnight: 41 Moreton Street was still, except for Ronnie, who made his way along the upstairs hallway towards the last door on the left.

The door was closed. He turned the handle and pushed it open. Only a foot. No more, as it would squeak. He had tested it that afternoon while everyone else was downstairs. But it was enough for him to enter.

A double bed stood in the centre of the room. Uncle Stan slept on the right-hand side, Auntie Vera on the left. Though the room was in darkness the curtains were flimsy and the street light provided illumination.

He crept towards Auntie Vera, treading carefully to avoid the creaking floorboard near the window and trying not to shiver. It was cold and he wasn't wearing his dressing gown. If they woke he would pretend to be sleepwalking. Thomas had been prone to sleepwalking when Ronnie's age. Ronnie had heard Auntie Vera telling Mrs Brown about it.

Auntie Vera lay on her back, her mouth open, her breathing a dull rasp as opposed to Uncle Stan's thunderous snore. Her right arm lay across her chest. But it wasn't her right arm he was interested in.

Gently he lifted the quilt and blankets. The left arm lay by her side. It was no longer bandaged. The light wasn't brilliant but sufficient for him to make out the damaged skin. He stretched out his fingers, wanting to touch it but holding back for fear of waking her. Seeing it was enough. To know that it existed.

Many children in his class had roller skates. Sally Smith's grandmother had tripped on one and broken her ankle. Sally had told them in class and a half-formed idea had suddenly taken shape. A broken ankle would have been good. But a scarred arm was even better.

His mother said that Auntie Vera didn't mean to be unkind. That she was a nice person really. But he didn't believe her. Auntie Vera thought his mother was stupid. Auntie Vera liked making his mother cry. Auntie Vera wanted his mother to have him adopted and sent away to strangers so they would never see each other again.

But he would never leave his mother. One day, in spite of what she said, his father *would* come and take care of them both, but until that day it was his job to take care of her. And Auntie Vera had better not try and have him sent away because if she did . . .

Well, she'd just better not. That was all.

Back in his own room he gazed down at his mother. She lay on her side, breathing softly, looking like a princess in a book of fairy tales. A tuft of hair stuck up at an angle. Moistening his fingers, he brushed it down.

No one was going to hurt her. He would not allow it because she was his mother and he loved her. And she loved him because he was her little Ronnie Sunshine, who made her happy when skies were grey. He was the best boy in the world, she told him, and he made her proud because he was handsome and clever and good.

But he wasn't always good. Sometimes he did bad things and was glad to have done them. He wanted her to be glad and praise him, but when he even hinted at them she was shocked because little Ronnie Sunshine never did bad things. Little Ronnie Sunshine didn't even think bad thoughts.

And if she knew the things he thought and did she might not be proud any more. She might not love him anymore.

She was smiling in her sleep. Her face was soft and lovely. He imagined it hardening. Growing cold. 'Go away, Ronald. You're bad and wicked and I hate you. You're not my little Ronnie Sunshine any more.'

Then there would be no one to love him and he would be alone.

The image terrified him. He burst into tears.

In her dream it was Christmas morning. She was nine years old and opening her stocking. Her father was smoking a pipe and her mother was telling him how much he looked like Ronald Colman while the family cat miaowed loudly as if complaining about the smell. Her brother John had been given a harmonica and was trying to play 'Hark the Herald Angels Sing' while they all laughed and sang along . . .

When she woke the laughter seemed to have followed her. But as her head cleared she realized it was the sound of crying. Ronnie stood beside the bed, shivering in the cold of the room and sobbing as if his heart would break.

She folded him in her arms, covering his wet cheeks with kisses. 'It's all right, Ronnie. Mummy's here.' Gently she rocked him, making soothing noises while a train rushed by outside, filling the room with noise and light.

'What was it, darling? A nightmare? Did a dream frighten you?'

He nodded.

'What did you dream?'

He opened his mouth, then shut it again, shaking his head.

'You don't have to tell me. All that matters is that it's over and I'm here and you're safe.' She stroked his hair. His eyes were wide and fearful. She remembered her thoughts in the café and felt ashamed. He was just a baby. He would never willingly hurt anyone.

'Do you want to sleep in my bed? I'll keep the monsters away. I promise.'

They lay down. She pulled the blankets over them while he wrapped himself around her. She continued to stroke his hair, humming a lullaby to help him drift back to sleep.

Monday evening, two weeks later. Ronnie sat on the floor next to his mother's chair, reading a book. Auntie Vera and Uncle Stan sat together on the sofa in front of the fire.

The wireless was on. A programme of classical music. 'Now a symphony from Haydn,' said the velvet-voiced announcer. Auntie Vera nodded approvingly. Haydn was one of Mrs Brown's favourites. Uncle Stan, who would have preferred jazz on the other station, tried to look enthusiastic.

Auntie Vera was wearing a thick jumper. In the past, even when it was really cold, the sleeves would have been pushed up. But not now. As she listened to the music her fingers kept stroking the wool that covered the damaged skin.

She realized that Ronnie was watching her. Their eyes locked.

'Does it hurt?' he asked.

'A little.'

'I wish it didn't.'

His mother was sewing. Mending one of his shirts. She stroked his hair. He gazed up at her, his face sad. The sort of face she would expect from little Ronnie Sunshine.

'Good boy,' she whispered.

He tried to concentrate on the words on the page. But the motion of Auntie Vera's hand kept disturbing him. Drawing his eyes like moths to the flame.

Spring 1953.

Langley Avenue was a terrace of elegant, grey stone houses, built at the turn of the century. The residents of Langley Avenue liked to say it was the best address in Hepton, but when one considered what a dreary place Hepton was, this wasn't saying much.

June and Albert Sanderson had moved there forty years earlier when Albert had been an ambitious young lawyer and their two sons only babies. Now both were lawyers themselves with families of their own and Albert, whose health was poor, spent his days expanding his stamp collection and trying to guess the culprit in detective novels.

Up until six months ago old Doris Clark had been their cleaner, coming every Saturday to work her magic on their over-cluttered home. When Doris announced her retirement, an acquaintance called Sarah Brown had suggested a possible replacement. A young woman called Anna who had no husband, a small son to support and the need to earn more money.

On this particular Saturday June sat in her kitchen, writing a letter to her cousin, Barbara. Anna sat beside her, polishing the silverware.

June finished writing and rose to her feet, trying to stretch the arthritis from her hand. 'Some tea,' she announced.

'I'll make it,' said Anna.

'Don't you worry. I'm up now.' June filled the kettle and put it on the stove. From the living room Ivor Novello's voice harmonized with Albert's snores. Anna carried on polishing, doing a thorough job. She was a good worker. A good person too. Always willing to listen to an elderly couple who missed their sons and often had only each other and the wireless for company. June felt lucky to have found her.

'How is Stan?' she asked. 'Is his cold better?'

'Much better, thank you.'

'And Vera? How is she?'

'Well too.' Anna's eyes remained on the silverware. Though she rarely talked about her life in Moreton Street, June was perceptive enough to sense that it was not easy. Sarah Brown had told her that Vera was a dreadful snob who was not pleased to have a relative working part time as a cleaner, and June had thought to herself that it took one to know one.

The kettle boiled. She filled three cups, poured lemon squash into a glass and covered a plate with biscuits. 'Come through, dear,' she told Anna. 'You've earned a break.'

On entering the living room she cleared her throat. Albert's eyes opened. 'Not asleep,' he said hastily. 'Was I, Ronnie?'

Ronnie shook his head. He was sitting at a table by the window, drawing on a pad. Anna often brought him with her, apologizing profusely for doing so, but he was always as good as gold. June's neighbour, Penelope Walsh, had said that she would never employ a cleaner who had an illegitimate child, but June refused to condemn someone for what was nothing more than simple human frailty.

She gave Ronnie his squash and offered him the biscuit plate, urging him to take two. 'Thank you very much, Mrs Sanderson,' he said. His manners were beautiful. A real credit to his mother. On the pad was a drawing of ships at sea. For a boy of not quite eight it was remarkably good.

'That's wonderful, Ronnie,' she told him.

'It's for you.'

'What a lovely present. Isn't it good, Albert?'

Albert nodded. 'You've got a talented boy there,' he told Anna, whose face lit up with pleasure, making her look like a child herself.

Ronnie sat beside his mother. She put her arm around him while Albert told them about the television set they were buying so they could watch the Queen's coronation. Ronnie said that the parents of a boy in his class called Archie Clark had just bought one but had no idea how to work it.

Anna smiled down at Ronnie, her eyes full of uncomplicated love. Once, during a rare exchange of confidences, she had told June that she had promised to buy Ronnie a big house of their own in the country. Perhaps she would, but it was hard to see how on her meagre wages.

June wished she could do something to help. But there was nothing.

Summer 1953.
    '. . . *always polite and attentive. Ronnie learns his lessons well.*'

October 7th 1953. The evening Thomas didn't come home.

At first no one was worried. As they sat down to supper Auntie Vera was more angry than anything. 'What a waste of good food! He'll feel the rough side of my tongue when he decides to show his face.'

But by the end of the meal her mood had changed. Anger replaced by apprehension. Such behaviour was out of character for Thomas. 'He'll be with that no-good Johnny Scott. Peter, go round to their house and fetch him.' Peter did as he was told and returned with the news that none of the Scotts had any idea of Thomas's whereabouts.

Time passed. Other friends were visited and all gave the same answer. Auntie Vera's anxiety increased. Uncle Stan tried to calm her. 'He'll be all right. He's not a baby.' It didn't work. 'He's only twelve! He shouldn't be out this late. Not without telling us. God, where can he be?'

Anna suggested calling the police. Auntie Vera began to panic. 'You think something bad's happened to him, don't you? Don't you!' Ronnie's mother denied it. Said that it was only a precaution. Ronnie sat with Peter, watching the scene, their respective bedtimes forgotten in the atmosphere of rising dread.

The rest of the evening was a blur. The house filled with people. Mrs Brown and her husband. The Jacksons from next door. Neighbours from Baxter Road they had barely seen since moving. The air was full of anxious voices, Auntie Vera's increasingly shrill. The clock above the fireplace ticked away, oblivious. Ten o'clock. Eleven. Midnight.

The police arrived. Questions were asked. Notes taken. One of them advised Auntie Vera to get some rest. She screamed at him. Called him an idiot. 'How can I sleep when my child's missing?' All the while she kept rubbing her left arm with her hand, not seeming to care that the sleeve of her blouse had slid up and the damaged skin was visible to all.

At last the house emptied. The five occupants were left alone. Stan and Auntie Vera sat by the fire, holding hands, telling each other to be brave in voices that dripped with fear. Peter crouched at their feet while Ronnie sat on his mother's knee. 'You should be in bed,' she whispered. He shook his head and she did not force the issue.

Eventually he slept and dreamed that the police returned, saying that Thomas had been found safe and well before leading in a skeleton dressed in Thomas's Sunday best. When he woke it was nearly dawn. Everyone was sleeping except Auntie Vera, who was rubbing her damaged arm while tears rolled down her cheeks.

At first he just watched her. 'Don't cry,' he said eventually.

'I can't help it. This is unbearable. The worst thing that could happen.'

'Worse than your arm?'

'Much worse.'

He leant forward. 'Why?'

'Because that happened to me. I was the one who was hurt. Now Thomas might be hurt.' She began to sob. 'He might be dead and there's nothing I can do. That's the worst pain in the world. When something bad happens to someone you love. It hurts far more than my arm ever did.'

'But . . .'

She wiped her cheeks. 'Go to sleep, Ronnie. I don't want to talk any more.'

Obedient as always, he closed his eyes.

October 9th. Mrs Jennings watched the third years pray for the safe return of Thomas Finnegan in the same classroom where five years earlier Thomas himself had sat.

There was still no news. Though Thomas had never been one of her favourite pupils, Mrs Jennings dreaded the thought of harm befalling him and raised her own prayer that it would turn out to be youthful misadventure and not something far worse.

A soft giggle disturbed her thoughts. Naughty Alan Deakins, the class troublemaker, was making faces at his friends, Robert Bates and Stuart Hooper. Mrs Jennings glared at them and three pairs of eyes quickly closed. Now all but two of the class had their eyes shut.

Pretty Catherine Meadows in the front row kept looking anxiously at Ronnie Sidney. Catherine had a childish crush on Ronnie and was clearly upset for him.

And Ronnie himself, next to little Archie Clark in the second row, stared in front of him, his brows knotted as if weighed down by the thoughts that whirred inside his head. Mrs Jennings liked Ronnie. He was a good boy; polite, hard working and bright. Imaginative too. Sufficiently so to be afraid for the well-being of his cousin Thomas.

She tried to catch his eye, give him a sympathetic smile. But he remained lost in his own thoughts and did not notice.

October 10th. Thomas came home.

He had been with Harry Fisher, an older boy and regular truant who attended another school in the area. Harry's mother was dead; his father a habitual drunk who had gone away for a week, leaving Harry to look after himself. But Harry had had other ideas; stealing some of his father's savings, intending to have a few days' fun in the West End and wanting someone to keep him company. Thomas, impressionable and easily led, had been the one he had chosen.

The police were angry. 'You've been a very stupid young man. Wasting our time and upsetting everybody.' Vera was beside herself. 'I don't know whether to kiss you or kill you!' In the end she did the former, lavishing Thomas with cake and lemonade. Peter, indignant, announced that he was going to run away too if this was the outcome and received a clout from Stan for upsetting his mother.

Anna, almost as relieved as Vera, hugged Ronnie to her. 'You must never frighten me like that, Ronnie. I couldn't bear to think of something bad happening to you.'

He hugged her back. 'I never will, Mum. I promise.'

December. Two days before the start of the Christmas holidays. Mrs Jennings finished reading the class a revenge story about a man called Horatio who had been robbed for his money and left for dead. After years of searching, Horatio had tracked down the culprit and killed him in a duel. Her colleague Miss Sims had expressed concern at the darkness of the subject matter but in Mrs Jennings' experience, even the most angelic of children liked their stories laced with gore.

'Did you all enjoy that?' she asked.

A chorus of yeses and nodded heads. Alan Deakins suggested that Horatio should have boiled the robber in oil and Catherine Meadows told him not to be horrid.

'Horatio had his revenge, Alan. That's the important thing.' Mrs Jennings closed her book. 'Now . . .'

'No he didn't,' said Ronnie Sidney.

'Yes he did, Ronnie. He killed Sir Neville.'

'Duh!' said Alan Deakins. A few children laughed.

Ronnie shook his head. 'Sir Neville was married. He loved his wife. Horatio should have killed her. That would have hurt Sir Neville more and been better revenge.'

Mrs Jennings was taken aback. 'Well, I don't know about that, Ronnie . . .'

'It would.'

Alan blew a raspberry. More giggling. Catherine told him to be quiet.

'Yes, well, perhaps you're right, Ronnie. Now for the rest of the lesson I want you all to draw pictures of Sir Neville's castle.'

Five minutes later all heads were bent over pieces of paper, Ronnie Sidney's included. Mrs Jennings watched him. His comments had taken her aback but perhaps it wasn't really so surprising. She knew he read a lot with his mother. Perhaps they had started looking at Shakespeare. The tragedies, possibly. Though Ronnie was too young to really appreciate it he would have understood something. He was a bright boy, after all, who learned his lessons well.

She began to think about what she would cook for supper.

September 1954.

'Anna,' said June Sanderson, 'there's something we need to discuss.'

'Have I done something wrong?'

'Far from it. I have a proposal to put to you.'

The two of them sat in June's kitchen. Albert was upstairs,

showing Ronnie recent additions to his stamp collection.

'I have a cousin. Barbara Pembroke. I think I've mentioned her.'

'The one who's moved to Oxfordshire?'

'That's right. A town called Kendleton. She has a house by the river.'

Anna nodded.

'I've told Barbara about you. About how highly Albert and I think of you. Barbara's an old lady. Her health isn't good. She has a weak heart and doesn't have long to live.'

Another nod. The eyes were confused.

'And she's lonely. She has no family near by. Her only son is working in America and she's looking for someone to act as a companion. Live in the house with her. Just keep her company. There'd be a little housework, but not much. She's a wealthy woman who already has a cook and a cleaner. A gardener too. There's even a nurse who visits her regularly. It's companionship she's after.'

'And you thought of me?'

'She'd pay well, Anna. Very well for the right person. She's a good woman. A little set in her ways perhaps, but kind. And . . .' June hesitated, choosing her words carefully. 'And generous. A woman who would remember a good companion in her will.'

'I see.'

'I know you want to get away from here. Build a new life for yourself. Have a home of your own. This could be the means to achieve that.'

Anna put down the tray she had been polishing. 'Do you think she'd want me?'

'You'd need to meet her, of course. But I'm sure she would. As I said, I've told her all about you. Sung your praises.' Another laugh. 'Cutting off my nose to spite my face, really, as the last thing I want is to lose you.'

Anna's expression became wistful. 'When I was a child, just before the war, my parents took my brother and me for a holiday on a narrow boat. We went through the London canals and out into the country. It was a wonderful holiday. The weather was glorious and we helped to work the lock gates. We passed through Oxfordshire and it was beautiful.'

'It still is. The Chilterns. The Goring Gap. Oxford itself. Home of the best university in the country.'

'Better than Cambridge?'

June looked indignant. 'A thousand times better.' Then she smiled. 'But my brother and Albert were at the same Oxford college. The two of them became friends and that's how we met, so perhaps I can be allowed a little bias.'

Anna smiled too. 'I think so.'

'It's a very different world from here.'

Anna's eyes began to shine. 'The sort of world I want for Ronnie. Somewhere green and beautiful. What are the schools like in Kendleton?'

June felt a tightening in her stomach. 'There's a catch, Anna. Barbara needs peace and her doctor is adamant that she mustn't have a child living in the house. Ronnie would have to stay with Stan and Vera.'

The smile faded as quickly as it had come. 'Then she'll have to find someone else.'

'But . . .'

'No.'

'Anna, think . . .'

'No! Absolutely not. Ronnie's all I have. I could never leave him. Never!' Anna flushed, her voice softened. 'I'm sorry. I don't mean to be rude. You've always been kind to us and I'm grateful but this isn't possible.'

Anna picked up the tray and continued her work. Upstairs June could hear Albert laughing at something Ronnie had said. On the far wall was a picture of the Tower of London. Another of Ronnie's efforts. Exceptional for a boy of not quite nine.

'It wouldn't be for ever, Anna. A few years, maybe less. You could come and visit. Kendleton's not that far away. Albert and I would keep an eye on Ronnie. He could visit us whenever he wanted. You know how fond we are of him. Please don't just dismiss the idea. Promise me you'll think about it.'

Silence. Upstairs the laughter continued.

'What's the matter, Mum?'

'Nothing, Ronnie.'

'Yes there is.'

They sat in the window of the Amalfi café. Ronnie had moved on from dissecting jam tarts and now ate chocolate éclairs. The café was crowded, the buzz of conversation almost drowning out the Alma Cogan record playing on the newly installed jukebox.

She told him what June Sanderson had said. 'Will you go?' he asked when she had finished.

'No. I told Mrs Sanderson that her cousin would have to find someone else.'

He nodded.

'Which she will.'

'They won't be as nice as you.'

'Thank you, Ronnie.' Anna sipped her tea. At a nearby table Emily Hopkins, sister of her one time suitor, Harry, talked with a younger woman called Peggy. Both kept looking over, making Anna feel uncomfortable. Harry had married Peggy the previous year and they were expecting their first child at Christmas. Peggy had dull hair and a mean mouth. Anna's friend, Kate, thought that Harry was a fool. That Peggy didn't have Anna's looks or sweet nature. But she didn't have an illegitimate child either.

Ronnie was staring at her. His eyes were troubled. Now it was her turn to be concerned. 'What is it?'

He didn't answer.

'Ronnie?'

He swallowed. 'You should go.'

She put down her cup. 'Do you want me to?'

'No. But . . .' He didn't finish his sentence. There was no need. She knew what he was thinking. What she was thinking herself.

'I don't want to leave you, Ronnie.'

'I'll be all right. I'm not a baby.'

There was cream on his lip. She reached out and wiped it away. 'No, you're not,' she said softly. 'You're my big, clever, grown-up boy, aren't you.'

Emily and Peggy were still glancing over. Uncharacteristically Ronnie made a face at them. Both quickly looked away. Anna suppressed the urge to laugh. 'That was naughty,' she told him. 'I'm very angry.'

He made a face at her too. A nice one this time. She thought of what she would have gained through marrying Harry. A decent, hard-working husband. A home of her own. Respectability. More children perhaps. The only price losing Ronnie for ever.

His hand was on the table. She gave it a squeeze. He squeezed back.

'I love you, Ronnie Sunshine. More than anything in the world.'

'I love you too, Mum. I don't want you to go away. But if you do I'll be all right.'

'Finish your éclair. We'll talk about this another time.'

He took a bite. Made a display of eating. But when they left the café half the éclair still remained on his plate.

October. While her husband snored in front of a quiz show on their new television set, Mrs Fletcher studied entries for a picture competition she had set the fourth-year class. The theme was 'An Important Person in My Life'. The winner was to receive five shillings and have their picture displayed on the school noticeboard for a week.

Most of the children had drawn their mothers. Naughty Alan Deakins had drawn that tart Marilyn Monroe, but Alan's mother looked like a tart so that was rather appropriate. Stuart Hooper, bottom of the class and eager to curry favour, had drawn what was supposed to be a flattering portrait of herself resembling a gargoyle. Some had drawn their fathers. Patriotic Catherine Meadows had drawn the Queen. Archie Clark had drawn his cat.

But one entry stood head and shoulders above the rest. Ronnie Sidney's drawing of his cousin Thomas.

It was an unusual drawing. Thomas himself did not appear. Ronnie had drawn a graveyard; at its centre a tombstone guarded by a stone angel with its wings spread out and its hands clasped in prayer. On the stone was carved: 'Thomas Stanley Finnegan. Born 12 November 1940. Died 7 October 1953'.

Mrs Fletcher thought back to the previous October when Thomas had gone missing. Her colleague, Mrs Jennings had told her how the whole class had prayed for Thomas's safety and of how worried

Ronnie had been. Scared that Thomas might be dead. Fortunately it had all worked out well.

But it could have been so different. That was what the drawing showed.

It was clever. Imaginative. Like Ronnie himself.

But it was also disturbing. Not the sort of thing to be displayed on a noticeboard. It might give the first-years nightmares.

She decided to award the prize to another child. There would be other competitions for Ronnie to win.

January 1955.

Ronnie stood on a platform at Paddington Station, talking to his mother at the window of her train. Uncle Stan and Peter, who had helped carry her luggage, waited near by.

'I'll write every day,' she told him. 'Tell me if you can't stand it. I can come back. I don't have to stay.'

'Don't worry, Mum.' He gave her his best Ronnie Sunshine smile. 'I'll be all right.'

The guard blew his whistle. It was time. She leant through the window. Hugged him as best she could while late arrivals pushed past trying to find seats.

The train began to move, sending clouds of white steam into the air. She remained at the window, waving. He waved back, fighting the urge to run after her and beg her to stay.

Then he walked back towards the others.

'All well, then, Ronnie,' said Uncle Stan in a tone of forced joviality.

He nodded.

'Let's have a plate of chips somewhere. I'm sure your aunt won't mind this once.'

'Thanks, Uncle Stan.'

'You two wait here for a minute. I need to get some cigarettes.'

'Aren't you going to cry?' demanded Peter once they were alone.

'No.'

'Yes you are. Come, on cry-baby bastard. Start blubbing for your mummy.'

Ronnie shook his head.

'You're only staying with us because Dad told Mum it would look bad if we didn't keep you. Otherwise you'd be in the orphanage with all the other bastards.'

A lump was growing in Ronnie's throat. The tears he had been battling against all day were very close. Peter's eyes shone as if sensing this. As Ronnie looked into them he remembered Auntie Vera lying on the kitchen floor. He imagined Peter lying there instead; screaming as boiling chip fat ate away his face.

Laughter bubbled up inside him, melting the lump into nothing.

Peter's smile faded, replaced by confusion. 'Cry!'

'Or what? Going to leave one of your roller skates for me to fall over?'

Peter flushed. 'Cunt!' He went to join his father.

Ronnie turned, wanting a last glimpse of his mother's train. But the platform was empty and she was gone.

4 February 1955

Dear Mum,
Thank you for your letter. It came this morning and I read it
at breakfast. Auntie Vera was cross but I didn't care. I took it
to school and read it three more times there. I am going to
read it in bed too!

I am fine. Thomas has a cold and has given it to Uncle Stan
but not me. Mrs Fletcher gave me a book to read called King
Solomon's Mines. *It is very good. We had a maths test and I*
came top with Archie. Last night Mr and Mrs Brown came for
dinner and Auntie Vera made fish stew from a recipe book. It
took her all day and I heard Mrs Brown tell Mr Brown that it
was the most horrible thing she had ever eaten.

Yesterday I saw Mr and Mrs Sanderson. They said to send
you their love and Auntie Mabel and Uncle Bill did too. Mr
Sanderson gave me a penny red stamp and some American
stamps and an album to put them in. There are different pages
for different countries. Archie's uncle lives in Australia and he
is going to give me stamps too.

Catherine Meadows sat next to me at school today. She said

that she is going to look after me while you are in Oxfordshire
but I told her that I don't need to be looked after. My job is to
look after you.

Lots and lots of love
from
Ronnie Sunshine

Mabel Cooper stood in her corner shop, listening to Emily Hopkins
talk about her brother Harry's newborn son, John. 'Such a beautiful
baby! And clever too. Do you know . . .' Mabel nodded politely,
while wondering whether Emily was actually going to buy anything.

Ronnie Sidney entered the shop, dressed in his school uniform. In
his hand was a white envelope.

'Hello, Ronnie, dear. What a nice surprise.'

'How are you, Auntie Mabel?'

'All the better for seeing you.'

He approached the counter. Emily's mouth tightened. She looked
him up and down as if trying to find fault with his appearance.
'How's your mother getting on?' she asked curtly.

'Fine, thank you.'

'Well, I must be off. Next time, Mabel, I'll bring a photograph of
John.'

'And a shopping list,' muttered Mabel as Emily left. Then she
smiled at Ronnie. 'Is that letter for your mother?'

'Yes.' He held out a shilling. 'Can I have a stamp, please?'

She gave him one. 'Did you send her our love?'

He nodded, while fixing the stamp to the envelope.

'And how are *you* getting on, Ronnie?'

His head remained lowered. 'All right.'

'Really?'

He looked up. Managed a smile. 'Really.'

She gave him a chocolate bar. The biggest one they had. 'Have this
too.'

'Thanks, Auntie Mabel.'

'Have tea with us soon. Bring some of your pictures. We'd love to
see them.'

'I will. Goodbye, Auntie Mabel. Say hello to Uncle Bill for me.'

She watched him make his way out of the shop. His second-hand uniform was too big but he would grow into it in time. A group of boys were playing football on the street outside, making the most of the last few minutes of daylight. One of them called for him to join them but he shook his head and carried on his way.

Once, years ago, she had heard a psychiatrist talking on the wireless, saying that often creative people needed solitude to truly hear the music inside themselves. Ronnie was something of a loner and he was artistic. Her husband, Bill, had a hunch that Ronnie would be famous one day. Perhaps he was right. Perhaps, twenty years from now, people would be asking her about *the* Ronnie Sidney and she would tell them: 'He was always contained. Solitary. But that was how he needed to be. Couldn't waste energy on the mundane. Not if he was to hear the music inside himself.'

Little Ronnie Sidney. A great man of the future? She hoped so. But only time would tell.

Another customer entered. She prepared to make a sale.

All the lights were off in 41 Moreton Street. Ronnie, wrapped in his dressing gown and using the moon for illumination, sat on the window ledge of his bedroom drawing a picture for his mother.

It was a copy of his favourite painting. Ophelia drowning with flowers in her hair. It wasn't as perfect as the original. He wasn't as skilled as Millais. Not yet. But one day he would be a famous artist and everyone in the world would know his name. It was what his mother wanted for him. He wanted it for her.

Her bed was stripped bare now. Uncle Stan had told him that he could sleep in it if he wanted. A change from the camp bed, which was almost too small for him. But he had refused. It was his mother's bed. He didn't want it to be used by anyone else, not even himself.

The moon was full. A great white orb high in the cold night sky. He stopped his work and gazed up at it, imagining as he had so many times before that he could see his father's plane flying across its face. In spite of his mother's pleas he refused to give up hope. One day his father *would* come and then the three of them would be together. He and his mother would finally be members of a proper family rather than just unwanted attachments to the family of others.

It would happen one day. He knew it would.

A train rattled past in the darkness, filling the room with noise and light. In the world behind his eyes he was walking towards a beautiful mansion by a river where his parents stood waiting while the train came off its railings, careering down the bank, smashing into the house he had left behind, wiping out the lives of those who slept there like a careless hand crushing a family of insects.

The drawing was finished. Good, but not good enough. Tearing it up, he began again, focusing all his energies upon the page, shutting out all background noise to better hear the music inside himself. Bundles of jumbled notes that in time would swell and grow into concertos and on into symphonies. And where those melodies would lead him only time would tell.

Little Ronnie Sunshine, a pocket full of rye.
Little Ronnie Sunshine, slugs and snails and puppy dogs' tails.
Little Ronnie Sunshine, a Mozart in the making.
Little Ronnie Sunshine . . .

Part 2

Oxfordshire: 1952

Osborne Row. A quiet street of terraced houses on the west side of Kendleton. Susan Ramsey lived at number 37 with her parents and a million photographs.

Every available surface was covered in framed images. Faded portraits of the grandparents she had never really known. Pictures of her father as an impish schoolboy or handsome in the uniform he had worn during the war. Pictures of her mother on childhood holidays or outside the church on her wedding day. But most of all there were pictures of Susan herself. Dozens of them. Every one of her six years lovingly chronicled for all to see.

Sometimes, when visitors were expected, her father would remove her pictures from the hallway and living room while her mother smiled and shook her head. When the visitors arrived Susan would hide on the stairs, looking at one of her books and waiting to be called down.

And as she entered the room, gazing curiously at the strange faces around her, the adult conversation simply died away.

Then it began, just as it always did. The talk of actresses known to all except herself. Vivien Leigh. Gene Tierney. Jean Simmons. Ava Gardner. Most were usually mentioned. But the one always discussed was Elizabeth Taylor. Susan knew nothing about Elizabeth Taylor except that she had once owned a beautiful collie dog called Lassie but then given it to a boy called Roddy McDowall. This meant that Elizabeth Taylor must be stupid, as if Susan had owned a dog she would not have given it to anyone. A dog was the thing she wanted most in the world.

Well, second most.

She would sit beside her mother on the sofa, eating sponge cake and telling the visitors about the things she was learning at school and Charlotte Harris who was in her class and lived in the same street and was her best friend. The visitors would smile and nod while her mother stroked her hair and her father, unnoticed, pulled faces so that eventually she would burst out laughing, spraying crumbs everywhere. Her father would then adopt a serious expression, remarking on how quickly poisons took effect and making her laugh even harder.

Sometimes, after being excused, she would sit in front of her mother's dressing-table mirror, studying the face that caused such excitement in others. It was heart shaped, framed by thick, dark hair. Blue-black, her father said. The skin was pale, lips red and full, nose slim and elegant. Huge eyes, rimmed by dark lashes, were so blue as to be almost purple. Violet, her mother said. The sort of face, said others, that men would one day die for.

But for now it was just her face. Quickly she would become bored and return to her own room with the bedspread decorated with moons and stars, the shelves full of books and toys and the conch shell her father had bought her while on holiday in Cornwall and which she had only to press to her ear to hear the sound of the sea.

In the centre of the room was a wooden crib that her paternal grandfather had made. Inside it, covered in a blanket, was a china doll that had been a present from her paternal grandmother. Both had died before her second birthday. She had no recollection of either but still she missed them. Her father talked about them often, keeping both alive in her mind.

She would kneel beside the crib, rocking it gently, singing the songs she had learned at school and feeling suddenly sad because the thing she wanted more than anything in the world was a brother or sister. A real-life doll that she could love and protect, just as her parents loved and protected her.

There would never be a baby. That was what her father had said. 'Why would we want another child,' he had gone on to ask, 'when we have the perfect one in you?' Though he was smiling his eyes had been sad and she had known that this was all part of some strange adult mystery that she did not yet understand and could only accept.

But still the longing remained, and as she sang to the doll she would stare into its painted eyes, willing it to live and make her dreams come true.

Kendleton, like most small towns, had its exclusive addresses.

The most prestigious was The Avenue: a collective description for the grand houses to the south-east of the town centre, all with huge gardens that backed on to the Thames. Susan's parents were not friends with any of the residents of The Avenue, but one of Susan's classmates, Alice Wetherby, lived there, and Susan and her friend Charlotte had been to Alice's house for a party. During the party Alice's elder brother Edward had thrown Charlotte's glasses into the river and made her cry, so Susan had punched Edward in the mouth and made him cry, immediately being sent home in disgrace and so bringing to an end her association with Kendelton's elite.

But she still had connections. The next most desirable address was Queen Anne Square; a quadrangle of beautiful red-brick houses in the shadow of Kendleton Church and home to Susan's godmother Auntie Emma and her husband Uncle George. The two of them had married the previous summer and Susan had been bridesmaid, sharing the honours with a girl called Helen, who had thrown a tantrum because she didn't like her dress and then been spectacularly sick when they were halfway down the aisle.

The heart of Kendleton was Market Court: a huge oval space at the centre of the town with streets running off it like the strands of a spider's web. The wealthier members of town lived on the east side, where houses were larger and streets wider, and 'crossing the Court' was something that many a west-side resident longed to do.

Market Court was full of shops, including Ramsey's Studio, which belonged to Susan's father. He was a photographer, specializing in portraits. Two years earlier a local newspaper had run a competition to find 'Little Miss Sparkle' and Susan's father had submitted her portrait. She had won and received ten shillings, a book of fairy tales and the honour of having her picture in the paper under the heading 'Little Susan Ramsey sparkles like a star'. Her father had had the article framed and hung on the wall of his shop so that everyone could see.

And from that day on she was always his little Susie Sparkle.

*

July 1952.

Until it happened, Susan had no idea that her mother was ill.

There were no obvious signs. Though her mother had complained of tiredness she often had trouble sleeping. And if she was quieter than usual, it was Susan's father who had always been the exuberant one.

It happened on a Wednesday afternoon. A hot, sticky afternoon two days before the start of the school holidays. Susan and Charlotte walked home with Charlotte's mother, whose turn it was to collect them, their satchels bouncing against their thighs as they made plans for the summer. Charlotte's cousins from Norfolk were coming to stay and Susan said that they should build a den in the woods to the west of the town. Her father had built dens there when he was a boy and had promised to show them a good place.

They reached number 22: Charlotte's house. Charlotte's mother asked Susan whether she wanted to come in and play but Susan said that she had promised to be home promptly. After saying goodbye she ran on to number 37 and knocked on the door.

She waited but the door remained closed. After counting to twenty she knocked again. Still nothing. She opened the letterbox. 'Mum, it's me. Let me in.' The wireless was playing in the background. Her mother must be there. Why wasn't she opening the door?

She stood on the doorstep, unsure what to do. Mrs Bruce from number 45 passed by, carrying her shopping basket and battling with her dog, Warner, who was pulling in the other direction. She gave Susan a wave. Susan waved back while wondering whether to call Charlotte's mother.

Then the door did open. But only an inch. From behind it she heard footsteps moving away. Slow and heavy. Like those of an old person. Not like her mother at all.

For a moment she hesitated. The first pricklings of fear starting within her.

Then, pushing the door open, she walked in. From the living room came the sound of movement, so she entered it.

Her mother was sitting on the sofa, wearing a dressing gown. Both her feet were bare. A hand kept tugging at a lock of hair. On the coffee table was a teapot and two cups, a huge plate of sandwiches and an apple with a candle burning in its centre.

'Mum?'

No answer. The wireless was broadcasting a play about sailors.

Susan began to approach. Her mother turned. For a moment her eyes were so blank it was as if she didn't know her daughter at all. Then the light of recognition. But faint. Like a flickering bulb that could blow at any moment.

'Sit down. Eat your tea.' The voice was flat. Empty. Not like her mother's voice at all. The hand continued to pull at the lock of hair.

Susan looked at the table. The sandwiches, neatly cut and trimmed, were empty. Just pieces of bread curling in the heat of the room. Wax from the candle slid over the apple and down to the table beneath.

The fear kept growing inside her. She didn't understand. What was happening? Why was her mother acting like this?

Her mother pointed to the apple. 'Make a wish.'

'Mum?'

'Make a wish. Wish for something nice. Wish . . .'

The voice faded away. The hair was so frayed it was starting to break. The wireless played on regardless while outside boys rode past on their bicycles, ringing their bells and laughing.

'Mum, I don't understand . . .'

Her mother began to cry. A soft, whimpering sound like a wounded animal. Susan put her arms around her, hugging her as tight as she could and starting to cry too.

The phone rang in the hallway. She ran to pick up the receiver and heard her father's voice. 'Dad, something's wrong with Mum. Come home, Dad. Come home, please . . .'

The rest of the day was a blur. Her father sent her to play in her room. Auntie Emma arrived to take her to Queen Anne Square. 'It's just for tonight,' she was told. 'Don't worry about Mum. Everything will be fine.'

In the end she stayed with Auntie Emma for most of the summer. Her father visited every evening. Her mother never came.

Auntie Emma and Uncle George were very kind. Auntie Emma,

young and pretty, took her on picnics by the river and trips to Oxford for new clothes and toys, and once to see *Peter Pan* at the theatre. Uncle George, homely and nudging middle age, was an architect who helped her draw pretend cities and told her stories about New York, where he had lived for three years and which was the most exciting city in the world.

Auntie Emma and Uncle George had a friend called Mr Bishop who was a lawyer and also lived in Queen Anne Square. When he came to visit he told Susan to call him Uncle Andrew. He had a sports car and once took Susan and Auntie Emma for a drive in the country with the roof down and the wind blowing in their faces. He thought that Susan looked like Elizabeth Taylor too.

Whenever she asked about her mother they said that there was no need to worry. 'Mum's gone on holiday but she'll be home soon and wanting to know all your news.' The explanation came with smiles that were just a little too bright and told her that they were lying.

Sometimes, when she couldn't sleep, she would creep downstairs to eavesdrop on their conversations. From these she gathered that her mother had had something called a breakdown, that she was in a special hospital and that they were all very worried about her.

She never told them what she had heard because she knew they didn't want her to find out. They didn't want anyone to find out.

But of course people did.

A hot Monday in September. The first day back at school. Susan's teacher was taking the class for a nature walk.

They took the path by the river that led west out of town and on towards Kendleton Lock. They walked in pairs, the boys wearing caps, the girls hats, to keep the sun off their heads. Their teacher, Mrs Young, kept up a running commentary on the surrounding fauna but no one listened, all too busy exchanging waves and greetings with the people on the brightly coloured narrow boats that were waiting to pass through the lock and continue their journeys down river.

Eventually the high spirits boiled over. As they walked through a field of bored looking cows the boy at the front of the line started hurling the caps of his friends into the river. The line came to an abrupt halt as Mrs Young scolded him and a good-natured boatman tried to rescue the fast-sinking caps with a fish hook.

Susan and Charlotte, standing near the back, discussed which narrow boat they liked best. Susan favoured one called *Merlin*, less for the castles painted on its side than for the yellow dog sunning itself on the roof. Charlotte was just telling Susan which boat she liked when Alice Wetherby announced that people who wore glasses were ugly.

Charlotte fell silent. She was the only person in the class to wear glasses and hated doing so. Charlotte's mother and Susan were always telling her that they looked nice but she didn't believe them.

'People who wear glasses are ugly,' said Alice again. Louder this time.

'I'm not ugly,' Charlotte told her.

Alice grinned, pleased to have provoked a reaction. She was a pretty girl with long blonde hair. 'Yes you are. You're the ugliest person in the world.'

'I'm not!'

Alice began to prod Charlotte with her finger. 'Ugly ugly ugly.' Alice's gang took up the chant, surrounding Charlotte and prodding her too. They enjoyed picking on people. The previous term they had taken against a girl called Janet Evans and tried to stop all the other girls from speaking to her. Janet had been very upset.

As was Charlotte. She shook her head, close to tears. Charlotte was afraid of Alice. But Susan wasn't. She pushed herself into the circle and shoved Alice away. 'You leave her alone. You're the ugly one.'

'Shut up!'

Susan began to prod Alice. 'Make me.'

'Stop it!'

'Make me!'

'Stop it, loony mother!'

Susan stopped. 'What?'

'Your mother's a loony.'

'No she's not.'

'Yes she is. She's in a loony bin.'

63

'She's on holiday.'

'She's in a loony bin. Everyone knows.'

'She's not!'

Alice's eyes began to shine. 'Loony mother! Loony mother!' Again her gang took up the chant, while on the river the yellow dog jumped into the water to chase the ducks that swam by the boat. 'Samson!' bellowed his owner. 'Come back 'ere!'

'Loony mother!' continued Alice. She started to dance around in front of Susan, pulling crazy faces. 'Loony! Loony!'

Susan grabbed Alice by the hair, marched her off the path and into the field of cows. 'Get off!' Alice yelled. 'Leave her alone!' shouted Alice's friends. 'Susan Ramsey! Stop that this instant!' bellowed Mrs Young. Susan ignored them all. She dragged Alice on until she found the perfect spot then shoved her hard. Alice fell forward, landing on her stomach in a cow pat much to the surprise of the cow chewing grass near by.

'Cows eat people covered in poo,' Susan announced. 'Come on, cows. Lunch!'

Alice jumped to her feet and ran screaming across the field, terrifying the cows, which parted before her like the Red Sea before Moses. 'Alice Wetherby, come back here,' cried Mrs Young, giving chase as fast as her ample frame would allow and looking rather like a lumbering cow herself.

Susan began to laugh. Others did the same while Samson emerged from the river, shaking himself dry and drenching them all.

'She said things about Mum.'

'What things?'

'Horrid things.'

It was six o'clock. She sat on her father's knee in the living room of their home. Now that term had started she was living with him again.

'What things, Susie?'

'That Mum was a loony. That she was in a loony bin.'

'She's on holiday.'

'That's what I told Alice.'

'Good girl.' He smiled down at her. His eyes were grey, his hair light brown. Her colouring came from her mother. She didn't want to upset him but she had to know.

'What's a breakdown?'

The smile faltered.

'She *is* in a loony bin, isn't she?'

'Susie . . .'

'Isn't she?'

'Listen . . .'

'Is it my fault?'

'Oh, Susie.' He pulled her close, kissing the top of her head. 'No, my darling, it's not your fault. None of this is your fault.'

She rested her head against his chest. On his finger was a signet ring that had once belonged to her grandfather. She twisted it back and forward, watching it catch the light. 'What's a breakdown, Dad?'

'Nothing bad, Susie. No matter what anyone says. It means that Mum . . . that Mum . . .'

'What?'

Silence. His eyes were thoughtful. She waited expectantly.

'When you fought with Alice were you scared?'

'I'm not scared of her.'

'But Charlotte is, isn't she?'

'Yes.'

'You still like Charlotte, though, don't you? You don't think bad things about her because she was scared.'

'No. She's my best friend.'

'When someone has a breakdown, Susie, it means that they've become scared of everything. That's what's happened to Mum. So she's gone away to learn how to feel brave again and when she does she'll come back home.'

Again he smiled. A reassuring gesture. One she did not return.

'What if she gets scared again?'

'She won't.'

'But what if she does?'

'She won't, I promise.'

'But what if she does? Will she have another breakdown? I don't want her to go away again. Not ever.'

'She won't get scared, Susie. Shall I tell you why?'

'Why?'

'Because we won't let it happen. We'll protect her. Just like you protected Charlotte.'

She nodded. They would. No matter what it took, they would.

After supper they walked by the river. The same path she had taken earlier in the day. A wind was rising, sending banks of clouds galloping across the sky.

They sat by the river bank, dangling their feet in the water, throwing pieces of bread to the ducks while the last of the boats passed through the lock. Her father made up stories about them, pretending they were pirate ships off to seek treasure on the Spanish Main. One came to moor beside them. An old man sat in the stern, smoking a pipe and smiling at the stories while his wife cooked a meal in the galley and their small black dog ran up and down the bank.

'You tell the best stories in the world,' she said when he had finished.

'Not me. Your grandfather. He used to bring me here when I was your age. Your grandmother would make us sandwiches and as we ate them he'd tell me the stories I'm telling you. Only he told them much better. Your grandmother said he should get them published but he never did. He said that they were just for me. Now they're for you.'

The dog came to sit beside them. The old man told them that his name was Bosun. 'You've got a friend there,' he said, winking at Susan. His wife appeared, carrying mugs of tea and biscuits for Bosun.

It was growing late. The light started to drip out of the sky. A swan landed on the water, sending circles to stretch across its surface. The old couple went down to the galley to eat, leaving Bosun on the river bank with his head in Susan's lap. She made a chain of flowers to hang around his neck while the cold water lapped at her toes.

'I wish you'd known my father, Susie. He would have been so proud of you.'

'Why?'

'Because you're strong.'

'I'm stronger than Alice.'

He touched her chest. 'I mean strong in here. Strong inside. Stronger than either your mother or me. Your grandfather was the same. He was a quiet man. Shy. Private. Not a noisy little baggage like you. But he had this strength inside him. Something very few people have. You felt safe around him because you knew that no matter what you asked of him he'd never let you down.'

The wind blew hair across her face. He brushed it back. 'You don't understand what I mean, do you?'

'No.'

'You will one day.' He turned, looking at the field behind them. The cows were lying down now, bedding in for the night. 'Is that where you pushed Alice over?'

'Yes.'

He pretended to look cross, then the smile that was so much a part of him spread across his face. 'I love you, Susie Sparkle. Don't ever change. Always stay the way you are.'

Suddenly he raised his foot, spraying her with water. She did the same. Soon both were drenched while Bosun ran around barking, frightening the unfortunate cows almost as much as Alice had done.

Noon, the next day. Susan's class sat in rows of double desks, copying the names of capital cities on to maps of Europe.

'I'm going out for a minute,' Mrs Young told them. 'Work in silence until I return.'

At first her order was obeyed. Then Alice Wetherby said, 'I'm glad my mother's not a loony.'

'I'm glad I'm not ugly,' said one of her gang.

Susan pointed to the window and let out a gasp. 'Run, Alice! The cows are coming!'

Everybody laughed. A few boys made mooing sounds. Charlotte gave Susan their special best-friend smile. Smiling back, Susan carried on with her work.

In November her mother came home.

She returned on a Friday. All week Susan had been unable to

concentrate, her head too full of everything she wanted to tell her mother when they were finally reunited. But as she entered the house and saw her mother standing there all words went out of her head. She started crying and couldn't stop; the fear and dread of the previous four months discharging themselves in a tidal wave of pure joy.

On Sunday they went to Auntie Emma's for tea. Auntie Emma had made scones, and as Susan ate she told her mother about the cities she had drawn with Uncle George and the picnics she and Auntie Emma had shared. Her mother tried to thank them but neither was having any of it. 'It was our pleasure,' said Uncle George. 'It was just as much fun for me,' said Auntie Emma. 'We found lots of lovely places, didn't we, Susie? We gave them special names too. You'll have to show them to your mum.'

'Next summer,' said Susan's mother, 'we can all have picnics together.'

Susan nodded. 'We can go to the pirates' lair. That's my favourite.'

As she spoke she noticed her father's expression become troubled. Uncle George's too.

But Auntie Emma was smiling. 'Of course we can.' She offered another scone to Susan. 'Eat up. I made these especially for you.'

Susan looked again at her father and Uncle George. Both nodded encouragingly. 'Go on, Susie,' said Uncle George. 'You'll never grow up to be an architect if you don't eat your scones. That's all my parents ever gave me and look at me now.'

They all laughed. She did as she was told.

December. Susan stood in Market Court, holding her mother's hand and listening to the Kendleton church choir, who were gathered around the Norman cross at its centre, singing carols.

It was late afternoon and already dark. A light dusting of frost covered the ground. The choir sang 'Once in Royal David's City', using old-fashioned lanterns for illumination; their breath condensing before them like ghosts dancing in the air. A crowd had gathered, many carrying shopping baskets full of presents. The bus from Oxford arrived and most of the passengers came to listen too.

The choirmaster asked for one of the children to choose the next carol. 'Hark the Herald Angels Sing,' cried Susan, knowing that it was her mother's favourite. The choir began to sing. 'Thank you, Susie,' said her mother, giving her hand a squeeze.

Her father came to join them, his cheeks red from the cold. 'Not this dreadful dirge,' he said, and began to hum out of tune, while her mother, laughing, told him to stop.

The carols came to an end. The crowd began to disperse. The three of them stood together, looking up at the cold, dark sky. Her father told her that when he and her mother had first met they had stolen a rowing boat and sat together all night on the river watching the stars. Her mother told her that the owner of the boat had reported them to the police and that her parents had forbidden the two of them from ever meeting again.'

'You didn't take any notice, though,' said Susan's father.

Susan's mother shook her head.

'More fool you.'

They kissed each other. Again her mother was laughing. She looked beautiful and happy. Not scared of anything.

As they moved through the crowds Susan saw Alice Wetherby standing with an elderly couple she didn't recognize. Visiting relatives probably. Alice was tugging at the woman's coat and pointing at Susan's mother. The woman began to stare. Susan stuck her tongue out. Quickly the woman looked away. Alice made a face back. Susan mouthed a single 'moo' and Alice, scowling, looked away too.

Her mother, who was talking about the carols, didn't notice. Her father, who was nodding in agreement, did. The two of them exchanged winks as they continued on their way.

April 1953.

It was a Saturday. Susan's mother was spending the day in Lyndham, a nearby village, visiting an old aunt. Susan and her father were going to the cinema.

There was no cinema in Kendleton so they had taken the bus to Oxford. The film they had chosen was *Singing in the Rain*. Susan's parents had taken her to see it the previous weekend and she had loved it so much that she had begged to be taken again.

They sat together in the auditorium, waiting for the lights to dim and the film to start. Most of the seats were full. One of the few empty ones was next to Susan. 'Smudge could have sat there,' she told her father.

'You're obsessed with that cat!'

Smudge was a ginger tabby with a black patch around his nose. Auntie Emma had given him to Susan in January as a seventh birthday present. Her father had taken a photograph of her sitting on the sofa with Smudge on her knee and Auntie Emma and Uncle George on either side. All three were wearing party hats and grinning for the camera.

That had been the last time she had seen them. Two days later they had left England for Australia, where Uncle George had an important new job. Auntie Emma had assured her that it wouldn't be for ever. That they would be back before she knew it. So far she had received three letters and a picture of a kangaroo which she had taken to school to show her friends. Mrs Young had pointed Australia out on the map. 'It's the other side of the world,' she had told the class, and Susan had suddenly felt sure that in spite of all their promises she would never see Auntie Emma and Uncle George again.

The feeling returned now, like a blow struck by an invisible fist. She lowered her head, staring down at her hands. On her wrist was a tiny bracelet. Another present from Auntie Emma, bought the previous summer while her mother was in hospital.

'What is it, Susie?'

'I hate it when people go away.'

'But they come back. You just have to be patient.' He took her chin in his hand, gently stretching her lips into a smile. It tickled and lifted her mood. He stroked her hair, telling her about when he was a boy and had come to this very cinema to see silent films just like the ones they were making at the start of *Singing in the Rain*.

'I wouldn't have liked those films,' she said.

'Oh yes you would. An orchestra used to play and the audience would shout and cheer. The stars were wonderful then. Buster Keaton was my favourite but there was Charlie Chaplin and Douglas Fairbanks. Your grandfather used to say that none of the modern stars could hold a candle to them.'

'Not even Elizabeth Taylor?'

He tweaked her nose. 'Well, perhaps her.'

The lights dimmed. She felt happy to be with him, there in the dark, waiting to be swept up in the excitement on the screen.

The film was wonderful. Even better the second time. When Donald O'Connor sang 'Make 'em Laugh' and inadvertently leapt through a wall they laughed so hard that the woman in the row behind began to complain. During the interval he bought choc-ices from a girl with a tray. As they ate them she waved to a boy in her class who was sitting near by.

It was raining when the bus dropped them in Market Court.

'How about a cream cake?' he asked.

She thought of the supper waiting for them. 'Mum will be cross.'

'Not if we don't tell her.' He took her hand and began to hum 'Singing in the Rain'. She did the same and they danced through the raindrops, drawing amused smiles from passers-by.

They sat in Hobson's Tea Shop, he sipping coffee while she chose a custard slice from the trolley pushed by a uniformed waitress.

'Have you enjoyed your day, Susie?'

'Yes. *Singing in the Rain* is the best film ever!' She bit into her cake. Sweet cream and flaky pastry merged in her mouth. A middle-aged couple at another table kept glancing over. She heard the woman whisper the word 'beautiful'.

Her father heard too and smiled. 'Perhaps you'll be in films one day. You'll live in Hollywood and your mother and I will go and see you at the cinema and tell everyone that the big star on the screen is our little Susie Sparkle and that we're more proud of her than we can say.'

She carried on eating. He sat, watching her. A kind man with untidy hair, twinkling eyes and a smile that could light up a whole room, just as it was doing now.

Then, suddenly, it faded.

She put down her fork. 'Dad?'

His eyes widened as if in shock.

'Dad?'

He put his hand to his chest, the colour draining from his face. 'Oh, Jesus Christ . . .'

'Dad!'

He slid sideways on his seat, his other hand grabbing at the tablecloth, pulling the contents of the table down with him as he fell to the floor.

The man from the nearby table crouched down beside him. She did the same but the woman who had called her beautiful pulled her away. 'It's all right, dear,' she said soothingly. 'My husband's a doctor. He knows what to do.'

The owner of the shop ran over. 'It's a heart attack,' said the man. 'Phone an ambulance. Quick!'

Susan tried to break free from the woman. People moved between them and her father so she couldn't see him any more. She told herself not to be frightened. That this was just one of his jokes. That he would soon appear and start teasing her for being such a baby.

But when the crowds parted he was still lying there. And this time she could no longer see his face. The owner of the shop had covered it with a towel.

In the days that followed it seemed as if the whole world had lost its voice. People spoke in whispers, their faces exaggerated masks of sorrow, so that in her dazed state she began to believe that she was trapped in one of those silent films her father had loved so much.

His funeral was like a dream. A long, tiring ceremony that did nothing to make what had happened seem any more real. She sat next to her mother in the front row of Kendleton Church, listening to the vicar say that her father would never truly be dead as long as he lived on in their hearts. She tried to understand but her head felt as if it would burst with all the thoughts that jostled inside. Her father *was* dead, and that meant he was gone and would never come back. But if he never came back she would never see him again and that wasn't possible. But if he did come back then he wouldn't be dead and . . .

When it all grew too much she shut her eyes, hiding in self-imposed darkness and seeking comfort in the warmth of his remembered smile. But when she opened them again she was still in the church, the vicar was still speaking, her mother was crying and the pain in her head was so bad that it made her want to scream.

Mrs Young told the class that she was very brave and didn't mind when she failed to pay attention during lessons. The other children made her a huge card and decorated it with wild flowers. All were kind to her, though some would stare at her warily as if her loss were an infection they could all catch.

She longed for Auntie Emma and Uncle George to come but they never did. Her mother said that Australia was too far away. Others came, though. An endless stream of visitors eager to recite their platitudes and wallow in the drama. 'Such a shock,' they told her mother. 'We couldn't believe it when we heard. Only thirty-six, poor man. It's always the good that die young, isn't it? But life must go on.'

They fussed over Susan, praising her for being 'such a grown-up girl'. 'You keep it up, dear,' said one neighbour whom she barely knew. 'Your mother needs you to be brave.' She had nodded and promised that she would.

But it was her mother who needed to be brave.

An early evening in June. The two of them sat on the living-room sofa while Smudge chased a ball of paper around their feet. From the house next door came the sound of singing. A party to celebrate the coronation. Her mother had tried to make her go but she had refused.

'We'll be all right, Mum.'

'How can we be without money?' Her mother stubbed out her cigarette and lit another. She had always been a light smoker but in recent weeks her consumption of tobacco had increased. As she smoked she twisted her wedding ring round and round her finger.

'Mum . . .'

'Your grandmother always said I was a fool to marry him. No practical sense. Just a dreamer with his head in the clouds. She was right too.'

'No she wasn't.'

The fingers continued to twist the ring. 'And this is right? Leaving us with barely enough money to survive. What sort of man does that to his family? A weak, selfish man. That's what he was.'

'No he wasn't! Don't say that about him. Don't!'

Her mother's face was in shadow. For a moment the eyes looked as blank as on the day of the breakdown. Just a trick of the light but enough to fill Susan with terror. Next door, people were laughing as someone sang the national anthem. When her father had been alive their house had been full of laughter but now he had gone and taken all the joy with him.

'Don't be scared, Mum. Please don't be scared.'

Silence. She stared into her mother's face. A soft, nervous version of her own. 'Susan has her mother's looks but her father's spirit.' That was what people said. Perhaps they were right. All she knew was that she loved them both and having lost one could not survive losing the other.

'Mum?'

'I'm sorry, Susie. I didn't mean that. Your father was a good man. I just miss him, that's all.'

A lump came into her throat. She tried to swallow it down. If she cried it meant she wasn't brave and that was something she had to be. For both of them.

'We'll be all right, Mum. I'll look after you. I won't let you get scared.'

They hugged each other. Her mother started to cry. In spite of her determination so did she, while next door the national anthem ended to a chorus of cheers.

A Saturday afternoon in August. Susan returned home from Charlotte's house. She knocked on the door, then waited, watching Mrs Bruce from number 45 wage the usual battle of wills with Warner.

Her mother let her in. 'Mr Bishop is here, Susie.'

'Who?'

'Mr Bishop. Auntie Emma and Uncle George's friend.'

She walked into the living room. Mr Bishop, or Uncle Andrew as she knew him, was sitting on a chair by the window, stroking Smudge, who was perched on his knee. He gave her a big smile. 'Hello, Susie.'

'Hello.' On the coffee table was a huge doll's house. 'Whose is that?'

'It's yours.'

'Mr Bishop brought it for you,' said her mother. 'Isn't it a lovely present?'

'Thank you, Uncle Andrew.'

'Mr Bishop,' her mother corrected.

'Uncle Andrew is fine. We're old friends, aren't we, Susie?'

Smudge jumped off Uncle Andrew's knee and scampered towards her. Picking him up she sat down on the sofa. 'Uncle Andrew took me and Auntie Emma for a ride in his car,' she told her mother.

The doll's house had three floors and nine rooms. 'It belonged to my grandmother,' Uncle Andrew told her. 'It's one hundred years old.'

'It's so generous of you,' said Susan's mother. 'Isn't it, Susie?'

She nodded. Uncle Andrew looked pleased. He had a round face, dark hair and grey eyes like her father. His smile could not light up a room the way her father's had but it was nice all the same.

Her mother cut her a slice of sponge cake. 'So how is the world outside?' Uncle Andrew asked. Susan told him about Mrs Bruce and Warner. Her mother shook her head. 'It's madness. She's over sixty, less than five foot tall and the dog is an Alsatian! He's always running off and causing trouble.'

'Once,' said Susan, 'he jumped up on Mrs Wetherby in Market Court and she dropped all her shopping. It was really funny.'

Her mother frowned. 'It wasn't funny.'

'It was. Mrs Wetherby's horrid.'

'Susie!'

'Well, she is. She wanted to have Warner shot and he was only playing.'

'Is that Mrs Wetherby who lives in The Avenue?' asked Uncle Andrew.

'Yes. Her daughter Alice is my class. She's horrid too.'

'Susan Ramsey!'

Uncle Andrew started to laugh. Eventually Susan's mother followed suit. As Susan ate her cake she looked at the doll's house. There were tiny dolls in each room, all dressed in Victorian costume, lounging on miniature chairs or cleaning miniature grates. She had never had much time for dolls except for the one her grandmother had given her but Uncle Andrew was watching her anxiously so she made a show of playing with his gift while Smudge stretched out on her knee, purring contentedly.

Time passed. Uncle Andrew said that he had to go as he was expected at a dinner in Oxford. 'With some of my fellow lawyers,' he explained.

'I'm sure that will be nice,' said Susan's mother.

'Nothing of the sort, sadly. Three hours discussing the latest developments in drainage law. Hardly a prospect to fill the heart with joy.'

They all laughed. He rose to leave. 'Thank you for the present,' Susan told him.

'Perhaps next weekend I could take you both for a ride in my car.'

Susan's mother looked uncertain. 'That's very kind. I'm not sure . . .'

'Go on, Mum. It'll be fun.'

'Well, perhaps. If the weather's good.'

It was.

They drove through country lanes, Susan in the back seat, while her mother sat up front with Uncle Andrew. The roof was down, the wind blowing in her face, blasting her hair and making her cheeks tingle.

Later they walked in the woods to the west of the town. Pine trees stood in rows like pillars in an outdoor cathedral while banks of flowers covered the ground like coloured marble. She ran ahead, searching for her favourite oak tree while her mother and Uncle Andrew followed behind. When she found it she prepared to climb, squinting up at the sunlight that shone through the branches and feeling the familiar rush of excitement.

Then she stopped.

Her father had loved these woods. The two of them had spent many afternoons hunting for new trees to climb. This oak he had christened the Golden Hind because its branches were like the rigging of a giant ship. She would climb as high as she could, pretending she was in the crow's-nest while he would stand below with an imaginary telescope; the two of them on a voyage of exploration, their discoveries limited only by the powers of their combined imagination.

Now it was just a tree. All the magic had gone. He had taken it with him and it would never return.

She stood at its base, close to tears, fighting them back, determined to be brave.

Uncle Andrew approached with her mother. His eyes were sympathetic, as if understanding her feelings. 'Go on, Susie,' he said, gently. 'I'd love to see you climb.'

For a moment she hesitated. But her mother was smiling; looking relaxed and happy. And that made her happy too.

Seizing the lowest branch, she began to pull herself up.

'What a lovely afternoon,' said her mother that evening.

'Can we go again next weekend? Uncle Andrew said he'd take us.'

'I don't think so, darling. Uncle Andrew's a busy man. We mustn't take up too much of his time.'

But in the weeks that followed they took up an increasing amount.

There were more drives in the country and walks in the woods. There was dinner at a smart hotel in Oxford where Susan was allowed a sip of wine and marvelled at all the different knives and forks around her plate. One Sunday he cooked them lunch at his house. 'Very badly,' he joked as he carved the joint of beef. He made a lot of jokes. They weren't as funny as her father's but still made her smile. His house was very tidy, full of old furniture and with paintings hanging on every wall. Susan spilled a drink on the carpet, much to her mother's horror, but Uncle Andrew said that he was always spilling things and that it didn't matter at all.

There were presents too. A book about famous explorers. A new basket for Smudge. A bicycle with a red seat and a shiny bell. Her mother expressed concern that she was being spoilt but Uncle Andrew said she deserved a bit of spoiling after losing her father, and then her mother would nod and agree that he was right.

One Saturday they went to the cinema to see a Disney film. The first feature was a history of comedy in cinema with clips of Buster Keaton and Charlie Chaplin whom she found just as wonderful as her father had promised. During the interval her mother went to buy ice creams. A small thank-you to Uncle Andrew, who had paid for the tickets.

'You're thinking about him, aren't you?' he said, when they were alone.

She nodded.

'It hurts, doesn't it?'

'Yes.'

'The pain will go away, Susie. You probably don't believe me but it's true.'

She looked up into his face. He was smiling. She smiled back.

'Your mother's very proud of you. She thinks you're the bravest girl in the world.'

'She's brave too.'

'You love her very much.'

'More than anyone.'

'She went away once.'

'Yes. She got scared.'

'Scared?'

'Scared of everything. That's what Dad said. But then she got brave so she came back home.'

'Do you think of what would happen if she became scared again?'

She remembered the blank look in her mother's eyes. A chill swept over her. 'I won't let her get scared.'

A lock of hair had fallen across her cheek. He brushed it back. 'That's a big responsibility for someone as young as you.'

'I'm not a baby.'

'I know that. But it's still a burden. Perhaps I can help.'

'How?'

'By being your friend. Someone you can talk to if you get scared now your father's not here. You do get scared, don't you?'

Silence.

'You do, don't you? It's nothing to be ashamed of. Even the bravest girl in the world is allowed to get scared sometimes.'

She wanted to deny it. But his eyes were sympathetic. Understanding. Just like her father's had been.

'I get scared Mum will go away and never come back.'

'Is that what scares you most in the world?'

'Yes.'

He took her hand. Squeezed it gently. 'Thank you for trusting me with that, Susie. I'll keep it secret. You can trust me. I'm your friend. You know that, don't you?'

She nodded.

'Good.'

Impulsively she kissed his cheek. He blushed slightly. Again he squeezed her hand. A woman in the next row smiled at her. She smiled back, happy to have a friend like Uncle Andrew.

A wet November day. Susan's class were spending their mid-morning break indoors.

Susan sat on a desk with Charlotte, talking to Lizzie Flynn and Arthur Hammond. Lizzie was small, dark and spirited and lived above the tiny pub her father ran. Arthur was small, blond and timid and lived in one of the grand houses in The Avenue.

'I wish I didn't have to go,' said Arthur. He was leaving Kendleton at the end of term for the boarding school in Yorkshire that three generations of his family had attended. His elder brother, Henry, was already a pupil there.

'So do I,' said Lizzie.

'If you stayed here,' said Susan, 'you could go to Heathcote. My mum says it's really good.' Heathcote Academy was a private day school on the outskirts of the town that took boys and girls from the age of eleven. Most Kendleton parents aspired to send their children there but the fees were a barrier for many.

Arthur shook his head. 'My father says I have to go to Yorkshire.'

'Your father's stupid, then,' said Lizzie bluntly.

'Henry says they beat up new boys and put their heads down toilets.'

'Henry's just trying to scare you,' Lizzie told him. 'He's stupid too.'

Susan nodded. 'He must be. He's friends with Edward Wetherby.'

Lizzie laughed. Rain pounded the window. Outside the skies were black. Alice Wetherby, sitting near by, looked over. 'What are you talking about?' she demanded.

'Mind your own business,' replied Susan.

'Yes. Go and sit in a cow pat,' added Lizzie.

They all laughed except Charlotte, who was quieter than usual. 'What's the matter with you?' Susan asked.

'My mum says your mum's going to marry Mr Bishop.'

'No. He's just our friend.'

'Well, that's what my mum says and she says that when that happens you and your mum will go and live in Queen Anne Square.'

'My mum's not marrying Mr Bishop.'

'But my mum says . . .'

'I don't care what your mum says.'

Alice approached with a girl called Kate, who was the only member of her gang not to have been struck down by a flu bug. 'You're going to have a loony as a neighbour,' Alice told Kate, who lived in Queen Anne Square herself.

'She'll probably kill everyone,' said Kate.

'No, Kate,' said Susan sweetly. 'Only you.'

Even Charlotte laughed at that. Lizzie began to hum 'Old MacDonald had a farm'. Alice, lacking her usual number of reinforcements, sneered then walked away.

'I hope your mum doesn't marry him,' said Charlotte, 'because if you live in Queen Anne Square then you'll be crossing the Court and we won't be best friends any more.'

'Yes you will,' said Arthur. 'Lizzie and I are best friends and we live across the Court.'

'Not for much longer,' Lizzie told him, 'now you're going to stupid Yorkshire.'

'I wish I didn't have to go.'

'So do I.'

'If you stayed,' said Susan, 'you could go to Heathcote . . .'

And so the conversational circle continued.

Evening. Susan lay in her bed. Her mother sat on its edge. Smudge, who was supposed to sleep in a basket on the floor, purred on the pillow.

'Are you going to marry Uncle Andrew?'

'Why do you ask that?'

'Because that's what people at school said.'

'And what did you say?'

'That you weren't. That Uncle Andrew was just our friend.'

She waited for her mother's agreement but it didn't come.

'Are you going to marry him?'

'He's asked me to.'

'Oh.'

Silence.

'How would you feel, Susie, if I did?'

She didn't answer. Her feelings were too complicated to express. She liked Uncle Andrew. He was kind and he was generous and he was her friend.

But he wasn't her dad.

'You like Uncle Andrew, don't you?'

'Yes.'

'So do I.'

'As much as you liked Dad?'

'No. Not as much as your dad. No one could ever be quite that special.'

She nodded. Her father had been special. The most special man in the world.

'But Uncle Andrew's special too, Susie.' A pause. 'In his own way. He makes me feel . . . I don't know . . .'

brave?

Perhaps. But the sentence remained unfinished.

'If you married him, would we live in his house?'

'Yes.'

She thought of old furniture and paintings. Clear surfaces. Neatness and order. Her father had been untidy. One of the qualities she had inherited from him. It drove her mother mad. But when she had spilt a drink on Uncle Andrew's carpet he hadn't minded at all.

'Would I have to call him Dad?'

'Not if you didn't want to.'

'I don't. He's my friend but he's not my dad. Are you going to marry him, Mum?'

'I don't know, Susie.'

They hugged each other. Her mother left the room, turning out the light. Susan lay in the darkness, waiting for her eyes to adapt and for the familiar shapes to appear. The wardrobe and cupboard. The shelves with her books and toys. The cradle her grandfather had made her. All as familiar as her own face in this, the only bedroom she had ever known.

She rose and walked towards the shelves, lifting Smudge on to her shoulder, ignoring the sting of his claws as she reached for the conch shell and pressed it to her ear. The roar of the sea filled her head, transporting her to a beach in Cornwall. A beautiful beach with miles of white sand where she and her father had built a giant sandcastle, decorating its ramparts with shells and stones, then watched, laughing, as the waves swept in, soaking their feet and wiping their creation away.

It had been a magical day. Every day spent with him had been magical. Her dad. The only one she would ever have or want. The one she missed so badly that sometimes the pain made her want to scream.

But screaming wouldn't bring him back. Nothing would.

She started to cry, standing there in the dark with the shell against her ear.

February 1954.

They married in a register office, two weeks after Susan's eighth birthday. Susan, her mother's spinster aunt Ellen and a work colleague of Uncle Andrew's called Mr Perry were the only guests. After the ceremony they ate lunch at a nearby hotel where a string quartet played in the foyer. Uncle Andrew ordered champagne and insisted that Susan be allowed a glass. Susan expected objections from her mother but none came. Just a nod and a smile that fell just short of the eyes.

Aunt Ellen, over eighty and not renowned for her tact, drank two glasses in quick succession. 'Your mother's very quiet,' she said to Susan in a whisper loud enough to wake the dead. 'Well, she's bound to have mixed feelings, poor love. This chap's a right bore compared to your father but at least he's got money.' Uncle Andrew and Susan's mother pretended not to hear, but Mr Perry choked on his champagne and had to have his back pounded by a waiter.

Later, when her mother had taken Aunt Ellen to the ladies' room and Mr Perry had returned to the office, Susan sat alone with Uncle Andrew. He too had consumed a great deal of champagne and seemed in very good spirits, impersonating the cellist, who was slashing away at the strings with his bow like a woodsman hacking down trees. It made her laugh. He laughed too.

'Your mother looks beautiful today, doesn't she?' he said.

'Yes.'

'So do you. The most beautiful bridesmaid in Oxfordshire.'

'I wasn't a bridesmaid.'

'A sort of bridesmaid.' He stroked her cheek. 'You make me proud. I never dreamed I'd have a little daughter as beautiful as you.'

'I'm not your daughter,' she told him.

'That's right. I'm your friend. Your special friend who you trust. You do trust me, don't you, Susie?'

She nodded.

Again he stroked her cheek. His hand was warm and dry. One finger tickled the back of her neck, making her giggle. He smiled down at her with eyes that were as soft and warm as her father's had been. He wasn't her father but he was her friend. And she did trust him.

Her mother approached with Aunt Ellen. As she waved to them Uncle Andrew's hand slid quickly away.

They honeymooned in Paris while Susan stayed with Charlotte and her family.

It was a happy stay. She rode her bicycle up and down the street with Smudge in the basket and Charlotte clinging on behind. She helped bathe Charlotte's little brother, Ben, and read him bedtime stories. She visited Charlotte's father in his shoe shop and tried to balance on six inch heels. Best of all, she lay awake with Charlotte, the two of them scaring each other with ghost stories and planning what they would do when they were grown up.

Only one thing spoiled her enjoyment. Passing number 37 and seeing new curtains in the window. It was now the home of the

Walters family, who had moved to Kendleton from Lincolnshire, just as Ramsey's Studio was now a dress shop. She knew these things were inevitable. But they still hurt.

'You'll still be my best friend, won't you?' asked Charlotte as they lay in their beds on the last night of her stay. 'Even though you're crossing the Court.'

'Of course. We'll always be best friends.'

'Promise.'

'Is my finger wet? Is my finger dry? God strike me dead if I tell a lie.'

'I wish God would strike Alice Wetherby dead.'

'I wish he'd turn her into a cow. Then she'd have to stand in a field all day, trying to look superior as she poos cow pats.'

They both began to laugh, making so much noise that Charlotte's mother had to shout upstairs for silence.

Uncle Andrew's house had three floors. Uncle Andrew and her mother slept on the first floor. They had separate bedrooms. 'I snore like a foghorn,' Uncle Andrew explained. 'Your poor mother would never get any sleep if she had to share with me.' Susan, aware that her mother often slept badly, was pleased at the arrangement.

Her own bedroom was on the top floor at the end of a corridor that also included Uncle Andrew's study and a bathroom in between. It was bigger than her last one with sensible furniture and a window looking out on to Kendleton Church. The bed was bigger too. 'A grown up bed for a grown-up girl,' said Uncle Andrew. Her toys and books lay in boxes on the floor. Her mother helped her unpack. 'You must keep your room tidy, Susie. Uncle Andrew doesn't like mess.' She promised to try.

They ate supper in the dining room. Beef stew cooked by her mother. A favourite dish of her father's that Uncle Andrew liked too. There were candles on the table and expensive chinaware. Uncle Andrew insisted that Susan be allowed a small glass of wine. 'This is a celebration for me. It's not every day I gain a new family.' The room was dark and austere with no photographs anywhere. The ones from Osborne Row were packed in boxes except for a picture of Susan's father that she had insisted on having by her bed.

As they ate, Uncle Andrew told her about Paris. 'There are wonderful cafés where artists draw your picture. One of them drew your mother and said I had the most beautiful wife in the world.' Susan said that the artist had been right while her mother gave Uncle Andrew a quick peck on the cheek. He smiled but did not return the gesture.

'Do you like this room?' asked her mother while tucking her into bed.

'I wish Smudge was here. He'll be scared in the kitchen.'

'I'm sure Uncle Andrew will soon let him stay up here with you. Remember that he's never had an animal in his house before. Now settle down and happy dreams.'

The window was behind her bed. A full moon shone through a gap in the curtains, bathing the room in pale light. Everything looked strange and cold. She could not imagine sleeping one night here. But this was her home now and she would grow used to it in time.

Her father's picture was on the bedside table. Hugging it to her chest, she shut her eyes and tried to sleep.

So began her life in Queen Anne Square.

In the weeks that followed a routine began to develop.

Each morning her mother would wake her. When she had dressed the two of them would eat breakfast in the kitchen. Uncle Andrew, who worked in Oxford, had usually left the house before she rose, but sometimes he would allow himself a late start so that the three of them could eat together.

Her journey to school had changed. She had to cross Market Court and could not go and knock on Charlotte's door as she once had. Generally her mother walked with her, but as she was a big girl of eight increasingly she walked alone. Sometimes Charlotte would come and wait for her at the Norman cross so that the two of them could go the rest of the way together, holding hands and bumping satchels just as they had in the old days.

The school day over, it was time for homework. One full hour between five and six. Uncle Andrew was very particular about this. When she had finished she would want to go and play with Charlotte but there was never enough time. Dinner was always at half past six and eaten in the dining room. Two other points on which Uncle Andrew was insistent. Charlotte's family had a television and often ate in front of it but Uncle Andrew said that television killed the art of conversation and refused to have one in his house.

Not that there was much actual conversation. Uncle Andrew did most of the talking, describing the events of his day. Her father had been the same, though she did not remember him growing angry over incidents the way Uncle Andrew did. When his voice began to rise, she would start to feel anxious, but then he would diffuse the tension with a joke and she would laugh and relax.

Occasionally there were guests for dinner. Clients of Uncle Andrew to whom she would be introduced and fussed over by. It was the same as when guests had visited her parents in Osborne Row, though she didn't remember her father praising her quite as effusively as Uncle Andrew did. 'Isn't she beautiful?' he would ask. 'The loveliest child you've ever seen?'

The guests agreed that she was. 'That's because she takes after her mother,' said one elderly man with sleepy eyes, causing Susan's mother to blush and shake her head. Uncle Andrew told her not to be modest. 'You are beautiful, darling. That artist in Paris said I had the most beautiful wife in the world. I'm going to have his drawing framed and hang it in my office.' He was always talking about doing this yet never managed to find the time.

Twice, Charlotte had come to the house to play. On the second visit Lizzie Flynn came too and broke a vase. Uncle Andrew had flown into a rage, shouting at them, but when Charlotte burst into tears he had apologized and taken them out for milk shakes. 'He didn't mean to get angry,' Susan's mother told her afterwards. 'He'd had a busy day at work and he's not used to having lots of children in his house. Perhaps you should stop asking them to come over. Just for a little while, that's all.'

She went to bed at eight o'clock, after her nightly bath. Her mother would always tuck her in. Smudge continued to sleep in the kitchen. Her mother kept promising to ask Uncle Andrew about Smudge sleeping with her but never seemed to find the right moment.

Sometimes, late at night, she was woken by the sound of footsteps. Uncle Andrew coming upstairs to work in his study. She would lie in bed, watching the glow of the landing light through her door frame, and know that he was there.

One night the footsteps continued past the study, coming to a halt outside her door. She called out a greeting but was answered only by silence. The footsteps moved away, she went back to sleep, and in the morning her memory of the incident was so faint that it seemed like nothing but the fragments of a broken dream.

In May Aunt Ellen was taken ill.

It wasn't serious, just a stomach bug, but Susan's mother decided to visit for a weekend. She wanted to take Susan but Uncle Andrew persuaded her to change her mind. 'She'll be bored and besides I'll be lonely without you. Susie will be company for me.'

Saturday was warm and sunny. In the morning they went for a drive, then walked in the woods which were full of bluebells. Uncle Andrew helped her pick some. They found the Golden Hind and she climbed into its branches while Uncle Andrew stayed on the ground, the two of them playing the game of exploration her father had invented. It still hurt to think about him but not as much as it once had. The pain was fading just as Uncle Andrew had said it would.

They had lunch at a pub, sitting at an outside table, drinking Coca-Cola from bottles with straws. In the afternoon they went to the cinema to see an Elizabeth Taylor film. 'You're just as beautiful as she is,' Uncle Andrew whispered as they sat together in the dark. 'One day I'll be watching you up there on that screen.'

'That's what my dad said,' she whispered back.

'Of course. He was very proud of you, Susie. Just as I am.'

That evening he cooked supper. Fish and chips. Her favourite meal. Later they sat together in the living room and he read her a story about smugglers, using different accents for different characters just as her father would have done. His voice was soft. It made her drowsy. The clock on the wall showed that it was past her bedtime. She waited for him to send her upstairs but he continued reading, stopping only to pour himself another brandy from the bottle on the table. As her yawns increased he put an arm around her, pulling her close, running his fingers through her hair. He felt warm and safe, just as her father had done. She rested her head against his chest, closed her eyes and drifted into sleep.

When she woke he was still stroking her hair.

She was lying in her bed, covered by blankets right up to her neck. He sat on its edge, facing her.

'It's time,' he said.

The room was in semi-darkness. The only light came from her bedside lamp. As her tired eyes adapted she saw that he was wearing his dressing gown. Below it his legs were bare. How late was it? Was he going to bed too?

His hand slid through her hair, tugging at the curls, starting to caress her cheek. 'You're so beautiful. I've never seen anyone as beautiful as you.' His fingers were clammy. They made her uncomfortable. She squirmed in bed, felt the sheets rub against her skin and realized that she was naked. Her pyjamas were kept under her pillow. Why wasn't she wearing them? Did he not know they were there?

He was smiling, but there was something strange about his eyes. They seemed brighter somehow. Clearer. As if until that moment she had only ever seen them through a screen.

And they made her afraid.

'I want my mum.'

He shook his head.

'I want my mum.'

'Not tonight. Tonight is just for us. I love you, Susie. Do you love me?'

'No. I loved my dad. You're not my dad.'

'You can love me too. You have so much love to give. I sensed it the moment I first saw you. It was incredible. As if God had made you just for me.'

His hand was on her throat, stroking her skin, one finger lifting the top of the bed covers. Instinctively her own hands moved upwards, clutching at them, holding them tight against herself. 'You mustn't be afraid,' he said. 'We both know this was meant to be.' His voice was soft yet rigid with tension. Velvet backed with steel.

He leant forward, bringing with him the smell of sweat and

alcohol and something else she couldn't identify. A dank, ripe odour that filled her nostrils so she felt she couldn't breathe. Dark chest hair poked through the top of his dressing gown.

'Don't,' she whispered.

'I won't hurt you. I just want to touch you.'

'Please.'

'Hush. Lie still.' He moved over her, his body blocking the lamp and swallowing the last of the light.

When it was over he remained on the bed. This time he kept his back to her; his eyes focused on the far wall. In time he began to speak.

'I'm not a bad person.'

She didn't answer. Just lay there.

'I'm not a bad person. It's just that I can see things in you that others can't. They think that because you're beautiful you're also good. But you're not. You're wicked. As wicked as the queen in *Snow White*.'

She swallowed. Her throat was dry. She wanted a glass of water. She wanted him to be gone.

'You made me do this. You wanted this to happen.'

She found her voice. 'No . . .'

He turned towards her. His eyes were no longer strange. Once again they were warm and soothing. Eyes that she had learnt to trust. And when he spoke his voice was warm and soothing too.

'It's true, Susie. You are wicked. A special wickedness that very few children have. I see it in everything you do. And if someone else found out about tonight they'd see it too. If your mother found out . . .'

He stopped. Sighing, he shook his head.

'If she found out, she'd get scared again. She'd have another breakdown. Only this one would be much worse. She'd never recover. She'd go away, you'd never see her again and it would be your fault. So we have to keep this secret, Susie. No one else must ever find out because if they do they'll tell your mother. You know how to keep a secret, don't you?'

She nodded.

'So do I. I don't care that you're wicked. I still love you, Susie. I'll teach you how to be good. It will take time but I'll do it. All you have to do is trust me.'

Silence. They stared at each other. She tried to picture life without her mother but she couldn't. It was too terrible even to think about. Like every nightmare she had ever had rolled into one.

She began to cry. Gently he wiped her tears away.

'I don't want Mum to go away.'

'She won't. Not if we keep our secret. I'll never tell anyone. You can trust me, Susie. Can I trust you?'

'Yes.'

He kissed her forehead. His lips were cool and dry. 'I'm thirsty,' she whispered.

'I'll get you some water.'

He rose to his feet, walked towards the door. When he reached it he turned back.

'I love you, Susie. More than anyone else in the world. You're the apple of my eye, you know.'

Then he was gone.

Half past eleven the next morning. They sat together in the dining room, eating a late breakfast. Bacon, eggs, tomatoes and fried bread. All the things she liked. She had no appetite but ate anyway. They always breakfasted in the dining room on Sunday so he could read the papers and watch the world go by.

The bay window looked out on to the square. There was a small garden at its centre where an elderly couple sat on a bench and Mrs Hastings from number 22 pushed her son Paul on a swing. Others walked by on the pavement; returning from church or enjoying the sun.

Her plate was almost empty. She chewed on fried bread that tasted like chalk. His newspaper had a picture of the Queen on the front page. She tried to read the headline but her brain refused to process the words. The bluebells stood in a vase at the centre of the table. A surprise for her mother, who would be returning after lunch, eager to know what they had done in her absence.

He closed his paper. 'Finished?'

'Yes.'

'Good.' He was smiling, just as he had been all morning. Happy and cheerful and making no mention of the previous night. True to his word he was keeping it secret, even between the two of them.

'What shall we do today?' he asked.

'I don't know.'

'Perhaps a walk by the river. We can't waste such a lovely day sitting indoors.' The doorbell rang. 'Who can that be?'

As he went to find out she watched Mrs Hastings push Paul higher and higher. Paul had blond hair and blue eyes. Her mother thought Paul a very good-looking boy.

She wondered whether Paul was wicked too.

There were footsteps in the hall. He re-entered the room, followed by Mrs Christie from number 5 and her daughter Kate, who was one of Alice Wetherby's gang, both dressed in their church clothes. Mrs Christie took Kate to church every Sunday. Twice sometimes. Kate was always complaining about it at school.

'You've caught us still at breakfast,' Uncle Andrew told Mrs Christie. 'We're being very lazy today, aren't we, Susie.'

She nodded. Kate was scowling. She had tightly curled dark hair and big features. Alice called her 'Golliwog'. Alice could be cruel even to members of her gang.

Mrs Christie was talking about a fête the church was running in the summer. Raising money for charity. Uncle Andrew said that he would be pleased to help. Mrs Christie was delighted. 'It will be such fun for the children. Kate's friends are all going to get involved. Bridget and Janet and Alice Wetherby. It would be lovely if Susan joined in too.' Uncle Andrew agreed that it would.

Kate, safe beside her mother, made a face at Susan. Normally Susan would have retaliated, but not this time.

Was Kate wicked? Was Bridget, Janet or Alice?

Or am I the only one?

Mrs Christie pointed at the bluebells. 'What beautiful flowers.' Uncle Andrew explained that Susan had picked them the previous day. 'A present for her mother as they're her favourites.' Mrs Christie beamed at Susan. 'What a lovely thought. Your mother's lucky to have such a kind daughter.'

'No she's not.' The words were out before she could stop them.

Uncle Andrew frowned. So did Mrs Christie. 'Whyever not, dear?'

Because I'm bad. Because I'm wicked.
And I don't know why.
They were all watching her. Unable to stand it she ran from the room.

Dragonflies danced on the surface of the river, catching rays of sunlight and irritating the swans that glided by the narrow boats waiting to pass through the lock. One boat moved in front of another. The two owners exchanged words.

She crouched at the base of a tree, hidden from view. Needing to be alone to try to make sense of the thoughts that swarmed like angry bees inside her brain.

She was wicked. Uncle Andrew had said so. He was a grown-up. He was her friend and she trusted him. If he said so it must be true.

But she didn't know why.

If her father had lived she would still be living in Osborne Row. Her mother would not have married Uncle Andrew and the previous night would never have happened.

Would it?

Suddenly she was back in her bed, watching Uncle Andrew's face close in upon her. Except that this time it was not Uncle Andrew. It was her father.

If her father had known she was wicked would he have forgiven her? Would he have carried on loving her like Uncle Andrew did?

She wanted to believe it. But in her head his face grew cold. 'You're wicked, Susan. Bad and wicked and I hate you. You're not my Susie Sparkle any more.'

The voices inside her brain grew louder and louder. A hurricane of sound that threatened to split it in two. Burying her head in her knees, she started sobbing while a spider crawled up her leg and began to weave a web in the folds of her dress.

When she was too tired to cry any more she raised her head. It was cooler. A wind was rising in the east, blowing clouds across the sky and making the boats bob in the water. It found her through the branches of the tree, lifting her hair and blowing it across her face. She brushed it back.

And in that moment she was with her father again; the two of them sitting together by the river bank on the day she had fought with Alice Wetherby.

I wish you'd known my father, Susie. He would have been so proud of you.

Why?

Because you're strong. Your grandfather was the same. You felt safe around him because you knew that no matter what you asked of him he'd never let you down.

Strong.

She rose to her feet, as if the word were a rope to pull her up.

Strong.

To be strong wasn't wicked. To be strong was good.

It *was* good, wasn't it?

Or at least it was a start.

Her father had said that they would protect her mother. That they would not let her be scared ever again. But now he was gone and it was up to her.

And she would do it. Whatever it took. Whatever secrets she had to keep. It was what he had asked of her and she would not let him down. She was strong. She would prove that she was good.

The noise inside her head died away. She felt empty. Drained of everything except a single thought.

I am strong and I will survive this.

She wiped her eyes. There would be no more crying. Tears were for the weak and she had to be strong. For her father. For her mother. And for herself.

Turning, she began the walk home.

The front door was open. Her mother stood in the doorway with Uncle Andrew.

'Susie, where have you been?'

'By the river.'

'You shouldn't have been away so long. We were worried. It was naughty.'

Wicked.

'I'm sorry, Mum.'

'It's all right. At least you're here now. Did you have a nice time while I was away?'

Uncle Andrew was watching her, his expression anxious. Was he worried she would tell their secret? She put on the brightest smile she could find.

'I picked you some flowers, Mum. Bluebells. Uncle Andrew helped me. We put them in a vase. Do you want to see?'

Her mother smiled too. 'I'd love to.'

She led her mother into the dining room. Uncle Andrew followed behind.

June.

It was almost midnight. She lay on her side in bed, staring at the frame of the door. Watching for the light. Listening for the footsteps. Wondering whether this would be the night.

He had visited her four times. Or was it five? As the weeks passed she found it harder to keep count.

When it was over she would ask him why she was wicked. Whether she was the only one. What it was she had to do to be good. 'I don't want to be wicked,' she would tell him. 'Please help me be good.' He would answer but his words were confusing. She would tell him that she didn't understand and he would smile and say that in time she would.

The light went on. He was coming. Her heart began to race. She knew that he was her friend. That he wanted to help her. But still the prospect of his visit filled her with dread.

She reached under her bed for the conch shell hidden there. As the footsteps drew closer she pressed it against her ear, listening to the sound of the sea, remembering that day by the river with her father. Remembering that she was strong.

Remembering that she was going to survive.

July.

Quarter to nine on a Tuesday morning and already the sun was climbing into a cloudless sky. Edith Bruce stood in Market Court, clutching her basket and wrestling with her dog, Warner, who wanted to chase an aloof-looking poodle that an equally aloof-looking woman was walking. When the poodle passed out of sight he turned, gave her one of his sheepish grins then jumped up, licking her face and almost knocking her over in the process.

'Oh, Warner, what am I going to do with you?'

She knew the answer. Give him to someone who could control him. A twenty-stone wrestler probably. But she couldn't do it. Her husband was dead and Warner was the only family she had. He was a terror but he was hers and she would have been lost without him.

The Court was filling: women with baskets, waiting for the shops to open; parents leading small children with satchels towards the primary school on the west side of town. The children were generally in high spirits. Excited at the prospect of a summer holiday that was only days away. Little Susan Ramsey, her former neighbour, walked with her stepfather, Andrew Bishop. Edith gave her a wave and promptly dropped Warner's lead.

'Hell! Warner, come back here!'

Warner bounded away, chasing an alarmed-looking pug and having to be stopped and returned by Mr Bishop.

'You've got a lively fellow here,' he told her.

'I certainly have. Thank you so much. Hello, Susie.'

Susan stoked Warner's head. 'Hello, Mrs Bruce.'

'Looking forward to the holidays?'

'Yes.'

'We're going to have a lovely summer, aren't we, Susie?' said Mr Bishop. 'Lots of fun.'

Susan nodded but said nothing. Normally she was a chatterbox but not today.

'I've got a late start this morning,' Mr Bishop explained. 'So I'm saving my wife a job by taking Susie to school.'

'How is your mother, Susie?'

'Fine, thank you.'

'Give her my love, won't you.'

Again Susan nodded. She looked tired. As if she had slept badly. Excitement at the holidays, probably. Warner started licking her face. Mr Bishop looked amused. 'You've got a friend there, Susie.'

'Typical male,' joked Edith. 'A sucker for a pretty face.'

Mr Bishop pretended to frown. 'Pretty?'

'Beautiful.'

'Absolutely. The most beautiful girl in the world. That's my Susie.' He looked at his watch. 'We must be off. Goodbye, Warner. Be good for your mistress.'

The two of them walked away. Edith watched them go. On her right was the dress shop that had once been John Ramsey's photographic studio. Poor John. A good man with a kind heart, a lively wit and a smile that could light up a cathedral. A man she had always liked and still missed.

Though not as much as if she had been his daughter.

But times changed. Susan had a new father now. A good man too, by all accounts. A new home. A new life. Was it enough to ease the pain?

She hoped so.

'Goodbye, Susie.'

Susan turned. For a split second her eyes seemed troubled. Frightened even.

But the sun was bright and she could have been mistaken.

Then came the smile. As big and as warming as her father's had been. And the wave that followed was warming too.

Little Susie Sparkle, all peaches and cream.

Little Susie Sparkle, sugar and spice and all things nice.

Little Susie Sparkle, hiding her wickedness behind a smile.

Little Susie Sparkle . . .

Part 3

Hepton
23 June 1959

Dear Mum,
Thanks for your letter. Sorry to be slow replying but at last the exams are over. We got three results today. I came top in Maths (88%), third in English (80%) and fourth in French (76%). Mr Cadman said that I'm getting the Maths prize. Hopefully I'll get History too and I'll definitely get Art. Archie did well but I don't think he'll win any prizes. One boy called Neville Jepps was thrown out of the Latin exam for cheating. Mr Bertrand stopped the exam and made a speech about how grammar school boys never cheat which was a joke as half the class were hiding crib sheets!

All is well here. Peter now prefers Eddie Cochrane to Little Richard but still thinks that the day Elvis went into the army was the worst day of his life. Yesterday I told him that Elvis had been shot by an escaped Nazi and he got really upset! Thomas has a new girlfriend called Sandra who works in a shoe shop on the High Street and is very boring. She came for tea at the weekend and spent so long telling us about different types of heels that Uncle Stan went to sleep! Auntie Vera is doing a correspondence course on English literature. It's the same one Mrs Brown is doing. Last week she showed Mrs Brown her first essay. I don't know what Mrs Brown said but when she'd gone Auntie Vera put it in the bin! Uncle Stan was off work with a bad back but is better now.

Auntie Mabel said that I could help her and Uncle Bill in the shop over the summer and earn some money. I haven't been able to cut the grass for the Sandersons because it's been raining so much but I'll do it as soon as the weather is better.

That's all for now. I'm missing you but everything is fine so don't worry about me.

Lots of love
Ronnie Sunshine

P.S. The father of a boy in my class says that Mr Brown is having an affair with his secretary. This is classified information!

Kendleton
28 June 1959

Darling Ronnie,
Thank you for your letter. I was THRILLED with your exam results and have been boasting to everyone who will listen about what a brilliant son I have. The poor women in the post office must be sick of the sight of me by now! Mrs Pembroke was very impressed and one of the ten shilling notes enclosed is from her. The other one is of course from me.

I'm sorry that the weather has been so bad and hope that it improves in time for your holidays. It is sunny and warm here and I have been for some lovely walks in the woods. The bluebells are long gone, sadly, but there are many other wild flowers and the countryside is full of colour. I wish you could see it and am sure that one day you will.

This afternoon Mrs Hammond from next door came for tea. We sat out in the garden and watched the boats. The river is full of them and Mr Logan, the lock-keeper, said that he's never known a summer so busy. Mrs Hammond was telling us about her sons, Henry and Arthur, who go to boarding school in Yorkshire. I think I may have mentioned them before – Arthur is only a month younger than you. They have just had exams too and done well by the sound of it, though nowhere near as well as someone else I could name! I don't think Mrs Hammond was very pleased to have me there – she's an even bigger snob than Mrs Brown – but Mrs Pembroke is very kind and insists that I be included in everything.

I hope that things really are well at home. You know you can tell me if they're not. I do worry about you, my darling, even though you tell me not to. Never an hour goes past without me thinking about you, wondering what you're doing

and wishing we were together.
  Counting the days until my next visit.

All my love
Mum

P.S. I cannot understand why any woman would want to have an affair with Mr Brown. This is classified information too!!!

July. Summer had arrived in Hepton and heat covered Moreton Street like a blanket. In the front bedroom he shared with Peter, Ronnie sat by the window finishing his homework.

It wasn't easy. Peter lay on his bed, singing along to an Eddie Cochrane record. They had shared for three years, ever since Thomas had demanded a room of his own, and Peter's greatest delight was disturbing Ronnie's work.

The window was open. A group of small boys played cricket in the street, using an old crate as a wicket. 'I'm Freddie Trueman,' shouted the bowler, hurling the ball at the head of the batsman, who ducked to avoid concussion while a woman bellowed at them to keep the noise down.

It was quarter to six. The end of the working day. Stan and Thomas approached the house. Thomas, nearly eighteen and as tall, thin and asthmatic as his father, had worked in the factory since leaving school. The two of them stopped to chat with a neighbour, Stan puffing on the cigarette he was forbidden from smoking in the house.

Ronnie's eyes returned to the essay he was writing. An account of the unification of Italy. Textbooks covered the desk. The history prize had yet to be awarded and he had no intention of falling at the last hurdle.

The record ended. Peter put it on again then went to study himself in the mirror on the inside of the wardrobe. Just sixteen, he had his father's height and mother's heavy build. His dark hair, worn in a lavish quiff, shone with Brylcreem. Picking up a dumb-bell, he worked on his biceps, admiring the powerful physique his white vest revealed. His half of the room was covered with pictures of singers and bodybuilders. Ronnie's was decorated with his own drawings. In the first months of sharing Peter had enjoyed defacing them and it was not until Ronnie had 'accidentally' smashed Peter's favourite record that a truce had been called.

Eddie Cochrane sang about the Summertime Blues. Ronnie had them now, trying to concentrate. Putting his essay to one side he began to reread his mother's most recent letter. Peter noticed what he was doing. 'And what does Mummy say?'

'None of your business.'

'Is she proud of her little Ronnie?'

'At least I give my mother something to be proud of.'

Peter, about to join his father and brother in the factory, adopted a sneer. 'What? Some stupid prizes. They won't get you anywhere in the real world.'

'They'll get me farther than big muscles and greasy hair will get you.'

'I'll do better in life than you.'

'Of course. Soon you'll be the new Charles Atlas. You've certainly got the brains.'

'Least I'm not queer. Only queers like art.'

Ronnie continued reading. Peter, denied a reaction, resumed work on his biceps.

Five minutes passed. Ronnie stared out of the window. Thomas was saying goodbye to the neighbour while Stan finished his cigarette.

'Looking for your dad, Ronnie? He's never coming. He doesn't even know you exist.'

Ronnie's eyes remained fixed on the street. The cricket game was breaking up amid accusations of cheating.

'And even if he did he wouldn't come. Who'd want some bastard queer as a son?'

'He'd be prouder of me than he would of you.'

'Least I know where my father is *and* that he wanted me. Two things you'll never know.'

The front door opened. Stan called out a greeting. 'Hello, Dad,' yelled Peter, placing emphasis on the second word. 'So win all the prizes you can, little Ronnie, but you'll still be the bastard queer of a stupid slut and a squaddie who was too drunk to remember her name.' Then he left the room.

Ronnie remained at his desk. To his left was a small photograph of his mother. He took it out of its frame to see the even tinier snapshot of his father hidden behind. His parents. A stupid slut and a drunken squaddie. Peter had Vera and Stan. A mother who didn't work miles away and a father who had always been there.

But he knew which set he would have chosen.

After kissing both pictures he continued with his work.

There were five for supper that evening: Peter's girlfriend Jane, a redhead of fifteen with a large bust and a taste for tight tops, took the place of Thomas, who was out with Sandra.

Vera served sausages and chips. Two sausages per person. Peter complained that it wasn't enough and Vera told him they weren't made of money.

'We are when it suits you. The Browns had steak when they came last week.'

'They were our guests.'

'Jane's a guest, too.'

Vera frowned. Her heavy face now played host to a double chin. 'Your guest, Peter, and when you're contributing to the family budget you can give her steak.'

'In the meantime I'll have his chips,' said Jane, spearing some with her fork. Vera's frown intensified. Vera did not like Jane.

'I'll be contributing soon enough, unlike someone else I could mention.'

'My mother contributes for me,' said Ronnie. 'And when I'm helping in the shop I can contribute too.'

'What are the Coopers paying you?' asked Vera.

He told her. Immediately she claimed the lion's share for housekeeping. 'That's a bit steep, Vera,' said Stan. 'Leave him something to spend.'

'It's perfectly reasonable. Do you know what it costs to keep him over the holidays?'

'I don't mind,' said Ronnie, who was being paid more than he'd said.

'How's your mother?' asked Stan. 'I saw you got a letter today.'

'Fine, thanks.'

'I should think so,' observed Vera. 'Cushy job like that.'

Ronnie swallowed a mouthful of sausage. Overcooked, as Vera's food generally was. 'It's not cushy. She works hard.'

Peter nodded. 'It's tough being a skivvy.'

'She's not a skivvy. She's a companion.'

Vera snorted. 'That's not a real job.'

'Yes it is. And she does it well. Mrs Pembroke thinks the world of her.'

'Well, your mother would say that, wouldn't she?'

'Actually Mrs Sanderson said it and she's Mrs Pembroke's cousin so she should know.'

'Don't play the smart alec with me, Ronald Sidney.'

'I'm not being a smart alec, Auntie Vera. I'm just saying . . .'

He stopped suddenly, his voice having shot up an octave. 'Little Ronnie's voice is breaking,' jeered Peter.

'Pity we can't say the same about your brain,' retorted Ronnie before he could stop himself.

Vera's face darkened. Fortunately Jane laughed, drawing maternal fury on to herself. 'We don't laugh at personal remarks in this house, miss.'

'Well, you should. That one was funny.'

'Whose side are you on?' demanded Peter.

Jane tapped him on the nose with a chip. Vera, scowling, complained to Stan about her latest essay assignment. Ronnie continued eating. Jane began whispering to Peter, who had a dopey expression on his face. Peter was always boasting to his friends that Jane was putty in his hands but Ronnie knew the opposite was true. Vera did too. As she ranted at Stan she kept looking daggers at Jane. Though it was a warm evening the sleeves of her blouse were pulled down, concealing the damaged skin on her left arm.

'Do you have a girlfriend, Ronnie?' asked Jane.

'No.'

'Little Ronnie doesn't like girls,' Peter told her.

'I bet they like him though. He's good looking.'

Peter flexed his bicep. 'Not as much as me.'

Jane licked Peter's cheek. He licked hers back. Vera's mouth was a thin line. 'There's a place for that sort of behaviour.'

'We're not doing anything, Mrs Finnegan,' said Jane breezily. Her eyes returned to Ronnie. 'You look like your mum, don't you?'

'Yes.'

'She must be pretty. Does she have a boyfriend?'

'No.'

'Do you think she'd tell you if she had?'

'She doesn't need a boyfriend. She's got me.'

Jane smiled. 'That's sweet.'

'What's the matter, little Ronnie?' asked Peter. 'Scared Mummy might love someone more than she loves you?'

'That's enough, Pete,' said Stan.

'Yes, don't be horrid,' added Jane. 'Or I'll hate you.' She grabbed Peter's hair, pulled his face towards hers and bit him on the lip.

'That's enough!' snapped Vera. 'What would the Browns think if they were here?'

'Where are our steaks?' asked Jane.

Vera lost her temper completely. Ronnie, following Stan's example, finished his meal in silence.

Later, as Peter played records for Jane in their bedroom and Vera complained about her to Stan in the living room, Ronnie went for a walk.

Boys were playing football in the tiny park on the corner, preening for the girls, who stood in groups, giggling and gossiping. Alan Deakins, the troublemaker from his primary school class, entertained one group with jokes. Ronnie recognized Catherine Meadows, another old classmate. She called for him to join them. He waved but did not stop.

The railway line ran along the far edge of the park. Climbing on to the ridge, he began to dig at the dry earth with a stick. A train rattled by, filling the air with smoke and noise. Once he had stood at his bedroom window, watching the trains and longing for the day when his father would come and take him and his mother far away. Now his mother *was* far away while his father remained nothing but an old snapshot. A dream that grew fainter with each passing year until eventually it would vanish altogether.

But not yet. Not when dreams were sometimes the only thing to make life bearable.

Catherine Meadows approached. For the last two years she had attended a boarding school in Berkshire, only coming back to Hepton in the holidays.

'Hello, Ronnie. My term ended yesterday. You haven't broken up yet, have you?'

'No.'

She sat down beside him. Her hair was blonde, her eyes pale blue. 'Do you still visit the Sandersons?' she asked.

'Yes.'

'You can visit me too if you like. We live at number twenty-five. I'll be here all summer except for a week in Devon with my grandparents. Have you been to Devon? It's boring.'

'It can't be as boring as here.' He carried on digging. Two footballers squared up to each other after an aggressive tackle. The other players separated them and the game resumed.

'Alan's still a show-off,' she told him. 'He says he's had sex with a girl in Southend. I don't believe him, though. I think if a girl wanted to have sex with him he'd be scared.'

'Maybe.'

'Would you be scared, Ronnie?'

'I don't know.'

'I bet you wouldn't.'

Another train raced by, drowning out her voice. She continued to mouth words, gesticulating with her hands like a silent film actress. It made him smile.

'How's your mum?' she asked when the train had passed.

'Fine.'

'You must miss her. I miss my family when I'm at school but when I'm at home they drive me mad.'

'At least you've got a family.'

They stared at each other. He imagined his mother sitting by the river in Oxfordshire with a man she liked. A man who might one day mean more to her than her own son.

But that would never happen. Could never happen.

Could it?

'Do you think I'm pretty?'

He nodded. All girls who looked like his mother were pretty.

'Do you want to kiss me?'

'No.'

'You will one day. Goodbye, Ronnie.'

'Goodbye.'

She returned to her group. He remained alone, hacking at the ground while the sun slid beneath the horizon, dragging the last drops of heat from the sky.

A wet afternoon in August. Anna poured tea for Mrs Pembroke and her guests.

Of all the grand houses in The Avenue, Riverdale was the most splendid. A red-brick Victorian mansion with oak-panelled rooms, a wide central staircase and a dozen chimneys. The furnishings, largely Victorian too, were ornate but comfortable, creating an atmosphere of affluent informality.

On this particular afternoon Mrs Wetherby sat on a sofa in front of the bay window that looked out on to the back garden and the river, flanked by her children, Alice and Edward. Mrs Pembroke was in her usual chair by the fireplace while Anna perched on a stool, ready to offer food and drink whenever the need arose.

Mrs Wetherby, a tall, raw-boned chain-smoker, was complaining about French hotels. Mrs Pembroke sipped her tea. Wrapped in a blanket, she looked as small and delicate as a bird. 'And how are things at school?' she asked the children.

'Edward was captain of his cricket team,' Mrs Wetherby told her, 'and Alice won her year's English prize and had two poems published in the school magazine.'

Edward nodded. At fifteen he resembled his mother, whose cigarettes he eyed enviously. Anna had seen him and his friends in Market Court, all smoking furiously with their collars turned up, trying to look like middle England's answer to James Dean. Alice smiled. At thirteen she was exceptionally pretty with long blonde hair, a doll-like face and predatory eyes, so immaculately dressed that she looked as if she'd been ironed. Both attended Heathcote, the expensive day school on the outskirts of town.

Mrs Pembroke offered congratulations. Mrs Wetherby looked smug. 'I'm lucky to have such talented children.'

'Anna's son, Ronnie, is talented too. He won four prizes this year.'

Mrs Wetherby's eyes widened. She nodded but made no comment. Alice, however, looked curious. 'Ronnie's my age, isn't he, Mrs Sidney? What prizes did he win?'

'Maths, history and art. His year prize too.'

'Given,' added Mrs Pembroke, 'to the boy with the best overall exam results.'

'That's only three prizes,' said Edward. 'Art doesn't count.'

Anna was taken aback. 'It does.'

'At *his* school, maybe. My school doesn't give prizes for non-academic subjects.'

'Well, perhaps they should,' suggested Mrs Pembroke.

Edward shrugged. Anna, keeping her anger in check, offered round a sponge cake.

'And how is Charles?' asked Mrs Wetherby. 'Mrs Pembroke's son is a history professor at an American university,' she told her children. Alice expressed interest while Edward continued to gaze longingly at the cigarettes.

'Not for much longer,' Mrs Pembroke told her. 'He's returning to England and will be living here for a while.'

'How lovely. He must come for dinner when he arrives.'

Anna masked her surprise. In the four and a half years she had lived in Kendleton, Charles Pembroke had never visited his mother. If Mrs Pembroke was hurt by such absence she never showed it, though on the few occasions his name arose she was often quick to change the subject. Just as she did now.

'I'm afraid I'm feeling rather tired. This wretched heart of mine.'

'Then we must go,' said Mrs Wetherby, quick to take the hint.

Anna showed them to the door. Mrs Wetherby lit another cigarette. 'Can I have one?' asked Edward.

'Certainly not. You're too young to smoke.'

'That's what you think, Mum,' said Alice meaningfully. Brother and sister glared at each other. As they walked down the drive Edward skidded on a wet stone and nearly fell. Restraining an urge to cheer, Anna shut the door behind them.

Mrs Pembroke, still wrapped in her blanket, gave her a weary smile. 'We never used to see so much of that awful woman.'

'You shouldn't have told her you were related to an earl.'

'Distantly.'

'But still related.' Anna smiled too. 'Are you tired? Shall I take you upstairs.'

'No, dear. I'll stay here.'

'Thank you for praising Ronnie.'

'Anything to deflate our guest. But it was my pleasure.'

'Would you like me to read to you?'

'Not now. Let's just sit.'

So they did, while outside the sky cleared, promising a brighter evening ahead.

'I didn't know Charles was coming,' said Anna eventually.

'I'm sure I mentioned it. Perhaps you forgot.'

'I must have done.'

'I think I'll sleep for a little.'

Mrs Pembroke shut her eyes. After checking that the blanket was secure, Anna crept from the room.

On summer evenings she liked to walk by the river.

That evening the path was less crowded than usual. The woman who ran the library said a cheery 'Good evening, Mrs Sidney'. She smiled back, stroking the silver band on the ring finger of her left hand. As far as the town was concerned she had been widowed during the war. A deception suggested by Mrs Pembroke to avoid the spiteful gossip that had plagued her in Hepton.

Ben Logan, the lock-keeper, was opening the gates to admit the last boats of the day. His face lit up when he saw her. ''Lo, Anna. How you doin'?'

'Better now the rain's stopped.' She stood, watching him guide boats into the lock. Her 'young man', as Peggy, the cook, called him. A private joke as Ben was seventy, bald and toothless. But he was her friend. Someone she enjoyed sitting and talking with when she had the time.

Ben went to help a woman tie a rope to a bollard. Though the lock was full, another boat tried to slide in. 'I don't think there's room,' Anna called to the man at the helm.

He glared at her. 'What's it got to do with you?'

Ben's face darkened. 'Mind your manners or you ain't comin' through my lock.'

'I'd better leave you to it, Ben. Talk to you tomorrow.'

'You do that, Anna.'

She walked on, past boats already moored for the night. Two teenage boys sprawled on the roof of one, exchanging jokes and ignoring the middle-aged man who ranted at them from the galley to make themselves useful. She sat down, shaking her head at the ducks that glided towards her in search of food. Across the river a fisherman landed a catch while swallows swooped over the water, hunting flies that danced in the evening breeze.

She wondered what Ronnie was doing. Whether he was missing her as much as she missed him. For a moment she hoped he was, then despised herself for the sentiment.

Was he seeing a girl? An innocent friendship that might blossom into something deeper? It was inevitable that he would one day fall in love, and though he would still be her son he would no longer be her Ronnie Sunshine. His heart would belong to another and as long as that person made him happy she would be happy too.

Or at least she would try to be.

She wondered what sort of girl he would choose. Someone like Alice Wetherby, perhaps. Attractive, intelligent and secure in the knowledge that no other girl in Kendleton could outshine her.

Except one. The girl who was walking along the path with a ginger cat perched on her shoulder.

She moved quickly, striding through the high grass, dressed in a childish cotton frock that only accentuated the graceful shoulders, long, lithe limbs and developing figure. Her feet were bare; her hair a tangled mane of ebony that she suddenly brushed back, allowing her glorious face to be seen. The boys on the boat fell silent as she passed. One made as if to call out but then changed his mind. The tension she radiated did not invite conversation, though she drew their eyes like a magnet.

She passed Anna, eventually coming to a halt farther downriver. As the ducks swam towards her she tossed them scraps of bread, her feet dangling in the water while the cat rubbed himself against the small of her back.

Over the years Anna had often seen her sitting there, lost in thought. Though tempted she had never called out a greeting, wary of disturbing another's obvious desire for solitude.

'That's Susie Ramsey,' Ben had said. 'Lives in Queen Anne Square with 'er mum an' stepdad. 'Er real dad died of an 'eart attack when she was seven. Dropped dead in front of 'er, poor little kid. A good man, John Ramsey. Used to bring Susie down 'ere all the time.'

The wind was rising, blowing clouds across the sky. Susan stared up at them, her lips moving. Talking to herself, perhaps. Or to her father. The cat climbed on to her knee, stretching up its paws like a child seeking comfort from an adult. She wrapped her arms around it, pulling it close, burying her face in the warmth of its fur.

Rising to her feet, Anna made her way back along the path. The boys were still on the roof of the boat. One was arguing with the middle-aged man in the galley. The other continued to gaze at Susan.

October. Anna, packed for a visit to Hepton, went to say goodbye to her employer.

Mrs Pembroke was sitting in bed, sifting through old photographs. 'My taxi will be here in a few minutes,' Anna told her.

'Sit with me until it comes. You look excited.'

'I suppose I am.'

'Of course you are. You're going to see Ronnie. I wish he could come and visit here but you know how particular my doctor is about noise.'

'It doesn't matter. Next week you'll see Charles.' Anna looked at one of the photographs that lay on the bed. Two boys, aged about ten and thirteen, sat together on a garden swing. She pointed to the elder one. 'Is that him?'

'Yes. That was taken in 1924. September twenty-ninth, to be precise. James's tenth birthday.'

Mrs Pembroke had had two sons, James and Charles. James had been killed during the war. Mrs Pembroke talked of him often and kept his picture on her bedside table. But this faded snapshot was the first likeness of Charles that Anna had ever seen.

'He looks nice,' she observed.

'He was just a boy then. This was him at twenty-one.'

Anna studied the image. A tall, serious-looking young man with dark hair, kind eyes and a strong jaw. An appealing face that missed the description 'handsome' by inches.

She wished that she knew more about him. Understood his relationship with his mother. But it was a subject on which she had never felt able to question Mrs Pembroke.

Mrs Sanderson might have told her something. But she had always felt it disloyal to a kind employer to interrogate one of her relatives. And as Mrs Pembroke had only moved to Oxfordshire five years ago there was no one else in Kendleton who knew her family history.

'He doesn't look like that now,' continued Mrs Pembroke. 'The war took a terrible toll on him.' She looked at the picture of James on her bedside table. 'On all my family.'

'And mine,' Anna said softly.

Mrs Pembroke touched her hand. 'Forgive me. That was a thoughtless thing to say.'

'No it wasn't.'

Her taxi sounded its horn in the driveway. Mrs Pembroke gave her some money. 'Here. Use this to treat Ronnie.'

'Thank you.'

'Not at all. A clever boy like Ronnie deserves it. When I'm dead you'll be able to treat him whenever you want.'

Anna felt embarrassed. 'You shouldn't talk like that.'

'Why not? It's true. Or are you saying you'd miss me?'

'Of course I would.'

Mrs Pembroke smiled. 'Yes, I think you would. You're a good girl, Anna. You've brought a lot of happiness into my life and I am grateful. Now give me a hug and be off.'

Obedient as always, Anna did as she was told.

Sunday evening. Anna sat on Ronnie's bed, watching him impersonate Mr Brown.

He waddled around the room, hands on hips, a pillow stuck down the back of his pyjamas, singing an improvised pop song:

'*Peggy Sue, Peggy Sue.*
Each night you pray I'll fall in love with you.
'*Cos I look like Elvis Presley*
And dance like him too-oo-oo.'

She didn't bother to muffle her laughter. The others were all in the pub.

'We shouldn't,' she said, 'but he really is an awful man.'

'Last time he came for dinner he spent the whole time leering at Jane.'

'And how did Mrs Brown react to that?'

'She looked sick but that was because of the food. Even by Auntie Vera's standards it was really disgusting.'

More laughter. He climbed into bed. 'This is like old times,' she said.

'Except that you sleep on the sofa. You should have my bed. I keep telling Auntie Vera but she says it wouldn't be right, you sharing with Peter.'

'It wouldn't. Anyway, I don't mind as long as I get to see you.' She brushed hair back from his forehead. 'You should wear it like this. Show off that handsome face.'

He looked sheepish. 'Mum . . .'

'It's true. You are handsome. I bet the girls think so.'

'Jane does. She says I look like Billy Fury but only to tease Peter.'

'You're better looking than Billy Fury. Anyone else?'

'Catherine Meadows. She's been writing to me.'

'What does she say?'

'Here's my maths homework. Send answers by Thursday.'

'So no special girl yet?'

'Only you.'

'My little man,' she said affectionately.

'I'm taller than you.'

'By a whole half-inch.'

'Three-quarters, actually.'

'And with a deep voice. Soon you'll have whiskers too.' She tickled his chin. As he wriggled away his top pyjama button came undone and she noticed a large bruise by his collarbone. 'How did you get that?'

'It's nothing.'

'Doesn't look like nothing.'

'Well, it is.' He tried to refasten the button.

She pushed his hand away. 'Did Peter do it?'

'It's nothing.'

'Were you arguing?'

'It's not important, Mum.'

'Did he say something about me? He did, didn't he? Oh, Ronnie! I've told you to ignore him when he says things like that. He's just wants to provoke you.'

'I know.'

'So don't respond. If you do then you're just being as stupid as he is. I don't care what he thinks about me. You shouldn't either.'

Anger flashed across his face. 'But I do.' He stared down at the bedspread.

She touched his arm. It was his turn to push her hand away.

'Ronnie?'

Silence.

'I'm sorry. I didn't mean to sound ungrateful. I'm proud that you defended me. I just don't want you to get hurt.'

His head remained lowered. She pushed at his lips, trying to turn his frown into a smile. After a moment's resistance he gave her fingers a soft kiss.

'Mum?'

'What is it, darling?'

'Do you think my father would be proud of me?'

The question took her by surprise.

'I know he's never coming. But that doesn't stop me thinking about him.'

'Of course he'd be proud. Any father would. You have the potential to do anything you want with your life and that's something very few people have. Your father didn't. I certainly don't. But you do and that means you don't need anyone's approval, least of all his.'

He raised his head, looking suddenly like the little boy she had sat with in the back bedroom all those years ago, teaching him letters and numbers as the trains rushed by.

'I need yours.'

'You've got that. Always.'

There was noise downstairs. The others had returned. Vera, her voice shrill with drink, called for Anna to come and make coffee.

'Let them wait,' he said.

'I can't. Better keep the peace.'

'You're going in the morning.'

'I'll be here for breakfast.'

'It feels like you've only just arrived.'

'Christmas isn't far away.'

'I love you, Mum.'

'I love you, Ronnie.'

'Ronnie Sunshine,' he corrected.

'Aren't you too grown up to be called that?'

'I'll always be your Ronnie Sunshine.'

'I know you will.'

They hugged each other while Vera continued to shout for service.

Monday afternoon. Anna let herself into Riverdale by the side door.

The kitchen was empty. Peggy the cook would be at home, returning in the evening to cook dinner. Mrs Pembroke would be having her afternoon nap, checked on from time to time by Muriel the cleaner until Anna could resume such duties herself.

But first she wanted a few moments to herself.

She sat at the kitchen table, worrying about Ronnie. Though he never complained he was clearly unhappy. She wanted to get him away from Vera and Hepton. When Mrs Pembroke died she would have the funds to do just that. But Mrs Pembroke had always been kind to her, and to long for such an event made her feel like a vulture hovering above a grave that had yet to be filled.

The hum of her thoughts drowned out the sound of footsteps in the corridor. The opening door took her by surprise. Startled, she looked up.

And saw the monster.

Letting out a cry, she jumped to her feet, backing away from the table.

Then realized it was just a man.

He stood in the doorway. Tall, heavily built and in his late forties. The left side of his face was quite handsome, topped with dark hair that was starting to grey. The right side was burnt flesh.

'I'm sorry,' he said quickly. 'I didn't realize anyone was here.'

She breathed deeply, waiting for her heart to slow. He turned his head, presenting her with his left profile while hiding the right. It made her think of her old idol, Ronald Colman, who had favoured one profile over the other too.

'I'm Charles Pembroke. You must be Anna.'

'Yes.'

'I didn't realize you were back. There was no taxi.'

'I walked the last part of the way. My bag wasn't heavy and I wanted some air. I thought you were coming on Wednesday.'

'My luggage arrives then. I came last night.'

Silence. Her face felt hot. Embarrassment at the way she had behaved and the poor impression she must have made.

He walked over to the sink. Poured himself a glass of water while keeping the right profile hidden. She wanted to tell him there was no need. That the shadows from the hallway had made it seem worse than it was. But that would only have added insult to injury.

'I'm very sorry, Mr Pembroke.'

'It doesn't matter. I understand you've been visiting your son. How is he?'

'Very well. I must go now. Your mother will be needing me.'

She hurried from the room, leaving him standing by the sink.

That evening she ate dinner with him and Mrs Pembroke.

There was little interaction between mother and son. Just some discussion of people they both knew, conducted with scrupulous politeness. Anna found herself the focus of most conversation. Mrs Pembroke spent an unusually long time asking about Ronnie while Charles Pembroke added the occasional query of his own. He was a good listener, giving an impression of genuine interest. As before, he tried to keep his right profile hidden. This and the strained atmosphere made her feel uncomfortable, and by the end of the evening she had come to wish that he had remained in America.

But in the weeks that passed she began to grow used to his

presence. Some of his days were spent in Oxford, teaching at one of the colleges. Others were spent in the study on the ground floor, writing a book on Russian history. She wanted to ask him about it so she could tell Ronnie but held back for fear of revealing her own ignorance in the process.

One afternoon, shortly before Christmas, she went to ask whether he had any letters for posting. He was standing by the window, looking out at the river. Quickly he hid his right profile from sight.

'You don't need to do that,' she told him.

'It isn't very pretty.'

'You were injured saving someone's life in an air raid. That's what your mother said.'

'And that makes it prettier?'

'Not pretty, but . . .'

He turned, displaying his full face. 'But?'

'It shows you have courage.'

'Is that so rare a thing?'

'In my experience, yes.'

'But you possess it. To a far greater degree than I.'

'Why do you say that?'

'Because you kept Ronnie.'

She lowered her head. 'I didn't think you knew.'

'My mother told me. She knows I can keep a secret.'

'It wasn't courage that made me keep him.'

'Then what was it?'

'Knowing, from the moment I held him, that I could never give him to someone else.'

'And do you ever think you made the wrong choice?'

'No. Not even for a second.'

'Neither do I.'

She looked up. He was smiling. The first proper one she had seen. She smiled back.

'Thank you, Mr Pembroke.'

'Thank you, Anna.'

New Years Eve. Stan and Vera were having a party.

It was nearly midnight. Ronnie stood behind a makeshift bar,

serving guests. Thomas and Sandra had just announced their engage-
ment and were being toasted. 'Sandra's a girl after my own heart,'
announced Vera, delighted that Thomas had chosen a wife she could
intimidate. Stan, for once allowed to smoke in the house, nodded in
agreement. Mrs Brown sipped sherry and looked superior while her
husband puffed on a cigar and leered at anything in a skirt. There
was no sign of Peter and Jane. Ronnie suspected they were upstairs,
enjoying a rather more intimate celebration.

His mother appeared from the kitchen, carrying a tray of sandwiches. She was wearing a blue dress and looked very pretty. Mr
Brown moved towards her, preparing to give her bottom its third
pinch of the evening. This time Ronnie was prepared. Hurrying
across the room he blocked Mr Brown's roving hand with a glass of
steaming-hot punch.

'Bugger!' roared Mr Brown, his cry drowned out by cheers for the
engaged couple.

'I'm terribly sorry.'

'I should think so! Bloody well . . .'

'I was just taking a drink to your wife.'

Instantly Mr Brown mellowed. 'Oh. Never mind, then. Accidents
happen, eh?'

'Thank you,' said his mother when Mr Brown had gone.
'I'm sick of this party. Everyone must have enough food and drink
by now. Let's go outside.'

They crept into the deserted street like conspirators. There was a
bench in the park on the corner. They sat together, their breath
condensing in front of them, staring up at the stars.

'Do you remember me teaching you the constellations?' she asked.

'Yes, but you got their names wrong.' He pointed to the Great
Bear. 'That's called Brownus Lecherus Slobbimus. And that one
there is Verata Witchita Maxima.'

She laughed. He felt pleased. No one could make her laugh the
way he did.

'Make a wish,' she said. 'Aren't you supposed to wish upon a
star?'

He shut his eyes and did so.

'What did you wish for?'

'It's a secret.'

'You can tell me.'

That my father would come.

'Ronnie?'

That I could stub a cigar out in Mr Brown's eye. That Peter would get hit by a train. That Auntie Vera would get cancer so I could watch it eat her alive. That I could get out of this fucking place before I explode.

'No, I can't. It won't come true if I do.'

She looked disappointed. Ronnie Sunshine didn't have secrets from his mother. There was nothing Ronnie Sunshine thought or did that he would not share with his mother.

I wish I could tell you everything. That's what I wish for most.

'I wished for more prizes this summer. I love winning prizes. Not for me but for you.'

The disappointment faded. A smile illuminated her face. She looked beautiful. His mother. The only person in the world who had ever mattered to him.

'Do you have a boyfriend, Mum?'

'Why do you ask that?'

'Jane asked me once if you did.'

'And what did you tell her?'

'That you didn't need one.'

'I don't. The only person I need is you.'

It was his turn to smile. Silently he made another wish. That she would never need anyone but him. He didn't want to share her ever.

Except with his father.

Cheers echoed down the street, followed by a raucous rendition of 'Auld Lang Syne'. 'Happy New Decade, Ronnie,' she said. 'I know it will be a glorious one for you.'

He hugged her while wondering what the future would bring.

March. Mrs Pembroke was having an afternoon nap. Anna stood in Charles Pembroke's study, watching him hammer away at a typewriter with one overworked finger. 'A woman at college is supposed to type for me,' he told her, 'but she can't read my handwriting.'

'Perhaps I could.'

'Doubtful. A secretary in America once told me I had the worst handwriting she'd ever seen. What were her exact words?' He adopted an American accent. 'You may be book smart, Charlie Pembroke, but you can't use a pen for shit.'

She laughed. He missed the key he was aiming for. 'Damn!'

Some of his notes lay in front of her. 'I can read this.'

'Prove it. Read aloud.'

She did. A few lines on Catherine the Great. 'She was German, wasn't she? Ronnie told me that.'

'He's right, and you're remarkable. But your time belongs to my mother. I mustn't encroach upon it.'

'You wouldn't be. She sleeps most afternoons and my evenings are free after she's gone to bed. I'd like to have something useful to do.'

'Then I accept.'

April. Mrs Pembroke sat up in her bed, nodding as Anna read from Ronnie's latest report. 'He's never come top in English before,' she observed.

'Actually he did come top in his English exam two years ago but he's never come top for the term, though he once came second and . . .' Anna shook her head. 'Sorry. You don't need to know all that.'

'Don't apologize. I asked to hear the report.'

'But if you hadn't I would have read it anyway.'

'You're proud of your son. That's a good thing. Ronnie is lucky to have a mother who loves him as much as you.'

'I'm the lucky one. Ronnie gives me more joy than I could ever have imagined. My love is the only thing I have to give back. It isn't much.'

'It's more than you think. Much more.' Mrs Pembroke's expression became troubled. 'Sometimes I think there should be a law against giving all your love to just one person. But who can legislate for the heart?'

'I wouldn't want to legislate for mine. Not when it comes to Ronnie.'

'I thought like that once. When I was young and didn't know what I do now.'

Silence. Anna, uncomfortable, picked up Ronnie's report. 'Perhaps I should go.'

'No, stay. I'm just a foolish old woman talking nonsense. Don't take any notice.'

'You're not foolish.'

'It's kind of you to say so. But then, kindness is one of the qualities that makes me like you so much. Charles likes you too. He's a good judge of character. And a good friend. Better than his brother ever was. Remember that when I'm gone. If a time should come when you need a friend then they don't come much better than him.'

And for a moment the troubled expression returned. Just for a moment. Then it was gone, replaced by an indulgent smile. 'Now back to the report. Which painter does the art teacher compare Ronnie to this term? Not Picasso, I hope. If someone painted me as a series of cubes I would be mortally offended!'

They both laughed. Anna continued to read.

June. There were now two desks in Charles Pembroke's study. Charles sat at the larger one in the centre of the room, its entire surface covered with books and papers. Anna sat at the smaller one by the window, its surface clear except for a typewriter and a vase of bluebells.

Having finished the latest batch of typing, Anna read a letter from Ronnie. It was full of news about school and anecdotes about Vera and the family, all told in a light, cheerful style. A skilful façade to convince her he was happy. She was grateful for the effort yet frustrated at not being able to make things better.

Not yet.

Charles was writing more notes for her to type, a pipe clenched between his teeth. 'All well with Ronnie?'

'Yes.' She upheld the façade. 'Plans for Thomas's wedding are coming on apace.'

He told her about a wedding he had attended in America where the groom's cousin had gone into labour when the bride was halfway down the aisle. It made her laugh. She liked his stories. As he spoke, clouds of smoke billowed up into the air. He had offered not to smoke when she was in the room but she liked the smell too. It brought back memories of her father.

'How was dinner at the Wetherbys'?' she asked.

'I would have enjoyed it more had Mrs Wetherby not kept hinting at how wonderful it would be if I'd give her son Edward private tuition. Though "hinting" is perhaps the wrong word. The woman is as delicate as a dentist's drill.'

Again she laughed. 'Will you tutor him?'

'Probably not. He seems a rather boorish young man. I doubt he'd be a very willing or rewarding student.'

She remembered how Edward had sneered at Ronnie's achievements and felt pleased.

'Then again I'm hardly the world's most exemplary teacher. Once I went to sleep on my feet while lecturing on Peter the Great's foreign policy and woke up to hear myself explaining why Laurel and Hardy were funnier than the Marx Brothers.'

She gasped. 'What did you do?'

'Assured my bewildered students that there would be no questions about 1930s film comedy in their Russian history exam then went and had a very strong coffee. I should stress that that was a one-off. An old friend had paid me a flying visit and we'd sat up all the previous night talking. Believe it or not I do take my teaching seriously.'

She did believe it. Sometimes she would ask him questions about his work and he would always take the trouble to answer them properly, never making her feel stupid or that she was wasting his time. He had the gifts of enthusiasm and clarity, combined with a melodious speaking voice. His students at Oxford were lucky to have him as a teacher.

Perhaps one day Ronnie would be among them. She hoped so. The day Ronnie gained entry to a university like Oxford would be the proudest of her life.

He finished writing and handed her a new pile of notes. 'I really need these by tomorrow. Would that be possible?'

It would, but only if she worked all evening. Outside it was a balmy late afternoon. She had hoped to go for a walk after dinner. But she wanted to be helpful too. 'Of course.'

'I don't know what I'd do without you.'

She smiled, glad to be appreciated.

'Perhaps I could take you out for dinner one evening. My way of saying thank you.'

'You don't need to do that.'

'But I'd like to. After all, you won't let me pay you.'

'It wouldn't be right. My time is already paid for by your mother.'

'Then let me show my gratitude with a meal. I promise not to fall asleep and talk about Stan and Ollie.'

Yet more laughter. He made her laugh more than anyone except Ronnie.

'May I take mirth as acceptance?'

'Yes.'

Wednesday evening. One week later.

Hawtrey Court was an Elizabethan mansion in a village on the outskirts of Oxford. Once a private house, it was now a luxury hotel with one of the finest restaurants in the area.

They sat at a table by the wall, Charles watching Anna eat goose. 'Is it good?' he asked.

'Delicious. This is such a treat.'

The restaurant was crowded. All the tables were occupied, each with a candle flickering at its centre. The constant hum of conversation was overlaid by a Chopin prelude, played by a pianist in the corner of the room. 'I hope this place doesn't compare too unfavourably to the Amalfi,' he said.

A smile. She had told him about the Italian café in Hepton where she took Ronnie. 'Not too badly.'

'And what kind of cream cake does Ronnie favour?'

'Anything with chocolate, though when he was younger it always had to be jam tarts. He used to eat the pastry first, then the jam, and it took for ever. I kept ordering more cups of tea for fear they'd throw us out!'

'My brother Jimmy was the same. He used to eat cream slices layer by layer. It drove our parents mad.'

'You must miss him.'

'Yes. Though not as much as my mother does.'

'It must have been a comfort to her to still have you.'

'Do you really think so?'

She looked awkward. He nodded reassuringly, not wanting her to feel uncomfortable. 'I don't know,' she replied honestly. 'I'd like to.'

'It puzzles you, doesn't it? My relationship with her.'

'Yes.'

'She's actually my stepmother. My father married her when I was very young and Jimmy was her son with him. My real mother died when I was born.'

'I'm sorry to hear that.'

'Don't be. It's difficult to miss someone you've never known. And Barbara is a good woman who deserved a better husband than my father.'

'She rarely talks about him. What was he like?'

'Superficially charming, but weak and self-centred. He adored my real mother and never really got over her death. He couldn't cope with a baby so my maternal grandparents took me in. He also couldn't cope with being alone so he married Barbara soon afterwards. She was younger than him and very much in love but all he wanted was someone to look after him and run the house while he carried on mourning my mother. The realization must have hurt her terribly, and when Jimmy was born he became the focus for all the love my father had made clear he didn't need.

'When I was ten my grandparents died and I returned home. And that just made things worse. I'd grown to resemble my mother and my father loved me for it in a way he never loved Jimmy. Of course that made Barbara resent me and love Jimmy all the more.

'The sad thing was that Jimmy grew up to be a more extreme version of our father. Utterly charming and totally irresponsible. He was only nineteen when Father died and had run through his inheritance within a couple of years. Barbara was constantly giving him money. She kept pushing him to start a career but he never had the discipline. The fact that I did and was bailing him out financially too only made her resent me more. When the war was over I moved to America and what was left of our relationship effectively broke down.'

'Do you regret that?' she asked him.

'Yes.'

'I think she does too and is glad you're here. I really do.' She smiled. 'Thank you for telling me. It won't go any farther. Like you, I know how to keep a secret.'

'A toast to secrets.'

As they clinked glasses he looked into her eyes. Two pale blue orbs, each with a trace of sadness at the centre. Even now, when she was enjoying herself, he could still see it. The only time it vanished was when she talked about her son.

Her hand brushed against his. It was soft and warm and he felt a sudden urge to caress it. Startled by the impulse, he downed the rest of his wine. A waitress came to refill his glass. His right profile was against the wall but when she asked whether he was enjoying the meal he turned his full face towards her. Momentarily taken aback, she spilt wine on the tablecloth.

'I'm terribly sorry,' she said, turning crimson. 'I'll have someone clear this up.'

'It doesn't matter. Accidents happen.'

She hurried away. 'Poor girl,' he said. 'Probably scared she's lost herself a tip.' He laughed, hoping Anna would follow suit. Instead she lowered her head, staring down at the stained cloth.

'What is it?' he asked.

'It does matter. The way she reacted to you. It's the same way I did and it's not right.'

'But it's natural. I'm scarred. I look different. People react to that.'

She looked up again, the candle sending shadows across her eyes. 'How do you face people?'

'Because I have to.'

'Vera is scarred. I've never told you that. She poured boiling chip fat on her arm. Now she always wears long sleeves so no one can see.'

'I was engaged when it happened. I've never told you that, either. Her name was Eleanor. She used to visit me in hospital and then one day she sent a note saying she couldn't marry me after all. For weeks afterwards I lay in a darkened room not wanting anyone to ever look at me again. But I knew I couldn't do that for ever. That I had no choice but to go out and face the world and hope that the people I met would learn to see behind the scars. And after the initial shock most of them do.'

She looked sympathetic. 'Eleanor must have hurt you terribly.'

'Just as Ronnie's father must have hurt you.'

'Do you still hate her?'

He shook his head. 'Do you still hate him?'

'How could I when he gave me Ronnie.'

'Has Ronnie always loved drawing?'

'From the first moment he could pick up a pen. When he was only two he could . . .'

And so she told him more about her beloved son, while in the background other diners carried on their own conversations and the pianist continued to play. Her eyes were shining, the trace of sadness temporarily banished. The sight made him glad.

And, for the first time, jealous.

In the assembly hall of Rigby Hill Grammar School, Archie Clark checked his answers to the end-of-year French exam. Desks were laid out in rows. To his right, Terry Hope wrote furiously while sighing loud enough to wake the dead. To his left, Ronnie Sidney, already finished, stared into space.

'Pens down,' bellowed the supervising teacher. 'Answers to the front.'

'Ronnie!' hissed Archie. 'How did you do?'

A shrug.

'I made a right mess of the third translation.'

'There was a *third* translation?' squeaked Terry.

'On the back page. Didn't you see it?'

Terry let out a groan.

'I wouldn't worry,' Archie told him. 'I'll get nought on it, unlike Brainbox over there.' He gestured towards Ronnie, feeling suddenly sad. Back at Hepton Primary both Ronnie and he had been considered brainboxes. They had been the only boys from their class to reach grammar school but now he was struggling while Ronnie still shone.

Terry left the hall. 'We'd better hurry,' said Archie. 'The bus goes in five minutes.'

Ronnie continued to stare into space.

'We don't want to miss it.'

No answer.

'The next one isn't for an hour.'

'Then piss off and catch it.'

'Why are you in a mood? You should be happy. The exams are over and soon it'll be the summer holidays.'

'And they'll be great, won't they? Six weeks stuck in Hepton working in the corner shop, listening to Auntie Vera rant about how spoilt and lazy I am compared to the brothers grim and, if I'm really lucky, a few days of watching my mother being ordered around and treated like she's nothing. I can't wait.'

Archie felt guilty. 'Sorry. That was a stupid thing to say.'

Ronnie sighed. 'Forget it. Go and get the bus. And don't worry about the translation. You'll have done fine.'

The hall was emptying; boys leaving in groups, talking excitedly about the forthcoming holidays. Archie packed up his belongings, wishing that Ronnie could be excited too.

Then, suddenly, he had a brainwave.

'Do you want to come to Waltringham? It's in Suffolk. We're going there on holiday in August and Mum said I could bring a friend.'

This wasn't strictly true. Waltringham was famous for its antique shops and Mr and Mrs Clark had spent their previous summer holiday browsing through every one of them, dragging a reluctant Archie in their wake. When he had complained his mother had told him that if he had a friend to go around with she would gladly forgo his company, but of course he didn't and there was no way he was wandering around a strange town on his own.

But if Ronnie was there too . . .

Ronnie's face lit up. 'Are you sure your parents won't mind?'

Archie told himself that it would be all right. His parents really liked Ronnie. Both referred to him as 'that charming young man'.

'I'm sure.'

Ronnie looked at his watch. 'The bus will have gone. I'll buy you a milk shake. Mum sent me some money and I need to spend it before Vera the Hun demands tribute.'

Archie laughed. Together they left the hall.

July 1960.
'An outstanding year, crowned by a superb performance in the exams. I predict that when Ronnie finally leaves us it will be to take up a place at either Oxford or Cambridge.'

August. Anna sat at her desk, typing up the latest batch of handwritten notes. The window was open. A faint breeze shifted the dark pipe smoke that Charles Pembroke breathed into the air. Outside it was a beautiful day. A narrow boat sailed past with three children sitting on the roof, all topless and brown as berries.

The handwriting was particularly bad this time. One sentence defeated her completely. She turned to ask her companion for clarification and realized that he was staring at her.

He was leaning forward in his chair, elbow on the desk, head resting on his hand and a faint smile on his face. The pipe was still clenched between his lips, clouds of smoke rising towards the ceiling like a signal from an Indian fire.

'Mr Pembroke?'

No answer. The eyes, unblinking, remained focused upon her.

'Mr Pembroke?'

He started. The smile faded, replaced by embarrassment. 'I'm sorry. Was I staring? I do that sometimes when I'm thinking through an idea.' A quick laugh. 'My secretary in America was always scolding me for it.'

'I can't read this sentence.'

She showed him the page. As he read aloud he scraped used tobacco from his pipe. 'Are there any other parts you can't decipher?'

'No.'

Returning to her desk, she continued to work. After relighting his pipe so did he.

Waltringham, an attractive coastal town, was a popular holiday resort.

Ronnie and the Clarks were staying in the Sunnydale Hotel, a small guest house. Though situated in a nondescript side street its location was excellent: only five minutes' walk from both the town centre and the beach.

They arrived on a hot, sticky afternoon. After they had unpacked, Mr Clark suggested a walk to show Ronnie his new surroundings.

The town centre, dating from the eighteenth century, was a maze of narrow streets converging on a small square with a fountain. 'One in every four shops sells antiques,' said Mrs Clark. 'Isn't that amazing?' Ronnie agreed that it was while Archie grimaced behind his mother's back.

One corner of the square opened on to a green surrounded by large houses with views of the sea. 'That's called The Terrace,' explained Mr Clark. 'The wealthiest people in Waltringham live there.' He smiled wistfully. 'Lucky things.' Ronnie told them about The Avenue in Kendleton and felt suddenly wistful too.

They ended their expedition sitting on a bench overlooking the beach, eating fish and chips. Though it was early evening people were still swimming or lying on towels soaking up the last rays of sun. Archie ate slowly, complaining of a headache. His mother began to fret, wanting to feel his forehead. Ronnie stared out at the vast expanse of water and huge, empty sky, experiencing a sense of euphoria at his temporary escape from the grey streets of Hepton.

'Have you been to the sea before, Ronnie?' asked Mr Clark.

'Once. Just for a day. Mum took me to Southend when I was little.'

'And how does Waltringham compare?'

'There's no comparison. This place is beautiful. Thanks for bringing me.'

'A pleasure. You must do some drawings for your mother while you're here.'

'I will.'

Mrs Clark continued to fuss over Archie. Mr Clark joined in. Ronnie remained silent, listening to the hiss of breaking waves, watching the gulls swoop over the water, tasting the salt in the air, allowing his senses to be filled by his new surroundings.

That night Archie started being sick.

He was still vomiting the next morning. A doctor was summoned to diagnose a particularly nasty stomach bug and prescribe the consumption of liquids and a week's bed rest. Mrs Clark, dreading a visit from the Grim Reaper, took up a vigil over the invalid while ordering her husband to keep himself and Ronnie out of the way.

'I'm sorry about this,' said Mr Clark as they ate lunch in a café.

'It's just a pity Archie's holiday is spoilt.'

'We must make sure yours isn't. What sort of things would you like to do?'

'Go swimming or exploring. The lady at the guest house told me about some good walks.'

Momentarily Mr Clark looked disappointed. 'More fun than antique shops, eh?'

'If you'd like to look at antiques, Mr Clark, I could entertain myself.'

'Can't have that. What sort of host would I be?'

'I don't mind. It's the least I can do after you and Mrs Clark have been so kind to me.'

'Well, if you're sure.'

Ronnie gave his most charming smile. 'Don't worry about me, Mr Clark. I'll be fine.'

The afternoon was hot. He sat on the coastal path, sketching the sea. The first time he had ever drawn it from sight rather than imagination.

An elderly couple stopped to admire his work. 'I'd give anything to have talent like that,' said the woman. Impulsively he offered her the picture, which she made him sign so she could show it to her friends when he had made his name.

The next day was hot too. In the morning he explored Rushbrook Down, a huge expanse of green with dense woodland all around that was a popular picnic site. At lunchtime he met Mr Clark to hear the latest on Archie's health, expressing concern while feeling none. There was so much to see and do in this exciting new place and Archie, with all the adventurous spirit of a dormouse, would only have slowed him down.

In the afternoon he went to the beach, plunging into the cold sea and swimming out as far as his arms would carry him. When exhausted he trod water, his body tingling with exertion, feeling the swell of the waves and the tug of the current while experiencing a strange sense of relief that his mother was not here to call him back lest he be drowned.

Later he sat on the beach, drawing pad in front of him, watching parents play with small children and elderly couples loll in deckchairs frowning at teenagers who lay on towels listening to rock 'n' roll on transistor radios. A father and son built a giant sandcastle. He began to draw it, embellishing its simple design with flourishes of his own, giving it ramparts, turrets, statues of dragons, a drawbridge and moat. Turning it into his own version of Camelot with the man and boy as medieval knights.

Three girls sat near by, all about sixteen and wearing one-piece bathing costumes, watching as a pair of slightly older boys arm-wrestled each other in an attempt to appear manly without damaging their carefully styled hair.

One of the girls noticed him drawing. She came to look, sitting down beside him in the sand. 'My name's Sally. What's yours?'

He told her. She had brown hair, large breasts and a sensual mouth. 'May I draw you?' he asked.

She nodded. Her gaze was direct and confident. 'You may.'

Her friends came to join them. One of them said he looked like Billy Fury. The other agreed.

In the end he drew all three while they asked him questions and talked about a party on the beach the following evening. Sally kept staring at him. 'You must come,' she said, her eyes warm and inviting. He stared into them, sensing her desire and feeling the sudden, unexpected heat of his own.

'I'll try,' he said.

The friends giggled, while in the background the older boys muttered to each other and the turning tide sent waves to besiege the castle and dissolve it into nothing.

The next morning the heavens opened. A summer storm blown out of nowhere and destined to vanish as quickly as it had come. Ronnie prowled from shop to shop waiting for the sun to return.

Eventually he entered a gentleman's outfitters in the central square.

It was a large shop. Assistants hurried about, serving customers. He stood by the tie rack, gazing out of the window. The rain seemed to be slowing.

'Can I help you?' A middle-aged assistant had appeared by his side.

'I need a new tie.'

'For a particular occasion?'

'My cousin's wedding.' Again he glanced out of the window. The rain was definitely easing. In the background a heavily overweight man complained that tailors were making trousers much tighter these days while his equally overweight wife rolled her eyes.

'Do you see any you like?'

He pointed one out.

'Would you like to try it on. There's a full-length mirror you can use.'

The rain was almost completely gone now. He decided to leave. There were other places to buy ties.

Then he saw the two boys from the beach.

They were standing by the fountain, their arms folded, looking bored and restless.

One of them noticed him in the window and nudged the other. Their faces darkened.

'All right, then.'

'The mirror's in that alcove.'

He turned in the direction indicated.

And heard a voice inside his head. A sudden bolt of pure instinct. *Leave. Leave now. Leave this place and never come back.*

But he couldn't leave. Not yet.

And what was there to fear? What could happen to him here in this public place?

Moments later he stood in front of the mirror, staring down at shoes which were still damp from the rain. His hair was damp too. A drop of water slid down his forehead and on towards the floor. He watched it fall.

There were footsteps behind him. Quick and purposeful. A hand came to rest upon his shoulder.

He looked up into the mirror.

*

Mr Clark checked his watch.

He was sitting in a café, waiting for Ronnie. They had agreed to meet for lunch at one o'clock and it was now a quarter past.

Anxiety stirred in him. Had Ronnie got himself into some sort of trouble?

But then it subsided. Ronnie was a sensible boy who would never do anything reckless. He had just lost track of time. That was all.

Beckoning to a waitress, he prepared to order.

From that day onwards his offers of lunchtime meetings were politely but firmly declined. 'It's very kind of you, Mr Clark, but I don't want to disrupt your day.' For the rest of the holiday he saw Ronnie only at breakfast and bedtime.

Except once. On a perfect summer afternoon, three days after the storm. While walking past The Terrace he noticed Ronnie sitting on the green, drawing pad on knee and pencil in hand, staring fixedly in front of him.

He decided against going over for fear of spoiling Ronnie's concentration. Instead he continued on his way.

Little Ronnie Sunshine, fourteen and restless.

Little Ronnie Sunshine, ready to leave childish things behind.

Little Ronnie Sunshine, alone in a new town, listening to the music inside himself.

During those long days of summer the jumbled sequence of notes at last took shape.

Allowing the first masterpiece to be heard.

October. Charles Pembroke drove Anna to the railway station.

It was raining heavily. The windscreen wipers swept sheets of water on to the road. As he drove she told him a story that her lock-keeper friend had told her. Something about a boat coming loose from its overnight moorings and drifting a mile downriver. Her voice was tight with excitement. The way it always was when she was going to see Ronnie.

It was warm in the car. He opened his window an inch, feeling a blast of cold air and the sting of raindrops on his cheek. 'Do you mind?' he asked, knowing that she would not. Not when she was going to see Ronnie.

She was wearing a blue dress; neat, simple and slightly old fashioned. She spent little on clothes, preferring to save her money for Ronnie.

But it didn't matter. She could have worn a potato sack and would still have looked lovely.

Her story reached its end. 'I bet you'll be glad to escape my prattling.'

'The rare luxury of a peaceful office.' He smiled to show he was joking while thinking of just how empty it would seem without her.

They reached the station. The rain was still heavy and she had no umbrella. He handed her his newspaper. 'Use this.'

'You haven't done the crossword yet.'

'There's no point. With you gone who can I swear at when I'm stuck on the last clue?'

She laughed. Her face was devoid of make-up. Not even lipstick. Ronnie didn't like it. Ronnie had told her she didn't need make-up to be beautiful.

He wished he could tell her too.

Instead he wished her a safe journey and a lovely break.

As she hurried across the station forecourt a youth on a motorcycle raced by, spraying her with water without stopping to apologize. He felt an urge to leap from the car, drag the cyclist from the bike and knock him to the ground.

But she didn't even notice. Too excited at the prospect of seeing Ronnie.

On reaching the entrance she turned back. A slim, pretty woman in a cheap blue dress, covering her head with a soggy newspaper. A woman who had experienced the full savagery of life but not become embittered. A woman with little in the way of education but who possessed a warmth that could fill a palace, let alone a book-lined study overlooking the river.

He gave her a wave, while feeling a raw ache in his heart.

I love that woman. I love her more than I have ever loved anyone in my life.

She waved back and then was gone.

*

Saturday lunchtime. Anna sat at the kitchen table with Ronnie, Vera, Stan, Peter and Jane, eating a chicken stew she had made. Her visits were always spent cooking. And cleaning. Doing all the jobs that Vera could possibly delegate.

Vera was griping about their new neighbours. Mr Jackson had moved away, leaving Mr and Mrs Smith to take his place. Though Vera had not liked Mr Jackson she had never complained about him as vehemently as she did about the Smiths. But then, Mr Jackson had not been black.

'It lowers the tone of the neighbourhood.'

'I don't think it does, dear,' said Stan soothingly.

'It does. Their sort always do. Mrs Brown thinks the same.'

'She wouldn't think so if Sammy Davis Junior moved in next door,' Peter told her. 'She'd be fighting to lead the welcome wagon.'

Vera frowned. 'What do you know about it?'

Peter began to whistle 'Old Man River', nudging Jane, clearly wanting her to join in. Jane smiled but kept silent. Anna knew that Jane enjoyed baiting Vera but on this occasion she seemed pre-occupied.

As did Ronnie. He sat beside her, eating slowly, saying nothing.

'Is the stew all right?' she asked.

He nodded. She gave him a smile. He smiled back; a quick gesture that barely reached his eyes. 'It's lovely, Mum. Thanks.'

She told herself that he was just bored. Perhaps he was.

But he had been the same on her last visit. For Thomas and Sandra's wedding at the end of August. Just after his holiday in Waltringham.

Vera was still complaining, growing increasingly shrill while a weary-sounding Stan tried to soothe her. It was a scene Anna knew by heart. As did Ronnie. Again she caught his gaze. Gave him a conspiratorial wink. This time he didn't respond.

The meal continued. Ronnie and Jane picked at their food while Peter and Stan had second helpings. So, in spite of her mental anguish, did Vera. 'I've nothing against the Smiths, personally,' she said between mouthfuls. 'They just don't belong round here.'

'So where do they belong, Auntie Vera?' asked Ronnie suddenly.

'Back where they came from.'

'And where is that exactly?'

'Well, I don't know the precise place.'

'But somewhere in Africa.'

'Yes.'

'Kingston, actually.'

Vera, now chewing hard, just nodded.

'Which is the capital of Jamaica. Which is in the West Indies. Which is even farther from Africa than Hepton is.'

Stan cringed. Anna felt herself tense.

Vera swallowed. 'Are you trying to be clever, Ronnie?'

'No, Auntie Vera. I just thought you'd like to know more about the Smiths. After all, they are your relatives.'

Vera put down her fork. 'My what?'

'Relatives.'

'I'm not related to coloureds!'

'Yes you are. Distantly at least. Your ancestors came from Africa, just as theirs did. They may even have lived in neighbouring mud huts for all we know.'

'My ancestors came from Lancashire!'

'Is that near Kingston?' asked Jane sweetly. Peter burst out laughing, spraying food across the table.

'All life started in Africa, Auntie Vera. I'm surprised you didn't know that because to hear you talk, anyone would think you knew all there was to know about everything.'

'That's enough, Ronnie,' said Anna quickly.

He turned towards her. 'Why?'

'Ronnie . . .'

'Why? Because it might rock the boat? Then I stand corrected. Kingston is in Africa and all life started in the Garden of Eden, except presumably for dirty niggers like the Smiths. Auntie Vera says so and who are we to argue with that?'

'Ronnie!'

'Look, let's all calm down . . .' began Stan.

Vera's face was crimson. 'I think that a certain person has forgotten what he and his mother owe Stan and me. He forgets that if it wasn't for our generosity he wouldn't have a home and his mother wouldn't have her job and they'd both be living in some refuge for mothers and bastards. I think that a certain person would do very well to remember that.'

Stan continued to call for calm. Peter was sniggering.

Ronnie's eyes remained fixed upon Anna. They were ice cold. Like those of a stranger. Silently she beseeched him with her own.

Don't do this, Ronnie. Please, please don't do this.

Then he turned towards Vera, his shoulders sagging, neck bent and eyes downcast. A flawless physical display of submission. And when he spoke his tone was submissive too.

'You're right, Auntie Vera. I was trying to be clever. I know how much Mum and I owe you and Uncle Stan and I am grateful.'

'Get out,' Vera told him. 'I don't want to look at you for the rest of the meal.'

'Who's a stupid little bastard, then?' jeered Peter.

'That's enough, Pete,' said Stan.

'Yes, shut up, Pete,' snapped Jane suddenly. 'Just shut up!'

Under the table Anna reached for Ronnie's hand. Pushing it away, he rose to his feet and left the room.

'You mustn't do that.'

It was later that afternoon. Anna sat with Ronnie in the Amalfi café.

He didn't answer. Just slouched in his chair, watching steam rise from his teacup.

'Ronnie?'

'Do what?' His tone was irritable.

'Make Vera look stupid.'

'Why not? Are you jealous?'

'Jealous?'

'It takes brains to make someone else look stupid. Even Auntie Vera. You've never been able to do it. I could do it when I was seven.'

His words, cruel and out of character, felt like a slap. 'Ronnie, that was a vicious thing to say.'

'And what about the things you say?'

'What things?'

'It won't be long. You said that when you went away. I was nine then. I'll be fifteen in a week and I'm still here. How much longer do I have to wait?'

'Not much.'

'What does that mean? Ten years? Twenty?'

'I know it's not easy for you . . .'

'No you don't. You're not the one stuck here having to listen to Auntie Vera and Peter say things about your mother all the time. And about you. Don't get above yourself, Ronnie. Don't forget who you are. Don't forget *what* you are. And I have to sit there and smile and say yes, Auntie Vera, of course, Auntie Vera, three fucking bags full, Auntie Vera!'

He began to make patterns in the steam with his fingers. She watched him, frightened by this unexpected display of anger and resentment.

'We'll be together soon, Ronnie. I promise.'

'Those are just words. They don't mean anything.'

'Yes they do.'

'Is that what my father told you?'

'What do you mean?'

He began to laugh. 'I love you, Anna. I think you're special. I promise I'll always be there for you. And you were stupid enough to believe him. You let him get you pregnant and then he couldn't get away fast enough.'

A lump came into her throat. She couldn't cope with this. Not from him.

'Shame on you,' she whispered.

He continued to play with the steam. 'It doesn't matter anyway. I don't need him and soon I won't need you. In a couple of years I'll have qualifications and can get a job and out of this place without your help.'

She looked down at her hands. They were shaking. The shock of a verbal beating from such an unexpected source. Softly she began to cry while he pounded the table-top with his fingers, playing a tune that only he could hear.

Then he stopped.

She looked up. He was staring at her. All anger was gone, replaced by mortification.

'Mum . . .'

'I've got something in my eye.'

'I'm sorry. I didn't mean any of that. I was angry with Auntie Vera and took it out on you. I had no right to do that.'

'Yes you did. I'm the one you should be angry with. I *do* know what you have to put up with. I see it every time I come here. You deserve better than this. Better than . . .'

'You?'

He stretched out his hand, gently wiping her tears away. 'Do you really think that?'

'Sometimes.'

'Don't. Not ever. When Peter's unbearable I feel sorry for him because his mother is Auntie Vera and you're worth a million of her. You're worth a million of anyone.'

She felt a warmth in her stomach. 'Do you really mean that?'

'You know I do.'

They stared at each other. She took his hand, pressing it against her cheek.

'What is it, Ronnie? What's troubling you?'

'Why do you ask that?'

'Because you're preoccupied. You were on my last visit too.'

'I'm fine, Mum.'

'If something's wrong I want to know.'

'Nothing is.'

'You can tell me anything.'

'I do. I could never have any secrets from you.'

Then he smiled. A glorious Ronnie Sunshine smile. He looked beautiful. Her son. Her darling. Her whole reason for living.

Two teenage girls sat at a nearby table. One of them kept staring over at Ronnie. Perhaps she knew him. Perhaps she found him beautiful too.

Oh God, let us be together soon. While he's still young.

While he's still mine.

Charles stood in Anna's bedroom, looking at the surface of her dressing table.

It was like a shrine. Every inch covered with pictures of Ronnie. A tiny baby lying on a bed, staring curiously about him. A chubby toddler grinning for the photographer in a cheap, backstreet studio. A small boy in swimming trunks, standing behind a sandcastle. A solemn teenager with his head buried in a book. And a collection of formal school photographs, eight in all, representing each completed year of education.

The resemblance to Anna was remarkable. The same colouring. The same features and smile. More like twins than mother and son.

Except for the eyes. Hers were soft, warm and nervous; perfect windows into her soul. His were like pieces of coloured glass. Beautiful but blank. Not windows so much as barriers, giving no clue as to what lay beneath.

Charles picked up the most recent school portrait and stared down at the face it revealed. Handsome, intelligent and charming yet somehow secretive. The face that Anna loved above all others. Ronnie; her perfect son.

Perhaps she was right. Perhaps Ronnie was perfect and his own doubts no more than the pathetic jealousy of one who yearned for a comparable hold on her affections.

But love could be cruel. Silver tongued and devious. Like a magic mirror that erased all flaws, showing those that sat in front of it only the images they wanted to see.

As he put the picture back in its place he caught a glimpse of his own reflection. A battered wreck of a face that no mirror in the world could ever make beautiful. No love could be so powerful as to weave that particular spell.

'I envy you,' he whispered to the boy in the photograph, who stared back at him with eyes that gave nothing away.

A cold November evening. Ronnie was drawing in his bedroom.

From the window he could see the railway line. He was back in the room he had once shared with his mother. Now that Thomas had left home Peter wanted a room of his own too.

He was working quickly, completing a sketch started earlier in the day. An image that had festered in his brain since Waltringham but which he had never yet dared commit to paper. When it was finished he crouched beside his bed, reaching under it, searching for the loose floorboard he had discovered as a small child. Vera and Peter often snooped through his possessions. But some things were private. Not for the eyes of others. His and his alone.

The picture hidden, he walked on to the landing. From downstairs came the sound of gunfire. Vera and Stan were watching *Danger Man*. He liked the show but Vera had been in a foul mood at dinner and would only give him a lecture if he appeared in the living room. Better to stay upstairs.

From Peter's room came the sound of music. Adam Faith singing in his nasal style. Jane liked Adam Faith. She was in the room too. He wondered what they were doing. Bored and wanting distraction, he crept towards the door. It was shut but not properly. He listened for muffled laughter, weak protests, eager sighs.

But there was none of that. They were whispering anxiously to each other, making plans that were theirs and theirs alone.

Saturday afternoon. Mabel Cooper stood behind the counter of her corner shop watching Ronnie refill the sweet jars. He now worked in the shop every Saturday afternoon as well as during his school holidays. A blessing as she and Bill were not so young any more.

She smiled as he dealt with the caramel creams. 'I know they're your favourite. Take some for yourself.'

Grinning, he put one in his mouth. She remembered the solemn little boy whose mother had bought him drawing pads and felt a sense of pride at the fine young man he was becoming. Not for him a menial job in the factory and dreams of fame as the latest pop sensation. Ronnie had prospects. Clever, disciplined and level headed. Handsome too. Teenage girls spent longer in the shop when Ronnie was there, huddling by the magazine rack, whispering to each other and giggling.

'Only a few, mind. Don't eat all my profits.'

Still grinning, he continued with his work.

'I'm sorry to hear Jane isn't well,' she said.

'It's nothing serious. Just a bug. But she's having trouble shaking it off.'

'What sort of bug?'

'She's sick a lot.'

'Oh, poor thing.'

'It's strange, though. She's only sick in the morning.' Ronnie finished dealing with the sweets. 'All done.'

Mabel stared at him, her brain whirring.

'Is everything all right, Auntie Mabel?'

'Yes. Could you price the tinned goods? They're out in the store cupboard.'

'Of course.' He went to do so.

Mabel vowed not to gossip. Bill was always scolding her for doing so. Calling her the biggest blabbermouth in town.

The bell rang. Mrs Thorpe from number 13 entered the shop. 'Hello, Mabel. What's the news today . . .?'

Wednesday evening. Ronnie sat on the stairs, listening to the row taking place in the living room.

'Were you even going to tell me?' bellowed a man with a deep voice. Jane's father.

'Of course.' Jane was in tears.

'Don't lie to me, girl!'

'I'm not!'

'Stop shouting at her!' Peter trying to be brave.

'Don't you tell me what to do. It's your fault she's in this mess.'

'Let's keep our voices down.' Stan, ineffective as ever. 'Think of the neighbours.'

'The neighbours!' Vera, piercingly shrill. 'It's a bit late for that now. The whole bloody street knows!'

'But how?' Peter again. 'We didn't tell anyone.'

'It doesn't matter how! The fact is they do. And that means it's too late to do anything. Nobody will believe it was a miscarriage. Not now.'

'Are you suggesting what I think?' Jane's father, shocked.

'Well, what else?' Vera, exasperated.

'My daughter's a Catholic. There's no way she's murdering her own child!'

'Dad!' Jane was still sobbing.

'The baby could be adopted.' Stan. A sensible suggestion for once.

'Yes, why not?' Peter eagerly clutching at straws.

'And leave my daughter with the stigma of giving birth to a child out of wedlock? Over my dead body! The two of them are getting married and sharpish . . .'

Later, when Jane and her father had left and Vera and Stan were drowning their sorrows in the pub, Ronnie crept into Peter's room.

Peter stood by the wall, staring down at the ground. 'Fuck off.'

'Are you all right?'

'What do you think?'

'When is it to be?'

'The kid's due at the end of May. It's got to be before then.'

'A ceremony won't change anything. Shotgun weddings never do. Most people round here will still consider the baby illegitimate and you know what that means.'

Peter looked up. 'What?'

'That soon I won't be the only stupid little bastard in the family.'

Then he began to laugh.

'Shut up!'

He shook his head, unable to stop.

Peter punched him in the mouth. 'Shut up! Shut up!'

But he couldn't. Even as he lay on the floor soaking up Peter's blows he just kept laughing as if his sides would split.

December 1960.

'An excellent term academically. As to conduct, however, Ronnie's performance has been less satisfactory. His teachers report that, though always courteous, he is often distracted and seems more involved with his own thoughts than the lesson in hand. This is not uncommon in boys of his age and does not give rise to immediate concern, but I would hope to see such behaviour corrected sooner rather than later. Someone with Ronnie's exceptional potential should not be developing habits that could hinder his future progress.'

February 1961.

Charles sat by his stepmother's bed. She never left it now. In recent weeks her bedroom had become her whole world.

He was reading from an expensively bound volume of Keats's

poetry. Keats was her favourite poet. On the front page, in flamboyant script, his brother had written, 'To my darling mother on her birthday. All my love, Jimmy.' The date was 17 May 1939. Only months from the start of the war that would take him from them both for ever.

'Which one would you like to hear now?' he asked.

'Ode to Autumn'.

He smiled. She had always loved autumn. Season of mists, mellow fruitfulness and Jimmy's birth.

And Ronnie's. Anna loved autumn too.

'I'll never see another one. That's what my doctor told me. Time to make my peace.'

'You don't have any peace to make.'

'Don't I?' She turned towards him. Her expression was anxious. Frightened even. A tiny, birdlike woman with skin as thin as rice paper. He had known that this conversation was inevitable and longed to tell her that it wasn't necessary. But it was. For her at least.

'I keep seeing you in my head. The way you were when you first came to live with us. A boy of ten who'd lost the only parents he'd ever known and been sent across the country to a strange house and relatives who were strangers too. When I picture it now I see how terrified you were. How much you wanted us to accept you. But I didn't see it then. All I saw was someone who might threaten Jimmy.'

'You had your reasons for feeling like that.'

'And that makes it right?'

'I understood.'

'You may do now but you didn't then. How could you? You were just a child.' Tears came to her eyes. 'The things you did to try and gain my affection. The way you tried and tried.'

'Just as Jimmy tried with father.'

'You should have hated me. I deserved your hatred. Instead you gave me more consideration than Jimmy ever did.' She pointed to the book. 'I know you bought that. Gave it to Jimmy to give me while you gave me a scarf in a colour I didn't like. You didn't want your present to upstage his.'

'Presents are just tokens. It's what you feel that matters.'

'And what did Jimmy feel? What was I to him, really? Just a never-ending source of credit. That's the truth. And yet I loved him. I couldn't help it. When he died I wished it had been you. I told you . . .'

She began to sob. Her hand, clawlike with arthritis, lay on the bed. He took it in his own, squeezing it as gently as he could.

'When Eleanor left you I was glad. I came to the hospital and told you that.'

'You were in pain. You weren't yourself.'

'And what about your pain? You must have hated me then.'

'Perhaps I did. But I also understood. You must believe that. Love can be a terrible thing. It can cause more pain than any physical wound. After Eleanor left me I never wanted to feel it again.'

'But now you do.'

Silence.

'Did you think I hadn't realized?'

'She'll never love me. I'm just a friend. I accept that.'

'Perhaps you won't have to. Not when I'm gone.'

'What do you mean?'

'Nothing. Nothing at all.'

Another silence. Her tears had stopped. She had said what she had needed to. He hoped that it had given her some peace.

'But Charlie, there's something you must understand. The boy will always come first. However much she might love you she will always love him more. For fifteen years he's been her whole reason for living, just as your brother was mine. And when you love like that, nothing can ever eclipse it, however much you might wish it could.'

'Do you wish that?'

'I have done. Now I only wish that I could see him again. Just once before I die. To see him smile. And to tell him . . . to tell him . . .'

Again she began to cry. 'Don't,' he said.

'Would you hug me?'

He leant towards her. Suddenly she shook her head.

'It doesn't matter,' he whispered. 'It's all right to pretend that I'm Jimmy.'

She put her arms around his neck, holding him to her with all the strength her feeble body possessed, as if he were a source of life itself.

*

In March Mrs Pembroke died peacefully in her sleep.

Her funeral was in Kendleton Church, attended by the few people in the town who had known her. Anna hoped the Sandersons would come from Hepton but both were too ill to travel. She sat with Charles in the front row, crying quietly as the vicar delivered his sermon. Since it had happened she had cried a great deal. Though happy that she and Ronnie could now be together, she had lost a woman who had shown her far more kindness and affection than her adopted family ever had.

Two days later Mrs Pembroke's lawyer, Andrew Bishop, came to the house to explain the provisions of her will. He sat at Charles's desk. A tall, plumpish man with a round face and grey eyes who had been a regular visitor to the house in previous months.

'I'm sorry to have kept you waiting,' he told Anna.

'You haven't.'

'How is your son? Ronnie, isn't it?'

'Yes. He's well, thank you. And your stepdaughter, Susan?'

'She's well too.'

'I often see her walking by the river. She's very beautiful, but I'm sure you don't need me to tell you that.'

'Just as long as you don't tell Susan. Her mother and I don't want her growing big headed.' He laughed, looking suddenly uncomfortable. 'And so to the will. It's a simple document. The bulk of the estate goes to Mrs Pembroke's son, Charles. However, there are also several generous legacies. One to the Sandersons, whom I believe you know. Others to her cook, her cleaner and gardener.'

'And to me.'

He rubbed his nose. 'That's the thing.'

'What do you mean?'

He cleared his throat. 'To Anna Sidney, my loyal companion and friend, I leave nothing because I believe others will provide for her.'

For a moment she was so shocked she couldn't speak.

'I know this must be upsetting. I think . . .'

She found her voice. 'That's not possible.'

'I'm afraid it is.'

'No! It's not possible! She would never have done this to me!'

He continued to speak but she could no longer hear him. A

thundering in her head drowned out all sound. Leaning across the desk, she snatched the document from him, telling herself that he had misread the provision.

But he hadn't. There it was in cold, hard type. A single sentence that destroyed all her hopes and dreams.

Half an hour later she was walking by the river.

It was raining. A harsh wind blew across the water. She had no coat but did not feel the cold. Too stunned by her employer's betrayal to register anything else.

Eventually she took shelter under a tree, leaning against the rough bark, her arms wrapped around herself, trying to comprehend how this could have happened.

And what she and Ronnie were going to do.

She would have to start again. But how? The last six years of her life had been wasted on hollow promises and she was drained. Too tired even to cry.

'Anna.'

Charles stood near by, under a huge umbrella, holding her coat. 'Put this on. You'll catch cold.'

'How could she do this to me? I don't understand.'

He looked down at the ground. 'I think I do. She was trying to help me. A misguided way of making up for the past.'

'What do you mean?'

'Haven't you guessed?'

'Guessed what?'

'That I love you.'

He looked up again. His eyes were frightened. Vulnerable. Like those of a child.

'I love you, Anna. I love everything about you. Your smile. Your voice. The way you laugh at my terrible jokes. The way you fiddle with your left ear when you're nervous. The way your face lights up when you talk about Ronnie. The way you manage to bring him into every conversation you have. The way that when we walk together by the water you have to describe every bird and every plant and the shape of every single bloody cloud as if it's the first time you've ever seen one. I love you more than I have ever loved anyone in my life and if I could call you my wife I would be the happiest man in the world.'

The ground felt unsteady beneath her feet. She pressed herself against the tree while the wind whipped at her skirt like a rogue hand.

'And this is how you do it?'

'Do you think I wanted this? If I'd known what she was going to do I would have stopped her. You must believe that.'

They stared at each other. He was her friend. She wanted to trust him. But she had trusted his mother too.

'What choice do I have?'

'You have two choices.'

'Marry you or back to Hepton. That's no choice.'

He shook his head.

'Then what?'

'The first choice *is* to marry me. We could live together here. Ronnie would join us and I would do my utmost to be a good father to him. I know you don't love me but you might grow to in time. Love can grow out of friendship.'

'And the other?'

'That I give you everything my mother has left me.'

For the second time that day she was unable to speak.

'The money and the house. They'd both be yours.'

'You can't do that.'

'I have money of my own. I don't need hers.'

'But what would you do?'

'Return to America, perhaps. I'm sure my old college would welcome me back.' He smiled. 'Provided I went on a handwriting course and promised not to fall asleep while giving any more lectures.'

She burst into tears.

'Anna . . .'

'I don't want you to go.'

'Why not?'

'Because . . .'

'Because?'

'You're my friend.' She wiped her eyes. 'A real one. Someone who's never judged me or tried to make me feel ashamed. There haven't been many people like that in my life.'

'I'll always be your friend. Don't you realize that? I know you won't marry me. You're young and lovely and deserve better than someone as old and ugly as I am. I accept that. But you have to accept that I will always love you and will always be your friend. Wherever I am in the world I will always think of you, and if you ever need me I will be here for you.'

She looked out at the river. A swan was moving across its surface, flapping its wings, rising majestically into the air.

He held out her coat. This time she put it on. 'Come back to the house,' he said.

'Not yet. I need to be on my own. To think. You understand, don't you?'

'Yes.'

'Thank you.'

She walked on down the river, staring up at the grey sky, watching the swan as it flew away.

April. Hepton High Street was crowded. Fifteen-year-old Catherine Meadows, home from boarding school for the holidays, studied her reflection in a shop window and smiled because no one could tell.

She was slim and dainty, dressed in a blouse, cardigan and knee-length skirt, her blonde hair held back with a band. She was pretty with big blue eyes and soft, delicate features. She looked like a girl who worked hard at school. A girl who had nice friends and no time for unsuitable boys. A girl who would never be a worry to her parents.

A girl, in fact, who never thought about sex.

But she did. Constantly. Her virginity had been lost the previous summer to a boy she had met on holiday who had written her poetry and said that he loved her. But she hadn't wanted love, just a physical experience, and once the act was over she had walked away without even a backward glance.

There had been two others since, both married. A friend of her father's whom she had known since childhood, and a handyman at her school whom she would meet on Sunday afternoons in a shed outside the grounds. Each had been chosen carefully. Older men with enough experience to make the act pleasurable and too much at stake to risk bragging of encounters with a girl still below the age of consent. Particularly a girl who projected so perfect a façade of respectability. Boys of her own age were of no interest. Too clumsy to be satisfying and too boastful to be safe. She would not waste time on any of them.

Except one.

Ronnie Sidney sat alone in the Amalfi café reading a letter. She walked inside, bought a cup of tea and went to join him. On the next table boys in leather jackets with Brylcreemed hair talked of a pop group they wanted to form. One of them winked at her. She turned away. He laughed, clearly thinking her intimidated. A frightened virgin who would scream if he so much as touched her hand. Inside she was laughing too.

Ronnie wore a grey jumper. His hair was neatly combed. A handsome, dignified-looking boy. Someone of whom her parents and grandmother would approve. All three complained constantly about the youth of today, their raucous music, flamboyant clothes and general rudeness. But Ronnie would have reassured them. Just as she did.

He looked up as she sat down. His grey-green eyes were far from welcoming. She felt a thrill in the pit of her stomach. He had always fascinated her. Even as a small child she would watch their teacher hold him up as an example of industry and courtesy and sense the danger that lay beneath the perfect exterior. Like a beautiful chocolate filled with acid.

'What do you want?' he asked.

'That's not much of a welcome.' She pointed to the letter. 'Is that from your mother?'

'Yes.'

'What does she say?'

'That she's coming to see me next week.'

'You don't sound very pleased. Don't you want to see her?'

'She's bringing a man with her.'

'Oh.'

His eyes returned to the letter. She watched him while the boys at the next table argued about whose turn it was to put money in the jukebox.

'It had to happen one day, Ronnie. She's still young and a son is only so much comfort.'

He looked up again, his face angry. 'What do you know about it?'

'More than you think.'

'You don't know anything.'

She smiled. 'I know about you. Good, sweet, clever Ronnie Sidney. That's what people think. But there's more to you than that.'

'Not according to my mother.'

'But she doesn't understand you.'

'And you do?'

She nodded. 'We're the same, you and me. My parents think I'm perfect but they don't know me at all. If they knew who I really was they'd disown me.'

'So who are you really?'

His hand was on the table. She covered it with her own. A chaste gesture to anyone watching. Like a girl with her brother. They couldn't see her thumb caress his palm.

'Come home with me and I'll tell you all my secrets.'

He didn't answer. Just stared at her.

'I think you're special, Ronnie. I always have. Come home with me. Let me show you who I really am.'

For a moment he didn't react. She carried on stroking his palm.

'I'd like that,' he said.

They rose to their feet. The boy who had winked now sneered. 'Off to do your homework?'

'Biology,' she told him, and led Ronnie outside.

Fifteen minutes later they sat together on a sofa in her parents' living room.

The decor was soft and feminine. Pastel colours and ornaments littering each surface. A large glass cabinet held rows of Victorian china painstakingly collected over many years. Most evenings during her holidays Catherine would sit on the same sofa, watching television and listening to her parents congratulate themselves on having produced such a model child while longing to tell them things that would wipe the self-satisfied smiles from their faces.

'I hate this room,' she told Ronnie. 'It sums my mother up. All pretty and sweet and nice. Everything she thinks I am but I'm not. I'm like you.' She stroked his chin. Still smooth. No beard yet. 'We even look alike. You could be my twin. Would you like that?'

'Maybe.'

'I wouldn't. Twins can't do this.' She leant forward, cupping his face in her hands, kissing him on the lips. His response was clumsy. His tongue too eager, his mouth too hard. Perhaps she was the first girl he had ever kissed. She found the idea exciting. Her fingers slid down his chest and belly towards the swelling in his groin, squeezing it gently and hearing him sigh. She bit down on his lip, then moved on to nibble at his ear.

'I understand you, Ronnie,' she whispered. 'What you are. What you need.'

'What am I, then?' he whispered back.

'You're bad. That's what makes you special. That's why I want you.'

'Why am I bad?'

She didn't answer. Too busy teasing his neck with her teeth.

He leant back. 'Why am I bad?'

'You just are. Like me.' She edged forward, eager to kiss him again.

He kept his distance. 'And why are you bad?'

'We can talk afterwards. Come on, Ronnie.'

'Why?'

Playfully she blew in his face. He kept his distance. 'Why? Because I won't be the first person you've had sex with? Is that the only secret you've got to tell me?'

'Isn't that enough?'

'No.'

'Yes it is.' She began to giggle. 'If my parents knew what we were going to do . . .'

'It's not bad. Not compared to what I could tell you. It's just . . . nothing.'

Her fingers crept back to his groin. 'This isn't nothing. You want me, don't you?'

'I want you to understand me.'

'I do.' Again she tried to pull him towards her.

He shoved her backwards, staring into her eyes. His were unblinking and so intense that for a moment she felt as if he were looking through her skin and inside her head.

'No you don't.'

'Ronnie . . .'

He rose to his feet. 'I'm sorry. I shouldn't have come here.'

'You can't go!'

'Yes I can.'

'Ronnie!'

He walked out of the room.

'Queer! Pansy! Fairy! You'll be sorry for this, Ronnie Sidney. I'm going to tell everyone what a little queer you are!'

No answer. Just the sound of footsteps, then the front door opening and shutting.

Frustrated, bewildered and hurt, she burst into tears.

Sunday lunchtime. Anna sat in the restaurant of the Cumberland Hotel with Charles and Ronnie.

The Cumberland was in Lytton. There were no decent restaurants in Hepton. As waiters and waitresses slid between the tables, Anna sipped her wine and listened to the conversation between her companions.

It was going well. Charles was being charming; asking Ronnie about school, finding out his favourite periods of history. Occasionally he tried to bring her into the conversation but she preferred to keep silent and observe.

'How is your beef?' he asked her.

'Lovely, thank you, Charles.' She controlled the urge to call him Mr Pembroke. It felt strange to be using his first name.

Ronnie was also charming. To Charles at least. To her he was polite but distant. Dressed in his school uniform, he looked handsome and very grown up. She watched him with a mixture of pride and apprehension.

They finished their main courses. A waitress approached with the sweet trolley. Charles rose to his feet. 'I'll go outside and smoke my pipe. Give you two a chance to talk.'

The motherly-looking waitress beamed at Ronnie. 'And what can I get for you?'

'Nothing.'

'You must have something. A growing boy like you. The chocolate gateau is very good. How about . . .'

'I said I didn't want anything. Are you deaf?'

The waitress flushed. Anna felt embarrassed. 'Ronnie, apologize at once.'

'Sorry,' he said sulkily.

'So am I,' added Anna, more graciously.

The waitress wheeled the trolley away. Ronnie lounged back in his chair, staring at the pepper pot at the centre of the table. 'What's got into you?' Anna demanded.

'Isn't there something you want to tell me?'

'What?'

'That you're going to marry him. You are, aren't you?'

'Yes.'

He picked up a napkin ring, rolling it back and forth on the tablecloth.

'How does that make you feel?' she asked.

'Proud. You make such an attractive pair.'

'Ronnie!'

'So what happens to me now?'

'You finish your school year here in Hepton. Then you come to live with us in Kendleton.' She smiled encouragingly. 'You'll like it there, Ronnie. It's a beautiful place. The house is beautiful too. Right by the river with a garden so big that it really does take a man a whole day to cut the grass. It's just like the one I promised you when you were little.'

'But you didn't promise we'd have to share it.'

'It'll be our home.'

'And his.'

Silence. At a nearby table a man laughed loudly at his own joke.

'Do you . . .' he began.

'No,' she said quickly. 'I don't love him. But he's a good man, Ronnie. He's been a true friend to me, just as he will be to you. Perhaps I will grow to love him. But one thing you must believe is that I will never love him as much as I love you.'

He looked up. 'Do you promise?'

'Do you need to ask?'

'I don't know.'

She covered his hand with her own.

'When I was thirteen God played a terrible trick on me. He took everything that gave my life meaning and destroyed it utterly. For three years I wished that he'd destroyed me too. I used to lie awake every night in the back bedroom in Baxter Road and wish that I was dead so that I could be with my family again.'

He swallowed. His hand continued to move the ring.

'And then I had you. My son. My Ronnie Sunshine who took all the pain away. From the moment I first held you in my arms I knew that I would willingly go through that pain a million times over provided you were waiting for me at the end of it. You are the most wonderful, the most glorious thing that has ever happened to me, and even if I were to love Charles more than any woman ever loved her husband it still wouldn't be the smallest fraction of the love I feel for you. Sometimes I look at you and feel as if my heart will burst with pride. My brilliant, beautiful, perfect son.'

His hand stopped moving. He began to cry. The sight caused her physical pain. 'Oh, Ronnie, darling . . .'

'But I'm not perfect. I want to be but I'm not. And if you knew . . . if you knew . . .'

'Knew what?'

He shook his head. She moved her chair closer, pulling him towards her, crooning over him as if he were a baby while his tears soaked through her blouse and on to her skin. The people at the next table, clearly embarrassed, kept glancing over. She ignored them. They didn't matter. The only person who mattered was Ronnie.

'Knew what, my darling? You can tell me. There's nothing you could do that would change how I feel about you. You know that, don't you?'

He wiped his eyes.

'Don't you?'

'Yes.'

She stroked his hair. 'Tell me, then.'

He looked up. Managed a smile. A faint Ronnie Sunshine smile.

'I was jealous of Charles. I was sitting here wishing he'd been killed in the war, not just injured, because then he couldn't marry you and take you away from me.'

'He's not taking me away from you. I'll always be yours, Ronnie. No one else's.'

'I love you, Mum. I want you to be happy. If Charles makes you happy, I'm happy too.'

'You make me happy. No one will ever make me as happy as you.'

She stroked his cheek. He kissed her hand. The people at the next table were still staring. One man muttered about people making exhibitions of themselves. Impulsively she blew a raspberry at him. Startled, the whole group looked away.

Ronnie began to laugh. She did the same. They hugged each other, neither caring what anyone else thought.

Charles stood in the doorway of the restaurant, watching Anna with Ronnie.

Her arms were wrapped around him. His head rested on her breast. The two of them locked together as completely as two pieces in a jigsaw puzzle.

People talked about the bond between fathers and daughters but to him it could not compare to that between mothers and sons. A mother nurtured her son in her womb and fed him from her body. Surrendered herself to him in a way that she would never do to any other man, not even her husband. And the son, on reaching manhood, would discover that no woman, not even his wife, would ever give herself to him as completely as his mother had done. It was a bond made up of contradictions. Pure yet sexual. Nurturing yet crippling. Creating a love so powerful that no one, not even God, could ever completely tear it asunder.

And if there were no other family members to dilute that love . . .

The boy will always come first. However much she might love you she will always love him more.

A woman near by was staring at his destroyed right profile. When he turned towards her she looked embarrassed. He wanted to tell her that it didn't matter. That he understood.

Even though it still hurt.

He walked through the restaurant towards the woman he loved above all others and the boy with the secret eyes who would always eclipse him in her heart. 'Is everything all right?' he asked hesitantly.

'It's fine,' Anna told him.

Ronnie raised his wineglass. 'A toast to the future.'

Charles did likewise. 'To our happiness.'

'To my mother's happiness.'

They clinked glasses. Anna smiled at him. Ronnie did too, with eyes that gave nothing away. Charles smiled back, telling himself that the future would be happy for all of them.

July 1961.

'Yet again Ronnie is a more than deserving winner of the year prize. Even by his own high standards, his performance in the exams was outstanding.

I am, however, still concerned by reports of restlessness in class which have grown ever more frequent in recent months. This may be due partly to excitement at his impending move but must now be brought into check as he enters the final years of his school career.

Ronnie's teachers join me in wishing him all possible success in the future . . .'

The morning of Ronnie's departure, and Vera was not herself. A strange madness had come over her which manifested itself in an obsession with four words: Oxford, professor, author and rich. She couldn't stop using them. Every sentence she uttered contained at least one. 'I keep asking myself,' she told the Browns, 'whether it's as prestigious to be a professor at an Ivy League university as it is to be a professor at Oxford. What do you think?' Mr Brown said that he didn't know. Mrs Brown said nothing, just looked sick.

The house was full that day. Vera and Stan. The Browns. Thomas and Sandra. Peter, Jane and their baby son. Mabel and Bill Cooper from the corner shop. Even Archie Clark. All there to say goodbye to Ronnie as he left Hepton for ever.

He sat on the sofa while Vera fussed over him. She had done a great deal of that since the wedding. 'Are you sure you've had enough to eat?' she enquired anxiously.

'Yes, thank you, Auntie Vera.'

'It's no trouble to make you something else.'

'I'll have something,' said Peter. He looked exhausted, as did Jane. The two of them shared the front bedroom that Peter had once shared with Ronnie. The baby shared it too, crying all night while his newly married parents shouted at each other, hinting at the long years of misery that lay ahead.

Stan was talking to Thomas and Bill Cooper about football. 'Talk about cricket,' Vera told him. 'Rich people like cricket.' She turned to the Browns. 'Did I tell you that Charles is related to an earl?' Mr Brown nodded while Mrs Brown puffed furiously on her cigarette.

'Actually he's not, Auntie Vera. His stepmother was.'

'Well, it's the same thing.' Vera sighed with pleasure. 'Who would have thought it? A cousin of mine marrying into the aristocracy.' Ronnie's mother, for years a despised relative of Stan's, had suddenly been elevated to the dearest of all Vera's kin.

A Bentley pulled up outside the house. His mother and stepfather had arrived. Vera led them into the living room, fawning over Charles as if he were royalty. His mother was wearing a new suit. Chic and expensive. Different from her usual clothes. It made her look older. Harder. For a moment she didn't look like his mother at all.

Then she saw him. Her face lit up like a child on Christmas morning and everything was all right again. She was still his mother. She was still his.

'Hello, Ronnie.'

'Hello, Mum.'

They sat together on the sofa, drinking tea while Vera forced expensive biscuits and cakes upon them. None of the cheap stuff the local shops sold. She had made a special trip to Harrods. Charles listened to Vera's gushing with good grace while Mr Brown asked about the drive from Kendleton and poor, henpecked Stan talked about cricket as if his life depended on it. In the corner of the room, Peter and Jane stared at Charles's damaged face. Jane whispered something and Peter began to snigger. He caught Ronnie's eye and gave him the usual sneer. Once it would have been accompanied by the mouthing of the word 'bastard', but not now.

His mother said that it was time to leave. Everyone crowded round to wish him well. Even Peter, after much prodding from his mother, offered his hand.

As did Mr Brown. 'So goodbye then, young Ronnie, and take my advice. If you can't be good then be careful.' His wife and the newly refined Vera cringed but Mr Brown just laughed. His hand was fat and clammy. The hand that had once dared to fondle Ronnie's mother. Ronnie laughed too, thinking of the letter that Archie would be posting in a week's time. An anonymous letter, addressed to Mrs Brown, giving a full account of her husband's philandering. Hopefully, after reading it, Mrs Brown would cut off her husband's hand along with something altogether more vital.

Vera suggested that he take some biscuits for the journey. 'I'll go and wrap them for you, dear.' She beamed at Charles. 'He loves his biscuits, does our Ronnie.'

'I'll come and help you, Auntie Vera.'

They stood together in the kitchen beside the table where he had had to sit in silence through countless meals while his mother's name was dragged through the mud. Vera smiled nervously. 'This is it, then, Ronnie.'

'I suppose so.' He smiled too, thinking of the fifteen long years they had spent together. They had had their ups and downs, that was for sure. But now it was over.

'How about a hug, then?'

He did as she asked. She smelt of cheap perfume, talcum powder and beer. He hated the way she smelt. He hated everything about her.

Pressing his mouth close to her ear, he began to whisper.

'You think the Browns are your friends but they're not. They despise you. Everyone in the street despises you. They used to come into the shop and laugh at you the way you used to laugh at my mother. You think you're better than her but she's worth a million of you. She always has been and she always will be. So goodbye, Auntie Vera, and don't ever expect to see or hear from me again unless you're dying in agony, because believe me I would walk through the fires of hell itself to see that.'

He kissed her cheek, his hand stroking her scarred arm. Then, still smiling, he walked back into the living room.

One hour later he sat in the car as it drove towards Oxfordshire.

They had left London and the countryside was opening up around them. It was a beautiful day and the windows were open. His mother sat in front, describing everything they passed, radiating happiness while the wind blasted her hair and Charles smiled indulgently at her.

'Am I talking too much?' she asked him.

'Absolutely not. Until today I had no idea what a cow looked like but now I do and my world will never be the same again.'

She began to laugh. A full, hearty sound. Ronnie had never heard her laugh like that before.

Except with him.

He laughed too, as loudly as her, masking the jealousy that churned inside him like a bag of snakes as the car sped on, carrying him away from his old life and on towards the new.

Part 4

Kendleton: 1959

A hot day in June. Mae Moss was cleaning for Mr and Mrs Bishop.

She enjoyed cleaning for them. Unlike their neighbours the Hastings, whose home always looked as if it had just been burgled, the Bishops were a tidy family. 'A place for everything and everything in its place,' was Mr Bishop's motto, and one of which Mae thoroughly approved.

She was working in the living room. Just a quick dusting of surfaces. Nothing else was needed. It was beautifully laid out; antique furniture, oil paintings and no television. 'My husband says it kills the art of conversation,' said Mrs Bishop. 'Young people spend their lives watching it and we don't want that for Susan.' Mae enjoyed television and never missed an episode of *Emergency Ward Ten*, but when she thought of the ghastly *Juke Box Jury* that her grandchildren adored she was forced to admit that Mr Bishop had a point.

After finishing the ground floor she moved upstairs. Mr Bishop's bedroom first, then his wife's. They were the only couple Mae cleaned for who slept apart. Her friend Dora Cox, who knew everyone's business, thought this was down to Mrs Bishop. 'She had a breakdown, poor love, and that's usually due to problems in the bedroom department.' Mae, whose husband snored loud enough to wake the dead, envied Mrs Bishop so understanding a spouse.

Finally she cleaned the top floor. Mr Bishop's study was full of files and papers, all meticulously arranged. He was a successful lawyer who acted for many of the wealthy families in The Avenue, including old Mrs Pembroke, who owned beautiful Riverdale and was reputedly as rich as Croesus. Mae was always telling her grandchildren to work hard so they too could become successful lawyers and live in Queen Anne Square, and they would roll their eyes and continue arguing over whether Cliff Richard was as good as Elvis Presley.

Last of all was Susan's bedroom, at the end of the corridor with a view of Kendleton Church. Mae could never enter it without feeling sad. On the bedside table was a framed photograph of Susan's father, John Ramsey. Ten years earlier, Mae had spent an afternoon in his studio with her twin sister, Maggie; the two of them in fits of laughter at his jokes as he took their portrait. Now Maggie was dead and pictures were all Mae had to remember her by, just as they were all that Susan had to remember John.

The room was as tidy as all the others. Books stacked neatly on shelves and school texts piled carefully on the desk in the corner. Everything else was packed away in cupboards and drawers except for a Victorian doll's house that stood by the wardrobe and a conch shell that lay under the bed. A far cry from the bedroom of Maggie's granddaughter, Lizzie Flynn, which was a shambles of dirty clothes, battered records and pictures of Alain Delon. Lizzie's father had died the previous year and an unsettled Lizzie was showing increasing signs of rebelliousness. Mae was glad that Maggie had not lived to see it and wished that Lizzie could find the sort of stabilizing father figure that Susan had in Mr Bishop.

Her work complete, she packed up her things and prepared to leave.

August. In his surgery near Market Court, Dr Henry Norris braced himself to break the news to the man with the round face who sat before him.

'Susan has gonorrhoea, Mr Bishop.'

A soft intake of breath. 'I was afraid of that.'

'Were you? Susan is only thirteen.'

'I know, but you see . . .' A sigh. 'I'm sorry. This is difficult for me. On a recent holiday Susan met an older boy at a party. He got her drunk and then . . .' A pause. 'Took advantage of her. Afterwards she was too ashamed to say anything, poor darling. She would have kept quiet for ever if she hadn't discovered that she was . . . um, unwell.'

'What of the boy? He forced himself on an underage girl. Have you told the police?'

'That wouldn't achieve anything. Susan can't remember his name or much about what he looked like. He was probably on holiday too and could be anywhere now.' A shake of the head. 'No, it really wouldn't achieve anything.'

'What does Susan's mother think about this?'

'She doesn't know. As you will have seen from Susan's records, her mother had a severe nervous breakdown seven years ago. She's not a strong woman emotionally and needs to be protected from shocks.' Another sigh. 'I did consider telling her but Susan made me promise not to. She's very protective of her mother and doesn't want her worried or upset.'

'Your wife's doctor is William Wheatley. I see that he was Susan's doctor too until she was nine but she's since moved twice. Why was that?'

'Though my wife likes Dr Wheatley I've always found him . . .' A conspiratorial smile. 'A little stuffy. Susan did too. A friend recommended Dr Jarvis but sadly Susan didn't take to him.'

'So you thought you'd try me.'

Another smile. This time ingratiating. 'And I'm very glad that we did.'

'Who is your doctor?'

'He's in Oxford. I work there so it's practical.'

'So each family member has a different doctor. That's unusual.'

'It's just the way things worked out.'

Henry nodded. It was plausible enough. The whole story was plausible.

It was the manner of its telling which troubled him. The confiding tone, awkward pauses and embarrassed sighs. All so seamless that it was like listening to an actor delivering lines that had been carefully rehearsed.

He studied the man who faced him. The earnest eyes, sad expression and clasped hands. Everything to suggest concern. Nothing to suggest guilt.

Except for faint drops of sweat on the forehead.

'So, Dr Norris, if we could . . .'

'I'd like to talk to Susan alone.'

The eyes widened like those of a startled owl. 'Why?'

'Is that a problem?'

A faint tremor of the Adam's apple. 'No.'

Henry remained at his desk. From the waiting room came the sound of whispering, then Susan Ramsey appeared in the doorway. A tall, slender girl with long dark hair and one of the loveliest faces he had ever seen. For a moment, in spite of his concerns, he was happy just to look at her. In a prosperous town like Kendleton prettiness was everywhere. As commonplace as rain. But real beauty was still rare.

'You wanted to talk to me, Dr Norris?'

He gestured to the chair her stepfather had vacated. 'Sit down, please.'

She crossed the room on coltish legs. Her movements were gangly and awkward, typical of a girl adjusting to changes in her body. But they were also erotic. Sensual and inviting. Ripened by knowledge that had come too soon.

He smiled, wanting her to trust him. She smiled back, her huge violet eyes full of suspicion. Like orchids spiked with razors.

'Your stepfather told me what happened. About the boy.'

A nod.

'What was his name?'

'I don't remember.'

'What did he look like?'

'Nice.'

'Just nice?'

'Yes.'

'There was no boy, was there, Susan?'

'I don't know what you mean.'

But she did. He could see it in the tightening of the lip and the finger that fiddled with a lock of hair. Unlike her stepfather, she was not an accomplished liar.

People told him he was lucky to live in Kendleton. Such a beautiful place, they said. But human nature was the same in any location. Secrets existed even in idyllic settings. Dark, ugly ones that could blight the lives of all they touched.

He leant forward, making his voice as soft as possible. 'Susan, what's happening to you isn't right. It's not your fault either. You're

not to blame no matter what anyone else has told you. If your
mother were to . . .'

'You mustn't tell my mother!'

'Susan . . .'

'You mustn't tell her. Not ever!'

She looked so genuinely frightened that he felt ashamed. As if he
were the one to blame for what she was living through.

But he wasn't and he wanted to help.

'Recently my sister discovered she had cancer. At first she didn't
tell me because she didn't want me to worry but eventually she did
and I'm glad because I love her and want to help her. Just as your
mother would want to help you.'

She lowered her head, staring down at shoes that shuffled on the
ground. He waited, hoping.

Then she looked up again. The fear was gone, replaced by a
composure so total that it seemed out of place in a girl so young. Just
as so much else about her did.

'The boy's name was Nigel. I remember now. He looked like James
Dean. He had horrid breath. I remember smelling it when he first
tried to kiss me. I told him to stop but he was stronger than me. The
next day I went looking for him to tell him what he'd done was wrong
but I couldn't find him and no one from the party knew who he was.'

Henry wanted to keep questioning but knew it would do no good.
The steel in her voice told him that.

Two years earlier another girl had sat in his office. A girl of around
Susan's age whose father had had a similar tale to tell. He had
spoken to the girl alone, trying to make her confide in him, but it had
done no good. She had stuck to the story she had been taught,
reciting it in a voice that was little more than a whisper. A sad, sweet
girl whose eyes were a heartbreaking mixture of shame, self-hatred
and total defeat. A girl who had given up on herself before she had
ever really had the chance to live.

He could see some of the same emotions in Susan's eyes. The
shame and self-hatred. But not the defeat. Her spirit, though
crushed, had not yet been destroyed.

'I'm sorry if I've upset you, Susan. I just want you to know that I'm
your friend. Someone you can talk to should you feel the need.'

'I won't.'

'Perhaps you'd ask your stepfather to come back in.'

On reaching the door she stopped, stood still, then turned back.

'I'm sorry about your sister, Dr Norris. I hope she gets well.'

'Thank you, Susan. I appreciate that.'

Half an hour later Susan walked home with her stepfather.

He was holding her hand, just as he often did when they walked together. It was early evening, warm and balmy. As they crossed Market Court a few people stopped to watch their progress. Perhaps they found his behaviour strange. Perhaps they thought it charming. She didn't know. Sometimes she felt as if she didn't know anything except how to be afraid.

It was with her all the time. The terrible, gnawing dread of discovery. Of exposure. Having her wickedness laid bare for all the world to see.

He was talking but she wasn't listening. In her head she was six years old again and returning home from school to a mother who had suddenly become a stranger. A mother who had left her for so long that it had seemed as if she would never return. A dreadful dress rehearsal for her father's death the following year.

'He knows,' she said.

'No he doesn't.'

'He does. What if he tells Mum?'

They entered Queen Anne Square. A neighbour called out a greeting from the other side of the road. Both responded brightly. Acting cheerful and relaxed. Giving nothing away.

'He won't tell anyone, Susie. He can't.'

'But he still knows.'

'Forget about him.'

'He said it wasn't my fault. That I wasn't to blame. That . . .'

'He's lying.' The hand tightened around her own. 'People like him always do. They pretend to be your friend then trip you up with lies. I'm your friend, Susie. The one who's protected you all these years. The one who's kept your secret safe and made sure your mother has never found out because we both know what would happen if she did.'

They crossed the north side of the square. The corner house was number 16, once the home of her godmother, Auntie Emma, who had left her too. Moved to Australia with Uncle George, so far away that she had feared never seeing her again. A fear that had been realized as Auntie Emma had died after unexpected complications following childbirth, leaving Uncle George to return a widower who now lived alone with his daughter, Jennifer.

Their own house was number 19. They stood outside it, facing each other.

'Your mother needs me, Susie. You know how vulnerable she is. How easily she can be frightened. I protect her from that. As long as we stick together she need never be frightened again.' He smiled, his eyes warm and reassuring. 'And we will, won't we?'

'Yes.'

He went to unlock the door. She turned towards number 16. Jennifer sat in the front window; a tiny, pretty girl of four playing with a doll. She waved to Susan, her smile as bright as a tiny sun. Susan waved back, masking her fear with a smile that was just as bright.

September. At Heathcote Academy the autumn term was just beginning.

Heathcote, situated just outside Kendleton, was in fact two schools facing each other across a country lane.

The boys' school, founded in the eighteenth century, boasted of having educated numerous politicians and an officer who had been instrumental in quelling the Indian Mutiny. It had also educated a viscount who had murdered his entire family then fled to the Continent to die of syphilis, but the prospectus kept silent on that. Its buildings were grand, its grounds vast and its sporting facilities the best in the area.

The girls' school, founded one hundred years later, had always been considered a poor relation. Its buildings were humbler, its grounds smaller and its facilities less impressive. Its academic record had been inferior too but in recent years it had begun to outshine its neighbour, leading to a fierce rivalry between the two sets of teaching staff, who groomed gifted pupils for Oxbridge entry like thoroughbreds being trained for the Grand National.

Charlotte Harris sat in a ground-floor classroom preparing a list of her holiday reading. Miss Troughton, the English teacher, required her pupils to produce one at the start of each term to check they were broadening their minds rather than rotting them in front of 'that infernal machine,' television. As Charlotte had spent her holidays doing just that, some fabrication was called for. Her list included *Silas Marner* and *Middlemarch*, the plots of both having been summarized for her by a kindly librarian the previous afternoon.

The classroom was still but not silent. Whispered conversations filled the air like the hum of bees while the profoundly deaf Miss Troughton marked essays obliviously. Kate Christie and Alice Wetherby watched Pauline Grant, whose grandmother was Russian and who, at the start of the previous term, had drawn rapturous praise for having read *Anna Karenina* in its original language. Alice, who considered herself the English star, had taken offence and ordered the rest of the class to pretend that Pauline had body odour and protest if they were made to sit near her. This had gone on for weeks, and Pauline had ended up with skin that was raw from excessive washing. Charlotte, who had lacked the courage to stand up for her, hoped that Pauline would not make the same mistake again.

A prefect strode by the window, a group of new girls trotting after her like chicks following a mother hen. All were dressed in blue blazers and dark skirts with satchels slung over their shoulders. One wore a blazer that looked shabby and second hand. A scholarship girl, probably. Plebs, as Alice and her gang called them. Alice thought girls whose parents couldn't afford the fees should not be admitted. She said so often and Charlotte, who was only there because of the generosity of a wealthy aunt and wore a second-hand uniform herself, would pretend not to realize that the comments were aimed at her.

Miss Troughton walked between the rows of desks collecting lists. 'Rather sparse,' she told Pauline.

'I'm sorry, Miss Troughton.' Though Pauline's tone was humble her voice was loud. One had to shout to be heard by Miss Troughton. The teacher in the next classroom was always complaining about it.

'Too much time watching that infernal machine.'

'Yes, Miss Troughton.'

Miss Troughton moved on. Pauline and Alice exchanged glances; Pauline's submissive, Alice's triumphant. The sight made Charlotte feel both angry and helpless.

Her parents told her she was lucky to attend Heathcote but often she would think wistfully of primary school and the friends she had had there: feisty Lizzie Flynn, timid Arthur Hammond and her best friend in the world, Susan Ramsey. Now Arthur and Lizzie were at different schools and, though Susan was sitting by the window less than ten feet away, it might as well have been a thousand miles.

She wished she understood what had gone wrong. Why Susan had changed towards her. Once they had been inseparable, always laughing and joking, playing games and exchanging confidences. Now they rarely spoke, and when they did Susan's eyes were wary and secretive, making Charlotte feel as if she did not know her at all.

It would have been easier if Susan had made new friends. If there had been others she could have blamed. But there was no one. Susan had no friends. Kept largely to herself.

And Charlotte didn't know why.

But still she had her memories. Susan pushing Alice into a cow pat. Susan teaching her how to whistle with two fingers. Susan facing her in a swing-boat at a local fair, the two of them screaming with excitement as they swung higher and higher. Often, when feeling hurt and confused, she would bring these memories out and study them like precious stones.

Miss Troughton continued to collect lists. Charlotte's was greeted with a nod, Alice's with praise. Finally she reached the row by the window. Marian Knowles was told that Dickens did not contain an 'h'. Rachel Stark that she was too old for Enid Blyton. Susan's list provoked a baffled frown.

'This is blank. Didn't you read anything?'

'No, Miss Troughton.'

'So what have you been doing all summer?'

'Feeding the loony,' whispered Kate, loud enough for all but Miss Troughton to hear. A soft giggle ran round the room.

Susan's back stiffened. 'That's right,' she said quickly. 'But at your age, Kate, you really should be trying to feed yourself.'

More laughter. Louder this time. Miss Troughton moved on to the next desk. Kate flushed while Susan turned and gazed out of the window. She looked both isolated and remote. Someone who did not belong, nor wanted to either.

But watching her, Charlotte felt a warmth in her stomach and sensed that somewhere the friend she missed so badly still existed.

A Friday evening in October. Susan ate dinner with her mother and stepfather.

The table was laid as if for a dinner party. The best chinaware, crystal wineglasses and candles. Uncle Andrew liked to make an occasion of Friday evening. 'The end of the working week,' he would say, 'and the chance to spend time with my family.'

They were eating *boeuf Bourguignon*, a favourite dish of his. As they ate he told them about his day. One of his partners was considering early retirement. Another was acting for a local politician who had been accused of accepting bribes. Old Mrs Pembroke had asked him to visit her house for a six-monthly review of her affairs. 'Which is a nuisance. I'll be glad when her son can bring her into the office.'

'Isn't he in America?' asked Susan's mother.

'He's moving back here. I did tell you. Don't you remember?'

'No.'

Uncle Andrew gave her an indulgent smile. 'You're so forgetful, darling. Mind like a sieve.' Reaching across the table, he patted her hand. Susan didn't remember him telling her mother either but perhaps she had not been there.

'And I doubt,' Uncle Andrew continued, 'that he'll take kindly to the gold-digger companion. Not when it's his inheritance she's after.'

'Are you sure she's a gold-digger? I've met her in town and she seems very nice.'

'You're too trusting. You'd see good in Jack the Ripper. It's lucky I'm here to look after you.'

Susan's mother lowered her eyes. 'I don't know what I'd do without you.'

'Hopefully you'll never have to find out.' Uncle Andrew gave her hand another pat, his own eyes locking briefly with Susan's. She sipped her wine, feeling a dull ache in her abdomen. Her period was approaching. Only a day away.

Uncle Andrew continued to describe his day. Susan's mother listened attentively, saying little herself. As Susan watched them she remembered meals with her father. The stories he had told. The impersonations he had performed that had been funny but not cruel. The way he had reduced her mother to tears of laughter. Looking at the demure, controlled woman who sat beside her, it was hard to believe she had ever laughed like that.

They finished their main course and her mother fetched a trifle. Another of Uncle Andrew's favourites. Everything they ate was a favourite of his. As she served she told him about a radio play being broadcast later that evening. 'It's a spy story. The sort you like. I thought perhaps we could listen to it together.'

He shook his head. 'You look tired, darling. An early night would do you good. Besides, I had to bring work home. I'll do it tonight in the study.' Again his eyes locked with Susan's. She stared down at her plate, her small appetite suddenly gone while the ache in her abdomen increased. The blood would soon be here. He did not like the blood.

But it would not come soon enough.

Her mother was watching her. 'You're not eating, Susie. Isn't it good?'

'It's lovely.' She took a large mouthful. The sweet taste made her want to gag. Instead she swallowed and smiled.

November.

'Are you my mummy?' asked Jennifer.

Susan shook her head. The two of them were in the bathroom of Uncle George's house. Jennifer sat in the bath, watching a toy boat bob through islands of foam bubbles. From downstairs came the sound of Beethoven playing on the gramophone and the click of the typewriter as Uncle George prepared a report on a new architectural project.

'Where is she?'

'In heaven, Jenjen, with my daddy, and they're watching us now and hoping we're not going to let the big monster eat the boat. Look out!' She pushed a rubber duck across the water, making growling sounds while Jennifer squealed and pushed it away.

'Are you clean now?'

'Yes.'

'Then out you get.' She held out the towel and Jennifer leapt into it like a jumping bean. Susan began to dry her hair. It was blonde with reddish tinges. Auntie Emma had had lovely golden hair. She hoped that Jennifer would grow up to have golden hair too.

'Anyway, how can I be your mummy if I'm your big sister?'

Jennifer frowned. 'Mrs Phelps says you can't be my sister 'cos you don't live here.'

'Do you want me to be your sister?'

'Yes.'

'Then I am, and if Mrs Phelps says different I'll smack her bottom.'

The frown faded, replaced by a laugh like the chiming of bells. Susan helped Jennifer brush her teeth then carried her along the corridor to the bedroom decorated in pink and yellow. The bedspread was covered in moons and stars, just as Susan's had been years ago. Smudge the cat lay purring on the pillow. She had given him to Jennifer at her mother's suggestion. Uncle Andrew had never been happy having an animal in the house. It had hurt but Jennifer loved Smudge and at least she could still see him whenever she wanted.

She helped Jennifer put on her pyjamas. 'Do you want Daddy to tuck you in?'

'No. I want you.'

Susan felt proud. Apart from Uncle George she was the only person allowed to do so. As she listened to Jennifer's prayers she had an image of herself at the same age, praying for a brother or sister of her own. Though her parents had never provided her with one her prayer had still been answered in the form of this motherless child, who was as precious to her as any sibling would have been.

Jennifer climbed into bed. Susan smoothed the blankets down. 'Shall I sing to you?'

'Yes.'

So she did. 'Speed Bonnie Boat', keeping her voice soft and soothing. One of Jennifer's arms was wrapped around Smudge. The other lay across the bedspread. Gently Susan covered the tiny hand with her own, feeling a wave of protective love sweep over her. In all the chaos and confusion of her life, Jennifer was the one perfect thing. Someone who made her feel that, in spite of all the badness inside her, there was perhaps just a little good too.

She sang until Jennifer was asleep. After kissing her on the cheek she crept from the room, leaving the door ajar so that the light from the landing and the sounds of music and typing would be a comfort should she wake.

December. Two days after the funeral of his sister, Henry Norris sat with a friend in a Kendleton pub sharing a companionable silence over a pint of beer.

'Thank you,' he said eventually.

'What for?'

'For not feeling the need to say how sorry you are. It's all I've heard recently, as if what happened to Agnes was somehow unjust.'

'People are sad, Henry. She was much loved.'

'I know and it was sad. But it wasn't unjust. She was sixty. She'd had a longer life than many and a happier one too. Far happier.' He sighed. 'A few months ago a man brought his daughter to my surgery. Only a child but she had the clap. He told me some story about a boy at a party but I knew he was the one who'd given it to her. She told me the same story herself while watching me with these suspicious eyes as if I was the one hurting her. Poor kid. Frightened and mistrustful of everyone. What sort of life is she going to have?'

'Perhaps a happy one. You never know. Things can change. They can get better.'

'I hope so. Such a beautiful kid too. Looks like a film star.' Henry laughed softly. 'Not something people would have said about Agnes. But she wouldn't have minded. Like I said, she had a happy life . . .'

March 1960.

Alice Wetherby hated Susan Ramsey.

There was no one else she hated. Not really. When her parents denied her something she would say she hated them. But she didn't mean it. And anyway, it happened so rarely. She was lucky in that.

But she was lucky in most things. Her mother was always telling her so, and when she could control her irritation she would see that it was true. Her family was one of the wealthiest in the town and she lived in one of the loveliest houses. She was clever and could shine in class. She was confident and outgoing and had always attracted a circle of adoring friends. 'But that's Alice,' her father would boast. 'A light around which moths flutter. Edward is the same.' Though Alice took major issue with her brother's claims to luminosity, of hers she had no doubt whatsoever.

And she was pretty. Exceptionally so. From an early age she had understood the power her appearance gave her. And now, as she grew older, its power grew too.

She was standing outside the school gates with Kate Christie. Boys and girls, on foot or on bicycles but all in the same blue-and-black uniform, approached from either direction on the tree-lined lane. A group of boys gathered outside the gates opposite, standing with hands in pockets, affecting indifference or doing stunts on their bicycles, all for the benefit of girls like Alice, who masked their own interest with outward disdain.

She watched Martin Phillips perform wheelies. Sixteen, handsome and a friend of her brother's, he winked at her then rode in circles with his hands in the air. She smiled triumphantly at Sophie Jones, who pretended not to notice. Sophie was smitten with Martin.

Fiona Giles, a horse-faced prefect, strode past. Kate made a neighing sound and Alice choked back laughter. Martin grinned, his lips red and full. She wondered what it would be like to kiss them. She had never properly kissed a boy, let alone done anything more intimate. When her crimson-cheeked mother had explained the mechanics of sex she had been revolted. An older female cousin had told her that the idea would grow more appealing but two years down the line it still left her feeling sick.

But it didn't matter. In fact it was a blessing. 'Your reputation is precious,' warned her mother. 'Never do anything to damage it because you can never win it back once it's lost.'

'Boys are all the same,' her cousin explained. 'They want what they can't have. Keep them believing that one day they'll get it and they're yours to command. Flatter and flirt. Hold hands. The occasional peck on the cheek. But that's all. It works for me. It'll work for you.'

And it did. Increasingly boys vied for her attention and competed for her smiles. She would giggle about them with her friends, revelling in her sense of power while a tiny part of her longed for one boy who would be her slave without longing for physical intimacy too.

Girls walked through the gates talking about the previous night's television, their latest pop star crushes or unfinished homework. Mousy Charlotte Harris scurried past. 'Boo!' yelled Alice, making Charlotte jump and Kate laugh while Martin rose up on his bicycle seat like a peacock performing just for her.

Then he stopped. His attention suddenly stolen by another.

Susan Ramsey approached. She walked quickly, her motions jerky yet strangely graceful. The drab uniform that turned other girls into black beetles had been casually thrown on yet looked as if it had been designed especially for her. Her hair was untidy, her face strained and tired, but in the cold morning light she still shone.

Martin began to circle her, trying to attract her gaze while other boys straightened their backs as if standing to attention. Susan ignored them all, staring straight ahead with a preoccupied expression on her face.

'Ever tried using a comb?' asked Kate sarcastically.

'Ever tried thinking before you speak?' retorted Susan without bothering to stop.

The bell for morning assembly began to ring. As Alice started up the school path she looked back. Martin was still on his bicycle. She waved but he stared straight through her as if she were invisible. Her own light extinguished by one that glowed infinitely brighter.

Susan walked ahead, her stride still quick. Alice followed more slowly, hatred swelling inside her like a tumour. There was nothing she could do about it. Not yet. But she would bide her time. Wait for an opportunity.

And when it came she would strike.

May.

It was nearly midnight. Susan lay in bed, watching the glow of the landing light creep under the door-frame.

Her stepfather was in his study. She could hear the creaking of his chair. Having spent so many nights listening for it, she could tell what each sound meant. The groan of the springs as he leant back and stretched. The rustling of fabric as he made himself more comfortable. Finally the sigh of the cushion as he rose to his feet.

Once it would have made her heart beat faster. But not now.

It was three months since his last visit. A stormy night in February just after her fourteenth birthday. He had sat on the bed while she had lain naked, feeling his clammy hand caressing her throat then moving over her breasts. A fat, five-legged spider crawling across her belly and on towards the soft down that grew between her legs while she had listened to the wind and rain and imagined that she was walking by the river, playing with Jennifer, anywhere but in that room.

Eventually he had sighed, his eyes dull and cold. In the preceding months she had felt a diminishment in the heat he brought. Now the last drop of warmth was gone.

He rose to his feet. 'Cover yourself. Don't lie there like that. It's wrong.'

'You told me to.'

'Only because you make me. It's your fault. Not mine.'

She had done as instructed while he had stood watching, his expression suddenly reproachful. 'You're so clever. A masterpiece of deceit. You fool everyone but me. They think you're good but you're not. They think you're beautiful but you're not that either. You were once. Now you're as plain and ordinary as everyone else.'

'You're still my friend, aren't you? You won't tell anyone?'

A sigh. The look of reproach remained. 'No, I won't tell.'

He had left the room, leaving her knowing instinctively that their strange and frightening ritual had been played out for the last time.

It should have been better after that. Her sleep, disrupted for so many years, should have been easier.

But it wasn't. She was so conditioned to listening for him that it was impossible to stop. She would lie awake for hours, feeling as if the room were spinning, clinging on to her bed for fear she would drift off into the sky. And when sleep finally came it brought dreams of a world where everyone ran while she stood still, screamed when she longed for peace, laughed when she wanted to cry. A world that made no sense and in which her place was at best uncertain.

Why had he stopped coming? She had tried to ask him but he had become angry and told her that she was never to mention it again, leaving her to struggle with questions that buzzed in her brain like angry wasps.

Did he no longer see the wickedness in her? Was she no longer wicked? Was she beyond redemption?

Perhaps you were never wicked at all.

The voice came from somewhere outside herself. Like the whisperings of a ghost, hanging in the air as fragile as a snowflake that would dissolve at the slightest touch.

The landing light went out. She heard his footsteps on the stairs, making for his own bedroom, leaving her alone to the spinning and the dreams.

Her father's picture stood on her bedside table. She imagined him standing beside her. But when she reached out to touch him he dissolved like a snowflake too.

A wet Saturday in July, one week after the start of the summer holidays. She sat by the window in the old reading room of Kendleton Library.

The library was in Market Court. The reading room, situated on a floor above the main library, was rarely used. It contained a few shelves full of redundant periodicals, a table and three chairs. Nothing else. The window that looked down on to the steps of the Town Hall was largely concealed by the eaves of the roof, enabling Susan to watch without being seen. A local businessman was presenting the mayor with a cheque to help repair the church roof. A crowd had gathered, sheltering beneath umbrellas as local journalists took photographs and the mayor, a pompous friend of Susan's stepfather, beamed like a Cheshire cat.

'Hello.'

A boy stood in the doorway, a pile of books under his arm. About seventeen with light brown hair. She recognized him from school.

'I was going to work here,' he said nervously. 'It's quieter than downstairs.'

She turned back towards the window, looking for a let-up in the rain. When it stopped she would take Jennifer to play on the swings.

The mayor was making a speech; as long-winded and boring as his dinner conversation.

The boy spread books across the desk, reading from each in turn while making notes on a pad.

'What are you doing?' she asked eventually.

'Research for an essay competition. Five thousand words on the causes of the English Civil War.'

'What were they?'

'I don't know. Hence the research.' He smiled; a gesture that transformed a pleasant face into an attractive one. 'You're Susan Ramsey, aren't you?'

'How do you know my name?'

'Everyone knows about you.'

She felt alarmed. 'What do you mean?'

'The most beautiful girl in school.'

'Oh.' A pause. 'Thanks.'

'You're in Alice Wetherby's class, aren't you? Her brother's in mine.'

'Do you like him?'

'He's all right. What about Alice?'

She grimaced.

'Really?'

'I can't stand her.'

'Actually I can't stand him either.'

They exchanged smiles. Conspiratorial. Confiding. Comfortable.

'Do you know who you look like?' he asked.

'Elizabeth Taylor. That's what people say.'

'They're right. Do you know who people say I look like?'

'Who?'

'My gran.'

She laughed. It was the sort of joke her father would have made. He looked a bit like her father.

'Why are you here on a Saturday?' he asked.

'Because it's raining.' And because it was better than being at home. But she didn't want to say that. 'What about you?'

'Because it's quiet. My father's at home and he can be noisy.'

'What about your mother?'

'She died last year.'

She felt embarrassed. 'I'm sorry . . . um . . .'

'Paul. Paul Benson.'

'I'm sorry, Paul. My dad died when I was seven. It's the worst thing that can happen, losing someone you love.'

'I think about her all the time. Silly, isn't it?'

'Why?'

'Because it won't bring her back.'

Silence. He resumed his work. Outside, the rain was slowing while the mayor still spoke to an audience of glazed faces. Mrs Pembroke's son, the disfigured man whom her stepfather had nicknamed Scarface, stood in the crowd whispering to the companion who was supposed to be a gold-digger. She had a nice smile, just like Paul.

Suddenly Susan thought of a way to make him smile again.

'Come here,' she said.

He did. She opened the window, shouted 'Boring!' then shut it again. The mayor, startled, lost his place while his audience, sensing escape, began to clap.

'I'd better go,' she said when they had finished laughing. 'Stop distracting you.'

''Bye, then.'

''Bye.'

As she reached the door he called her name. She turned back.

'I'll be here on Monday in case you want to distract me some more.'

'Maybe. If the weather's bad.'

Monday was a lovely day. The first since the holidays began.

But she did go back.

A beautiful August evening. Susan entered her house.

Her mother and stepfather sat together in the living room; her mother mending a torn blouse while Uncle Andrew nursed a glass of whisky. Classical music played on the wireless.

'Where have you been?' he demanded.

'Just for a walk.'

'You said you'd only be half an hour. You've been nearly two.'

'Sorry. I didn't realize.' She smiled to mask the lie.

'What were you doing all that time?'

'Just looking about. The countryside is lovely at the moment.'

And it was. Paul had said the same as they had walked together.

Uncle Andrew's face darkened. 'You should be in your room studying. I'm not paying a fortune in school fees for you to come bottom in everything.'

'I didn't.'

'As good as.'

For years her school performance had been poor. Too little sleep playing havoc with her ability to concentrate. In the past he had taken a relaxed approach to her academic failings but in recent months his attitude had hardened.

'Susan does her best,' her mother interjected.

'Well, you would say that, wouldn't you?'

'I just meant . . .'

'It's your job to keep her in line. That's not asking too much, is it, even of you? After all, it's not as if you have anything else to do except sit around all day.'

Susan felt uncomfortable. Uncle Andrew's manner towards her mother had always been patronizing but recently the apparent benevolence had been replaced by contempt. She didn't like it. But there was nothing she could do.

'It's not Mum's fault,' she said quickly. 'I'm the one you should be angry with.'

'I am angry with you.' He downed his drink then poured another. His alcohol consumption was increasing. Yet another change. Paul's father had also been drinking more recently, though he had always had a taste for the bottle. Paul had told her that.

He had told her a lot of things. That sometimes he still cried for his mother and that his father despised him for it. That his father was always taunting him for liking music and literature while not being much of an athlete. For not being enough of a man. His classmates taunted him too. Idiots like Edward Wetherby and Martin Phillips, who laughed and blew kisses at him while he would pretend not to notice, and she would long to hit them and knock the smirks off their faces.

She had told him things too. Her memories of her father. The nightmare of her mother's breakdown. There were other nightmares but she kept those secret.

'Go to bed,' Uncle Andrew told her.

She kissed him goodnight. His cheek was hot and damp. She hated the feel of his skin.

As she climbed the stairs he continued to lecture her mother, his tone as contemptuous as before.

Early September. Three days before the start of the new term. She walked along the riverbank with Paul.

It was a beautiful late summer afternoon. Ducks glided alongside them, calling for food. They walked past Kendleton Lock towards the bridge that led to the village of Bexley. Mrs Pembroke's son approached, listening to the gold-digger companion describe the shape of clouds. He gave them a smile then turned his damaged face away.

Past the bridge the path became overgrown. Few people came to this stretch of river, but she had always loved it. Her father had brought her here, carrying her on his shoulders, pointing out birds and plants, teaching her to enjoy the nature around them as much as he did.

Eventually she led Paul away from the water into trees so tightly packed together that their branches blocked out the sky. Then they parted, opening into a clearing with a large pond at its centre. Dragonflies danced over its surface, avoiding the eager tongues of frogs perched waiting on water lilies.

'I used to come here with Dad,' she said. 'We used to eat picnics and he'd tell me stories. He called this place the nymphs' grotto. He had names for every place we used to go. Secret names we didn't tell anyone else. Not even Mum.'

'But now you've told me.'

'Yes, now I've told you.'

A single tree stood by the pond, its branches casting shadows over the water. They sat beneath it. A clump of roots stuck out of the shallows of the pool. She pointed to them. 'Dad used to call them the troll's fingers.'

'And he called you Little Susie Sparkle.'

She felt a sudden emptiness inside. 'That was a long time ago.'

'My mother used to call me her little miracle. She thought she could never have children, you see, but then I came along. And now she's gone and all I have is Dad. Do you know what he calls me?'

'What?'

'My little pansy. That's what he thinks of me.'

'He doesn't mean it.'

'That's what they all think. Edward Wetherby and his friends. I hate it.'

'They're just idiots.'

He lowered his head, staring down at the ground. Overhead the air was full of birds.

'But I can't be a pansy because if I am then why do I want to kiss you so much?'

He looked up, staring at her with eyes that were like her father's except for the sadness at their centre. She wanted to make the sadness go away and never return.

'I want to kiss you too,' she said.

So they did. Her tongue parted his lips, caressing the inside of his mouth. He put his arms around her, pulling her close.

The girls in her class talked constantly of sex, giggling in corners about this wicked, wonderful act that none of them dared experience but which fascinated them all. And as they talked they would think of Emma Hill; an older girl who had become pregnant and been forced to leave school. A grim warning of the dangers in straying from the path of virtue, however sweet the temptations might be.

She kept apart from these discussions, fearful the girls would discover the nature of her own experience, while wondering whether this act she had been told she wanted but which had always left her feeling dirty and ashamed could ever be as glorious as they seemed to believe.

Paul stroked her cheek. He looked exposed. Vulnerable. Filling her with the same feelings of protectiveness she experienced with Jennifer. But his arms were strong and they made her feel safe.

Conflicting emotions that should have been confusing but instead left her with a glow she had never known before. It was stronger than desire. Better. Purer.

Perfect.

'I love you,' she told him.

They kissed again. She lay back in the grass, pulling him towards her, knowing what was coming and feeling no shame. Just a desire to be close to him, and make him happy.

He was clumsy. Nervous and hesitant. It was she who took the lead. Coaxing and soothing. Guiding him inside her. He thrust a few times then withdrew, juddering to a climax and pressing his face into the grass.

She whispered his name. He didn't answer. She tried again.

He turned towards her. 'I'm sorry.'

'Why?'

'I wasn't very good.'

She stroked his hair. 'Yes you were.'

'It's because it's my first time.'

'It was lovely, Paul. Really it was.'

'It's always difficult the first time.'

'That's right.' She smiled reassuringly. 'I've never liked it before but . . .'

His eyes widened. Suddenly she realized what she'd said.

'Before?'

Her heart began to race.

'Before?'

'Just once. With a boy at a party last summer. He got me drunk. It wasn't my fault.'

'You said you've never liked it. Plural.'

'No I didn't.'

'Yes you did.' The warmth left his face, replaced by hurt and anger. 'How many people have you brought here?'

'None!'

'So why me?'

'Because you're special.'

'Is that what you told the others?'

'There were no others!'

'How do I know that?'

'Because it's true.' She was close to tears, wanting him to hold her and say that he believed her. Instead he hacked at the dry earth with a stick.

'There weren't any others. That's the truth.'

He stood up. 'We should go. Your stepfather will be angry if you're out too long.'

They walked along the river bank in silence. Her heart was still pounding. The ducks accompanied them as on the outward journey. She wished she could turn the clock back to then. She wished that this had never happened.

They reached her house and faced each other on the pavement. 'There weren't any others, Paul. Just the boy at the party.'

He nodded.

'You're still my friend, aren't you?'

A smile. Faint but still a smile.

'You won't tell anyone, will you?'

'No.'

She watched him walk away. On reaching the corner he would normally turn and wave. This time he just kept going.

Martin Phillips was bored. He stood with Brian Harper by the Norman cross in Market Court waiting for Edward Wetherby, who was stealing cigars from his father's desk.

Paul Benson walked past. Feeling the need for distraction, he shouted out, 'Been to see your boyfriend?'

Paul ignored him.

'Benson, I'm talking to you!'

Slowly Paul approached. 'Why the long face?' demanded Brian.

'Probably still heartbroken that Eddie Fisher left Debbie Reynolds for Liz Taylor and not him,' joked Martin. 'Never mind, Benson. Montgomery Clift is still single.'

Paul shook his head. 'You don't know anything.'

'We know you're queer,' Brian told him.

'Why do you keep picking on me?'

'Because it's fun.'

Paul turned to go. 'D'you know something?' Martin called after him. 'We're starting a campaign to ban queers from Kendleton. Better pack your bags.'

Paul stopped. Stood still. Then walked back towards them.

'You seem very knowledgeable about queers. Sure you're not one yourself?'

'Fuck off!'

'How many girls have you had sex with, then?'

Martin felt uncomfortable. This was a delicate subject. None of his friends would admit to being a virgin though he was sure they all were. Just as he would not admit it himself.

'More than a queer like you.'

'I've had sex this afternoon.'

'What was his name?' jeered Brian.

'Susan Ramsey.'

'I don't believe you,' Martin told him.

'Don't, then. It doesn't matter. I know it's true.'

Martin remembered Edward boasting about a girl he had slept with on holiday in France. 'She loved it. We did it four times.' His tone had been aggressive, as if fearful that his lie would not be accepted. Not that there was any need to worry. His audience were all too anxious to have their own fantasies believed to dream of questioning those of another.

But there was no aggressiveness in Paul's eyes. Just a quiet certainty.

'Seriously?'

Paul nodded.

'You screwed the ice queen? God, Benson, I'm impressed.'

For the first time Paul smiled.

'What was it like? Come on, you can tell us. We're your friends.'

The smile became conspiratorial. 'I just hope I didn't catch something.'

'What do you mean?'

'She's not the ice queen you think she is . . .'

Alice Wetherby lay on her bed listening to records.

Her brother Edward entered her room. She threw a pillow at him. 'Try knocking!'

'Got any chocolate?'

'You've been smoking. I can smell it. Mum will go mad when she finds out.'

He threw the pillow back while Cliff Richard sang about pleasing his living doll. 'How can you listen to this rubbish?'

'Because I like it and so do you. You only pretend to like jazz because you think it makes you look mature when really it makes you look queer.'

'It doesn't.'

'It does. Soon you'll be making dresses with Paul Benson.'

'Paul's not queer, either. He's done it with Susan Ramsey and he's not the only one either.'

Alice felt disgusted. The idea of doing it with one person was bad enough. But to do it with several.

Then, suddenly, a light bulb went off in her brain.

Five minutes later she was on the phone to Kate Christie. 'You'll never guess what . . .'

The first day of the new term. Susan made her way along the lane towards school.

She walked quickly. The way she always did when she was anxious. A cyclist rushed by, ringing his bell. Alan Forrester from the year above. Charlotte liked Alan.

But not as much as she liked Paul.

They hadn't seen each other since the afternoon at the river. She had phoned but no one had answered. Perhaps he had just been busy. Perhaps.

She noticed a group of girls staring at her. One began to giggle. Some boys were staring too. Whispering to each other and smirking.

What was going on?

She approached the gates where the usual crowd was gathered. Alice Wetherby and her gang. Idiots like Martin Phillips posing on their bicycles.

And all were staring.

An anxious-looking Charlotte hurried over. 'It's not true, is it? What people are saying about you and Paul Benson.' An awkward pause. 'And all the others.'

She felt a lurch in her stomach.

'Everyone's talking about it. Alice is having a field day. I told her it was rubbish. I was right, wasn't I?'

She swallowed. Her throat felt dry.

Then, behind her, she heard a familiar voice.

Paul was approaching, Brian Harper by his side. The two of them talking together like old friends.

She stood, waiting. Paul didn't even stop. Just walked by as if she were invisible.

Charlotte took her arm. 'Come on. Let's go to assembly.'

Pushing her away, she followed Paul. As he reached his gates she called his name. He ignored her. She tried again.

This time he turned. His eyes were cold and contemptuous. 'Get lost, you tart,' he said before continuing on his way.

Alice and her gang were laughing. She wrapped her arms around herself, realizing that she was trembling, feeling as exposed as if she were naked. Her veneer of decency stripped away to reveal the wickedness that lay beneath.

Martin Phillips grabbed her waist. 'Forget him. I'm not doing anything tonight. Who knows what fun we could have.'

For a moment her legs threatened to collapse, sending her tumbling to the ground. Around her the laughter was growing while Martin's hands crawled all over her.

And then, from somewhere deep inside her memory, came a voice. One that had been silent for years. Deep, warm and resonant. As comforting as a hug.

Her father.

You're strong, Susie. Never forget that. You're strong and you can survive this.

Her spine straightened as if pulled by an invisible hand. She rammed her elbow into Martin's chest, making him cry out in pain. 'Go to hell,' she told him, before striding towards her own school gates, holding her head high, ignoring the whispers that chased after her like hungry insects.

Late afternoon. She walked home alone. Charlotte had wanted to walk with her but she had refused, unable to face the sympathy and the questioning eyes.

But Charlotte had been loyal; refusing to believe the stories that were spreading round school like wildfire, each more elaborate than the last. She would not forget that.

Market Court was crowded. Women with shopping baskets and men in work suits. She made her way towards the bakery, head still high, feeling as if all eyes were upon her. She was going to buy a chocolate shortbread cat. Jennifer's favourite. She was babysitting for Jennifer that night.

She passed Cobhams Milk Bar; a popular venue with the town's teenagers. Martin Phillips sat at a table near the window with Edward and Alice Wetherby. Kate Christie was there too, and Brian Harper.

And Paul.

They were all laughing about something. Her, probably. Paul's face was happy and relaxed. No longer the outsider, he had been welcomed into the fold. His admission a simple matter of her total humiliation.

She stood, watching him. The first boy she had ever cared about. For a moment his betrayal hurt so much that she wanted to curl up and die.

But that would have been the weak thing to do.

So she entered the shop.

When he saw her the smile faded from his face. As well it might.

'You're right,' she said, raising her voice so everyone could hear. 'There've been dozens. So many I've lost count and none of them were as pathetic as you. You were so bad it was all I could do to stop laughing.'

A chocolate milk shake stood on the table. She threw it over him. Some boys from another school began to cheer.

'So brag all you want if it makes you feel like a man, but just remember that the only things you made me feel were pity and boredom.'

The furious-looking proprietor marched over. 'I'm going,' she told him, staring contemptuously at Paul, who was wiping his face. 'There's nothing here worth staying for.'

The schoolboys continued to cheer. She blew them a kiss, turned and left.

*

Early evening. Uncle George described the contents of his kitchen. 'There's milk in the fridge and cocoa in the cupboard. A hot drink often helps her sleep.' She nodded while a pyjama-clad Jennifer bounced on the sofa beside her.

'You've got a contact number. Call if there're any problems.'

He walked into the hall. Jennifer followed him, wanting to help him put on his coat. He crouched down, smiling as she guided his arms into the sleeves before lifting her up and hugging her. 'Who's my special girl, then?'

'Me!'

He tickled her ribs, making her giggle. As Susan watched them she remembered the smell of her father. A mixture of cologne, pipe tobacco and musty old clothes. Suddenly her nostrils were full of it, transporting her back to a time when she had felt as safe and secure as Jennifer did now.

The tears she had been fighting all day finally came. She wept silently, struggling to hold on to a memory that threatened to slip through the fingers of her mind and be lost for ever.

The front door opened and closed. Then footsteps. Jennifer stood, watching her. She tried to smile but the tears kept coming, like a burst dam that could not be stopped through willpower alone. Jennifer climbed on to her knee, hugging her while she sobbed into the blonde hair with its reddish tinges, despising herself for being weak but unable to stop.

'I'm sorry, Jenjen,' she whispered when her emotions were under some semblance of control. 'I didn't mean to scare you.'

'Why are you sad?'

'I'm just being silly.' She wiped her eyes. 'I must look horrid.'

'You look beautiful. I wish I was beautiful like you.'

'You are. You look like your mum and she was beautiful too.'

A worried look came into Jennifer's face. She put her thumb in her mouth.

'What is it, darling?'

No answer.

'Jenjen?'

'My mum's in heaven.'

'That's right.'

'I don't want Dad to go there too.'

She was taken aback. It had never occurred to her that someone so young could dread the loss of a loved one. Gently she stroked Jennifer's hair. 'Does that thought scare you?'

A nod. Jennifer's lip started to tremble.

'Your dad won't go to heaven for ages, Jenjen.'

'Sam Hastings said he would.'

'Sam Hastings is a stupid baby who still wets his bed. What does he know? Your dad won't go to heaven until you're a big, grown-up girl with babies of your own who won't wet their beds because they'll be much cleverer than Sam.'

The lip continued to tremble. The sight distressed her. 'Don't you believe me?'

'Do you promise?'

She opened her mouth to do so.

But dad died when I was seven. Only two years older than she is. What if something happens to Uncle George like it happened to him? I can't promise that it won't.

'Promise?'

She took Jennifer's hand and pressed it to her cheek. 'Do you love me, Jenjen?'

'Yes.'

'Then I'm going to make you a very special promise. One that I will never, ever break. I promise that I will always take care of you. I will always protect you and I will never let anything bad happen to you because you're my little sister and because I love you too. I love you more than anyone else in the world.'

The last sentence was an afterthought, intended simply to comfort and reassure. But as soon as the words were spoken she realized with a shock that it was true.

Slowly Jennifer's face broke into a smile. The sight made Susan happier than being with Paul had ever done. Far happier.

'I'm sorry I frightened you, Jenjen. I'll never do it again. That's a promise too.'

Jennifer curled up on her lap. Susan cradled her like a baby, singing softly, watching her drift into sleep.

*

The next morning she sat in class staring down at a blank sheet of paper. Battles could be fought and won, empires rise and fall, but the ritual of the holiday reading list was as constant as the stars.

People were whispering. She felt eyes boring into her just as they had in assembly. It seemed the whole school knew about her. Alice, the most enthusiastic spreader of gossip, had done her work well.

She looked across at Charlotte on the other side of the room. Charlotte who refused to believe anything bad about her. Charlotte from whom she had once had no secrets.

But that had been a long time ago.

Charlotte nodded encouragingly, as if to say 'Don't let them get to you'. She nodded back as if to say 'I won't'.

Miss Troughton began to collect the lists. Hers was greeted with a frown. 'This isn't very impressive.'

'Don't be too hard on her,' hissed Alice. 'She's had her hands full recently.' Muffled giggles echoed round the room.

'Your brother being the exception. Thank God for microscopes and tweezers.'

More giggles. Shocked this time. Well, let them be shocked. Let them think ill of her. Let them think whatever they wanted.

What if someone tells Mum?

An icy hand squeezed her heart. She kept her breathing steady, refusing to give in to fear. If her mother found out anything she would simply deny it. Pass it off as spiteful gossip. Charlotte would back her up and no one could prove anything. If Paul challenged her she would call him a liar and a lot worse besides. She would fight back and she would beat him. She would beat them all if she had to.

Because she was strong. That was her weapon. She would be strong for her mother, just as she would be strong for Jennifer. And she would survive this.

She stared ahead, her back straight, ignoring the whispers and the eyes.

And the aching desire that just once someone would be strong for her.

That evening she told Uncle Andrew. She didn't want to but thought it best he knew.

She told him in his study while her mother cooked supper down-stairs. 'Are you absolutely sure you didn't mention me?' he asked when she had finished.

'Yes.'

He nodded, his face a patchwork of different emotions; concern, relief and something else she couldn't identify.

'I'm sorry,' she said. 'It wasn't supposed . . .'

'Did you enjoy it?'

She was too embarrassed to answer.

He leant forward. 'I need to know.'

'Yes.'

'Whose idea was it? Yours or his? Tell me, Susie. We don't have secrets from each other.'

'Mine.'

'Only fourteen but you took the lead.'

She swallowed. 'Don't.'

'But I must. It's important.'

'Why?'

'Because it means I was right. You're just as wicked as I always said.'

At last she identified the final emotion in his face.

Pleasure.

It made her feel dirty. She left the room.

A windy Saturday in November. She sat in Randall's Tea Room watching Jennifer finish a strawberry milk shake.

'Can I have another?'

'No. I told your dad I wouldn't feed you so remember to keep quiet.'

A waitress cleared their table while two others gossiped by the counter. There were only three other customers. Most people in town favoured Hobson's Tea Shop but Susan had never been able to enter it since the April evening seven and a half years ago when she had watched her father die.

The window looked out on to Market Court. Mrs Wetherby and Alice entered the dress shop that had once been Ramsey's Studio. Someone had told her that the shop was not doing well and she had felt a guilty pleasure.

While waiting for the bill she listened to Jennifer read from a story book, assisting with unfamiliar words. Not that there were many. At almost six Jennifer was an accomplished reader.

'Well done, Jenjen,' she said when the story was finished.

Jennifer looked proud. 'Miss Hicks says I'm the best reader in my class.'

'I bet you are. What shall we do now?'

'Go on the swings.'

Susan had visions of midair vomiting. 'Let's go to the river and feed the ducks. I've got bread in my pocket.'

Jennifer beamed.

'Do you need the toilet first?'

'Yes. You come too.'

The toilet was at the back of the shop. As Jennifer used the cubicle Susan studied her reflection in the mirror. There were bags under her eyes. Her problems with sleep continued. The wind had messed her hair. She smoothed it down. 'Are you all right, Jenjen?'

Silence.

'Jenjen?'

A flushing sound. Jennifer appeared. 'What's a tart?'

'What?'

'It says you're a tart.' Jennifer pointed to the cubicle. Again she looked proud. 'I read it all by myself.'

And there it was on the wall, in dark letters an inch high.

Susan Ramsey is the biggest tart in town.

It wasn't the piece of graffiti which upset her. She was already seeing worse at school.

It was the fact that Jennifer had seen it.

And that her mother might.

Jennifer came to stand beside her. 'What's a tart?'

'Nothing.'

'But it says . . .'

'It's nothing.'

'But . . .'

Deny, deny. Be strong, be strong.

'It's a joke. Someone thinks I look like a jam tart. Isn't that silly? Let's go to the swings after all. Would you like that?'

'Yes!' Jennifer grabbed her hand and tried to pull her towards the door. Instead she knelt down and put her hands on Jennifer's shoulders.

'Jenjen, promise me you won't tell anyone about this.'

'Why?'

'Because . . .' She struggled to think. 'Because Mum is proud that people think I'm beautiful. She'd be cross if she knew someone thought I looked like a jam tart. Just like your dad would be cross if he knew you'd had a milk shake.'

Jennifer nodded.

Susan put her fingers to her lips. 'So shush.'

Jennifer copied the gesture then tried to pull her forward. Again she held firm, soaking her handkerchief and trying to rub the words from the wall, managing to blur the letters so that her name could no longer be read. Only then did she allow herself to be led.

Christmas Day. She ate lunch with her mother and Uncle Andrew.

The atmosphere was strained. Uncle Andrew, who had been drinking continually since their return from church, prodded his turkey with a fork and pronounced it undercooked.

'Are you sure, dear?' asked her mother anxiously.

'Of course I'm sure. The potatoes are undercooked too. Everything is.'

Outside it was snowing. The square was dusted in white like a great cake. The Hastings family walked past the window, wrapped up against the cold. The previous evening they and other neighbours had been guests at a party Uncle Andrew had organized. He had been the perfect host, gracious and charming, giving no clue as to what he was really like.

It wasn't just the drinking. His temper was now so bad that any failing by her mother or herself provoked an explosion of rage. And if the mood took him and the failing did not exist he would simply invent one, just as he was doing now.

He began to drum on the table with his fingers. She felt herself tense. Outside the Hastings boys threw snowballs.

'How can you serve me this muck? Look around you. Look at where we live. Look at what we have. Do you know how hard I have to work to pay for it all? I give you everything and you can't even give me a decent meal.'

He poured himself more wine. Susan longed to tell him there was nothing wrong with the food but that would only have made things worse.

A snowball thudded against the window. Mr Hastings called out an apology and ordered his sons indoors. Uncle Andrew smiled and waved. All joviality and charm. Careful to give nothing away.

'Don't you remember what things were like after John died? The mess he left you in? Where would you be now if I hadn't come along? Not living in a lovely house like this. There aren't many men who'd marry a woman with your history. People told me I was a fool but I wouldn't listen, though God knows there have been enough times since when I wish I had.'

Her mother looked close to tears. Under the table Susan clenched her fists, nails digging into palms so hard they threatened to draw blood.

Don't say anything. He'll stop soon. He always stops.

Don't make it worse don't make it worse don't make it worse.

'But you're not grateful, are you? Oh, no. You probably wish John was sitting here now instead of me. A failure who couldn't even provide for his family. A pathetic nobody who couldn't . . .'

'Don't talk about my father like that!'

Her mother looked alarmed. 'Susan . . .'

'Why shouldn't I?' demanded Uncle Andrew. 'It's the truth.'

'No it's not. And even if it was he'd still be twice the man you are.'

His eyes widened. He looked as if he'd been struck.

Then he picked up his plate and hurled it against the wall. Her mother shrieked.

'You don't want to make me angry, Susan. Otherwise I might forget myself and say things better left unsaid. You don't want that to happen, do you?'

They stared at each other.

'Do you?'

Her heart was racing. She wanted to scream. Instead she shook her head.

Her mother was crying. He put his arm around her, making soothing noises as if comforting a frightened child. 'Hush, now,' he whispered, his voice suddenly tender. 'I only say these things for your own good. You know I love you. Who loves you more than me?' As he spoke he smiled at Susan. This man who claimed to be her friend. Who had always kept her secret hidden.

Just as she had hidden his.

She made herself smile back while realizing for the first time how much she hated him.

March 1961.

Half past ten in the evening. She sat with her mother in the living room, waiting for Uncle Andrew to return.

He had spent the afternoon at Riverdale, dealing with Mrs Pembroke's will. The gold-digger companion had been left nothing; a fact he had gloated over as if it were a personal triumph. Increasingly he seemed to relish the misfortune of others.

He should have been home for supper. But more and more frequently he was spending his evenings away from home, drinking in the Crown pub over the river in Bexley. It was the oldest pub in the area, dating back to the sixteenth century. Her father had taken her there sometimes on summer afternoons. She remembered sitting with him at an outside table, drinking lemonade from a bottle with a straw. But Uncle Andrew only ever went there alone.

She watched the clock on the mantelpiece, wondering what time he would eventually return. And what mood he would be in when he did.

'You should go to bed,' said her mother. 'It's me he'll expect to wait up.'

'Then I'll wait with you.'

'Susie . . .'

'You know what he's like when he's been drinking. Better we're both here.'

'He'll be angry if you're still up. He'll say it proves what a bad mother I am.'

'You're not bad. You're wonderful.'

Her mother shook her head.

'You are. If he says different he's wrong.' A pause. 'Though you'd better not tell him that.'

'You can stay up till eleven. No later.'

Eleven o'clock came and there was still no sign of him. Reluctantly she went upstairs, leaving her mother to wait alone.

Next morning the two of them ate breakfast in the kitchen. Uncle Andrew was still in bed. 'He's not due at work until noon,' her mother explained.

'What time did he come in?'

'Late.'

'And what was his mood like?'

'Not good, but I'm sure it will be better today.'

Susan didn't believe it but tried to look convinced. Though she had no appetite, she reached for another slice of toast. Her mother worried if she didn't eat.

The window was open. A moth flew into the room and hovered above the table. As her mother brushed it away the sleeve of her dressing gown fell back to reveal an angry bruise on her upper arm.

'What's that?'

'Nothing.' Hastily her mother covered it again.

She moved around the table, pushing up the sleeve. The bruise had rounded indents at the top. Like the knuckles of a fist.

'He hit you, didn't he?'

'I bumped into the door on my way to bed.'

'I don't believe you.'

'You should go. You'll be late.'

'But mum . . .'

'That's enough, Susie.'

They faced each other. She was taller than her mother now. Not that it changed anything. Ever since the breakdown she had always felt taller.

'You don't have to protect me, Mum. It's my job to protect you.'

'No it's not.'

'Yes it is. I promised Dad.'

'You were only a little girl then.'

'That doesn't matter. I meant it then and I mean it now.'

'You still miss him, don't you?'

'Every day.'

'So do I. He was a good man. The best I ever knew.' Her mother's lip began to tremble. 'And if I had one wish it would be . . .'

There were footsteps overhead. Heavy and ominous, making them both jump. Hastily her mother wiped her eyes. 'But your stepfather's a good man too, Susie. We're lucky to have him. Now go to school.'

'But Mum . . .'

'Please, Susie, just go.'

Feeling a hateful mixture of anger and helplessness, she made for the door.

Morning assembly was over. She walked along a corridor full of the smell of polish and the clicking of sensible heels on tiles. Dozens of voices bounced off the walls and ceiling, all shrill with excitement. The Easter holiday was only days away.

There was laughter behind her, soft and conspiratorial, following her like a bad smell. She tried to ignore it but the rage and frustration were still inside her. A Molotov cocktail of emotion that needed only a spark to ignite.

She swung round, confronting two girls from the year below. 'What's so funny?'

Both looked alarmed. 'Nothing,' said one quickly.

'You think it's funny to laugh at people behind their backs? To write things about them on toilet walls?'

'We weren't . . .'

'If you've got something to say then have the guts to say it to my face!' She took a step towards them, her fists clenched. They backed away, clearly frightened.

'What's going on?' A prefect hurried over. 'Susan? Alison?'

'She thinks we were laughing at her,' the girl called Alison babbled. 'But we weren't, honestly. We went to see *Spartacus* last night at the pictures and Claire was saying she thought Kirk Douglas looked sexy in his gladiator shorts.'

The girl called Claire nodded in agreement. Both looked weak and defenceless and Susan realized they were telling the truth.

She felt ashamed. As if she were as big a bully as Uncle Andrew.

'I'm sorry,' she told them. 'I didn't mean to scare you.'

'Then get to your lesson and stop causing trouble,' said the prefect.

Others had gathered to watch. Kate Christie mouthed the word 'loony' to Alice Wetherby. Both were smirking, happy she had given them something else to use against her.

Despising them and herself, she did as she was told.

Heathcote School
27 May 1961

Dear Mrs Bishop,
As you know, I am Susan's form teacher this year. I had planned to speak to your husband and yourself at last week's parents' evening but understand that he had work commitments and that you were unwell. I hope that you are feeling better now.

During her time with us Susan has never come close to achieving the academic success we would expect from so obviously intelligent a girl. In recent months the problem has been compounded by increasingly truculent behaviour. I have had reports of rudeness from many of her teachers, who consider her a disruptive influence on her classmates.

Susan is now fifteen. At the end of the next academic year she will sit her O-level exams and I need hardly tell you how important it is that she perform well. She still has the ability to do so provided she can improve her conduct and apply herself properly to her studies. I was wondering whether there was anything I could do to help this come about.

Forgive my writing this letter but Susan happens to be a girl of whom I have always been very fond. She is, I believe, one of those rare people who have the potential to do anything they want with their lives and I would hate to see that potential spoiled.

Please do let me know if I can be of any assistance.

Yours sincerely
Audrey Morris

A balmy morning in late June. Susan made her way towards school.

A younger boy sidled up to her. 'Hello, sexy,' he said, eager to impress his friends. 'Busy tonight?' Normally she would have slapped him down but this time she had more important things on her mind.

The previous evening Uncle George had told her that he had been offered an eighteen-month contract in Australia, starting the following January. He didn't think he would accept but she felt certain he would soon leave her, just as he had done when she was seven.

And this time he would take Jennifer. The one person who could make her smile no matter how bad she was feeling. Who helped her believe that there was still some good inside her. The person she loved more than anyone else in the world. Her little sister. The only perfect thing in her life.

In the distance Alan Forrester wheeled his bicycle and talked to Charlotte, who had had a crush on him for years. She hadn't realized the two of them were friendly. Charlotte was laughing, looking happy and excited.

The boy continued to pester her. 'How about us getting together?' he asked, trying to sound like an American gangster.

'Not tonight,' she told him. 'Ask again when your balls have dropped.'

He turned crimson while his friends jeered. Alan and Charlotte said goodbye outside the school gates. He kissed her on the cheek. She turned crimson too. In spite of her anxiety, Susan felt pleased. Charlotte considered herself plain and boring and needed someone to make her feel special.

Just as she needed Jennifer.

Don't let him take her away from me. Please God, don't let him take her away.

Monday evening.

She had been walking for hours, along the river then through the town, with no purpose except to escape the atmosphere of dread that filled the house like fog.

Uncle Andrew had missed supper. He would be in the Crown, all bonhomie and generosity, buying rounds and telling stories, charming his fellow drinkers as he consumed the alcohol that would act as fuel for the rage he would unleash on his return home.

Three days ago her mother had broken her finger. Caught it in a door frame. That was the story he had ordered her to tell and which she was too frightened to challenge for fear that he would leave her as he was always threatening to do. 'And where will you be then? You'll never survive without me. You need me and you always will.'

It couldn't go on. Susan knew she had to do something. But what?

She stood outside 37 Osborne Row. The house she had once shared with her father. She longed for him to tell her what to do but when she tried to summon his voice from inside her head she heard nothing but the whirring of her thoughts, like an orchestra of spinning tops all about to collapse.

Someone called her name. Lizzie Flynn approached with Charlotte, who was wearing a new blouse and skirt. Her hair was carefully styled and there was even gloss on her lips.

And she was crying.

'I found her in Market Court,' announced Lizzie. 'She'd been standing by the Norman cross for two hours. That prick Alan Forrester stood her up.'

'Why?'

'Because Alice Wetherby told him to. She was sitting by the window at Cobhams with her gang, all laughing their heads off. I was in there with my sister. That's how I found out what was going on.'

'Why would she do that?'

'Because I beat her in the English exam,' whispered Charlotte. 'You know what she's like about things like that.'

'So she gets Alan to pretend to be keen on Charlotte,' continued Lizzie. 'He's a friend of her idiot brother. Alan tells Charlotte he's taking her out, asks her to dress up smartly then leaves her standing there to be sniggered at by that bitch.'

'I'm sorry,' Susan told Charlotte.

Charlotte wiped her eyes. Lizzie frowned. 'Is that all you've got to say? It was a vicious thing to do. Alice needs to be taught a lesson.'

Wearily she nodded.

'So what are you going to do?'

'I don't know.'

'You must do something.' Lizzie's eyes were flashing. 'She can't get away with it.'

'Why can't you do it?'

'Because I don't go to Heathcote . . .'

'Or Charlotte? Why does it always have to be me?' Frustration overwhelmed her. 'I've got problems of my own. If Charlotte wants to teach Alice a lesson then why doesn't she stop being so bloody weak and try doing it herself?'

Charlotte flushed. Lizzie shook her head. 'You've really changed. I used to like you. You used to be worth something as a friend. Now you're only interested in yourself. You're just a selfish cow. You're no better than Alice.'

She couldn't listen to this. Pushing past them both, she headed for home.

Next morning she sat alone at the kitchen table.

Uncle Andrew appeared, fastening his tie. He was unshaven and looked tired. She had no idea what time he had come home the previous night.

'Where's Mum?' she asked.

'In her room.' He grabbed a piece of toast. 'I'll be in my study. I've got phone calls to make.'

She carried a cup of tea upstairs. Her mother was sitting in bed, wearing a nightdress and with a bandage on the middle finger of her left hand. The curtains were drawn and the window open, letting in the song of birds from the park at the centre of the square.

She put the cup on the bedside table then sat on the bed. Her mother stared down at the sheets, her face strained with pain.

'What happened, Mum? What did he do to you?'

No answer.

'Mum?'

The head rose. For a moment the eyes were as blank as they had been on the day of the breakdown. Her heart began to pound.

'Mum, it's me.'

Recognition. A cold smile. 'Why are you here?'

'What did he do to you?'

Her mother lifted her nightdress to reveal a row of bruises across her belly.

Susan gasped.

'Don't pretend you care.'

'Of course I care. He can't treat you like this. He can't . . .'

'It's your fault that he does.'

'What?'

'You're to blame for this.'

'How can you say that?'

'Because it's true. This is your fault. When he was pleased with you he was kind to me but now you just make him angry and I'm the one that suffers.'

'But Mum . . .'

'Just get out! Go to school. I don't want you here.'

She stood in the doorway, shaking with shock, hurt and anger, listening to Uncle Andrew laughing on the telephone. All warmth and affability. Her stepfather. The nicest man you could ever meet.

Walk away, Susie. Don't make it worse.

Walk away walk away walk away.

But she couldn't. Not any more.

So she went upstairs.

He was sitting at his desk, facing the far wall, so busy laughing that he didn't hear her enter. She shut the door behind her, reached over him and disconnected the call.

'What the hell . . .'

She turned his chair round and stared into his face. 'If you ever lay another finger on my mother I swear to God I'll make you sorry!'

His eyes widened. For a moment he looked frightened.

But only for a moment.

'Are you threatening me, Susie?'

'Leave her alone.'

'Or what?'

'You'll see.'

'You don't want to go making threats. They might make me angry, and who knows what could happen then.'

'You wouldn't tell her.'

'Wouldn't I?'

'You promised me!'

'Perhaps I had my fingers crossed.'

'You couldn't! Think what it would do to her.'

He was smiling, enjoying her desperation and his own power. 'Then no more threats, because one careless remark is all it would take. The cat would be out of the bag, and imagine how your mother would feel about you then.'

'And imagine how the rest of the town would feel about us both.' The smile faded.

'Because it's not just my dirty secret, is it? And if it got out do you really think you'd still be friends with the mayor and doing wills for people like Mrs Pembroke, because I don't. Not a chance. They wouldn't be able to drop you fast enough.'

His face darkened. He rose to his feet. 'You'd better stop this, Susie.'

She stood her ground. 'How do you think they'd feel, Uncle Andrew?'

He took a step towards her. 'I told you to stop.'

'I might lose Mum but you'd lose too. You'd lose everything. I'd make sure of it!'

'I said stop!'

'And what will you do if I don't? Hit me? Go ahead. I'm not frightened. I'm not Mum. But that's the point, isn't it? You wouldn't want to hit me. It's only exciting when the person is afraid.'

He slammed her against the wall, one hand gripping her throat. His breathing was ragged, his eyes narrowed into slits. He looked bestial. Murderous.

And at last she was afraid.

'And who is going to listen to anything you say? You. Susan Ramsey, the town bike. The girl every boy's ridden. I've heard the stories they tell about you. And if you try telling stories about me they'll just shake their heads and feel sorry for me. The man who took you into his home and gave you the best of everything. Who's been a far better father to you than your own ever was, but who still couldn't stop you going off the rails and acting like the spiteful little slut you really are.'

He was choking her. Her head was spinning.

'And your mother won't believe it either. Not coming from you. She won't allow herself to believe it because I'm the one she needs. She can't survive without me. She's barely surviving as it is. She's on the edge, Susie. One good hard push from me and over she goes, and this time she won't come back. You'll lose her for ever just like you lost your father.'

He put a finger to her lips.

'So if you want to stop that happening keep your mouth tight shut, because if you ever try and cross me I'll make you sorrier than you can possibly imagine.'

Then he released her, stepping backwards and folding his arms.

'Do you understand?'

She rubbed her throat.

'Do you?'

'Yes.'

'Now get out.'

Half an hour later she approached the school gates.

People surrounded her. Her head was in such turmoil that she was unable to process the voices around her, as if the rest of the world had started speaking a new language.

Charlotte walked ahead, shoulders sagging. Alice and Kate stood at the gates, waiting to gloat. Alan Forrester approached on his bicycle, whistling cheerfully, oblivious to the hurt he had helped cause.

And as Susan watched him something inside her snapped.

She called his name. He stopped alongside her, grinning inanely. 'What?'

Then she punched him in the mouth, knocking him off his bicycle and on to the ground.

Alice, realizing what was coming, tried to run. But others blocked her path. Susan strode towards her, shoving a protesting Kate to one side. 'We need to talk, Alice,' she announced, grabbing her by the hair and hurling her against the gates.

Alice tried to push her away. 'You pulled my hair out . . .'

Susan slapped her face as hard as she could. 'Listen!'

Then she leaned forward so their noses were almost touching.

'If you ever hurt someone I care about again I will get a knife and cut your throat. Do you understand?'

'You're mad . . .'

'That's right. I'm a loony, just like my mother, and that means I'll do it. Now tell me you understand.'

Whimpering, Alice rubbed her cheek.

'Tell me!'

'I understand.' Alice looked terrified. The sight excited Susan, making her feel strong. Making her feel better than she had done in a very long time.

She pulled her arm back as if to land another blow, watching Alice flinch, revelling in the fear she was causing and the power she possessed.

And heard her father's voice in her head.

This is wrong, Susie. This isn't strength. This isn't the way. You're better than this.

The euphoria faded, replaced by frustration so intense it made her want to scream.

Then what is the way? Who are you to lecture me? Who are you to make me feel bad? You left me when I needed you and now the only person I can depend on is myself.

And I don't know what to do.

She pointed a finger at Alice. 'Remember.'

Then forced herself to walk away.

Ten minutes later Charlotte entered the toilets on the first floor.

Susan stood by the basins, staring at her reflection in the mirror. Two first-year girls washed their hands while watching her warily, as if she were a dangerous animal. Charlotte gestured for them to leave then locked the door behind them.

'Susie?'

Susan continued to gaze into the mirror. She was shaking, her body discharging tension like electric waves.

'Susie?'

'Leave me alone.' The voice was tight. Like an elastic band about to snap.

'Thank you for sticking up for me.'

Silence.

'I should have been the one to do it, just like you said. You didn't have to.' A pause. 'But I'm glad you did.'

Someone tried to open the door. Charlotte waited in vain for Susan to speak.

'Do you want me to go?' she asked.

'Yes.'

Though hurt, she knew she had no right to show it. Instead she turned to leave.

'You're still my best friend, Charlotte. I didn't mean what I said last night. There's nothing weak about you.'

Charlotte turned back, a lump forming in her throat. 'You're my best friend too. You always have been and I wish you'd trust me like you used to.'

Susan shook her head. 'Don't . . .'

'But I must. I know things are wrong and I want to help but I can't if you don't tell me what they are. We never used to have secrets from each other and we don't need to now. You can trust me with anything. You know you can.'

Susan burst into tears. Charlotte made a move towards her but Susan held out an arm, keeping her at a distance.

'Susie . . .'

Susan began rubbing her temples, mouthing the word 'weak' over and over again.

'You're not weak, Susie. You're the strongest person I know, and sharing your problems with me won't change that.'

People hammered on the door. A prefect shouted that if it was not opened immediately there would be trouble. Susan breathed deeply, gaining control of her emotions. She ran a tap and washed her eyes. 'Better tell them I locked it. I'm in so much trouble already that a bit more won't make any difference.'

'Won't you tell me?'

'I can't.'

'Please, Susie.'

Susan took her hand and squeezed it. 'Thanks.'

Then went to open the door.

*

August.

Susan sat by the river bank with Jennifer, staring up at the sky. Though it was cloudless there was a dryness in the air that warned of an impending storm.

Both had their feet in the water, the current tugging at their toes. Jennifer threw pieces of bread to the ducks. 'Susie, will there be ducks in Australia?'

She nodded, masking her sadness with a smile. Uncle George had accepted the job just as she had feared he would.

Swans glided over, searching for food, scattering the ducks like ninepins. Sighing heavily, Jennifer tossed them some bread.

'What is it, Jenjen?'

'I wish you were coming.'

She wished it too. More than anything. To escape from Kendleton and its whispers and sneers to a place where no one knew her.

But what would happen to those she left behind?

Uncle Andrew had not hit her mother since their confrontation. In fact he was being kinder to her. As patronizing as ever, but kinder. He was drinking less too. And when Mr and Mrs Wetherby had come to complain about her own 'vicious assault on poor Alice', he had taken her part, diffusing their anger with apologies and winning them over with charm. There had been no comparable visit from Mr and Mrs Forrester, but then Alan was hardly going to make an issue of being floored by a girl.

She wanted to believe she was responsible for this improvement. That she had frightened him into changing his ways. But in her heart she knew she hadn't. He wasn't frightened of her. She was the one who had reason to be afraid.

Things *were* better. That should have been enough to make her happy.

But until she knew the reason why, her sense of unease would remain.

'Why won't you come?' asked Jennifer.

'Because I have to stay here and take care of my mum.'

Jennifer looked reproachful. 'You promised you'd take care of me.'

'I will.'

'No you won't.' Jennifer started to cry. It was like a blow. Susan tried to hold her but was pushed away. Instead she stroked her hair. It was turning gold in the sun, looking more like Auntie Emma's every day. She remembered how hurt she had been when Auntie Emma had left. A woman who had been a surrogate mother to her, just as she had been to Jennifer. A mother and a sister.

She tried again. This time Jennifer allowed herself to be held.

'I'll always take care of you, Jenjen. Even when you go away, and that's not for four whole months, I'll still be with you in here.' She touched Jennifer's chest. 'And if ever you feel sad you just think of me and know that I'll be thinking of you and if I'm doing that then I'll be taking care of you and that's the truth.'

It wasn't, of course. Just the best she could do.

But it made Jennifer smile and that was all that mattered.

'But you won't feel sad. You'll have too much fun. There are so many things for you to see and do . . .' She began to paint a picture of Australia as the most exciting place on earth. Perhaps it was. Whatever it was like it had to be better than here.

A narrow boat came down the river, stirring the water, disturbing the ducks and swans. A man with grey hair and a kind face stood at the helm while two bull terriers sat on the roof snapping at each other, fractious with the heat and the impending storm.

The man waved to them. She waved back, wishing she could climb aboard with her mother and Jennifer, sail away and never return.

Saturday morning. One week later.

She stood at the kitchen sink, helping her mother wash the breakfast things. Uncle Andrew had left early to play golf with Uncle George. The two of them had been seeing more of each other since the news about Australia. They had been friends for twenty years and would miss each other when the time came.

Though not as much as she would miss Jennifer.

She looked out at the back garden. The grass was withered, the ground parched. The storm of seven days ago had done nothing to break the heat that blanketed the town.' When are you collecting Jennifer?' asked her mother.

'In half an hour.'

'She'll enjoy the fair.'

'So will I.'

Her mother smiled, looking more relaxed than she had in months.

'Why don't you come too, Mum?'

'I've got things to do.'

'You need to have some fun.'

'You sound like your father when you say that.'

'And he was always right. Please come.' She smiled too. 'They've got swing-boats.'

Her mother shuddered.

'Remember when we went on swing-boats at Lexham fair with Dad and Charlotte?'

'Don't remind me. You sat on my knee and Charlotte sat on your father's and you swung us so high I was terrified that after all the candy floss you'd eaten you'd both be sick!'

'Liar. You were scared because you don't like heights. I remember you shouting, "No, Susie! Not so high! For the love of God not so high!"'

'And your father kept singing "Swing Low Sweet Chariot"!'

'And then that stuck-up cow on the next boat complained about him singing "nigger music", so he did his Al Jolson impression and started calling her mammy!'

Both of them were now laughing hard. As she wiped her eyes Susan had a sense that somewhere her father was watching and laughing too.

'Please come, Mum. I know you'll enjoy it.'

'Very well. But we must finish this first. There's a plate in your stepfather's study that needs washing too.'

'I'll get it.'

As she walked upstairs she realized that she felt happy. Suddenly the reasons for Uncle Andrew's changed behaviour were not important. The change itself was enough.

His study door was open. The plate was on his desk, sitting on top of a pile of papers. She picked it up.

And saw the brochure underneath.

Collins Academy – A good place to learn

She turned to the first page.

Founded in 1870, Collins Academy has a long history of academic success. A boarding school for girls between the ages of 11 and 18 situated in the beautiful Scottish countryside . . .

Scotland?
Her heart racing, she read on.
Five minutes later she re-entered the kitchen. 'What the hell is this?'
Her mother turned. When she saw the brochure she paled.
'I'm not going to boarding school!'
'It's just an idea.'
'Whose? Yours?'
'No.'
'His, then. I thought so. He's trying to separate us but it's not going to work. If he sends me away I'll just get expelled and sent home again. Don't think I won't!'
'But Susie . . .'
'He's being nice now but how long do you think that's going to last? What if it stops when I'm not here? Who'll protect you then?'
'And what if it stops when you are here? Do you really think you'll be able to protect me, because I don't. Not when it's your fault he acts like that in the first place.'
'That's not true!'
'Yes it is! He's a good man. He only acts badly because you make him angry.'
'Who are you trying to convince, Mum? Me or yourself?'
'He *is* a good man. He is!'
'And you need him, don't you? That's what you believe. What he's taught you to believe. That you need him far more than you need me.'
Silence.
'I'm right, aren't I?'
Her mother lowered her eyes.

'Thought so.'

'Susie . . .'

'You don't have to come to the fair. Like you said, you've got things to do.'

She put the brochure on the table then left the room.

A Monday morning at the start of September. The first day of the school term. After finishing her breakfast Susan went upstairs to brush her teeth.

She was wearing her Heathcote uniform. Since her discovery of the brochure her mother had made no mention of boarding school. Neither had Uncle Andrew.

But that didn't mean he wasn't thinking of it.

And what will he do to Mum if I refuse to go?

As she reached the second floor she heard voices coming from his study. Uncle George was visiting. She knew she should say hello but did not feel sociable. Instead she tiptoed down the corridor so as not to alert them to her presence.

She stood in the bathroom between the study and her bedroom. In the mirror she noticed a piece of loose thread hanging from her sleeve. Picking up a pair of nail scissors, she prepared to cut it off.

Their voices carried easily from the study. She assumed they were talking about the previous day's golf. Idly she began to listen to their conversation.

And realized they were discussing something very different.

'It's not that I don't want to take her,' said Uncle George. 'Of course I do. She's my daughter. But there's going to be so much travelling. I could be away for weeks at a time.'

'And that would mean leaving her with strangers in a strange country. It wouldn't be fair when she's so young.'

'I still wonder if I should tell them I've changed my mind.'

'You can't do that.' Uncle Andrew's tone was forceful. 'You've been saying all along that this job is a once-in-a-lifetime opportunity, just as I've been saying all along that leaving Jennifer with us is the perfect solution.'

'But it's such an imposition.'

'No it's not. We love Jennifer. And she could come to you in the holidays when you've got time to spend with her. That way she doesn't have to be uprooted from her home, her school and her friends.'

'I wish Susie was going to be here too. You know how Jennifer adores her.'

'Yes, but it can't be helped. It's just not working at Heathcote and there are no other suitable schools in the area, so from next term it will have to be boarding school.' A pause. 'One good thing, I suppose. Jennifer can have Susie's room. I'm sure she'd like that.'

'I'm sure she would too.' Uncle George sighed. 'Well, if you're certain.'

'I am, so stop worrying. I'll take good care of Jennifer. She'll be the apple of my eye . . .'

Susan grew cold all over.

The conversation continued. She tried to listen but suddenly it was like the day her father died and all the sound had drained out of the world, leaving her trapped in a silent movie with only the cue cards of her thoughts for company.

But this time they were not just collections of random words. They had form and they had structure. To read them was as simple as breathing.

And at last everything was clear.

Her right hand hurt. The scissors had cut into her finger. Blood from the wound dripped into the basin. The same dark liquid that had proclaimed her womanhood and freed her from Uncle Andrew's attentions.

But Jennifer was still a child. A sweet, pretty, vulnerable child who believed implicitly in the goodness of others. A child who would believe anything a trusted adult told her. A child no one could consider wicked. Not unless they were truly wicked themselves.

She pictured Jennifer lying in the bed she had lain in, listening to the sounds from the study, watching for shadows in the hall, knowing that she was wicked and that this frightening ritual was her own fault. Knowing but not understanding. Praying for Uncle George to come and save her yet convinced he would hate her if he discovered just how wicked she was.

Praying for Susan to come and save her . . .

You must never tell anyone, Jenjen, because if you do they'll tell your father and he'll stay in Australia and you'll never see him again. You'll lose him for ever, Jenjen, just like you lost your mother.

She gazed into the mirror. In her mind's eye she saw her own father looking just as he had on the day he died. A kind man with untidy hair, twinkling eyes and a smile that could light up a whole room. But he wasn't smiling now. His expression was fearful, as if sensing the violence that was stirring inside her.

This is wrong, Susie. This isn't the way. Listen to me. Please listen . . .

But she wouldn't. Not to a ghost from an earlier life that seemed more like a fairy tale than anything real. He couldn't help her. The only person she could depend on was herself.

Stretching out her hand she touched the glass. 'Goodbye, Dad,' she whispered. 'I love you and I'll always miss you.'

His image faded. Drops of blood slid down the glass. She drew a line across them with her finger, turning them into a row of crosses that seemed to grow before her eyes, filling the room, turning it into a crimson graveyard where every tomb bore the same name.

Suddenly a voice broke through the silence. Her mother's, shrill and anxious. 'Susie, where are you? You're going to be late.' There was no sound from the study. Who knew how long she had been standing there, lost inside the dark caverns of her mind.

But now she was back.

And she knew what she had to do.

Half past two that afternoon. Audrey Morris, an elderly teacher, stood in the entrance hall of the girls' school, waiting for one of the fifth-years to arrive.

Two boys stood with her, both wearing the blue-and-black uniform. Fifth-years too and new that term. The rest of their class were in the art room with the fifth-year girls, listening to a lecture from a successful local painter. Art was the one field where the girls' school had facilities to outshine its rival across the lane.

One boy explained why they were late. Something about administrative procedures. His companion apologized for any inconvenience they had caused, speaking with a faint London accent.

Normally Audrey disliked regional accents but this one, delivered with a courteous smile, had a certain charm.

She heard footsteps. Susan Ramsey approached. Beautiful, wilful Susan Ramsey who had slept with half the boys in town if the stories about her were to be believed. But Audrey didn't believe them. She had always been fond of Susan.

Quickly she made the introductions. The boy with the London accent offered his hand. As Susan took it Audrey was struck by what a handsome couple they made. Like a pair of film stars meeting for the first time on a glamorous Hollywood set.

Greta Garbo, meet John Gilbert. Vivien Leigh, meet Laurence Olivier. Lauren Bacall, meet Humphrey Bogart.

Susie Sparkle, meet Ronnie Sunshine.

Part 5

Kendleton: September 1961

They faced each other in the hallway. Two people meeting for the first time and performing the rituals such an event demanded. The shaking of hands, the exchange of names and smiles and the masking of any negative feelings the encounter might provoke.

She didn't register a person. Just a body. Nothing about him made any impression. She had other things to occupy her mind.

He saw a girl of his own age, as tall as he was and beautiful enough to be arrogant. In his experience beautiful girls were always arrogant. Convinced they could win any boy they wanted with a smile.

But not him. He could never desire a girl with nothing in her face to remind him of his mother.

She told him her name. Her eyes were like violets. Deep and dangerous. The sort an unwary boy could fall into and be lost for ever. But not him. He stared into them calmly, sure of his immunity to their power.

And suddenly he knew.

It was like an electric shock inside his brain. An absolute certainty that had nothing to do with logic or reason. It was something far more primitive. A bolt of pure animal instinct.

You are my kind.

'This way,' she said.

The art room was crowded. Boys and girls sat at desks around a table where books, fruit and a globe were carefully arranged. Pencils scratched against paper while the local painter explained the techniques of still life and Mrs Abbott, the art teacher, kept reminding them of how lucky they were to have so distinguished a guest.

She sat near the back, staring straight ahead, watching the film that played on a screen behind her eyes. The one with the girl who lay awake night after night, heart racing and throat dry, listening for the footsteps and watching for the shadows. A film that was soon to be remade with a new actress in the lead. One who would be crushed by the demands of the role and whose casting she would oppose with all the strength she possessed.

She waited for the fury, the dread and desperation. All the emotions she had learned to understand if not to welcome. But since that morning all she had felt was a calmness so alien that it seemed to belong to someone else. Another person who had no time for apprehension or fear. Not when it was clear what had to be done.

Time passed. She continued to watch the screen, unaware of her hand moving pencil over paper like that of a medium guided by a spirit.

He sat near the window, studying his new surroundings. The school buildings were far smarter than those he had left behind in Hepton. Those across the lane were smarter still, with facilities to make his former classmates gasp. A vast library, a brand-new science laboratory, a swimming pool and half a dozen sports pitches all mown and marked and ready for use.

His new companions worked around him, taking their sur-roundings for granted in a way he never could. It was strange to think he now lived in a grander house than any of them. Two boys cracked jokes, prompting frowns from the teacher and giggles from some girls. His fellow new boy followed suit, eager to fit in and gain acceptance. He could have done the same. Made a better job of it too. But first he would have had to have wanted their good opinion, and none had yet done anything to stir that wish.

Except for the girl whose violet eyes were focused on a view a million miles from the room they sat in.

The teacher told them to stop. The painter moved between the desks, commenting on each drawing. When he saw the girl's effort he frowned. 'What is this supposed to be?'

'I don't know.'

'It looks like a cross.'

'Perhaps that's what it is, then.' Her voice was flat and as distant as the moon.

'Why didn't you draw what you were asked?'

'There was no point.'

'Why not?'

'Because when I leave school I'm going to become a prostitute and in that line of work no one cares if you can draw a decent bowl of fruit.'

A gasp went round the room. Even the jokers looked shocked. 'To the headmistress this instant!' cried the teacher when she had finally regained the power of speech.

He watched her cross the room, looking for signs of embarrassment or attention-seeking but finding neither. She seemed completely detached from her surroundings. He wondered where her thoughts had led her and if there was room for him too.

The flustered-looking painter continued his inspection. The work of a pretty, blonde girl drew praise. Alice Wetherby, one of his new neighbours, now looking very pleased with herself. His own effort drew another frown. 'This isn't what you were asked to do.'

'Isn't it? I'm sorry. I was late arriving and must have misunderstood.'

'This is very good, actually. You have real talent.'

'Thank you. I want to be an artist when I leave school.'

'Which artists do you admire?'

'Hogarth for his realism. Turner for his colour. Blake for his imagination. And Millais. His Ophelia is my favourite painting.'

'It's one of my favourites too.' The painter smiled. 'Well, best of luck . . . er . . .'

'Ronnie. Ronnie Sidney.'

'That's a good name for an artist. I'll watch out for it in the future.'

Alice was staring curiously at him. One of the jokers mouthed the word 'queer'. He looked down at his drawing, liked what he saw and smiled too.

Twenty minutes later she walked out into the afternoon. Boys and girls from the art room stood in groups on the main steps. The buzz of conversation died away when she appeared. Charlotte rushed over. 'What happened?'

'A week's suspension. Another slip and I'll be expelled. From now on I'm to be a perfect young lady.'

She began to laugh while others watched, whispering and judging. Once their condemnation would have hurt. Now it was as trivial as rain.

'It's not funny, Susie!'

'Isn't it?'

'Why are you acting like this?'

'Maybe I'm possessed.'

'What are you talking about?'

'I'm not talking at all. This is someone else's voice.'

Charlotte looked upset. 'What will your parents say?'

'My mother will say whatever my stepfather tells her to. But he's not going to care. He has other things to think about.'

'What things . . .?'

'Excuse me.'

One of the new boys stood beside her. He handed her a drawing. 'This is for you.'

'Why have you drawn me?'

'Because I think you're interesting.'

'No, you think I'm cheap. But I'm not. Like all prostitutes I only fuck for money. Not for scruffy little sketches like this.'

She ripped the drawing in two, letting the pieces fall to the floor before making for the main gate. Charlotte followed, spouting words Susan didn't want to hear, so she blocked them out as easily as if there were a volume control inside her brain.

And still the sense of calm remained.

He watched her walk away. Some boys called out things but she ignored them, keeping her dignity and her head held high.

His ruined drawing lay on the ground. The present she didn't want, just as she didn't want to know him.

But in time she would.

Alice watched Ronnie Sidney pick up pieces of paper. Her curiosity intensifying, she walked over. 'May I see?'

He shook his head, lowering his eyes as if shy. She liked that.

'Go on. I promise not to say anything horrid.'

He gave her the fragments. 'You're really good,' she told him.

'Thank you.'

'And she's really beautiful.'

'Do you think so?'

'Isn't that why you drew her?'

'No.'

'Why, then?'

Again he looked shy.

'Tell me.'

'Because you had your hand over your face.'

Surprise was eclipsed by delight. A smile spread across his own face, tentative at first then growing brighter. He was very good looking. More so than she had first realized.

'You're Alice Wetherby,' he said. 'You live in my street.'

'Why haven't you come and said hello, then?'

'I would have but . . .' Another shake of the head. The shyness had returned but the smile remained. It was a lovely smile. Really lovely.

She felt a fluttering in her stomach.

Kate Christie appeared beside them. 'Why have you drawn that loony?'

'Ronnie, this is my friend Kate.'

Ronnie offered his hand. Kate giggled. 'You look like John Leyton. I really like him.'

'What do you want?' demanded Alice, trying not to sound irritated.

'If you're coming for tea we'd better go.'

'I'm not.'

'But you said . . .'

'That I'd come on Friday.'

'No . . .'

'Yes. See you tomorrow.' Her tone was firm.

Kate left, once again giggling. 'Sorry,' said Alice. 'She can be very childish.'

'But nice, though. She must be if she's a friend of yours.'

The fluttering sensation returned. 'Are you going home now, Ronnie?'

'Yes.'

'Shall we walk together?'

'I'd like that.'

Two boys watched them as they set off. She had flirted with both in the past, relishing the sense of power it gave. Boys were all the same. Coarse, blundering creatures interested in only one thing and willing to suffer any humiliation in its pursuit.

But Ronnie seemed different. Courteous and charming. A lone gentleman in a landscape of oafs.

They entered the lane. The sun was high above the trees. 'It's beautiful here,' he said. 'In Hepton, where I come from, everything is grey and dull, but here it's like a painting.'

'Will you do a painting for me?'

'If you promise not to rip it up when I give it to you.'

'Of course not.' She touched his arm. 'I'm nothing like her.'

'Is she really a loony?'

'Absolutely. She attacked me last term for no reason. It was really frightening.'

'It must have been.' He looked concerned. 'Tell me what happened . . .'

She entered Market Court, Charlotte following at her heels like an anxious puppy. It was full of people all moving in slow motion and speaking without sound. Her calmness was like a tranquillizing drug, dulling her senses and turning the world into a dream.

Until the moment she saw Jennifer, when everything became real again.

She was with another little girl outside a sweet shop, both of them wearing the same red-and-brown primary school uniform that Susan had once worn and eating ice creams. She ran over to Susan, who hugged her so tightly that it provoked cries of protest. 'You're hurting me!'

'Sorry.' Susan relaxed her hold. 'I'm just pleased to see you, that's all.'

'My new teacher's called Mrs Boyd. She made us read aloud and said I was the best and she taught us a new song called 'Land of the Buffalo'. Listen.'

Jennifer began to sing. Her mouth was covered in chocolate sauce. Gently Susan wiped it away. 'Can I tell you a secret, Jenjen?'

'What?'

'We're never going to be parted. We'll always be together.'

Jennifer's face lit up. 'Always?'

'Always.' Susan licked sauce from her finger then wiped it clean. 'Is my finger wet? Is my finger dry? God strike me dead if I tell a lie.'

Jennifer was smiling. It was bright and pure and full of trust. The smile of a child who knew nothing of wickedness, shame or fear.

And never would.

'Now go and finish your ice cream and I'll see you later.'

Jennifer did as she was told. Rising to her feet, Susan watched the people around her, all going about their business as if everything was normal. From now on she would do the same. There would be no more suspensions. No more behaviour that drew attention to herself and raised questions in others. She would be restrained and controlled, projecting a surface so perfect that no one would ever guess at the ugliness that lay beneath.

Hesitantly Charlotte approached. 'Susie . . .'

Susan pointed to the two little girls eating ice creams without a care in the world. 'Remember when that was us?'

'What's the matter, Susie? What's going on?'

'Nothing. I just feel a bit mad today but I'll be sane again tomorrow.'

'Shall I come home with you? Moral support when you break the news.'

'No. I'm a big girl now. But thanks for caring. I'm lucky to have a friend like you.'

She kissed Charlotte's cheek then turned and walked away, humming a tune and wearing a smile as if everything were normal and she too had not a care in the world.

Two days later. Charles Pembroke ate breakfast with his wife and stepson.

The room was full of light. A cloudless sky promised another glorious day in a summer that showed no sign of ending. Charles, who was lecturing that morning, looked at his watch. 'If you want a lift, Ronnie, we must leave in five minutes.'

Anna frowned. 'There's fried bread in the oven. He must have some before he goes.'

Ronnie swallowed a mouthful of sausage. 'I'm full, Mum.'

'But I made it specially.' Anna turned to Charles. 'Can you wait a little longer?'

He couldn't really but wanted to make her happy. 'Of course.'

Anna left the room. Charles sipped his coffee and read the local paper. The mayor had just been re-elected. Andrew Bishop was quoted as saying that this was a good thing.

Ronnie was staring at him. Studying him with those eyes that gave nothing away. 'Everything all right, Ronnie?'

'I'm going to make you late, aren't I?'

'No.'

'I could easily walk.'

'Would you rather?'

'I just don't want to make you late.'

'You won't.' He smiled. 'Honestly.'

'Don't bet on it. I won't be allowed to leave until I've eaten enough to kill an elephant.' Ronnie smiled too. 'You know what Mum's like.'

'I do.'

'Not that I'm complaining. Auntie Vera's meals were either burnt or raw. Uncle Stan used to say that the only reason we didn't starve to death was because God gave us chip shops.'

Charles laughed.

'Mum's a wondeful cook, isn't she?'

'Absolutely. We're both spoiled.'

'Well, I am. She didn't cook me meals like this in Hepton.'

'Didn't she?'

'She couldn't afford to.'

'No, I suppose not.'

'Poor Mum. She hated it that we were poor. When I was little she used to promise me that one day we'd have lots of money. No matter what she had to do to get it.'

Charles ignored the dig. 'And now you do,' he said affably.

'And my stomach will burst because of it.' Ronnie's smile returned. Perhaps it hadn't been a dig. Perhaps.

Anna appeared with the fried bread. 'Made with egg the way you like it,' she told Ronnie.

'But I really am full, Mum.'

'I'm not listening.' She cut a piece and guided it into his mouth. Sighing melodramatically, he began to chew.

There was a knock on the door. Edna the cleaner entered, carrying a pile of clothes. 'Excuse me, Mrs Pembroke, I was wondering . . .'

Anna's face darkened. 'What are you doing with those?'

'I was going to wash them.'

'Those are Ronnie's clothes.'

'I know, but . . .'

'I wash Ronnie's clothes. How many times have I told you?'

'I'm sorry . . .'

'Next time do what I say and leave them alone. That's not too difficult, is it?'

Quickly Charles stepped in. 'Perhaps you could put them back in Ronnie's laundry basket, Edna. But thank you for the thought. It was very kind.'

'That was a little harsh,' he told Anna once Edna had gone. 'She meant well.'

Anna continued to look angry. Charles remembered how she had been at the start of their marriage. Her anxiety at finding herself mistress of so huge a house. The agonies of shyness she had suffered in dealing with the domestic help. How she had looked to him for reassurance at every turn, allowing him to be her guide and protector.

Until the day Ronnie came.

She did everything for him. Washed and mended his clothes. Cooked all his meals. Cleaned his room. Catered to his every need in a way that was both devoted and possessive. Keeping others at a distance like an anxious bird defending a frail chick.

He did understand. For six long years her time with Ronnie had been restricted to brief visits, and those constantly disrupted by Vera's demands. It was only natural that she would now seek to express the maternal love that had been frustrated for so long.

But still the intensity of that love worried him.

A piece in the paper caught his attention. 'Ronnie, do you know a boy at school called Paul Benson?'

'No. Why?'

'He's just won a national essay competition.'

'May I see?'

Charles handed over the paper. 'I bet you could have written a better essay,' Anna told Ronnie.

'You don't know that, Mum. He might be brilliant.'

'You're brilliant. The most brilliant boy in Kendleton.'

'I'll be the fattest too at this rate.'

'But you'll still be the most handsome. Now eat!' She tried to shovel more food into his mouth while he pushed it away, laughing. She wrapped her arms around him, kissing his cheek while he stroked her arm, their gestures fluid with familiarity. As Charles watched them Ronnie's eyes locked with his. For a moment the barriers seemed to vanish. The eyes flashed in triumph, as if to say, 'You see how it is. I come first and always will.' But did they really? Or was envy distorting his own perception?

He couldn't wait any longer. 'I'm sorry, Ronnie, but we must go.'

'Just a couple more minutes,' begged Anna. 'Please.'

'I don't mind walking, Mum. After all, it's a lovely day.'

'Then I'll walk with you as far as Market Court.'

'Do you remember walking me to Hepton Primary? There was that woman with curlers who stood on the corner of Knox Road.'

'I do. She was an awful woman. Always gossiping.'

'And her husband spent his whole life in the pub, though who wouldn't if it meant getting away from her . . .'

Charles listened to them talk about people who meant nothing to him. He felt shut out. Excluded. But it was only natural that they would sometimes want to talk about their past.

He made for the door, leaving Ronnie to his breakfast and his mother.

'Did you really enjoy your day?'

'Very much. Double chemistry and double Latin. What could be better than that?'

Anna laughed. She was sitting on Ronnie's bed. The night was warm and the windows were open, letting in the smell of the river. 'Do you think you'll be happy there?' she asked.

'The facilities are rather second rate but I'll try and make the best of it.'

Again she laughed. He did too, looking debonair in the silk pyjamas she had bought him. Once their cost would have been prohibitive. But not now.

A floorboard creaked in the corridor. Just the sigh of an old house but still she tensed, half expecting Vera to burst in and demand that she perform some meaningless task. Old habits died hard.

'Made any friends yet?'

'No.'

'What about Alice Wetherby? You walked home with her this afternoon.'

'That doesn't mean she's my friend.'

'She's very pretty.'

'And spoilt. I'd much rather walk on my own, but she seems to like my company and I can't just ignore her. She is a neighbour.'

She masked her relief with an indulgent smile. 'Of course she does. What girl wouldn't like the company of such a handsome boy?'

'Mum!'

'But it's true.' She stroked hair back from his eyes. His pyjamas made him look younger than he was. More like the little boy he had been than the young man he was fast becoming. She liked that.

'Charles says you can invite your friends here whenever you want.'

'Makes a change from Moreton Street.'

'This isn't Moreton Street. This is your home and you don't need permission. Charles wants you to know that.'

He nodded.

'You do like him, don't you?'

'Of course. He's your husband.'

'Is that the only reason?'

'No.'

'Then why?'

A troubled look came into his eyes.

'Ronnie?'

'Because he's not my father. My father hurt you. Charles won't ever do that.'

'Your father hurt you too.'

'Not really. I never knew him.'

'You wanted to, though. You used to talk about him all the time.'

'I was younger then. Just a baby.'

For a moment the troubled look remained. Then it was gone, replaced by a Ronnie Sunshine smile. As reassuring as a hug.

'Better go to sleep,' she told him.

He lay down in bed. From the window came the sound of swans fighting. The room was vast with a wonderful view of the river. An antique desk stood by a bay window. One of its drawers had a lock. She gestured to it. 'What do you keep in there?'

'Nothing.'

'Why is it locked, then?'

'Is it?'

'You should know. You have the key.'

'I'll keep it open if you like.'

'Not if you don't want to.'

'It doesn't matter to me.'

'Nor to me. You keep your secrets if you want to.'

'I don't have any secrets. Not from you.'

She gazed down at him, remembering the tiny bedroom they had shared in Hepton all those years ago. Its walls had been covered in the pictures he had drawn for her, each full of colour and joy. But there had been other pictures he had never shown her. The ones he kept hidden under the loose floorboard beneath his bed.

She had never told him she knew about the floorboard. Occasionally, when he was very young, she would open it up and study the dark, angry visions he kept there. But eventually she had stopped doing so. They were just drawings, after all. Images without meaning or significance. From around his seventh birthday they had remained undisturbed. About the time Vera had her accident with a pan of chip fat and a roller skate.

He smiled up at her. Another glorious Ronnie Sunshine smile that could banish all her worries like magic. Something he must have known, for no one knew her better than he did.

But she knew him better than anyone else too. And whatever secrets he had would be nothing more than summer storms. Fleeting disturbances that could not disturb the beauty of the season.

That's all they'll be. I know it.

'Goodnight, Mum. I love you.'

She hugged him while outside the swans continued to fight.

Next morning, while tidying his room, she studied the books on his desk.

The titles alone were enough to make her head swim. *A History of the Industrial Revolution, William Pitt: His Life and Times, Lord Byron and the Romantic Movement in English Culture, The Dawn of Democracy: Revolt and Reform in Nineteenth-century Europe.*' It was hard to believe her little Ronnie had read and understood them all.

But he wasn't her little Ronnie any more. In a month he would be sixteen. A man in the eyes of many and a far cry from the boy of nine she had been forced to leave behind in Hepton. A boy who had needed her in a way she had never been needed before.

But he still needed her now. Time hadn't altered that. The nature of the need might have changed but the need itself remained.

He's still my Ronnie Sunshine. However old he is he'll always be that.

Her leg brushed the drawer with the lock. She tried the handle, hoping it would open. But it remained shut.

Saturday afternoon. Susan walked into Market Court.

A crowd had gathered around the steps of the Town Hall watching Paul Benson receive his essay award from the mayor and be photographed for the local paper. She hadn't meant to be one of them, but as the moment approached had found that she couldn't stay away.

It was a beautiful day. Paul, bathed in sunlight, looked very smart in his school uniform. The mayor, pompous as always, made a speech about prizes he himself had won at a similar age and how they had helped make him the respected public figure he now was. She stood at the back, not wanting Paul to see her and conclude that she still had feelings for him. Because she didn't. None whatsoever.

Finally the mayor handed Paul the award. The crowd began to applaud. 'Say cheese,' said the photographer. Paul's grin almost split his face in two. As she saw it she realized that she still hated him, both for the cruelty with which he had treated her and for her own weakness in allowing herself to care.

And then it happened.

Something fell from the sky. Just at the moment the picture was taken. Something dark and heavy, landing on the heads of Paul and the mayor and fragmenting into pieces.

The applause died away, replaced by stunned silence. A brown lump stuck in Paul's hair. Others were plastered to his jacket. The mayor, similarly smeared, wiped at his clothes, his eyes widening in horror.

'It's a cow pat!' cried a man in the crowd.

Someone laughed. Others followed suit. Susan looked up at the window of the old library reading room but it was obscured by the eaves of the roof and the culprit could not be seen.

The mayor, his face crimson, began to rant about the outrage that had been committed. Paul, equally flushed, appeared close to tears. The photographer's eyes were shining. The potential headlines were a newspaper's wet dream. 'Mayor Attacked by Wayward Turd', 'Invisible Cow Spoils Student's Big Day', 'Hanging Too Good for Bovine Tearaway'.

The laughter continued to swell. Soon she was laughing too, so crippled with mirth she thought her sides would split.

Ten minutes later she was sitting on a bench in the corner of the square eating an ice cream. The crowd had now dispersed, most with smiles on their faces. Martin Phillips and Brian Harper, Paul's so-called friends, were riding their bicycles round the Norman cross. She wondered whether they had been responsible for the incident.

'Hello.'

A boy stood beside her. The one who had drawn her picture. Ronald something.

He sat down on the bench. 'Do have a seat,' she said sarcastically.

'Are you pleased?'

'About what?'

'You were there. I saw you from the window.'

'What window?'

'The one in the library.'

She bit into her ice cream. Martin, riding his bicycle with no hands, swerved to avoid a dog and promptly fell off. Brian cheered. She was about to do the same when she realized what Ronald had said.

'You did it?'

'Yes.'

'Why?'

'Because of the way he treated you.'

'Who told you about that?'

'Alice Wetherby.'

'You're friends with her but doing favours for me?' A snort. 'I don't think so.'

'She isn't my friend. We just live in the same street.'

'You live in the Avenue?'

'Yes.'

'So your mother's the new Mrs Pembroke.'

He nodded.

'And how does she feel about you throwing turds at VIPs?'

'Very proud. What mother wouldn't be?'

Unexpectedly she found herself laughing. He was watching her, his blond hair framing a handsome face and clever eyes. His clothes hung neatly upon him. He looked like a male version of Alice.

Her defences rose like a drawbridge. She knew what he was after. What all boys were after. And she knew how to make him sorry.

'There are easier ways to impress me. All you have to do is say the magic words.'

'What are they?'

'That I look like Elizabeth Taylor.'

'You look like who you are.'

'And who is that?'

'Someone special.'

'That's right. I am special. The only girl in town who'll do it with anyone. Just pay me a compliment and I'll spread my legs. That's what you think, isn't it?'

'How do you know what I think?'

'Because I can see through you like an X-ray. You believe gossip because it's easier than trying to find out the truth. Unless, of course that gossip is about your mother.'

He frowned. 'What about my mother?'

'Haven't you heard? I'm surprised. Everyone's talking about it.'

'About what?'

'About how she's a hard-faced gold-digger who'd have happily married a leper provided his bank account was big enough.'

'That's not true.'

'She married your stepfather for his looks, did she?'

'You don't know anything about her.'

'Don't I? If you're going to believe gossip about me then why shouldn't I believe it about her? It's a free country, after all, even for tarts and gold-diggers.'

He rose to his feet, looking so angry she thought he might hit her. But when he spoke his voice was calm.

'Maybe you're right. If wanting to have money and a nice home is being a gold-digger then that's what she is. But before condemning her you should know that when she was only thirteen she lost her entire family in an air raid. Her mother, father and brother all killed in an instant. She was only just seventeen when she had me. My father was dead, she had no money and was living with relatives who didn't want her and did everything they could to make her give me up. But she wouldn't, and all my life she's tried to give me the things she never had. That's why she came to work here and that's why she married my stepfather, and if that makes her a bad person in your eyes then so be it. But she'd never judge someone without knowing the facts, and if you do then perhaps you really are the stupid tart the gossips say.'

He turned and walked away. She told herself she didn't care. Tried to focus on her anger but found it eclipsed by another emotion she hadn't anticipated. Shame.

'Ronald, wait.'

He stopped, staring down at his feet.

'Come back.'

He did. They sat in silence, side by side in the afternoon sun, while women with shopping baskets passed by them, complaining about the price of groceries.

'Sorry,' she said eventually.

He didn't answer. She prodded him in the ribs, looking for a reaction. Her ice cream was melting so she dabbed some on his nose. 'Sulky,' she told him.

Still no answer. Again she prodded him. 'Come on, Ronald. Try smiling.'

'It's Ronnie. No one calls me Ronald.'

'I'm not surprised. It's a horrible name.'

'Blame Ronald Colman. Mum named me after him.'

'Why? Was he her idol?'

'No. She just couldn't spell Humphrey Bogart.'

Again she found herself laughing. At last his smile came. Warm and genuine. Perhaps he didn't look so like Alice after all.

'I'm sorry for what I said about your mother. I don't think she's a gold-digger.'

'Do others?'

She thought of her stepfather. 'Some. But they're just fools.'

'Sorry I got angry.'

'I'd get angry too if someone said things about my mother.'

'You think I'd be used to it by now.'

'What do you mean?'

'Nothing. Nothing at all.'

Her ice cream was liquid. She put it in the bin. 'That's sixpence down the drain.'

'I'll buy you another if you like.'

'It doesn't matter. I'd have paid ten times that to see the look on Paul's face.'

'You still can. I take cheques.'

'Why did you do it?'

'For you.'

'But why?'

'Because I want to know you.'

'I'm not worth knowing. Ask anyone.'

'I don't believe in gossip and I think you are.'

'So you want to be my knight in shining armour.' She shook her head. 'Don't waste your time, Ronnie. I don't need anyone to understand me.'

'I do,' he said quietly.

'Are you that complicated?'

'Perhaps.'

'You certainly like living dangerously. Did anyone see you in the library?'

'Do I look stupid?'

'Very.'

His smile returned. As attractive as before. But Paul's smile had been attractive too and the naive girl of twelve months ago was gone for ever.

She rose to her feet. 'Find someone else to understand you. It shouldn't be difficult with your looks. Girls will be queuing up. Just don't pick Alice. Beneath the sugary exterior lurks a vicious bitch, and that's not just gossip.'

'I'll see you again.'

'Of course. We live in the same town, don't we?'

'That's not what I meant.'

'But that's how it is. Goodbye, Ronnie.' A pause. 'And hey . . .'

'What?'

'Good shot.'

Then it was her turn to walk away.

Monday morning. She sat at the breakfast table listening to Uncle Andrew rant about the wildness of modern youth. The previous day's paper lay on the table. 'Prize Ceremony Disrupted by Prank,' read the headline. She had hoped for a more descriptive one but the accompanying photograph of a soiled Paul more than made up for that.

'Are you sure it was a young person?' asked Susan's mother. 'The paper said they didn't know who the culprit was.'

Uncle Andrew gave her a withering look. 'So what's your theory, then? Pensioners protesting at increased library fines? It'll be one of those hooligans from Holt Street.' He spread marmalade on to his toast. 'I blame television. It gives them all sorts of ideas.'

'Then thank goodness we never got one.'

'Though that didn't stop a certain person getting herself suspended, did it?' He jabbed his finger at Susan. 'You'd better behave yourself from now on.'

'I'm sure she will,' said her mother.

'Let's hope so. It would be nice if she could finish her last term at Heathcote without being expelled.'

Susan reached for a piece of toast, wearing an expression of glum resignation. They had told her about her move to boarding school the previous Monday, just after she had told them about her suspension. 'We'd hoped it wouldn't come to this,' Uncle Andrew had said, 'but after this incident there's really no choice.' His tone had been one of regret, masking his certain delight at how perfectly she had played into his hands.

She hadn't just accepted it, of course. An actress had to give the performance her audience expected. There had been protestations. Tears even. A perfectly executed display of distress that had eventually collapsed into sullen acceptance. Uncle Andrew was not the only one who could dissemble. She had years of hard-won experience under her belt.

And she was better at it than he was.

He continued his rant, blaming her peer group for all the evils of the world. She sat in silence, keeping her mask in place.

Half an hour later she made her way towards school.

She walked quickly, ignoring the whispers and stares. Acting as if she didn't mind, just as she had done every day for the past year. Only this time it was no act. The girl who cared about the opinions of others had vanished in front of her bedroom mirror a week ago, replaced by one who found it hard to believe that anything so trivial could ever have mattered to her.

The usual crowd were gathered around the gates. Alice was prattling away to Ronnie like a wind-up doll while looking daggers at Kate who kept trying to join in the conversation. Not that it was a real conversation. Ronnie just nodded, a faint but unmistakable look of boredom on his face. Perhaps Alice really was nothing more to him than a neighbour.

But it wasn't important.

Kate continued to interrupt, prompting further glares from Alice. Others were glaring too. Boys with whom Alice had once flirted now cast menacing looks at Ronnie. Briefly she felt concern for him. Hoped he wouldn't suffer for having stolen Alice's attention.

But it wasn't her problem.

Ronnie's eyes locked with hers. His expression was questioning. Having no answers for him she shrugged and looked away.

The following Sunday she took Jennifer to the local playground.

Hand in hand they walked across Queen Anne Square. It had rained solidly for the previous two days and Susan had feared the summer was over, but that morning the sky had been clear and the sun bright, so perhaps it hadn't ended yet.

As they approached the road that led to Market Court she saw Ronnie.

He was standing on the corner, hands in pockets, staring fixedly at her.

'What do you want?' she called out.

'To see you.'

'Well, I'm busy.' She carried on walking.

Jennifer tugged at her hand. 'Who's that?'

'Just some stupid boy. What shall we do first? Swings or slide?'

'Swings!'

'I'm going to swing higher than you.'

'No you're not. I'm going to swing as high as the sky!'

They crossed Market Court, exchanging polite greetings with people they knew. Jennifer kept looking over her shoulder. 'What is it, Jenjen?'

'That boy's following us.'

'Well, that proves how stupid he is. Let's sing him our song.'

So they did. A rhyme she had made up as a joke.

> *'Boys are stupid. Boys are sad.*
> *And girls who like boys are raving mad!'*

They left the Court and entered the side street that led to the playground.

'He's still following,' said Jennifer.

She nodded, trying to feel annoyed while realizing she was pleased.

The playground was situated close to her old house and had swings, a slide and a battered old roundabout decorated with pictures of horses. It was rarely used now, eclipsed by a bigger one that had opened the previous year. But Susan still brought Jennifer, just as her father had once brought her.

She led Jennifer towards the swings. Ronnie sat on a bench by the entrance. After making a face at him she gripped the ropes and launched herself forward, propelling herself higher and higher. As the air rushed past her face she shut her eyes and pretended she was flying. Feeling for a brief but glorious moment like the child she had once been whose life had been an adventure unclouded by worry or fear.

Beside her, Jennifer was squealing with excitement. 'I can swing higher than you, Susie. Look!' Instantly the adult side of her nature reasserted itself. She slowed herself down, opening her eyes to check that Jennifer did not go higher than was safe and realizing that there were now others in the park.

Martin Phillips and Brian Harper were perched on the round-about, smoking cigarettes and staring at her just like Ronnie. Their bicycles lay on the ground near by. Martin whispered something to Brian, who began to snigger. She told herself to ignore them. What did a bit of name-calling matter? Sticks and stones could break her bones but words could never hurt her.

But they might hurt Jenjen.

Brian continued to snigger. Jennifer had stopped swinging and was watching him warily. 'I don't like those boys, Susie.'

'Don't worry about them, darling. They'll go away soon.'

'That's not very friendly,' Martin told her. His speech was slurred. Susan knew he often stole alcohol from his father's drinks cabinet and began to feel anxious.

She gave Jennifer a reassuring smile. 'Let's go on the slide.'

'I've got something you can slide on,' Brian told her.

'Me too,' added Martin, his cigarette clenched between his thumb and first finger in the studied pose of a street tough. He took a long drag and promptly suffered a coughing fit. Though she knew it was dangerous, she burst out laughing.

He swallowed, his eyes watering. 'What's so funny?'

Contempt overcame wariness. 'The sight of a sad little boy trying to act like a man and failing miserably.'

'Better that than a stupid tart trying to act like a lady.'

She didn't want Jennifer to hear this. 'Come on, Jenjen. Let's go home.'

'Yes, piss off, tart,' sneered Martin. Once again Brian sniggered.

And then Ronnie said, 'Don't call her that again.'

'What's it got to do with you, new boy?' demanded Brian.

Ronnie walked over to the roundabout. 'She's not a tart,' he told Martin calmly. 'So please don't call her that again.'

Martin's face darkened. Susan's alarm increased. 'Leave it, Ronnie.'

'Yes, leave it, Ronnie,' echoed Brian. 'It's not going to get you anywhere with her. You need money for that.'

Ronnie punched him in the face.

The blow was poorly struck, glancing off Brian's jaw. But it was enough to make him roar. Both he and Martin jumped to their feet, Martin grabbing Ronnie round the neck while Brian punched him back. Both were older and stronger and in their drunken state looked set to hurt him badly like the bullies they were.

And she wasn't having that.

She positioned herself between Ronnie and Brian before another blow could be struck. 'Please don't,' she begged Brian. 'He barely touched you.'

'Get out of the way.'

'You can hardly have felt it.' She held up her hands in supplication. 'Please.'

He hesitated. Seizing her moment, she grabbed him by the shoulders and slammed her head into his face.

'Now that, on the other hand, has got to hurt!'

He screamed, covering his nose with his hands. She rammed her knee into his balls then turned to face Martin, blood pounding in her temples like a drum. 'You're next,' she told him. He released Ronnie, looking genuinely frightened. She raised her fists in a fighter's stance. 'What are you scared of? I'm just a stupid tart. What can I do to you?'

Brian began to rise. She kicked him in the backside, sending him down again. Martin moved away. 'Bloody psycho!'

'That's right. It runs in my family, didn't you know?'

Again Brian tried to rise. Again she kicked him. Martin grabbed his bicycle. She taunted him with clucking sounds, flapping her arms like a chicken.

For the third time Brian tried to rise. This time she let him. He hobbled towards his bicycle, rubbing his bruised testicles, clearly eager to follow Martin's lead and flee. She watched them go, the blood still racing inside her. When they reached the entrance Martin turned back. 'You should be locked up!'

'It'll take more of a man than you to do it.' Laughing, she made more clucking sounds.

And heard Jennifer sob.

She was cowering by the swings, her shoulders shaking and a terrified expression on her face. Susan's exhilaration vanished, replaced by shame. 'Oh, darling, come here.'

'I thought they'd hurt you. I thought . . .'

She wiped Jennifer's eyes, making soothing noises. 'How could they hurt me? They're just boys, and we know what we think of boys, don't we?' She began to hum their rhyme, making silly faces, trying to make Jennifer smile and eventually succeeding. 'That's better. You're a brave girl. The bravest girl in the world.'

Ronnie stood watching them. His lip was bleeding. She felt pleased. This was all his fault. He wiped the blood with his hand. 'Use a handkerchief,' she told him.

'I don't have one.'

'Oh, for God's sake!' She gave Jennifer a kiss, then walked over to him, holding out her own. 'Use this.'

He took it, dabbing at his mouth. 'Does it hurt?' she asked.

'No.'

'Pity. You're making a mess. Let me.' She pressed the handkerchief against the wound, feeling him wince. 'Hold still, Lancelot. And next time pick a fight with someone your own size. That way you might not get killed.'

'I wouldn't have got killed.'

'Oh, sure.'

'It's true. My cousin used to treat me like a punch bag and he makes those two look like a pair of pansies.'

'They are a pair of pansies. I'm glad your cousin beat you up. It's what you deserve.'

'I'm glad you're glad.'

'Why did he do it?'

'To teach me to have respect for tarts.'

She made herself frown. She was still angry with him. She really was.

'I'm taking Jennifer home. If you're going to follow then try not to get into any more fights. I'm not bailing you out again.'

She jabbed the handkerchief against the cut, making him wince for a second time. Then she returned to Jennifer.

Twenty minutes later Ronnie stood in Queen Anne Street, watching Susan take Jennifer home.

The handkerchief was still pressed to his lip. The cut was tender but he didn't notice. Too embarrassed at his reckless behaviour and the poor impression it must have made.

Susan, holding Jennifer's hand, knocked on the door of a house on the corner. It was opened by a middle-aged man with a kind face. Jennifer's father presumably. The man touched Jennifer's cheeks, obviously noticing the tear stains. Ronnie expected Susan to point the finger at him but she didn't. Just stroked Jennifer's hair, smiling down at her. It was a lovely smile. Really lovely.

The man took Jennifer's hand, leading her into the house. He indicated for Susan to enter too but she shook her head, gesturing that she had to go but would be back shortly.

The door shut. She walked towards him, moving like a dancer, radiating strength with every step. People had told him that he radiated strength too. Perhaps he did. But he didn't have her grace.

She held out her hand. 'My handkerchief.' Her tone was brisk, her eyes unblinking. Those glorious eyes an unwary boy could fall into and be lost for ever. The sort of boy he would never be.

Or so he had once thought.

'I'm sorry. I didn't mean to frighten Jennifer. Please believe that.'

'My handkerchief.'

He gave it to her. 'I'm sorry,' he said again.

She leaned forward and kissed him softly on the cheek.

'Idiot,' she whispered, before turning and walking away.

The next morning heralded another beautiful day. Susan, carrying her school bag, made her way across Queen Anne Square.

Ronnie stood on the corner, just as he had the previous day. This time it wasn't a surprise. She had expected him to be there even though she couldn't say why.

And she was pleased. Even though she didn't want to be.

'Don't you have anything better to do than hang around on street corners?'

'No.'

'Then you'd better walk with me.'

They entered Market Court. People were already queuing outside shops that had yet to open. His lip was swollen. Her forehead was bruised but she could cover it with her hair. 'Is Jennifer all right?' he asked.

'No thanks to you.'

'Or you. Even I was frightened.'

'And you a professional punch bag.'

'Now retired and seeking a more dignified profession. Toilet brush perhaps.'

She laughed while feeling uncomfortable at how easily he could make her do so.

They continued on, eventually reaching the school lane. Others walked beside them, whispering about this strange new pairing. Alice stood at the gate, her forlorn expression becoming one of horror when she saw who Ronnie was with.

'Your girlfriend's spotted us.'

'She's not my girlfriend.'

'Good. She deserves better than a professional urinal scrubber.'

It was his turn to laugh. She felt pleased. Even though she didn't want to be.

They faced each other outside the gates. Martin Phillips was watching her warily. He was frightened of her now and with good reason.

But was he frightened of Ronnie?

'Be careful,' she said suddenly.

'I can take care of myself.'

'Don't let anyone provoke you.'

'I'm not going to sit there and let people say things about you.'

'They're just words. They don't matter.'

'They do to me.'

'Then you're an idiot.'

'Of course. What else could a professional urinal scrubber be?'

People were staring. Ronnie didn't seem to notice, let alone care. There was a contained quality about him. A strength that was like a shield, causing all the stares to bounce off him. Maybe he really could take care of himself after all.

But she didn't want to take the risk.

'If people say things about me then don't react. Please, Ronnie. For me.'

He smiled. 'OK. For you.'

The bell rang. 'I'll wait for you after school,' he said. 'Buy you an ice cream to make up for the one I ruined.'

'I don't eat ice cream anymore.'

'Yes you do. No tart can live without ice cream. That's a medical fact.'

'And where did you learn that? *Boy's Own* comic?'

'No. *Emergency Ward Ten*.' A sigh. 'And people say it's just cheap drama.'

'Goodbye, then, Doctor.'

'Goodbye, Susan.'

'Susie. No one calls me Susan.'

'I'm not surprised. Stupid name.'

'Blame my grandmother. My father named me after her.'

'So she was Susan too.'

'No. Dad just couldn't spell Gwendolyn.'

Again he laughed. Turning, she walked through the gates, shrugging off the watching eyes like flies. All except his, which nestled like two warm lights in the small of her back.

She didn't want to like the feeling but she did.

*

Ten to four. She walked out of the school gates to find Ronnie waiting for her.

The path was deserted. School had ended twenty minutes earlier. She had spent the intervening time sitting in the library, hoping he would have left by the time she emerged. But as soon as she saw him she was glad he had stayed.

Half an hour later they sat by the river near Kendleton Lock, dangling their feet in the water with the sun on their faces and ducks and swans calling for scraps of bread. Ben Logan, the lock-keeper, paused from helping a woman tie up her boat to give them a wave.

'My mother loves it here,' Ronnie told her. 'Just before the war she had a holiday with her family on a narrow boat in this part of the world. She's always said it's her most precious memory of being with them.'

A fly buzzed around her head. She brushed it away with her hand. 'It must have been terrible for her. Losing her family when she was even younger than us.'

'You were only seven when you lost your father.'

'But I still had my mother.'

'I don't know what I'd do if I lost mine.'

'You really love her, don't you?'

He nodded, making waves in the water with his toes. She did the same, enjoying the coldness against her skin.

'Were your relatives really horrible?'

'They were to her.'

'And you by the sound of it. Your cousin using you as a punch bag.'

'It doesn't matter about me. I can take care of myself.'

'Yes, I think you can. Do you take care of her too?'

'Of course.'

'Just like I take care of mine.'

Silence. She waited for him to say something but he just stared across the river.

'Alice must have told you about my mother. I can't believe she'd have missed out something like that.'

'It must have been frightening. At that age you couldn't have understood what was happening to her.'

'I didn't. And it *was* frightening. Very.'

He turned towards her, his eyes sympathetic. 'Do you ever . . .'

'Yes. All the time. But it won't happen again. I won't let it.'

'She's lucky to have someone as strong as you to protect her.'

She struck a boxer's pose.

'That's not what I meant.'

'I know.' A pause. 'Thanks.'

The lock gates opened. Boats drifted out into the river. 'Mum had her holiday on a boat called *Ariel*,' he said. 'She still searches for it sometimes when she comes here.'

'She comes here a lot. I've often seen her. She looks really nice.'

'She is. You'd like her.'

'Your stepfather looks nice too.'

He nodded rather half-heartedly.

'Don't you like him?'

'Of course. He's her husband.'

'That's not a reason to like someone.'

'But it'll do.'

'What was your father like?'

He picked up a stone and skimmed it across the river.

'Your mother must have told you about him.'

A nod.

'It's awful him dying so young. How long were they married?'

'They weren't.'

She was taken aback. 'Really?'

'My father was a soldier. Mum met him at a dance when she was sixteen. He promised her that when the war was over he'd come back and marry her but the war ended and he never came.'

'Is that why your relatives tried to make her give you up?'

'Yes.'

'But she didn't. That was brave.'

'If you got pregnant and weren't married would you give your baby up?'

She had an image of Jennifer lying alone in the dark, watching shadows. Afraid but with no one to help her. 'No. I don't think I could.'

'Are you shocked?'

'Should I be?'

'People in Hepton were. Everyone was always gossiping about it. Using it as a way to put my mother down and make out that she wasn't as good as them.'

'Does anyone know in Kendleton?'

'Only my stepfather.'

'And now me.'

They stared at each other. 'Yes,' he said. 'And now you.'

'Thank you for trusting me. I promise I'll never tell. I know how to keep a secret.'

He skimmed another stone. More boats entered the lock. 'There are other things I could tell you,' he said eventually.

'Are there?'

He looked embarrassed.

'You can tell me, Ronnie. If you want to, that is.'

He took a deep breath. She waited expectantly.

'The capital of Albania is Tirana.'

For a moment she was confused. Then she burst out laughing. 'Idiot!'

'Hardly. I can recite pi to two hundred places.'

'I take it back. You're unbelievably clever.'

'Unlike you.'

'Tarts don't need to be clever.'

'Do you know which film star you really look like?'

'Who?'

'Norma Shearer. People said she had a face unclouded with thought.'

She kicked water at him. He kicked some back. Ducks paddled away from them, squawking reproachfully. 'I know her,' he said, pointing to one with a crooked wing. 'She's always at the bottom of our garden. Mum feeds her so much it's a miracle she doesn't sink.'

'It must be lovely having a garden on the water.'

'Come and see it.'

'I can't do that. Alice will put up roadblocks.'

'Don't worry about those. It's the landmines you need to watch out for. Come for tea next weekend. You can meet Mum.'

He was smiling again. As she looked at him she realized she was happy. That being with him made her feel happier than she had since . . .

Paul.

Her defences resurrected themselves. She was not going to allow another boy to distract her. Now, more than ever before, she had to cut all distractions out of her life.

'I can't. I'm looking after Jennifer at the weekend.'

He looked disappointed. She felt bad. But it couldn't be helped.

'You really love Jennifer, don't you?'

'Yes.'

'And I can keep a secret.'

'What do you mean?'

'Nothing. I just wanted you to know it.'

He was still staring at her. This handsome boy with his air of self-sufficiency and calm. Suddenly she ached to tell him all her secrets. To share her burden with someone who looked as if he might be strong enough to help her carry it. But she couldn't tell anyone. Not ever.

'I have to go, Ronnie.'

'Not yet. I still owe you an ice cream.'

'Another time perhaps.'

'If you go I'll throw myself in the river and the swans will kill me.'

'No they won't.'

'Yes they will. They believe that bathing in human blood keeps their feathers white. I heard that on *Emergency Ward Ten* too.'

Her lips began to twitch. 'Stop trying to make me laugh.'

'Why? It's easier than trying to make you think.'

She kicked more water at him, starting a battle that didn't end until both were drenched.

Fifteen minutes later they entered Cobhams Milk Bar.

All the tables were full with boys and girls from Heathcote and other schools. Martin Phillips sat with Edward Wetherby, but his presence didn't bother her, just as it didn't seem to bother Ronnie.

They stood at the counter, watching the waitress prepare their ice-cream cones. As Ronnie paid for them a girl came to ask for change to put a record on the jukebox.

Then Edward Wetherby called out, 'We've both had your girlfriend, Ronnie.'

The milk bar fell silent. People shifted in their seats, excited at the prospect of trouble. Susan's eyes locked with Ronnie's. He looked completely relaxed and she knew instinctively that whatever he did would be perfect.

Which it was. Without even turning, he replied in a voice clear enough to be heard by everyone: 'I know. And I'd like to thank you for giving her, collectively, the best five seconds of her life.'

The place erupted in laughter. Edward turned crimson. Susan touched Ronnie on the arm. 'Not five seconds, Ronnie,' she said, again loud enough to be heard. 'I told you it was more like seven.' Then leaning forward, so her face and Edward's were almost touching, she lowered her voice to a whisper. 'Just so we're clear, if you fight with him I'll fight with you.' A quick nod in Martin's direction. 'And I'll win.'

The laughter continued. She stood up, taking her ice cream from Ronnie.

'Bring Jennifer at the weekend. Mum won't mind. She loves children.'

'OK.'

'Good.'

They walked out of the milk bar, leaving Edward to his embarrassment.

Tuesday evening. Charles knocked on Ronnie's bedroom door.

Ronnie sat at his desk studying a textbook. 'Am I disturbing you?' asked Charles.

Ronnie shook his head, gesturing to a chair next to the desk. His textbook showed rows of mathematical formulae. Charles shuddered. 'Those look like hieroglyphics to me.'

'Didn't you like maths at school?'

'I hated it. My teacher had a speech impediment so we never understood a word he said. How any of us passed the exam is God's own mystery.'

'My old French teacher was Viennese so we learned to speak

French with an Austrian accent. It was so strong that when our class went to Paris no one there could understand it.'

They both laughed.

'I didn't know you'd been to Paris.'

'I haven't. Mum wanted me to go but couldn't afford the trip.'

Dig.

'She tells me we have guests this weekend.'

'Is that all right? She said you were happy for me to invite friends over.'

'More than happy.' A pause. 'Susan's a beautiful girl.'

Ronnie nodded.

'Do you like her a lot?'

'Yes.'

'You should take her to the pictures some time. Or to see a rock'n'roll group.'

Ronnie looked amused. 'Which group would you recommend?'

'Oh, I don't know. Cliff Richard and the Comets. The Everly Quintuplets.'

Ronnie laughed. Charles was pleased. 'Seriously, Ronnie, if you want to take her somewhere but are strapped for money then let me know. I'd be happy to help out.'

'That's kind.'

'Not at all. Anything to help the path of true love run smooth.'

'But she's not the sort of person who'd like someone just because they had money.'

Dig.

'Well, the offer's there if you need it.'

'I know.' Ronnie smiled. 'Thanks.'

'Is the lip hurting?'

'No. Is Mum still worrying?'

'A bit. But that's a mother's job. Actually, Ronnie, I've been thinking that her bedroom walls look bare. Why don't we have some of your drawings framed so they could hang there?'

'That's a great idea.'

Again Charles was pleased. 'We'll have to pick some out. Say, half a dozen?'

'I can do that. I know the one's she'll like.'

Dig.

But was it really? Were any of them?

'Of course. Let me know when you've chosen.'

'I will.'

Silence. Charles tried to think of something to prolong the conversation. He wanted the two of them to be friends. To be close. He had always longed to be a father and knew from Anna that Ronnie had always felt the absence of one. Now there was nothing to stop each fulfilling such a role for the other.

But only if Ronnie wanted it too.

He stared at the boy who faced him. This handsome, clever boy whose behaviour towards him was never less than gracious.

And who stared back at him with those barrier-like eyes.

What are you hiding, Ronnie? What's going on inside you?

Who is the real Ronnie Sunshine?

He rose to his feet. 'Better let you get back to your hieroglyphics.'

'OK. Thanks again for the offer.'

'My pleasure.'

Two minutes later he entered the living room.

Anna sat sewing name tags into Ronnie's school shirts. 'Where have you been?' she asked.

'Fetching my pipe and having a chat with Ronnie.' He sat down beside her. The television was on. A comedian told mother-in-law jokes to shrieks of laughter from the studio audience. Soon it would be time for a drama series they both enjoyed.

'How is he?'

Charles filled his pipe. 'As well as a boy with maths homework can be.'

'Do you think he's being bullied?'

'No. It was just a scuffle. My friends and I were always having them at school. If you think my face is a mess now you should have seen it when I was Ronnie's age.'

Silence. He had hoped for laughter or better still a gesture of affection. Instead she just sighed.

'You mustn't worry about him, darling. He's tougher than you think.'

'He's never got into fights before.'

'All boys have them occasionally. It's part of growing up.'

'If he got into fights I'd know about it. Ronnie doesn't keep secrets from me.'

'Which means he'd tell you if he were being bullied. If he hasn't then he's not.' He gave her arm a squeeze. 'So stop worrying.'

She continued to sew. He lit his pipe, breathing smoke into the air. Outside, the setting sun sent rays of red and gold across the surface of the river. 'If the good weather lasts,' he said, 'we could have tea in the garden on Saturday. Jennifer could feed the swans.'

For the first time she smiled. 'Is my cooking so bad she'd want to dispose of it?'

'It's inedible. Why do you think I'm putting on so much weight?'

'I think I'll stick to sandwiches and cake. The sort of things young children like to eat.'

'And middle-aged men too. Shaming though it is to admit.'

She laughed. Again he squeezed her arm while the television comedian finished his routine to loud applause.

'I'm glad he's made a friend,' she said eventually.

'I think Ronnie would like her to be more than that.'

'Do you?'

'She's very beautiful.'

'Yes, I suppose she is.'

'As are you.'

She ignored the compliment. 'But Ronnie's too young to be interested in girls.'

He'll be sixteen next month. The same age you were when you met his father.

'Anyway, he'd have told me if he felt anything for her. He tells me everything.'

'Of course.'

'We never have secrets. If he did keep something from me it would be trivial. Nothing that mattered or meant anything.'

He nodded. A strange thought crept into his head. As stealthy as a thief.

Who are you trying to convince, Anna? Me or yourself?

Do you think he's hiding something too?

Her hand slipped, the needle puncturing her finger. She winced, looking suddenly like a wounded child. Love swept over him like a wave. He ached to put his arms around her and hold her close. To keep her safe from harm and pain.

But he couldn't. Their marriage was about friendship, not romantic love. Separate bedrooms and no physical intimacy except for tiny gestures that amply displayed her fondness for him but could not begin to describe the world of emotion he felt for her.

Taking her wounded finger, he pressed it to his lips. 'Does it hurt?' he asked softly.

Her smile returned. 'Not now it's been kissed better.'

'Good.'

'Our programme starts in a few minutes. Shall I go and make some coffee?'

'That would be lovely. Thank you, darling.'

On reaching the door she hesitated, then turned back.

'I'll just check on Ronnie. But I won't be long so keep my seat warm.'

He did. But when the programme ended an hour later it was still empty.

Early evening on Thursday. Ronnie walked with Susan across Market Court.

His legs were aching. They had spent the late afternoon exploring the woods to the west of the town. Her knowledge of them was remarkable. She could navigate their paths almost blindfold and had shown him one, almost hidden by undergrowth, that led all the way to the river bank. 'No one else uses it,' she had told him. 'I don't think they know it's here.' He had found some wild flowers and she had helped him pick them for his mother.

They reached the corner of Queen Anne Square. 'I'll wait for you tomorrow,' he said.

'Don't you ever get tired of hanging around on street corners?'

'No. It's in my blood. I must be descended from housebreakers.'

She laughed. Someone called her name. A tall, plumpish man approached them wearing an expensive suit and a genial expression. 'Hello, Susie. Have you been walking?'

'Yes, Uncle Andrew.'

'And who can blame you on such a lovely afternoon.'

Ronnie held out his hand. 'I'm Ronnie Sidney.'

The man smiled at him. 'And I'm Andrew Bishop, Susie's step-father.' The handshake was firm and friendly. 'Sidney, eh? You're not Mrs Pembroke's son, are you?'

'Yes.'

'Well, welcome to Kendleton. How are you enjoying life here?'

'Very much. Mum said it was beautiful but her letters didn't do it justice.'

'Has Susie been showing you the sights?'

'Yes.'

'Then I'll know who to blame when her homework suffers.' Mr Bishop laughed affably.

Ronnie turned to Susan, relieved that his first meeting with a member of her family seemed to be going well. She smiled at him, looking just as she always did.

But something about her was different.

He knew it instinctively. A change he couldn't see so much as feel. Her physical presence was diminished. The aura of invulnerability reduced. This girl who had more courage than anyone he'd ever met. Who wasn't afraid of anyone.

But she's afraid of him.

'Are those flowers for your mother?' asked Mr Bishop.

'Yes, provided they haven't died before I get them home.' He laughed too, giving no indication that he had noticed anything. 'Actually Mum's invited Susie and Jennifer to come for tea on Saturday.'

'How kind of her.' Mr Bishop beamed at Susan. 'What a lovely treat for Jenjen.'

Susan nodded. 'Yes, she'll really enjoy it.' She was still smiling and her voice was steady but her body discharged tension like electric waves. Particularly when the abbreviation of Jennifer's name was used.

'We'd better get home,' said Mr Bishop. 'Susie's mother gets very cross if we're late for tea.' He grinned at Susan. 'Doesn't she, Susie?'

'Yes, Uncle Andrew. 'Bye, Ronnie.'

''Bye, Susie. Goodbye, Mr Bishop. It was nice to meet you.'

'And you, Ronnie. See you again soon, I hope.'

They walked away. Mr Bishop turned and gave him a wave.

Why is she afraid? What have you done to make her afraid?

Still smiling, he waved back.

Saturday afternoon. Charles sat in the garden with Anna, Ronnie and their guests.

They had an extra guest that afternoon: Mary Norris, widow of his friend Dr Henry Norris who had died of a stroke the previous winter. He and Henry had been undergraduates together and Mary had an open invitation to visit whenever she wanted.

It was proving a lively gathering. Jennifer was treating them to a medley of songs she had learned at school. A spirited performance of 'Land of the Buffalo' had just been eclipsed by an even more passionate rendition of 'Little Donkey'.

'Now I'm going to sing "My Old Man Said Follow the Van",' she announced.

'That's enough singing for now, Jenjen,' said Susan quickly.

'No it's not. Mrs Boyd said I sang it best in the class.'

'And I'd love to hear it,' added Mary.

'See.' Jennifer gave Susan a meaningful look then once again burst into song. Charles, fighting an urge to laugh, noticed Mary's lips also twitching. He caught her eye across the table and gave her a grin.

The table was laden with food. Sandwiches, crisps and an assortment of buns and cakes, all of which Anna had made herself. Jennifer, stopped singing mid-verse, gulped down some lemonade, gave a contented sigh and started up again. Charles's need to laugh increased. Biting down on his lip, he watched swans land on the water and swim towards the bank. Though the sun was bright there was a nip in the air, warning that autumn was finally on the way.

At last Jennifer finished. 'That really is enough now, Jenjen,' said Susan firmly.

'But it was a lovely treat,' Mary told her. 'You sing very well.'

'Thank you.' Jennifer gave her a dazzling smile, then turned to

Charles and gave him one too. Something she had been doing on a regular basis since her arrival. He smiled back, careful to keep the damaged side of his face from view.

'Would you like some chocolate cake, Jennifer?' asked Anna.

'Yes please.'

'Would you like to be a singer when you grow up?' asked Mary.

Jennifer nodded. 'Or a cowboy. I know a song about cowboys.'

'Which you're *not* going to sing,' Susan told her.

Jennifer looked indignant. 'Why don't you sing it to us after tea?' suggested Mary, and was rewarded with another dazzling smile. As was Charles, though he wasn't sure why.

More swans approached the bank. 'We can feed them later,' Anna told Jennifer.

'Do you like swans, Jennifer?' asked Mary.

'Yes. Susie and I feed them bread by the lock.'

'Then you don't want to be a cowboy,' Ronnie told her. 'There aren't any swans where cowboys live. Only buffaloes and coyotes and Red Indians with tomahawks.' He gave an Indian war cry that made her giggle. Susan smiled, but only briefly. She seemed subdued and not entirely comfortable.

'Would you like some more food?' Charles asked her.

'No thank you, Mr Pembroke.' She sipped her lemonade, staring down at the table. On first arriving she had appeared sure of herself but that confidence had quickly evaporated. Again he wondered why.

'Did you ever want to be a cowboy, Ronnie?' asked Mary.

'Ronnie always wanted to be an artist,' answered Anna, looking proudly at her son. 'From the moment he first picked up a pencil.'

Mary turned to Susan. 'And what about you, dear? What would you like to be?'

'I don't know.'

'No ideas yet?'

Susan shook her head. She seemed particularly awkward with Mary, though there was no need to be. Mary liked young people and they usually liked her too. Jennifer certainly did.

And Susan had seemed to at first. The two of them had been talking quite happily.

Up until the moment when Mary revealed who her husband had been.

Charles felt a rumbling at the back of his head. The hiss of a memory yet to take shape.

'Of course,' continued Mary, 'you could be a model with your wonderful looks.'

'My dad says that too,' Jennifer told her between mouthfuls of cake.

Mary nodded. 'My cousin's daughter is a model and she's nowhere near as beautiful as you. She lives in London now and is always going to parties with actors.'

'That's what Susie should be,' said Ronnie.

'What? An actor . . . I mean actress?'

'Not just an actress. A film star. That's what she looks like. A film star.'

'You're right,' agreed Mary. 'She does.'

The rumbling in Charles's head grew louder.

And suddenly, the memory came.

He was sitting in a pub with Henry, listening to him talk about a girl patient he had treated for venereal disease. A disease she had contracted from her father.

Such a beautiful kid too. Looks like a film star.

And how many girls in Kendleton looked like Susan?

Her father would have been dead by then. Long dead.

But not her stepfather.

He couldn't be sure, of course. Yet he was.

A shiver ran through him. As if someone had walked over his grave.

Jennifer gave him yet another smile then turned to Susan and said, 'Was Mrs Hopkins in the library brave in the war?'

'Why do you ask that, dear?' asked Mary.

'Because she's got a horrid face.'

'Shut up, Jenjen!' hissed Susan.

'But you said Mr Pembroke had a horrid face 'cos he was brave in the war.'

Susan turned crimson. Everyone else looked flustered except Jennifer, who just looked confused.

'I don't think this is a horrid face,' Charles told her. 'At least not as horrid as this one.' He stuck out his tongue and began to wiggle his ears.

Jennifer shrieked with laughter.

'Or this one.' He struck another pose.

The others relaxed. Mary and Ronnie began to laugh too.

'And look at this.' He performed an optical illusion, seeming to remove his thumb and then replace it. Jennifer squeaked, her eyes almost popping out of her head.

'It looks like magic, Jennifer, but it's easy really. Shall I show you how to do it?'

Jennifer leapt from her seat and rushed to stand by his. 'Show me!'

So he did. Teaching her the trick while the others offered encouragement. He kept glancing at Susan but her eyes remained focused on Jennifer and she didn't seem to notice.

Half an hour later, he sat smoking his pipe and watching the others feed the swans.

'Mr Pembroke.'

Susan stood beside his chair, looking as awkward as she had earlier. 'I wanted to say that I'm very sorry . . .'

'I'm extremely flattered you think I'm brave. That's a great compliment to pay someone.' He smiled. 'However undeserved.'

The awkwardness vanished, replaced by a smile of her own. He realized that she reminded him of Eleanor, the girl he had been engaged to before his accident. Susan was more beautiful but the resemblance was still there.

'So please don't feel embarrassed. There's no need. Especially as it gave me the chance to display my prowess as a magician.'

'Which is very good.' A pause. 'Unlike Jennifer's singing.'

'I disagree. Her rendition of "Little Donkey" had real pathos.'

'She sings all the time! It's like being with a walking jukebox except that unlike a jukebox you can't switch her off.'

He laughed. Jennifer, helped by Ronnie, climbed into a tree that hung over the water. 'That's the wonderful thing about being that age,' he said. 'You know no fear. Life is one big adventure. It's only as you grow older that you learn how to be afraid.'

Her eyes became thoughtful. He waited for a reply but none came.
'Wouldn't you agree?'

'Not for her.'

'We're all afraid sometimes. Even the bravest of us.'

'She won't ever be if I can help it. I want her to stay just the way she is.'

'She's lucky to have you as a friend.'

'Why?'

'Because you strike me as someone it would take a great deal to frighten.'

Another smile. 'Don't you believe it. All sorts of things frighten me.'

'Like what?'

'School lunches. French homework. Not getting picked for the lacrosse team.'

And what your stepfather did to you in the dark when there was no one there to help.

Jennifer called out to Susan. 'You're being summoned,' he told her.

She nodded, turned to go, then turned back.

'Thanks, Mr Pembroke.'

'My pleasure.'

He remained in his seat, breathing smoke into the air. Jennifer sat in the tree, throwing bread to the swans beneath. Susan climbed up beside her, holding her round the middle, whispering into her ear. Briefly Jennifer looked over in his direction. He gave her a wave and received a huge grin in return.

Anna stood with Mary, observing the scene just as he was. He hoped she had enjoyed the afternoon and had seen Susan for what she was. Genuine. Warm hearted. And no threat.

Time passed. Susan said they had to go. Jennifer ran over to where he sat. 'Thank you for teaching me the trick,' she told him before kissing him on the cheek. He was touched that a child would want to kiss so damaged a face. As, perhaps, Susan had intended.

He watched them walk away. Ronnie was going with them as far as Market Court. Jennifer held Susan's hand, swinging her arm through the air. A pretty little girl with reddish blonde hair who loved to sing and knew nothing about being afraid.

But Susan did. He was sure of it.

A very great deal.

'What charming girls,' observed Mary. 'It's lovely they're so fond of each other.'

He nodded, keeping his worries to himself.

Ronnie stood on the corner of Queen Anne Square, waiting while Susan walked Jennifer the rest of the way home.

His shoulders ached. Jennifer had sat astride them for much of the journey, singing yet more songs. Not that he had minded. He liked Jennifer.

As they crossed the square, Susan's front door opened. Mr Bishop appeared, calling out to them. They stood waiting for him, Jennifer bouncing up and down excitedly while Susan smiled and seemed diminished. Just as she had before.

Mr Bishop squatted on his haunches and said something to Jennifer. She started to laugh. He tickled her ribs then picked her up, throwing her into the air and catching her, stroking her hair and kissing her cheek. Still laughing, she kissed him back.

And Susan shuddered. Even though her smile remained in place.

Suddenly Ronnie was back in Hepton, watching Vera humiliate his mother. Sitting in silence at the kitchen table, night after night, masking the fury that burned inside him like acid at the pain being inflicted on someone he loved with all his heart.

Just as he loved Susan.

He knew it now. As clearly as he knew his own name. This girl who was like no one he had ever met before. Whose beauty, strength and courage left all others in the shade. But who was still capable of being hurt.

And no one could hurt someone he loved. He would not allow it. Anyone who did so would be sorry. Vera had already discovered that.

Now Andrew Bishop would discover it too.

Sunday morning. Susan made her way downstairs to breakfast.

She tiptoed past Uncle Andrew's bedroom. He had still not returned from the pub when she had gone to bed the previous evening. It had been the same story four nights earlier. His drinking, briefly curtailed, was now as bad as before. As was his temper. Their joint return bewildered her mother but not her. She understood what was happening. What was going on inside his head.

He's getting impatient. He can't wait until January. He wants Jenjen now.

On reaching the bottom of the stairs she heard his voice. So he was up already. Her heart sank.

But he sounded excited. Animated. Unheard of when he was battling a hangover.

What was going on?

She stood behind the dining-room door, holding her breath and listening.

'So he'll go, then?' asked her mother.

'I should think so. Why wait until January if they want him to start in November? It's all sorted this end except for a tenant for the house, and estate agents will take care of that.'

'But do you really think it's a good idea for Susie to move in the middle of a term?'

An impatient snort. 'Why not, for heaven's sake? It's an excellent school and they don't seem to mind her coming early.' A laugh. 'Mind you, they'll be getting an extra term's fees so they're hardly going to complain.'

'It just seems so rushed.'

'Well, it's not.' Again the impatience. 'They're not expecting her until mid-October so you've got at least three weeks to get her ready. That's plenty of time, even for you.'

Three weeks? I could be in Scotland in three weeks?

Her heart began to race. This couldn't be happening. She needed more time to think and to plan. Much more.

A floorboard creaked beneath her foot. 'Is that you, Susie?' her mother called out.

She entered the room. Uncle Andrew frowned. 'You're late. We eat breakfast at nine o'clock on Sunday.'

'Only by five minutes.' She struggled to keep her voice steady.

'But still late.'

'I'm sorry.' She kissed his cheek. His breath reeked of stale alcohol. He was still frowning but his eyes looked through her as if she were a spectre. The ghost of midnights past, now being rushed from the stage to make room for the ghost of midnights still to come.

After kissing her mother she sat down, pouring herself some tea and spreading butter on to toast. Keeping her breathing steady. Forcing herself to be calm. When they told her about the changed plans she would look upset but resigned. Keeping up the façade. Giving nothing away.

It's just acting, Susie. You can do it. You know you can.

'Did you sleep well?' asked her mother.

'Yes, thanks.'

Uncle Andrew gestured towards the window. 'It looks like being a nice day. We should all go for a walk this afternoon. Down by the river, perhaps.'

'That sounds like a lovely idea,' said her mother.

'Then it's agreed.' Uncle Andrew leant back in his chair and stretched. 'Susie, you must bring Jenjen. She loves it by the water.'

Her mouth was full of toast. For a moment she needed to retch. She couldn't bear him being close to Jennifer. Touching her. Holding her. Making her laugh. Teaching her to trust him. Just as he had done with another little girl not so many years ago.

Three weeks. That's all I've got. Three weeks.

But I can do it. I can. For Jenjen I can.

Oh God, I hope I can.

She swallowed and smiled.

'That would be nice,' she said.

'What's the matter, Susie? What's going on?'

'Nothing.'

Monday afternoon after school. She walked deep into the woods with Ronnie.

She hadn't wanted to see him. Had tried to avoid him in fact. Leaving for school far earlier than usual and sitting in the library at the end of the day. But when finally she had emerged through the gates he had been waiting.

And she had been glad. Even though she hadn't wanted to be.

She sat on the trunk of a fallen tree. He sat beside her. 'These woods are supposed to be haunted,' she said. 'There's a story that hundreds of years ago a mother had a picnic here with her daughter. After they'd eaten it the mother went to sleep and the daughter wandered off and was never seen again. The mother went mad, so the story goes. She spent the rest of her life searching these woods. and now if you come far enough in and sit and listen you can still hear her calling for her daughter to come home.'

'Have you ever heard her?'

'I thought I did once but it was only my imagination. It's just a story, like I said.'

'I could tell you a story. One that nobody knows but me.'

She scratched at the earth with a stick. 'Tell me, then.'

'I hated my aunt. Of all my relatives she was the one I hated most. Not for the way she treated me but for the way she treated my mother. Ordering her around like a skivvy. Humiliating her in front of others. Always reminding her that she could yank the roof from over our heads whenever she wanted.

'One day she made my mother cry and I couldn't stand it any more. I decided I was going to make her sorry. So I hid a roller skate by the cooker while she was making supper. She tripped on it and poured boiling chip fat down her arm. It left her scarred. Even now, when it's really hot, she wears long sleeves to hide it.

'No one ever guessed it was me. They thought it was an accident. I tried to tell my mother once but she wouldn't listen. I'm her perfect son, you see, and perfect sons don't hurt people. But I'm not ashamed of what I did. As I see it, if someone hurts a person you love then you hurt them back. I hurt my aunt because she hurt my mother, and if someone else were to hurt her then I'd hurt them too.'

She turned towards him. 'Why are you telling me this?'

'Because your stepfather's hurting you.'

Silence. Except for the wind stirring the branches of the trees.

'I've got eyes, Susie. I see how you are with him.'

'And how is that?'

'Afraid.'

She began to tremble. The need to unburden herself was like a physical pain. But it was too dangerous.

'Tell me.'

'I can't.'

'Yes you can.'

Another silence. She looked at the trees that surrounded them. The leaves were changing from green to brown. Soon they would be falling, covering the ground like a blanket.

'He does hurt you, doesn't he?'

'Not any more.'

'What did he do to you? You can trust me. You know that, don't you?'

'He told me that once.'

'But I'm not him.'

She stared at him. This boy with his contained strength who defended her when others tried to put her down. Who made her feel happy. Who made her feel . . .

. . . safe.

'You have to swear on your life that you'll never tell.'

'Not on my life. On my mother's, because that's the most precious thing I have.'

'Swear it, then. On her life.'

'I swear.'

So she told him. The secret she had kept hidden inside herself for nearly eight years. The wind caught her words as soon as they were spoken, dashing them against the trees as if trying to help keep her secret too. He listened, saying nothing, just watching her with eyes that were warm and did not judge.

'He gave me gonorrhoea when I was thirteen. The doctor who treated me was Mary's husband. We told him a story about a boy at a party but he knew what was really going on. When I realized who Mary was it brought it all back. Not that she'd know. Doctors can't talk about their patients, not even to their wives.' She gave a hollow laugh. 'I should be a doctor. I'd be good at the secrecy part.'

He shook his head. 'Oh, Susie . . .'

'What frightens you? I mean more than anything else?'

'Never finding anyone who really understands me. Of always feeling alone.'

'For me it's a dream I've had since it started. In it I've died and gone to heaven to be with my father. I'm so excited about seeing him again that I'm crying. But when we meet he tells me that he hates me. He says I'm wicked and that everything that's happened is my fault. That I wanted it to happen. That he's ashamed to even look at me, let alone call me his daughter.'

'But dreams aren't real, Susie. You know what happened wasn't your fault. How could you stop it? You were only a little child. If your father were here now he'd say the same thing. And he'd tell you that he was proud to call you his daughter, not ashamed.'

A lump came into her throat. She tried to swallow it down. Determined to stay strong. 'It doesn't matter what he thinks, anyway. He wasn't so special. Just some man who ran a photography shop, told lousy jokes and was hopeless with money. He left us in debt when he died. That's how wonderful he was. Good riddance, I say.'

Then she burst into tears.

He tried to put his arm around her but she pushed him away, pounding her temple with her fist, giving physical expression to the anger she felt with herself. 'Weak. Weak!'

'You're not weak, Susie. That's the last thing you are.'

'But Jennifer is.'

'What do you mean?'

'He's going to start on her. He's been planning it for months. I'm being sent away and she's being moved into my bedroom. She's only six! Just a baby. He thinks I can't stop him. He knows no one will believe me if I tell them. Not when it's his word against mine.'

She took a deep breath. The air was damp. Rain was only moments away.

'But I *can* still stop him. There's one final thing I can do.'

'Kill him.'

'Yes.'

They stared at each other. She wiped her eyes, feeling suddenly weightless. The burden she had carried alone for so long had at last been lifted.

'I'll do it for you,' he said.

For a moment she thought she'd misheard. 'What?'

'I'll do it for you.'

'Why?'

'Because I love you.'

A drop of rain fell on to his cheek. She felt one land on hers too.

'I love you, Susie, and I'll do it for you. All you have to do is ask.'

'We can't stay here,' she said.

They made their way back through the woods, leaving the ghost mother to cry unheard.

By the time they reached town the rain was heavy. They took shelter in Cobhams Milk Bar.

It was nearly empty. Most of their peers were eating their tea at home. They sat at a table in the corner, far away from wagging ears, drinking coffee and watching each other through the rising steam.

'I meant what I said,' he told her.

'No you didn't.'

'You think I'm afraid to do it?'

'Aren't you?'

'I told you what frightens me.'

'And murder isn't on the list?' She shook her head. 'You're mad.'

'That's why I should do it. You're frightened. I'm not.'

'Of course I'm frightened! Imagine if it went wrong. Imagine getting caught.'

'That won't happen.'

'But what if it did?'

'Then I'd take the blame. I'd say it was all my idea. That you knew nothing about it. And they'd believe me because I know how to act. I'm good at it. I've been acting for people all my life. Even my mother.'

'And you'd do that for me?'

'I would.'

She gazed into his eyes. Two beautiful grey-green orbs with centres of steel. The eyes of someone who would not allow themselves to be crippled by fear. Who had real strength.

But she had strength too.

'I don't want you to do it, Ronnie.'

'But . . .'

'Not alone. We do it together. I'm not afraid any more. You don't have to help me if you don't want to. If you change your mind I'll understand. But if we do it together then we sink or swim together and that means that if we get caught we take the blame together.'

'We won't get caught. We can do this. We're both clever and we both know how to act. Nothing can stop us. Not if we're together.'

'And we are.'

'I love you, Susie.'

A lump came into her throat. Just as it had in the wood.

'I love you too.'

She did.

'You should have told me you were going to be late.'

'I'm sorry, Mum.'

Eight o'clock that evening. Anna watched Ronnie eat a supper of roast beef. Charles was away, attending a university dinner in Oxford.

'I thought something might have happened to you.'

'You worry too much.' He smiled at her. 'I'm a big boy now.'

'Of course I worry. I'm your mother. That's my job.'

'Well, you don't need to. I can take care of myself.' He cut into his beef, his knife slipping and splashing gravy on to the tablecloth.

It was her turn to smile. 'So I see.'

He looked sheepish. 'Sorry.'

'Never mind. It can be washed. Are you enjoying it?'

'It's delicious. Thanks, Mum.' He took another mouthful, a contented look on his face. It put her in mind of an old saying: the way to a man's heart is through his stomach.

But Ronnie's not a man. Not yet.

And I already have his heart.

'It's nice being just the two of us, isn't it?'

He nodded.

'I keep expecting Vera to barge in and start giving orders. I'm surprised she hasn't been in contact since you left Hepton.'

'She won't be in contact. Not ever.'

'How can you be so sure?'

'Just a feeling,' he said, though his tone was certain. She nodded and found herself thinking of the locked drawer where he kept his secrets. Except that he had no secrets. Not from her. At least none that meant anything.

'How's Susan?'

'Fine. She really enjoyed Saturday. She was saying how much she liked you.'

'Did Jennifer like me?'

'Yes, but not as much as she liked your cakes.'

'And how much do you like her?'

'She'd be perfect if it wasn't for the singing.'

'I meant Susan.'

A nod.

'Well?'

'I like her a lot.'

'How much is a lot?'

'She's a good friend.'

'And a beautiful one.'

Another nod.

'I liked her, too.'

He continued eating. She watched him, wishing he would open up. Not wanting to appear inquisitive.

Not wanting him to know she was jealous.

'Have you met her parents?'

'Only her stepfather. He seemed very nice.'

'Ben Logan says he drinks. Ben often sees him walking past the lock looking the worse for wear.'

'Perhaps he drinks to forget.'

'Forget what?'

'Jennifer's singing.' He began to hum 'The Good Ship Lollipop', while sticking roast potatoes on the end of his knife and fork and making them skip like Charlie Chaplin's dance of the bread rolls in *The Gold Rush*. The sight rendered her helpless with laughter. He watched her, grinning. She knew he liked being able to make her laugh more than anyone else.

Can you make Susan laugh this hard too? And are you as happy when you do?

Or even happier?

He continued the performance. She focused on her amusement, trying to push the questions from her mind.

Tuesday afternoon. Alice Wetherby walked home with Kate Christie, who kept talking about a boy she had met at a family party the previous weekend. 'Can't you talk about something else?' Alice snapped. 'He sounds incredibly boring.'

Kate frowned. 'Don't take it out on me because Ronnie doesn't like you.'

'I don't care about that. I didn't like him anyway.'

'Not much you didn't. Serves you right, too. You're always acting like you can have any boy you want. Looks like you were wrong.'

'That's the point. I *didn't* want him. Who'd want some pathetic mother's boy. He's probably queer anyway. Boys who like art usually are.'

'Maybe you should ask Susan if he's queer. She should know.'

'I don't care,' said Alice forcefully. 'It doesn't matter to me.'

Except, of course, that it mattered a great deal. Ronnie was the first boy she had ever had feelings for and to discover that he preferred someone else had hurt more than she could have imagined. Especially when that someone was Susan Ramsey.

She needed to take her pain out on someone but Kate was not proving a satisfactory target.

Then they entered Market Court and she saw a better one.

Ronnie's mother was entering Fisher's Bookshop. Pretty, timid, common Anna Sidney, who adored her precious son and had married a deformed freak in a pathetic attempt to buy them both respectability.

'Do you want to have some fun?' she asked Kate.

Anna stood in the art section of the shop, looking for birthday presents for Ronnie, relishing the fact that expense was no longer a consideration.

She found a book about Millais and began to skim through its pages, checking that his favourite painting of Ophelia was included among the illustrations.

And heard someone say his name.

Two people were talking about him, both female, on the other side of the shelves.

'I like him. He's really nice.'

'That's why Susie's chasing him. Nice people are more fun to hurt.'

The first voice was unfamiliar. The second belonged to Alice Wetherby.

'Paul Benson was nice too.'

'And look what she did to him. He'd just lost his mother and she comes along and is all nice and concerned and I really care about you and isn't it a shame your father doesn't. She really damaged that relationship. Edward says that before she got involved Paul and his father were close but now they don't get on at all.'

'Ronnie's really close to his mother, isn't he?'

'Not for much longer. She'll find a chink and start scratching at it. Your mother doesn't care about you, Ronnie. Not now she's got her rich husband. Ronnie's mother's nice but she's a bit pathetic. Susie will eat her alive.' A sigh. 'Oh well. It's not my problem. I can't see that book. It must be out of stock. Let's go.'

Footsteps moved away. A bell rang as the door of the shop opened and shut.

Anna remained where she was, the book on Millais still clutched in her hand.

She told herself that it was nonsense. Alice had been attracted to Ronnie but he was attracted to someone else. Her words were prompted by jealousy and spite.

She paid for the book. The assistant complimented her on her choice. 'It's a birthday present for my son,' she explained. 'Millais is his favourite painter.'

The assistant smiled. 'He's lucky to have a mother who knows what he likes.'

And it was true. She did know what Ronnie liked. She knew him better than anyone. Their bond was as strong as steel and no third person could ever break it.

Not that any such person existed. It was all spite.

It was. She was sure of it.

She walked out of the shop. Two elderly women stood on the

pavement talking about the weather. One tapped the other on the arm and pointed. 'What a beautiful couple.'

Ronnie and Susan were walking through the Court. They moved slowly, arm in arm, deep in conversation and with their heads almost touching. Others were watching them too, but they didn't seem to notice. Too wrapped up in each other to care.

And they *were* beautiful. Radiant and magnetic. Like a pair of young film stars carefully paired so their colouring would enhance that of the other while completely extinguishing all those who came into their orbit.

'The girl is Susan Ramsey,' one of the women said, 'but I don't know who the boy is.' Anna wanted to tell them he was her son but held back, suddenly fearful that she would not be believed.

Ronnie's mother's nice but she's a bit pathetic.

Too pathetic to hold on to Ronnie if someone else chose to steal him away?

But Susan didn't want to steal him. She was a nice girl. She was. She really was.

He'd just lost his mother and she comes along and is all nice and concerned . . .

She'll find a chink and start scratching at it.

But that would never happen. Ronnie needed her as much as she needed him. She knew him better than Susan ever could. There were no secrets. Nothing she did not know.

But what about the drawer?

Ronnie and Susan continued on their way, still attracting stares as they took the path that led to the river, drawing some of the light after them.

Half an hour later. Anna sat on Ronnie's bed, staring at the desk drawer.

It was locked, just as it always was. He kept it so believing he had the only key.

Unaware that she had kept one too.

She held it in her hand, the metal cool against her skin. A quick look. That was all. Only a second and it would be done.

Rising from the bed, she walked towards the desk.

Then stopped.

She couldn't do it. He was her son. Her Ronnie Sunshine. And the contents of the drawer would be sunshine too. No darkness. No shadows. Nothing to make her afraid.

Everything is all right. Susan is no threat. Ronnie is yours and whatever secrets he has are meaningless.

It's true. You know it is.

She walked out of the room, leaving the drawer undisturbed.

Thursday evening. Andrew Bishop sat in the living room of his home.

He was feeling irritable. Susan had invited Ronnie Sidney for supper without asking permission first. Not that it would have been granted. The last thing he wanted at his dinner table was tedious adolescent chatter. He had considered revoking the invitation but decided against it. Ronnie's stepfather was a rich and useful contact. Better not risk giving offence.

And it wouldn't happen again. Within weeks Susan would be in Scotland.

Besides, there were consolations. Jennifer was having supper with them too. 'She likes Ronnie,' Susan had explained. 'You don't mind, do you?' And he had shaken his head and said, 'Of course not. She's almost family, isn't she?'

Jennifer sat at his feet, wearing a blue dress, playing with the doll's house he had given Susan after her father died. Moving dolls from room to room, singing to herself.

'Having fun, Jenjen?' he asked.

She nodded.

'Are you making up a story?'

'Yes.'

He patted his knee. 'Come and tell it to me.'

She climbed into his lap, the fabric of her dress sliding up to reveal her thighs. He felt an ache in his groin. The desire to touch them was almost overwhelming.

But he could be patient. Not much longer now.

Jennifer prattled on, beaming from ear to ear. She was very pretty. Just as Susan had been. He put his arms around her, tickling her ribs and kissing her cheek. Giggling, she kissed him back. She didn't yet know that this would soon be her home. When she found out she would be upset, but not for long. She loved her Uncle Andrew. Just as Susan had.

She continued to smile. Her pale blue eyes wide and trusting. But knowing too.

Just as Susan's had been.

She wants it to happen. Deep down I know she does.

A bottle of whisky stood on the table at the centre of the room together with a box of chocolates. Presents from Ronnie. It was good whisky. He would enjoy drinking it when the time came.

From the distance came the sound of clattering pans. His wife was making chicken casserole. There were voices in the hallway. Susan was talking to Ronnie. He could see them through the half-open door. Susan's face was anxious. Troubled.

His curiosity roused, he began to watch.

Susan touched Ronnie's arm. He smiled at her, looking suddenly uncomfortable. She leant across and kissed his face. Still smiling, he moved very slightly away, then wiped his cheek. Susan looked hurt. Rejected.

Andrew experienced an odd sense of déjà vu. Though why he couldn't say.

Jennifer continued to tell her story. Susan entered the room. 'I'm going to help Mum.' Ronnie remained in the doorway, still looking uncomfortable.

'Enjoying school, Ronnie?' he asked.

'Yes. The facilities are amazing. Especially the sports pitches. At my old school all we had was a patch of grass marked out with weedkiller.'

'I'm sure it wasn't that bad.'

'Well, there was a good side. If you wanted to get out of games you just fell on a patch of dead grass and started screaming about industrial burns.'

He laughed. Jennifer frowned. 'What are 'dustrial burns?'

Susan reappeared. 'Uncle Andrew, Mum says could you come and taste the casserole. She's not sure if she's put enough salt in.'

'Of course. I'll come now.'

The kitchen was hot and stuffy. He tasted the casserole while his wife watched him anxiously. 'Fine,' he told her. She nodded while Susan stood by sniffing.

'Getting a cold?' he asked.

'I think so.'

'Well, try and keep it to yourself.' He made his way back to the living room, choking down irritation as Susan gave a thunderous sneeze.

When he reached the doorway he stopped and stared.

Jennifer and Ronnie were crouched together by the doll's house. Jennifer was poking around in the rooms, completely wrapped up in her imaginary story. Once again her skirt had slid up revealing her thighs.

And Ronnie was stroking them.

His fingers slid over them so lightly they barely touched the skin. Not enough contact for Jennifer to even notice. A gesture that could possibly be taken as one of innocent affection, were it not for the look of frustrated desire on his face.

A strange tremor ran through Andrew. A mixture of shock and recognition.

And excitement.

He cleared his throat. Both looked round. Jennifer gave him a wave. Ronnie's eyes widened with alarm.

'Having fun?' he asked, smiling and pretending to have noticed nothing.

Instantly Ronnie relaxed. 'Jennifer's telling me a wonderful story.'

'I'm sure she is.'

Susan appeared, still sniffing. 'Jenjen, come and help me lay the table.'

'I can help too,' said Ronnie.

'Don't worry. Jenjen and I can do it.' Her tone was civil but cool.

Susan and Jennifer left the room. Ronnie rose to his feet. Fleetingly Andrew glanced at his groin, noticing a faint bulge that could have been the fold of his trousers.

Could have been.

'Jenjen's got quite an imagination,' he said affably.

Ronnie nodded. 'Carol did too.'

'Carol?'

'The daughter of our neighbours in Hepton. I used to babysit for her. It was an easier way to earn money than having a paper round.'

I bet it was.

'Thanks again for the whisky. I'll enjoy it.'

Ronnie gazed longingly at the bottle.

'Do you like whisky?'

A guilty look. 'I've never tried it.'

'Really?'

The expression became sheepish. 'Well, a couple of times.'

'And did you like it?'

'Yes, but it doesn't like me. I had some at my aunt's Christmas party and ended up telling Mum I'd cheated in one of my exams.' A grimace. 'She was horrified.'

'I'm sure I cheated in the odd exam when I was your age.' A quick wink. 'And I used to sneak the odd whisky too from my father's cabinet.'

'And then fill it up with water?'

'Yes.'

Ronnie grinned. 'So did I. Carol's father had a bottle in his cupboard. I was sure he'd notice but fortunately he never did.'

What else didn't he notice? What else did you do when you and Carol were alone?

And will you tell me? When a few swigs of whisky have loosened your tongue?

The ache in his groin had returned. He swallowed. His throat was dry.

'Susie says you like history.'

'Yes.'

'I've got some eighteenth-century prints of Kendleton in my study. Perhaps, after supper, you'd like to come up and have a look.'

'I'd like that. Thank you, Mr Bishop.'

'My pleasure, Ronnie. My pleasure.'

Saturday afternoon. Susan stood on a street in Oxford, looking at her watch.

Someone called her name. Charles Pembroke approached. 'Hello, Susan. What are you doing here?'

'Just some shopping.'

'Did you come by bus?'

'Yes.'

'My car's here. I could give you a lift home but I wouldn't mind a coffee first. Will you join me?'

'I'd like that.'

Five minutes later they sat together in a smart tea shop.

'Ronnie not with you, then?' he asked.

'No. I'm trying to find him a birthday present. I think he's doing some homework, though he said he might go for a walk.'

As had Uncle Andrew. The two of them might even run into each other.

'So what have you bought him?'

'Nothing yet. He's difficult to buy for. Clever people always are.'

'And he's certainly that.'

'Do you think he'll get into Oxford?'

'Yes, if he wants to. As will you.'

'I won't. Not a chance.'

'There's every chance for someone with your brains.'

She smiled. 'What brains? You should see my school reports.'

'And you should have seen mine. I was the despair of my teachers.'

She was taken aback. 'You're really clever.'

'But I hated school. Not because it was an awful place but because I had an awful home life.'

'Why?' she asked, and then felt embarrassed. 'Sorry. It's none of my business.'

'Don't apologize. I brought it up. It was because of my father. He could be charming when he wanted to but he also had a temper, and when he drank, which he did a lot, he took it out on my stepmother and younger brother. I always felt it was my job to protect them but I never knew how. I used to worry about them and him all the time and it affected my ability to concentrate.'

'So how did you learn how to concentrate?'

'My history teacher befriended me. I think he realized I wasn't quite the simpleton others believed me to be. He encouraged me to confide in him and advised me on how to deal with the situation. Just being able to share my worries with someone really helped.'

He smiled at her. His eyes were kind. Just as his teacher's must have been.

Just as her father's had been.

Suddenly she felt the urge to tell him everything. To confide in him. To have him advise her on what she should do.

But Uncle Andrew had once reminded her of her father too. And she already knew what she had to do.

'I don't have that excuse. My home life's fine. I'm just lazy.' Quickly she changed the subject. 'Jennifer's learnt some new songs.'

For a moment she thought he looked disappointed. But she could have been mistaken.

Then he smiled again. 'And you're happy about that?'

'Not as much as the farmers. She sings when we walk near their fields and now all their cows have stopped giving milk.'

He burst out laughing. A woman on a nearby table gawped at his damaged face. The sight made Susan angry. 'Can we help you?' she called out. Flushing, the woman looked away.

'That was a bit hard,' he told her.

'She was staring. It's rude.'

'But it's natural. Besides, it doesn't bother me.'

Something told her that this wasn't completely true. But perhaps it was.

She hoped so.

'Anyway, Ronnie's mother screamed when she first saw me and now we're married. Trust me, our fellow diner will have decided I'm the love of her life before she's finished her cream slice.'

It was her turn to laugh. He looked pleased. His eyes really were like her father's. She remembered the way he had put her at ease the previous Saturday and felt a warmth in the pit of her stomach.

I like you. You're a good man. You really are.

Again she felt the urge to confide. But she suppressed it. He wasn't her father and the only person she could depend on was herself.

And Ronnie.

Eight o'clock that evening. On the pretext of going to post a letter, she met Ronnie.

'It went perfectly,' he said.

'Did anyone see you?'

'No. People saw him, though. The lock-keeper for one.'

'He was drinking at lunchtime. Nearly a bottle of wine.'

'It made him a bit unsteady on his feet. The lock-keeper will have seen that too.'

How long were you together?'

'An hour. He brought Carol up after fifteen minutes. Casually, like it wasn't important. I didn't say anything explicit. Just enough to make sure he'd want to meet again.'

'When?'

'Next Sunday. Like we agreed. With whisky this time to loosen my tongue.'

She nodded.

'I can do it alone. You don't have to be there.'

'Yes I do. We have to alibi each other.'

'We don't need alibis. It'll be a drunken accident. That's what everyone will think.'

'We do it together, Ronnie. That's how it is.'

'Then that's how it will be.'

'I'm scared. That's stupid, isn't it?'

'No. Just unnecessary. I love you, Susie, and I won't let you down.'

'I know you won't.'

They kissed each other, slowly and tenderly.

Then turned and made their separate ways back home.

Eleven o'clock. Anna sat in bed trying to read a novel but finding herself unable to concentrate. Too many other things were occupying her mind.

There was a knock on the door. Charles entered. 'Is it too late to disturb you?'

'No.'

He sat on her bed, bringing with him the comforting smell of pipe tobacco. 'So what's bothering you?' he asked gently.

'Nothing.'

'And does that nothing concern Ronnie?'

'Why do you say that?'

'Because I know you.' He stroked her hand with his finger. 'And I also know what they say. A nothing shared is a nothing halved.'

She smiled. 'Even with my appalling arithmetic I know that calculation is flawed.'

'But my hearing isn't. Try me.'

'It's stupid.'

'Let me be the judge of that.'

'He went for a walk this afternoon. I said I'd go with him but he didn't want me to.'

His finger continued to stroke her hand. She looked down at the bedspread, feeling foolish. 'Told you it was stupid.'

'He wanted to be on his own. We all want that sometimes. It doesn't mean anything.'

'I know.'

'So?' His tone was encouraging.

'It's just that I didn't think it would be like this. Ever since I came to work for your mother I've dreamed about having him here with me, and now he is and he's . . .' She paused, searching for the right words.

'Not nine years old any more?'

'Yes.'

'Growing up doesn't mean growing away. There's a saying. If you want the bird to stay then keep your hand open. If it's free to go it will always come back.'

'You think I want to cage him?'

Silence. She looked up again. His eyes were sympathetic.

'Do you?'

'Perhaps. Just a little.'

She felt hurt. 'So I'm smothering, am I?'

'I didn't mean it like that, darling. You know I didn't.'

She did. And she knew he was right too.

But she didn't want to admit it. Not even to herself. It made her feel weak. Powerless.

Pathetic.

She shook her head. 'It's more than that. It's her.'

'Who? Susan?'

'He's been different since he met her. More secretive.'

'I don't think so.'

'Well, you don't know him the way I do.'

A strange look came into his eyes. There for a second and then gone. It looked like pity, but she was upset and not in the best mood to judge.

'And I know that girl is bad for him. She'll hurt him. I'm sure of it.'

'You're being too hard on her.'

'Am I? She wants to make trouble between us. I'm sure of it.'

'That's not true. Do you know where she was this afternoon? In Oxford, trying to find him a birthday present. We had coffee together and she asked me what you were giving him so she could make sure her gift didn't overlap.'

She felt betrayed. 'How nice for you,' she said archly.

'It was. She's a genuinely likeable girl. There's no malice in her.'

'I know her type. Spoilt and spiteful.'

'That's not true.' His tone was firm. 'She's a good person. One who's had a harder life than you think but not let it spoil her.'

'And your instincts are infallible, are they?'

'Of course.' His tone softened. 'That's exactly what they told me about you.'

Silence. His hand squeezed hers. Again she knew he was right. It was Alice who was spoilt and spiteful. Susan was different. Susan was good.

And beautiful and clever and strong. Someone who could cast a shadow over all the other people in Ronnie's life. Even his own mother.

'Why do you think she's had a hard life?'

'I don't know. Just a feeling. All families have skeletons, don't they?'

'I don't. Not with Ronnie.'

And it was true.

Except for the ones he kept in his drawer.

'You can't stop him caring about her but you can stop letting it upset you. People grow up and fall in love. That's a fact of life. But they don't stop loving their parents because of it. Especially not when the bond with that parent is as close as the one Ronnie has with you.'

'It *is* close. I know him better than anyone.' A pause. 'And I always will.'

He was gazing at her, his expression tender and protective. As if she were a child herself. Someone weak, who needed to be protected.

Someone pathetic.

'I'm tired,' she told him. 'I want to sleep.'

He leant forward to kiss her cheek. She moved her head away. Only an inch but sufficient to indicate distaste. Briefly he looked hurt. It made her feel strong. Even though she despised herself for it.

'Sleep well, darling,' he said.

'Thank you.'

He left the room. She tried to read but the buzz of her thoughts was like a drill inside her head, causing the page to vibrate and turning the words into blurs.

Tuesday evening. Anna stood in Ronnie's room.

It was empty. He was in Oxford on a school trip to the theatre.

The key to the drawer was in her hand, growing sticky as her palm began to sweat. She didn't want to look yet couldn't stop herself. She had to know. Knowledge was power, after all, and power meant an end to feeling weak.

She walked up to the desk and put the key in the lock, trying to ignore the voice that screamed inside her brain.

Don't do this. Throw the key away. Bury it. Hurl it in the river.
For what is seen can never be unseen.

But there would be nothing to see. Nothing that mattered. Nothing that could hurt. She knew it because she knew Ronnie. Better than anyone. A million times better.

So she turned the key, opened the drawer, looked inside.

And found what she found.

One hour later. Charles, who had been asleep in his study, walked out to find the house in darkness.

He stood in the hallway, feeling confused. Had Anna gone to bed? Would she not have come to say goodnight first? Or had she done so and decided not to wake him?

Assuming this was the case, he went to the living room to watch the news.

The room was in darkness too. He switched on the light. Then jumped.

Anna sat on the sofa, staring into space, blinking at the sudden illumination.

He said her name but she didn't seem to hear. Her face was as pale as marble.

'Darling, what is it?'

Still no reaction. Alarm surged through him. 'Has something happened to Ronnie?'

A shake of the head.

'Then what?' Crossing the room, he sat down beside her, putting his hand on her shoulder.

'Don't touch me!'

Again he jumped. She pulled away from him. 'You're always touching me. Always trying to handle me.'

'But it's just affection. It's not . . . what you think.'

'I don't love you. Not like that. I married you for companionship and so Ronnie could have all this.' She gestured at their surroundings. 'This house. This life. All the things you take for granted that he's never had before but always deserved. And he does deserve them. He does!'

She began to cry. Plaintive, heart-wrenching sobs like those of a child who returns home to find her house and family destroyed, leaving her to face a cold, uncaring world alone. The child she had once been and still was inside.

He pushed his own hurt to one side. 'What is it, darling? Please tell me. I can help.'

'No you can't.'

'How do you know if you don't tell me? I accept that you don't love me but you must accept that I love you more than anyone else in this world and if something's hurt you I want to help you bear the pain. That's all I've ever wanted. To protect you from pain.'

She turned towards him, her eyes wide and frightened. Again he put his hand on her shoulder. This time she allowed it to stay.

'Tell me,' he whispered. 'I'll do whatever it takes to make the pain go away.'

They stared at each other. He waited.

Then suddenly the sobs stopped. Her back straightened. She wiped tears from her eyes, her manner brisk and businesslike. And when she spoke her voice was businesslike too.

'I was asleep when you came in and having a terrible dream. When you woke me I thought the dream was still going on. I was confused and frightened, that's all. I didn't mean what I said earlier. I was just upset. We all say things we don't mean when we're upset.'

He swallowed down his frustration. 'Anna . . .'

'It was just a dream, Charles. Now it's nothing.'

Then she rose to her feet and walked out of the room.

Eight o'clock the next morning. He sat reading the paper and drinking coffee while Anna tried to persuade a reluctant Ronnie to eat more food. The three of them performing the same ritual of breakfast they acted out every morning.

Ronnie worked his way through a plate of bacon, sausage and egg, protesting that his stomach was about to explode. Anna stood behind his chair, offering encouragement. Her voice was as warm as ever but there was a new hardness around her mouth. It aged her face as delicately but irreversibly as a wrinkle.

He could see it. Could Ronnie?

The phone rang in the hallway. A call from college that he had been expecting about rescheduling a tutorial that took only a moment to answer.

He returned to the dining room, stopping just outside the door, wanting to observe.

Ronnie had nearly cleared his plate. Anna was still behind his chair.

'I really am full, Mum.'

'Are you sure?'

'Yes. But it was lovely. You spoil me.'

'Of course.' A kiss on the cheek. 'You're my sunshine, aren't you?'

'I know.'

She stroked his hair, as gently as if it were the fur of an injured kitten. 'No one else could ever come close. It'll always be you and there's nothing you can do to change it. Not even something truly bad. No matter what you've done I'll always love you and you'll always be my Ronnie Sunshine. You know that, don't you?'

Silence.

'Don't you?'

'Yes, Mum. But I'll never do anything bad. You know that too, don't you?'

Her fingers continued to slide through his hair. 'Yes, Ronnie. I do.'

What has he done? You've found out something, haven't you? Something bad.

Something truly bad.

He re-entered the room. Anna took Ronnie's plate through to the kitchen. Ronnie remained in his chair, sipping a glass of milk, looking just as he always did. There was no change in his face. Like Dorian Gray, he would stay the same while his mother grew twisted and withered like the picture in the attic.

What clouds have you cast, Ronnie Sunshine? What storms have you summoned?

And what can I do to banish them?

'Looking forward to today, Ronnie?'

'Yes. We start with double hieroglyphics. What could be better than that?'

He forced out a laugh, managing to make it sound natural. Ronnie laughed too, watching him with those eyes that gave nothing away.

Sunday.

It was still dark when Susan woke, fleeing the old, hated dream about her father, escaping into the day when she hoped to leave it behind for ever.

She lay in her bed, looking at the shapes in her room. The desk with her books piled neatly on top. The wardrobe and chest of drawers. The doll's house. And a pile of clothes bought in Oxford the previous day for her new school in Scotland.

Birds began to sing outside her window, hailing the dawn. Light crept under the curtains and across the room, dispelling the shadows that crawled into the corners to die. From this day on there would be no more shadows. Not for her mother, Jennifer or herself.

Rising, she walked to the window, preparing to pull the curtains back, bracing herself for the rain clouds that could threaten everything they had planned.

But the sky was clear. A dull orange sun promised a mild, dry day. A typical Sunday in early October, except for it being the one on which Uncle Andrew would die.

Time passed. She remained by the window. On the ledge was the conch shell her father had bought her in Cornwall. The one that had soothed her with its song as she had lain awake night after night, frightened and alone in the dark. The fear was still with her but the darkness was gone and she was no longer alone.

And it would be all right.

Pressing the shell to her ear, she stared out at the day.

A quarter to eight. Anna brought Ronnie an early-morning cup of tea.

He was sitting on top of his desk, cross-legged, staring out at the river.

'Ronnie?'

He turned, still cross-legged, and gave her a grin. His red dressing gown and sleep-ruffled hair making him look like a little boy. She walked towards him, ignoring the locked drawer. Once, in a dream, she had looked inside it and been frightened by what she had found. But dreams weren't real. When the light came you buried them in the farthest corners of your mind, leaving them to wither and die so you never had to look at them again.

'It's a lovely day,' she remarked. 'We should go for a walk later.'

'I can't. I said I'd meet Susie.' His eyes were apologetic. 'You don't mind, do you? She leaves for Scotland in a week.'

She didn't mind. With Susan gone he would be hers again, which was as it should be. After all, she knew him better than anyone, in spite of dreams that tried to tell her that she didn't know him at all.

'You'll miss her, won't you?' she said.

'A bit. But I'll make other friends.'

'Of course you will. Who wouldn't want to be friends with you?'

'Mum!'

'It's true.' She sat down on a chair while he remained perched on the desk like an elf, telling her a funny story about one of his teachers. She laughed while daylight streamed through the window, banishing shadows and protecting them both from dreams.

Half past one. Susan sat at the dinner table, eating roast chicken and watching Uncle Andrew drink wine.

Her mother asked him about a colleague at work. She listened to his voice with ears programmed to register its every cadence, searching for the tightness that denoted excited anticipation and finding it present and correct.

They finished the main course. As her mother fetched the pudding he poured the remains of the wine bottle into his glass. Only a few millimetres. Irritation flashed across his face. She gestured to a jug of water in the middle of the table. 'Would you like some?'

'Yes. I'll get it. You should go and help your mother.' His speech was excessively slow and clear. The way it always became in the early stages of inebriation.

She stood just outside the door, listening for the clink of bottles. He hated water, but not when flavoured with whisky. Within seconds the telltale sound came.

Ten minutes later he stretched in his chair. 'It's stuffy in here. I'm going for a walk.'

'Don't you want coffee?' asked her mother.

An irritated snort. 'If I wanted it I'd ask. I'll get my coat.'

He left the room. Susan remained at the table. Her mother looked at her anxiously. 'The food was all right, wasn't it?'

'It was lovely, Mum. He said so when you were in the kitchen.' In the distance she heard the front door open then shut. He was gone.

Her heart began to race. This was it.

She sat in silence, counting the seconds, not wanting to appear too eager, while her mother talked about the proposed menu for the evening. One minute. Two. Three.

'Mum?'

'Yes.'

'I said I'd see Ronnie this afternoon. I'm supposed to meet him in a bit. You don't mind, do you?' A sigh laced with just the right amount of reproach. 'I won't be able to see him after next week.'

Her mother nodded. 'Of course.'

'Leave the washing up. I'll do it when I get back.'

'Don't worry. I'll do it. You have a nice time.'

'Thanks.'

She rose to her feet and made for the door.

Five minutes later she entered Market Court.

There were not many people about. A dozen at most. But some she knew, and all were an audience. Fighting the urge to run, she kept her stride measured.

Ronnie was leaning against the Norman cross, his head buried in a book. When she called his name he looked up, waved then continued reading until she reached him.

'*Sons and Lovers,*' he told her. 'We have to read it for English.'

'We did too. It's awful, isn't it?'

'You're telling me. And I thought *Silas Marner* was bad. Come back, little Eppie, all is forgiven.'

She laughed. A woman passer-by overheard the exchange and looked amused.

'Shall we go for a shake?' she suggested.

'Later. I had a huge lunch. Let's have a walk first.'

'OK.'

They set off, arm in arm, complaining about school just like any other pair of teenagers.

Ten minutes later they entered the woods and left the town behind. Her urge to run increased. His grip tightened on her arm. 'Slow down.'

'What if you miss him?'

'There's no chance of that. I didn't give an exact time. Between half past two and three, assuming I was even going for a walk at all.'

An elderly couple ambled towards them, arm in arm just as they were, with a small dog at their heels. Instantly Ronnie began to ask questions about the wildlife, playing the ignorant town dweller while she flaunted her rural expertise. The couple gave them friendly nods. Both smiled back while the dog chased a squirrel up a tree.

They continued through the woods, on to where it became overgrown and wild and people rarely came. Frightened, perhaps, of meeting a ghost mother searching for her lost child.

Until at last they came to the forgotten path that led to the river bank.

He looked at his watch. 'Twenty to three exactly. Check yours says the same.'

It did.

'Be there at half past. No earlier. I need time to make sure he's ready.'

'He will be. He was hardly abstemious at lunch.'

'Good.' He pulled a pair of leather gloves from his pocket and put them on.

Then they stared at each other.

'This is it,' he said.

She nodded.

'You don't have to come. I can do it on my own.'

'We do it together, Ronnie. That's how it must be.' She kissed his cheek. 'For luck.'

'We don't need luck.' He kissed her back. 'We have each other.'

He vanished down the path. She remained where she was, arms wrapped around her body, feeling herself tremble while the first leaves drifted to the ground and the birds sang oblivious overhead.

There was an old hut near the path.

Once it had been used by a long-dead woodsman. Now it was abandoned and almost derelict. She had played in it as a child with her father, just as he had once played there with his. Now she sat inside it, staring down at her watch as the minute hand moved ever forward.

Until she couldn't wait any longer.

She crept outside, listening for voices and footsteps that would signal another human presence, hearing nothing but the sighing of the trees and the thundering of her own heart.

She made her way down the path, hemmed in by trees and bushes that often blocked out the sky, moving on legs that felt as if they could collapse beneath her while breathing air that was heavy with the smell of earth.

Until, up ahead, she heard voices.

They were there. Together.

Suddenly, unexpectedly, calm descended.

A few more yards and the path opened up. She stood on the edge of a clearing with a pond and a tree by its edge. The tree under which her father had once told her stories. The tree under which she and Paul had made love on that fateful summer's day the previous year.

And under which Ronnie now sat with Uncle Andrew.

They were sitting very close, their heads almost touching. A strategy of Ronnie's to ensure their voices remained soft. Uncle Andrew sipped from the almost empty whisky bottle then passed it to Ronnie, who suffered from poor circulation and wore gloves to protect his hands from the cold. Tilting his head, Ronnie pretended to swallow, fooling his companion, who was far too drunk to notice the deception.

She looked across the clearing to the trees that acted as a barrier from the river. Again she listened for sounds of life but heard nothing. Just as she had expected. Few people ever came to this stretch of the river, especially outside the months of summer. Her father had loved such places for that reason and taught her to love them too, while never dreaming of the use to which such knowledge would one day be put.

Ronnie handed the bottle back, checked his watch and looked up. Their eyes locked.

For a moment he did not react. Then he nodded.

She walked into the clearing. Ronnie rose to his feet. Uncle Andrew followed his cue, staring at her with drink-befuddled eyes. 'Why are you here?'

'I'm here for Jennifer.'

'Jennifer?' He took a step towards her, wobbling unsteadily. Ronnie put an arm around him. Supporting. Guiding. Manoeuvring him towards the designated spot by the water's edge. Close to where the tree roots broke the surface. The ones her father had called the troll's fingers.

'What do you mean?' he asked.

'That I'm here to watch you die.'

'Die?' He turned to Ronnie and began to giggle. 'She's mad.'

Ronnie nodded. He was smiling but then his expression became one of surprise. 'What's that?' he said, pointing to a spot over Uncle Andrew's shoulder.

Uncle Andrew began to turn, still holding the whisky bottle. Ronnie dropped down, put his hands around Uncle Andrew's ankles and gave a gentle tug. In Uncle Andrew's unsteady state that was all that was needed. He fell forward, too disoriented to cry or put out his hands before his head slammed against the troll's fingers.

He lay with his head in the water, the dropped whisky bottle by his side. She watched him, her throat dry. Was he unconscious? Or would they have to hold him down and risk leaving telltale bruises. Ronnie had assured her that they wouldn't. That he would be too incapacitated by the blow and by drink to struggle. But she didn't want to take the chance.

Twenty seconds passed. Thirty. Forty. He remained motionless. Ronnie could hold his breath for a minute and a half. She for nearly two.

But they were younger and fitter than he was.

Ronnie came to stand beside her, treading gingerly, careful to avoid the one spot in the clearing where the ground was damp enough to register footprints. He took her hand and squeezed it. She squeezed back.

One minute. Two. She waited for him to start moving. But he just lay there.

Three minutes. Four. Five.

It had worked.

'It's done, Susie.'

'But . . .'

'He's dead. We have to go. Now. Before someone comes.'

They made their way up the path, still hand in hand. Leaving the river and returning to the woods. She was running, feeling as if her feet were made of air. Wanting to scream and cry and laugh all at the same time. Terrified and exhilarated. Dizzy with adrenalin.

Back in the woods, he led her to the hut. 'We have to stay here for a few minutes,' he told her. 'You musn't appear excited when we go back. You have to be calm.'

'How can I? We did it.' Laughter erupted from her throat. 'We did it!'

He began to laugh too, while trying to cover her mouth with his hand. She pulled away, opening her mouth to laugh some more. Again he covered it, only this time with his own.

Desire exploded through her like dynamite. She kissed him back, savagely, greedily, wanting to devour him completely. His eyes were shining and she knew he felt it too. That sense of union. Of oneness. I am yours and you are mine and not even death can break this bond we have between us.

So their union became physical, there in the hut, while outside the ghost mother cried for her child and kept other watchful eyes away.

Half past six. She stood in the hallway of her house, breathing in the smell of supper.

For the last two hours she had been sitting in Cobhams Milk Bar with Ronnie, forcing herself to drink a strawberry shake and talk about school, Scotland, films, music. Anything except what had taken place by the river.

'Is that you, Andrew?'

'No, Mum. It's me.'

Her mother appeared from the kitchen, looking anxious. 'Your stepfather's not back yet. You don't think he's gone to the pub, do you?'

'It won't be open yet. He's probably just lost track of time. Last weekend he went for a walk and was gone for hours.'

'I suppose so.' Her mother sighed. 'I'm making a casserole. He likes that, doesn't he?'

'Very much.' She forced a smile. 'Don't worry, Mum. He'll be back soon . . .'

Twenty to seven. From the kitchen window Anna saw Ronnie coming up the drive.

She walked out to meet him. 'Did you have a nice time?' she asked.

He nodded, looking sad. Overhead the evening star climbed into the night sky.

'She hasn't left yet, Ronnie.'

The sadness remained. 'It's just the thought of someone I like going away. It reminds me of what it was like in Hepton, always watching you go away.'

'And is this as bad?'

'No. Nothing could ever be as bad as that.'

She felt a warmth in her stomach. 'It's only until Christmas. That's not long.'

But by then you won't care. I'll see to it that you don't.

Another nod.

'What did you do?'

'Had a walk in the woods, then went to Cobhams.' His expression became guilty. 'Where I ruined my supper with a chocolate milk shake.'

'That's a pity. I'm making your favourite lamb chops with mint sauce.'

'Really?' His face lit up into a perfect Ronnie Sunshine smile. 'Thanks, Mum. You always know how to cheer me up.'

'Of course. It's my job. Who knows you better than me?'

'No one.'

Together they walked back into the house.

A quarter to nine the next morning. Susan stood in the hallway with her mother, both of them staring at the telephone.

'You have to call them, Mum.'

Her mother reached for the receiver, then pulled her hand back again. There were bags under her eyes from lack of sleep. Neither of them had slept the previous night.

'He's probably just stayed with a friend. If I call the police and they come round he'll be angry. You know what he's like.'

'And you know he's never stayed out all night before. What's he going to do? Wake the mayor at midnight and say sorry but I'm too drunk to find my way home?'

'We don't know he was drinking.'

'He was out all evening. What else will he have been doing? Anyway, it doesn't matter what he was doing last night. The question is where is he now?'

Again her mother reached for the receiver then pulled back her hand.

'Mum, he's got an important meeting this morning. Don't you remember him talking about it? He should have left for the office an hour ago but he's still not here. That's got to tell you something.'

Her mother was looking frightened. Susan ached to put her out of her misery and tell her that he would never be coming back. But of course she couldn't.

'He drinks at the Crown. Why not call them first. Ask if he was there.'

'I'm not sure . . .'

'Or ask Ben Logan. If Uncle Andrew did go to the Crown he'll have had to walk along the river bank and Ben will have seen him. Ben sees everybody.'

'You should go to school. You're late already.'

'I'm not leaving you.'

'If he comes back and finds you here he'll be angry with me. Please, Susie.'

She didn't want to go. But she didn't want to stay either. Even the best actresses needed the occasional break from the stage.

'OK. But I'm coming home at lunchtime, and if you haven't heard from him by then we're calling the police . . .'

The following afternoon. She walked home from school with Ronnie.

Neither spoke. She knew what he was thinking. What she was thinking herself. When would they find him? When would the real performance begin?

Her mother had phoned the police the previous lunchtime. Two officers had come to take a statement. She had stayed home all afternoon, sitting by her mother's side, looking anxious, saying nothing.

Except that if he had gone to the Crown then Ben Logan should have seen him.

Everyone who knew Uncle Andrew had been called. Uncle George, who had spent the previous evening at their house. The mayor. Other friends. The landlord of the Crown. Nobody knew anything.

Though Ben Logan had seen him walking by the river the previous afternoon, looking a little unsteady on his feet. And not for the first time either.

They reached the corner of Market Court. A police car was parked outside her house. Were they there to ask more questions? Or to break the news?

'This could be it,' she said.

'It was an accident. That's how it looks and that's what they'll think.'

'I hope so.'

'Let me come too.'

'No. It might seem strange. I have to do this on my own.'

'Are you ready?'

She took a deep breath. 'Yes.'

He kissed her cheek. 'Lights.'

She kissed him back. 'Camera.'

'Action.'

As she walked towards the house the light around her seemed to fade, like the darkness that fell over an auditorium at the start of a film. In her head she was seven years old again, sitting in the cinema with her father, holding his hand and watching the girl on the screen who looked like an older version of herself. The girl who was in danger and needed all her wits about her to survive. The girl who felt sick with fear, just as she did.

But her father wasn't frightened. He was smiling, keeping her hand safe and warm in his. 'Don't be scared, Susie,' he whispered. 'She can do this. She can do anything because she's my daughter and she makes me proud. I wish she were here so I could tell her that but she's not so you'll have to tell her for me. Keep the knowledge safe in your heart so that one day years from now when she really needs to know it she will.'

I do know it. I love you, Dad.

And I can do this.

She opened the door. From the living room came the sound of voices. Her mother appeared, her eyes red from crying. 'Oh, Susie . . .'

'Mum, what is it?'

Her mother burst into tears. A policeman stood in the doorway, shifting from foot to foot, clearly uncomfortable at witnessing another's grief.

'Mum?'

'Oh, Susie, he's dead.'

Inside her head the camera whirred and the music swelled. She thought of her father. She thought of her audience. Surrendering to the scene, she began to cry too.

Wednesday evening. Charles listened to Mary Norris on the phone.

'There was an empty bottle beside him. At least, that's what I heard. He was partial to the bottle, by all accounts. Often in the Crown three sheets to the wind.' A sigh. 'Poor Susie. How must she be feeling?'

He didn't know for sure. But he could guess.

Happy? Free? Safe?

Guilty?

The thought stuck in his brain like a tick. He didn't want to believe it. Susan was someone he liked a great deal. A genuinely warm and likeable human being. He had learned to trust his instincts about others and those he had about her had always been good.

But he couldn't say the same about Ronnie.

And good people could do bad things. If they felt trapped. If they were afraid.

Where there's a will there's a way.

Susan had the will. Had Ronnie shown the way?

As Mary prattled on he shook his head as if trying to dislodge the thought. But it clung on like the parasite it was, feeding and growing stronger.

The next morning he sat in his study, smoking his pipe and trying to work.

A subdued-looking Anna entered. 'Would you like some lunch?'

'No thank you. I'm not very hungry.'

'Neither am I.'

He put down his pen. 'It's a terrible business.'

'The funeral is on Saturday. We must go. Show support.'

'Saturday is Ronnie's birthday.'

'So?'

'Nothing. I was just pointing it out. I know how you've been looking forward to it.'

'We can celebrate another day. The funeral is more important.' As she spoke she began to fiddle with her left ear. The way she always did when she was nervous.

'Of course it is,' he said soothingly. 'And of course we'll go.'

'All three of us will. You, me and Ronnie. He wants to go. He said so last night.' The hand continued to fiddle with the ear. 'And that's how it should be. He and Susie are such good friends. People would think it strange if he wasn't there.'

He nodded, breathing out clouds of tobacco and watching her.

You suspect him too. You don't believe it was an accident any more than I do.

He asked about the time of the service. She answered, her voice tight. Again he saw the hardness in her mouth. But this time it seemed even more pronounced. Another wrinkle in the picture Dorian Gray kept in his attic.

She continued to speak. Suddenly tears came into her eyes. Concerned, he rose to his feet. 'Darling, what is it?'

'Someone dying so unexpectedly. It brings it all back with my family. One minute they're there and the next they're gone.' She shook her head. 'It's so stupid. You'd think I'd be over it by now.'

'It's not stupid. You never get over something like that. Not totally.'

'I wish I could.' She swallowed. 'I wish I was brave.'

'You are.' He walked towards her. 'I told you that the first time we ever really spoke. Here in this study. Do you remember that?'

'Yes. You said I had courage because I'd kept Ronnie and I said it wasn't courage that made me do it. It was knowing as soon as I held him that I could never give him away. That he was mine.'

She leant forward, resting her head against his chest. He put his arms around her, stroking her hair, feeling her tremble.

She's frightened. Frightened of what he's done. Frightened of him being caught.

But it had been an accident. That was what everyone else seemed to think. He hoped they kept thinking it. For her sake. And for Susan's.

'It'll be all right,' he whispered. 'You're not alone any more. You've got me and I'll get you through this.'

Did she read the message in his words? Perhaps. Though she would never tell him so.

But her head remained pressed against his chest, allowing him to feel, for a brief but precious moment, that he was needed.

Saturday. Cold and clear. Susan stood next to her mother in Kendleton churchyard, watching Uncle Andrew's coffin being placed into the grave.

The vicar began to say a prayer. She lowered her head, staring down at her black shoes which had been bought especially for the ceremony, just as so much had been bought for her in previous weeks. The clothes for Scotland still lay on the floor of her bedroom waiting to be returned to the shop. This should have been the day of her departure but she would not be leaving now. Not when her mother needed her.

The prayer ended. Her mother threw a handful of earth on to the grave. She did the same, feeling the weight of eyes watching her performance of grief. In her stomach she felt the fluttering of butterflies. She was nervous, though not excessively so. The autopsy had revealed high levels of alcohol in his system and though the inquest would not be until Tuesday the release of his body for burial suggested it would be a formality. That was what one of the policemen had told her mother, and there was no reason to doubt him.

Who, after all, would suspect her? To the world Uncle Andrew had been a good and decent man. A little too fond of a drink, perhaps, but that was hardly a crime. She had been lucky to have had a stepfather like him. That was what people would think, and her loss would inspire their pity, not suspicion.

Uncle George threw earth on to the coffin. Jennifer remained by her side, holding her hand, gazing up at her. 'Are you OK, Jenjen?' she whispered.

A nod. 'Are you?'

'Better because you're here. Much better.'

Jennifer's face broke into a smile. Bright and full of trust. A wave of love swept over her, together with a sense of calm. Jennifer was safe. She had done what needed to be done and she had no regrets.

Ronnie stood on the other side of the grave, flanked by his mother and stepfather. He looked sad, though not as sad as she did. He was performing too. Both of them giving their audience what was expected.

For a moment their eyes locked. Then both looked away.

Wednesday afternoon. Mary Norris, grocery-shopping in Market Court, saw Anna emerge from the post office. Quickly she made her way over. 'How are you, dear? I haven't seen you since that lovely tea party in your garden.'

'I'm fine,' Anna told her.

But she didn't look it. Her features were drawn and there were bags under her eyes. Mary felt concerned. 'Are you sure? You seem a bit under the weather.'

'I'm quite well, thank you.' Anna smiled but there was an uncharacteristic brittleness to her voice. Perhaps she wasn't sleeping well. Mary, who sometimes slept badly herself, knew that the resulting tiredness could make her brusquer than she meant to be.

'Did you see yesterday's paper?' she continued. 'I don't think they needed to include so much detail about his drinking. It's not very pleasant for Susie and her mother, is it?'

Anna shook her head.

'Did you know he drank? I didn't but my friend Moira Brent's husband Bill said he was always in the Crown. Part of the furniture, were Bill's words, though . . .'

'Don't you have anything better to do than gossip?'

The tone was glacial. Mary was taken aback. 'I only meant . . .'

'He's dead. It was a tragic accident like the coroner said, and you're not helping Susie and her mother by raking over it.'

'But I'm not. I was just . . .'

'I have things to do. Goodbye.'

Anna turned and walked away. Hurt and bewildered, Mary watched her go.

Thursday morning. While the rest of the English class debated the pros and cons of Dr Faustus selling his soul, Susan watched raindrops hit the window by her desk.

The classroom was full of noise, just as her house had been in recent days. An endless stream of people had come to offer support and wallow in the drama, just as they had when her father had died. A colleague of Uncle Andrew's had brought details of the will. Everything had been left to her mother. 'A very tidy sum,' they had been told. 'I know it doesn't make the loss any easier but at least you won't have to worry about money.' For all she cared he could have left them destitute, but for the sake of her mother's peace of mind she was glad.

Uncle George visited each evening, eager to help them bear their grief and, perhaps, share the pain of his own. His move to Australia had been cancelled. 'Something like this makes you realize how important it is to be close to people you care about,' he had told Susan. 'And who Jennifer cares about.'

Raindrops continued to slide down the glass like racing pearls. She traced the path of one with her finger and noticed Miss Troughton watching her. Instead of a lecture on the perils of inattention she received a sympathetic smile. Everyone was being kind to her, although, as when her father had died, she would occasionally catch other girls looking at her warily, as if her loss were an infection that could spread as easily as flu.

The bell rang for mid-morning break. As the classroom emptied Charlotte came and sat beside her. 'I didn't think you'd come in this week.'

'Mum insisted. She didn't want me to miss any more school.'

'How is she?'

'All right. She's still got me and I know how to look after her.'

'And how are you?'

'Tired of people asking me that.'

Charlotte looked apologetic. 'Sorry.'

'Don't be,' she said quickly. 'It's natural to ask. But since it happened it's the only thing people talk to me about, and it would be nice, just for a bit, to talk about something else.'

'Like what?'

'Like you. What's been happening in your life?'

'Nothing,' Charlotte told her. Then began to blush.

'What's going on?'

'I've . . . er . . . made a new friend.'

'Who?'

'Colin Peters.' The blush deepened. 'He goes to Lizzie Flynn's school but he's leaving at the end of term to become a mechanic.'

Susan remembered the debacle with Alan Forrester and felt protective. 'Do you like him as much as you liked Alan?'

'Much more! He's nothing like Alan. This is real.' Charlotte's tone became conspiratorial. 'He's a fantastic kisser.'

Susan burst out laughing. 'Charlotte Harris!'

'He keeps giving me love bites! I have to wear my collar up all the time so Mum and Dad can't see them!'

By now they were both laughing. Laughing and sharing secrets, just as they had when they were Jennifer's age. Before her mother's illness and her father's death had changed her world completely.

But she could change it back, and herself too. Back into the Susie Sparkle who knew that life was to be enjoyed, not endured. Now Uncle Andrew was gone she had everything she needed to be happy. Her mother. Jennifer. Charlotte.

And Ronnie. Ronnie most of all.

'Are you sure you want to know this?' Charlotte asked her. 'I mean . . .'

'Of course! I'm your best friend, aren't I? I want to know everything . . .'

Twenty to four. Alice Wetherby climbed into her mother's car. The school lane was full of them, all driven by parents who didn't want their little angels to catch cold.

Her mother lit a cigarette and gazed up at the sky. 'I hope Edward will be all right.'

'Why wouldn't he be? You know how much he loves his stupid rugby practice.'

'It's not stupid. He's their top scorer.'

'Only because the rest of the team are so useless they might as well be in wheelchairs.' Alice brushed away smoke with her hand. 'And can you blow that somewhere else?'

'There's no need to be rude. I didn't have to come out and fetch you.'

'And I didn't ask you to either.'

Her mother frowned. 'What's the matter with you?'

'Nothing. Everything's fine.'

Or it would be if she could only stop thinking about Ronnie.

She didn't want to think about him. He was just a boy and boys were only fit to be laughed at. Not longed for, day after day, so badly that it hurt more than any pain she had ever known.

Her mother steered the car down the path, muttering at people who were slow to move out of her way. Alice brushed more smoke away from her face and saw Ronnie walking with Susan Ramsey, the two of them sheltering under a huge umbrella.

As the car passed them she turned to look back. Ronnie, who was carrying the umbrella, was listening to something Susan was telling him. His face was full of concern, and something else that made it shine and made him more beautiful than anyone she had ever seen.

Love.

Poor Susan had lost her stepfather. Their teacher had made a speech the previous day reminding them of how kind they must be to poor Susan. After all, it wasn't the first time poor Susan had suffered a bereavement. Poor Susan was to be pitied. And people did pity her. Even Kate Christie, who had always hated her, had said that it was sad.

But Alice didn't feel pity. Not for someone she couldn't outshine or outwit. Not for someone she couldn't dominate or intimidate. Not for someone who had never hidden the fact that they utterly despised her.

Did Ronnie despise her too? Had Susan taught him to do that?

Or had he done so all along?

The pain became unbearable. She wanted to lash out. To wound and scar.

Her mother continued to talk. She sat in silence, breathing in cigarette smoke and choking down the dark emotions that churned inside her. They were going to be sorry. Both of them. How, she didn't know. Not yet.

But she would find a way.

Saturday morning. Two weeks later. Susan stood in her bedroom with her mother, looking at the doll's house Uncle Andrew had given her after her father died.

'It's not as if I ever play with it,' she said.

'Jennifer might, though.'

'She's got her own toys, Mum, including a doll's house that's even bigger than this.'

'You should still keep it. It's valuable. Anyway, your children might like playing with it someday.'

'Not if they're anything like me. They'll be too busy building dens and climbing trees. I'll take it to the thrift shop this morning. Charlotte's mother helps out there and she says there's a girl in Holt Street who'd love to have it.'

'Well, it's a very generous thing to do.'

She nodded, knowing that generosity had nothing to do with it. She had always hated the doll's house. It reminded her of him, and now he was gone she wanted it gone too.

'It's heavy,' her mother pointed out. 'Can you carry it on your own?'

'Ronnie's going to come and help.'

Her mother smiled. 'Why doesn't that surprise me?'

'You do like him, don't you, Mum?'

'Yes. He's funny, just like your father was. But much better looking. The best-looking boy in town, I'd say, so it's only right he'd like the best-looking girl.'

She felt self-conscious. 'Mum!'

'It's true. You're a beautiful girl, Susie. And you're strong. Unlike me you'll never be frightened of being alone.'

'You're not alone. You've still got me and you always will have. I'll look after you, Mum. You don't ever have to be frightened as long as I'm alive.'

Her mother stroked her hair. 'You make me proud, Susie. Proud of the person you've grown into.' The smile returned. 'And I know your father would be proud of you too.'

They hugged each other. The conch shell her father had bought her lay on the window sill. Unlike the doll's house it wasn't worth a penny. But it held memories of its own and she wouldn't have parted with it for all the money in the world.

*

That afternoon she sat in Cobhams Milk Bar with Ronnie and Charlotte.

Others were there too. Lizzie Flynn. Arthur Hammond, her old friend from primary school, who was home from his Yorkshire boarding school for a long weekend. And Colin Peters, the budding mechanic who had given Charlotte her first love bite.

It was a lively gathering. As they drank coffee or milk shakes, Ronnie entertained them with descriptions of some of his neighbours in Hepton. A couple called the Browns sounded particularly grim. 'She was the biggest snob you've ever met and he was the biggest lecher and convinced he was irresistible. If Marilyn Monroe moved into our street he'd think she'd done it just to be close to him.'

Everyone laughed. 'Not much chance of that happening,' Lizzie pointed out.

'But that doesn't stop him trying. He keeps writing to her in Hollywood, sending her maps of East London and photographs of himself in his vest and underpants signed, "Come and get me, baby".'

More laughter. Susan watched Colin wipe coffee from his lip. He was heavy set with a nondescript face and little to say that did not involve motorcycles. But he also had a nice smile, a friendly manner and clearly adored Charlotte, and that was enough to make her like him immensely.

Ronnie continued to tell anecdotes, provoking more mirth in his audience. As he spoke he caught her eye and gave her a quick wink. She winked back.

'How's school?' she asked Arthur.

'As wonderful as ever.' Arthur rolled his eyes. He was small, blond and delicate and looked like a flimsier version of Ronnie. 'Henry's head of house now but says he'll stand down if we don't win the inter-house rugby championship.'

'That's tempting fate,' observed Lizzie.

'I know. The whole team are planning to go lame on the big day just to make sure.'

Yet more laughter. 'Have you met Arthur's brother Henry?' Charlotte asked Ronnie.

'Ronnie hasn't had that pleasure,' Susan told her.

'And it is a pleasure,' added Arthur. 'Believe me.'

'He's a complete idiot,' elaborated Lizzie. 'You can tell that from the fact he's friends with Edward Wetherby. No one but a moron would want to be friends with him.' She turned to Charlotte. 'Do you remember that party we went to at their house when we were about six and he threw your glasses in the river?'

Charlotte giggled. 'And then Susie punched him in the face and made him cry.'

Colin put his arm around her. 'If he ever does anything like that again I'll be the one that makes him cry.' He gave Susan a grin. 'But thanks for stepping in for me.'

Arthur went to put an Eddie Cochrane record on the jukebox. Susan noticed Uncle George standing by the door, looking self-conscious in such a predominantly teenage environment and holding a beaming, balloon-clutching Jennifer by the hand.

'She saw you through the window,' he explained, 'and wanted to come and say hello.'

'Can I stay with Susie?' Jennifer asked her father.

'If she doesn't mind.'

Susan patted a space between Ronnie and herself. Uncle George kissed Jennifer on the cheek. 'Be a good girl for Susie, darling.'

Jennifer nodded. She was wearing a blue dress that matched her balloon and looked very pretty. 'Have you been to a party?' asked Charlotte.

Jennifer nodded. 'We played games and sang lots of songs.'

'But you're not going to sing now,' Susan told her.

Ronnie made his hand into a gun and pointed it at the balloon. 'Or old Bluey gets it.' Jennifer giggled. Lizzie offered her some milk shake. 'Don't give her too much,' said Susan anxiously.

'Or what? Going to throw me in a cow pat like you did Alice Wetherby?' Lizzie grinned at Ronnie. 'Did you know your girlfriend was a thug?'

'Yes. But she's not my girlfriend. She's my soulmate.'

Susan, feeling a mixture of embarrassment and extreme pleasure, sipped her coffee and tried to act nonchalant.

'You've gone red,' Jennifer told her.

'Just drink your shake and be quiet.'

'What's a soulmate?'

'A soulmate,' answered Ronnie, 'is the most special person in your life. So special that you can sit with them for hours and they'll never ever want to sing.'

Everyone laughed. Lizzie and Charlotte asked Jennifer what songs she was learning and discovered they knew them too. They began to sing, deliberately mixing up the words while Jennifer earnestly corrected them. Susan felt Ronnie's hand stroke the back of her neck and realized that for the first time in years she was completely and utterly happy.

They smiled at each other while the others continued to make a mess of songs and suffered Jennifer's correction.

Half an hour later she walked through Market Court with Ronnie, each holding one of Jennifer's hands and swinging her through the air to shrieks of delight. It was growing dark and housewives rushed by them, all eager to finish their shopping and return home, while a group of boys collected money for a Guy Fawkes celebration that was taking place the following evening.

Someone called her name. Turning, she saw Paul Benson coming towards her. Taken by surprise, she stood waiting.

'How are you, Susie?' he asked.

'All the worse for seeing you, I expect,' said Ronnie.

'I wasn't asking you,' Paul told him.

'But I'm telling you anyway. Get lost. She has nothing to say to you.'

'I've got something to say to her.'

'What? More names to call? Shouldn't you wait until there's a bigger audience?'

Paul shuffled from foot to foot, looking deeply uncomfortable. 'So what do you want to say?' Susan asked him.

'That I'm sorry about your stepfather. I really am.'

She nodded. Jennifer tugged impatiently at her hand. 'Susie, I'm getting cold.'

'Isn't there something else you should be sorry for?' Ronnie asked Paul.

Paul continued to shuffle.

'Well?'

'Leave it, Ronnie,' Susan told him.

'I'm sorry for how I treated you,' said Paul suddenly. 'It was wrong and it was cruel.' He swallowed. 'And for what it's worth I'm ashamed.'

She stared at him, waiting for the sense of triumph. Remembering how she would once have given anything to have him apologize and then throw the words back in his face. But that had been before meeting Ronnie.

And now the words were spoken she felt nothing except an unexpected sense of pity.

'It doesn't matter. It's ancient history.' A pause. 'How are things with your father?'

Relief swept over his face. 'Better.' He smiled. 'Thanks.'

'I'm glad,' she told him.

Jennifer was still pulling at her hand. This time she allowed herself to be led.

After seeing Jennifer home she walked back across Queen Anne Square with Ronnie.

'Can't you stay out a bit longer?' he asked.

'Not tonight. I need to be with Mum. You understand, don't you?'

'Of course.'

'Did you really mean what you said about me in Cobhams?'

He nodded. 'Every word.'

'More fool you, then.'

He smiled, his eyes twinkling in the dusk light. 'Sad, isn't it?'

'What?'

'Having a tart for a soulmate.'

'Not as sad as having one who's a bastard.' She stroked his cheek. 'And a common one at that.'

They kissed each other. 'I knew it the moment I saw you,' he said. 'That we belonged to each other. That we were meant to be together.'

'I didn't. Not then. I wish I had.'

'It doesn't matter. You know it now.'

She caressed his lips with her tongue. An elderly couple walked past, muttering about the youth of today. 'Imagine if they knew,' she said.

'No one will ever know.'

'I don't feel ashamed. I keep expecting to but it never happens.'

'It never will. We did what had to be done. That's all you need to feel.'

Again they kissed. Slow and tender. 'I have to go,' she whispered. 'Mum's waiting.'

His arms tightened around her. 'But I'll see you tomorrow.'

'Of course. We could go to the firework party. The others are going.'

He shook his head.

'Didn't you like them?'

'Yes. But I want tomorrow night to be special. I want it to be just about us.'

She smiled. 'Then it will be. But now I must go.'

His hold remained firm. 'In a minute.'

They continued to kiss, there in the dwindling light, while the elderly couple shook their heads, clucked their tongues and predicted the imminent decline of Western civilization.

The following evening Charles ate dinner with Anna, Ronnie and Susan.

A Guy Fawkes celebration was taking place across the river. Fireworks filled the sky with noise and light to an accompaniment of cheers from the crowd gathered beneath.

He sat at one end of the table, Anna at the other, while Ronnie and Susan faced each other in the middle, all of them eating roast beef washed down with red wine.

'How is your mother coping?' he asked Susan.

'Quite well, thank you, Mr Pembroke.'

'And you? How are you managing?'

'I'm fine.' She sipped her wine and gave him a smile that combined warmth with sadness. A perfect gesture in a flawless performance. He longed to tell her that she didn't need to act for him. That whatever the rights and wrongs of her behaviour he was on her side and would never betray her.

Or Ronnie.

'I'm glad to hear it,' he said, smiling back with just the right mixture of kindness and concern. Playing the benevolent, unsuspecting patriarch. Matching her performance with one of his own.

Anna poured herself another glass of wine. Her third of the evening. 'I'm glad too,' she told Susan. Her tone was friendly but her features were drawn. She looked tired and anxious. Could Susan see it? he wondered. Could Ronnie?

Or were they so in love that they could see only each other?

Ronnie swallowed a mouthful of beef and complimented his mother on her cooking. Acting the part of a loving, dutiful son. Except that it wasn't acting. Ronnie loved his mother. That was real, but what else about him was? With Ronnie he wondered whether anyone could tell where illusion ended and reality began.

Fireworks filled the sky with red and gold. As Susan watched them through the window, Anna studied her with eyes that were deep pools of hostility. Dropping her own mask for just a second. Exposing her real emotions to the air.

The meal drew to its end. Ronnie cleared his throat. 'Do you mind if Susie and I go to my room? There are some drawings I want to show her.'

Anna fixed the smile back on her face. 'Of course not.'

'Thank you for the meal, Mrs Pembroke,' said Susan.

'My pleasure.'

They left the room. Anna poured herself yet more wine. When first married she would never drink more than one glass. But things had been very different then.

She saw him watching her. 'Well?'

'You think it, too, don't you?'

'Think what?'

'That her stepfather's accident was no accident at all.'

Her eyes widened. She looked frightened. 'You don't have to be afraid,' he said quickly. 'I'm on their side. I'd never say anything to hurt them. On my life I wouldn't.'

Then the fear was gone. 'You've had too much to drink,' she said coldly. 'Of course it was an accident. Only a fool would think otherwise, and I didn't marry a fool.'

He opened his mouth to protest. She shook her head. Rising to her feet, she began to clear the table, her mask securely back in place.

Susan stood in Ronnie's bedroom, watching him lock the door. 'Why are you doing that?' she asked.

'Because I don't want us to be disturbed.' Taking her hand, he led her towards the window.

The fireworks continued to illuminate the sky. 'They're beautiful,' she said.

'Not as beautiful as you.'

They kissed. 'Your breath smells of wine,' she told him.

'So does yours. Did you enjoy your meal?'

'Yes, though your mother seemed a bit subdued.'

'She's OK.'

'Do you think she suspects?'

'How could she? I'm her perfect son and perfect sons never do anything bad.'

'Was it really bad?'

He shook his head. 'Just necessary. He was going to hurt Jennifer the same way he'd hurt you. He had to be stopped. That's all there is to it. I'd never let anyone hurt you, Susie. You know that, don't you?'

'Just as I'd never let anyone hurt you.'

Again they kissed. 'Soulmate,' she whispered.

'That's why you trusted me, isn't it?'

'Yes.'

'And that's why I can trust you too. With a story I know you alone will understand.'

She nibbled on his lower lip. 'What sort of story?'

'A story about someone who hurt me once. A long time ago.'

She ran her fingers through his hair. 'Who? Your aunt? Your cousin?'

He shook his head. 'Someone else. Someone who should have known better."

'Who?'

He moved away from her, towards the desk beneath the window. Reaching into his pocket, he produced a tiny key that he used to unlock a drawer. 'It's all in here,' he said.

She looked inside. The drawer was full of paper. On the top was an old newspaper, the print faded.

'Have you heard of a place called Waltringham?' he asked. 'It's on the Suffolk coast. I went there once on holiday with a friend from school. A boy called Archie, who was ill, so I was on my own most of the time.'

She turned towards him. His eyes were shining.

Suddenly, for no reason, she felt a vague sense of alarm.

'One day it rained. As I waited for it to stop I went into a men's clothes shop and pretended I wanted to buy a tie. There was a mirror in an alcove. The shop assistant told me that I could go and try it on there . . .'

* * *

. . . he stood in front of the mirror, staring down at shoes that were still damp from the rain. His hair was damp too. A drop of water slid down his forehead and on towards the floor. He watched it fall.

There were footsteps behind him. Quick and purposeful. A hand came to rest upon his shoulder.

He looked up into the mirror.

A man of about forty stood beside him. Tall, well built, expensively dressed and holding a sports jacket. 'You don't mind, do you? The assistant says it's my size but I'm sure it's too small.'

He didn't answer. Struck dumb by the sight of the man's face. It was older now but it was still the same face he had looked at every day since he could remember. The one in the tiny snapshot he kept hidden behind the framed photograph of his mother.

His father.

He opened his mouth, trying to speak words that refused to come. His father stared at him with his own grey-green eyes. 'Are you all right?' The voice had a slight lisp. On the neck was a tiny birthmark shaped like a map of England. Just as his mother had described.

He managed a nod. His father tried on the jacket, studied his reflection and exhaled. 'I was right. Too small. Sorry to have disturbed you.'

Then he turned and walked away.

Ronnie's mind screamed at him to follow but he found himself frozen to the spot. Some wicked fairy had turned his body to stone at the moment he needed it most.

The middle-aged shop assistant appeared. 'Will you take the tie?'

And the spell was broken and he could move again.

Dropping the tie and ignoring the muttered complaints, he rushed into the main shop. There was no sign of his father. He ran out into the square. The boys from the beach who had been watching him earlier had gone in search of fresh sport. His father was striding away through the puddles while overhead faint patches of blue spread across the sky.

'Excuse me.'

His father turned. 'Hello again. Did I drop something?'

Again he searched for words. Trying to deal with the reality of an encounter he had longed for all his life while never dreaming it would come like this.

His father frowned. 'Well?'

'I'm Ronnie.'

'And I'm in a hurry. Can I help you with something?'

'My mother's Anna Sidney.'

'Who?'

'Anna Sidney.' A pause. 'From Hepton.'

He stared into his own eyes, searching for the things he had always yearned for. Recognition. Pleasure. Pride.

Love.

And saw nothing but blank incomprehension.

She was nothing to you. Not then. Not now. Not ever.

And neither was I.

Pain shot through him in waves, as if an invisible hand had reached into his chest and was squeezing his heart. A lump came into his throat. He swallowed it down. Trying to be strong. Wanting to keep his dignity.

'Well?' his father demanded.

'I'm sorry. I thought I knew you but I was wrong.'

His father nodded. Then once again turned and walked away.

Ronnie remained where he was. The lump returned. A passer-by stopped momentarily to stare at him. He touched his face and realized that he was crying.

His father reached the corner of the square. A woman appeared from a nearby side street and called out, 'Ted!' An abbreviation of Edward. The name his mother had used in the stories she had told him when he was a child.

The woman was weighed down with shopping bags. His father went to help her. Was she his wife? She looked about his age.

Unable to control his curiosity, he began to move closer.

A girl followed behind the woman. Tall and good looking with his father's features and the woman's colouring. His father said something to her and she slapped his arm playfully and exclaimed, 'Dad!'

But that wasn't possible. She was at least sixteen. Possibly older. Certainly older than himself. How could his father be her father too when before leaving Hepton he had promised his mother that he would come back and marry her?

Unless he had been married with a child at the time.

The sun came out, creeping through the thinning clouds and casting its light across the square. He felt its warmth against his face just as something warm inside himself died.

You cheated my mother. You cheated us both. You damaged our lives and you don't even care.

Suddenly the pain vanished, replaced by a calm so alien that it seemed to belong to someone else. He swallowed and found the lump gone. A last tear dribbled past his lips. He licked it away. It was salt and water, nothing else.

But in his mouth he tasted blood.

The following morning he sat on the green in front of the beautiful houses of The Terrace, all with their views of the sea. Bathed in sunshine and with his drawing pad on his lap, he stared at the one that belonged to his father.

The door opened. His father appeared, leading a little boy by the hand. A boy of about five or six, no older. A handsome little boy with pale blond hair and a bright smile. A boy who looked much as Ronnie would have done at the same age.

Rising to his feet, careful to keep his distance, he began to follow.

They spent the morning on the beach, building a huge sandcastle, just like the father and son he had drawn two days earlier. His own father took the lead, constructing ramparts and a drawbridge while the merry little boy who was his half-brother collected shells to decorate the walls. When they had finished they sat together eating ice creams, his brother laughing at seagulls that swooped down from the sky and waving to sailors on the boats out at sea while his father cradled him in his arms and covered his blond curls with kisses.

He bought an ice cream himself and ate it slowly, remembering the day when he had been his brother's age and his mother had taken him to the beach at Southend. It had been such a treat for him. His mother had had to save for weeks to afford it. They had gone by bus and she had bought him a bucket and spade and paid a beach photographer to take his picture because she had no camera of her own. He remembered posing for it, smiling to make his mother happy while watching other boys with their fathers and wondering when his own would come and rescue him and his mother from Auntie Vera's rules and the dull, grey streets of Hepton. Take them away to somewhere beautiful.

Somewhere like this.

At noon his father and brother ate lunch at a restaurant in the centre of town. He could see them through the window; his little brother eating sausages and chips while other diners beamed at him, waitresses fussed over him and his father watched him with eyes that were full of warmth and pride and love and all the things he had longed to see but hadn't.

When the two of them left the restaurant his brother sat astride his father's shoulders, squeaking with delight and waving to passers-by as he was carried back to his beautiful house in this beautiful town. Basking in the sunshine of this beautiful life that he and his sister took for granted.

And of which others could only dream.

Two days later, he stood inside a bookshop, browsing through the books on display while listening to his father's wife talk to his half-sister on the street outside.

'Well, I'm sorry, but you'll just have to. That's all there is to it.'

Margaret scowled. That was his sister's name. He had learnt that from his surveillance and he had learned some other things too. In particular that there was a boy called Jack with whom she was very taken and of whom her parents did not approve.

'Alan's your brother, Margaret. It's only right you should look after him sometimes.'

More scowling. 'I don't see why.'

'Because I say so. And your father does too.' Phyllis's tone softened. That was the name of the woman his father had married and then cheated on with his mother and perhaps other women besides. Phyllis. A heavy-set woman with none of his mother's attractiveness but the cut-glass vowels of someone who had never known what it was to scrimp and save to give her son a day at the seaside. 'I'll make you up a nice picnic. You could go to the beach.'

'The beach is boring.'

'Rushbrook Down, then. He likes it there and so do you. Please, Margaret. It's not much to ask.'

A sigh. 'All right.'

They walked away. He remained where he was, thinking. Analysing. Planning.

The owner of the shop approached him. 'Do you need any help there, young man?'

His brain continued to whirr. Ideas clicking into place like the pieces of a mental jigsaw puzzle. One piece, then another, until at last the whole picture was revealed.

And it made him smile.

'No thank you,' he said politely. 'I don't need any help at all.'

The next afternoon was the hottest of his holiday so far. He sat on the grass of Rushbrook Down, feeling the sun cook the back of his neck and send drops of sweat to cool his skin, pretending to read a book while watching Margaret and Alan and all the others who were picnicking that afternoon.

Margaret sat on a blanket in the centre of the grass, watching Alan chase a red beach ball. Jack sat beside her, his arm draped around her shoulder. A tall, heavy youth with greased back hair and a cocky smile who reminded Ronnie of his cousin Peter. The two of them were talking, their heads bent so close together that they were almost kissing.

Which they soon would be. He was sure of it.

Counting on it.

Alan, looking increasingly bored, was throwing his beach ball into the air and chasing after it. At one point he threw it at Margaret. Angrily she kicked it away. 'Go and play over there,' she told him, gesturing to a spot to the right. Closer to the woodland that surrounded them like a high green wall. As Alan did so she and Jack began to kiss, becoming oblivious, at least briefly, to anything except each other.

And so it was time.

Rising to his feet, he walked towards Alan, past others who were playing games of French cricket or eating picnics or just lying soaking up the sun. As he moved he kept his head lowered and allowed his shoulders to sag, folding his body in upon itself to reduce his physical presence. A trick he had learned years ago in his dealings with Vera, making himself as inconspicuous as possible to better avoid being the target of her rage.

Alan threw the ball in his direction, chasing it with all the focused concentration of a dog chasing a rabbit. Keeping his pace steady he let it roll towards him, then kicked it hard into the trees before continuing on his way.

Alan stopped, looking momentarily bewildered. Then hurried after it.

He kept walking, maintaining his pace and his crumpled posture while checking that no one was watching.

Then, turning, he made his way into the trees.

Alan Frobisher, nearly six and a big, grown-up boy, according to his parents, hunted for his beach ball.

Eventually he saw it, buried in a clump of bracken. He reached in to fetch it but there were thorns. Quickly he pulled back his arm, not wanting to get hurt. Wishing Margaret were there to help.

'Hello, Alan.'

He turned. A boy was standing beside him. Not as big a boy as Jack but still big. Bigger than any of the boys at his school, and some of them were eleven.

'Hello,' he said back, and then felt naughty. His mother had told him that he must never talk to strangers, and here he was doing just that.

But the big boy had known his name so perhaps he wasn't a stranger after all.

'I'm Ronnie,' the big boy told him with a smile. It was a nice smile. He had eyes just like Alan's father, and that was nice too. Alan smiled back.

'Shall I help you get your ball?'

'Yes please.' He watched Ronnie reach into the bracken and pull it out. 'Thank you.'

Ronnie kept holding the ball. 'Shall I tell you a secret?'

'What?'

'There are fairies in this wood.'

Alan gasped.

'Would you like to see them?'

'Yes!'

Ronnie put a fingers to his lips. 'We have to keep very quiet. Fairies are scared of people. If they hear us coming they'll run away and we won't see them at all.'

Alan nodded. 'I'll be quiet,' he whispered.

'Promise?'

'Promise.'

Again Ronnie smiled. Holding the beach ball under one arm, he held out his free hand. 'Come with me.'

Excited, trying not to giggle, Alan took it and followed Ronnie deeper into the woods.

Ronnie led Alan through the trees, along the paths he had explored on his second day alone in Waltringham. The one before he had met his father.

They came to the route that was blocked by barbed wire and a sign that read 'Danger – Keep Out'. The barbed wire was only three foot high. He lifted Alan over it, then jumped over himself. 'Don't worry,' he told Alan. 'We're nearly there now.'

They continued on. Down the path which was silent except for the song of birds overhead. On and on until they came to the ridge that led to the quarry.

It had long been abandoned. They stood at its summit, looking down at sheer stone walls that were covered in clumps of moss and valiant sprouts of grass. Its base was full of brackish, stagnant water.

Alan tugged at his hand. 'Ronnie, where are the fairies?'

He pointed to the water. 'In there.'

A frown. 'I can't see them.'

He put his hand on Alan's shoulder. 'You need to look more closely,' he said.

Then pushed.

Alan fell twenty feet, slamming into the water. Sinking deep below its surface before emerging, gasping with shock and struggling to find something to hold on to but finding only smooth stone. Trying to cry out with lungs that were paralysed with fear and fast filling with water before sinking under once again.

Ronnie remained where he was. But in his head he was back in Hepton on the night that Thomas had not come home. The night when a distraught Vera had told him that there was no pain worse than the suffering of a loved one.

That's the worst pain in the world. When something bad happens to someone you love. It hurts far more than my arm ever did.

And it was true. He knew it was true.

Now his father would know it too.

There was a noise behind him. He swung round, fearing discovery and the ruination of his plans. But it was just a fox. He made a hissing sound and it scampered away.

He looked down into the quarry. The fight for life had ended. A tiny body lay motionless on the surface of the water.

'Looks like you scared the fairies away,' he whispered.

The beach ball lay at his feet. He kicked it into the water. It bobbed up and down a couple of times, then, like its owner, lay still.

The penultimate morning of his holiday. He sat beside a recovered Archie on a bench that faced out to sea.

Behind them was The Terrace. As Archie talked endlessly about nothing of interest, he turned to see a police car pull up outside his father's house. In the two days since Alan's disappearance dozens of people had been searching the woods around Rushbrook Down. Now it seemed that the search was over.

'I'm going to get an ice cream,' Archie told him. 'Coming?'

'No. I'll stay here.'

Archie wandered off. Ronnie watched a policeman knock on the door of the house. His father answered, his wife beside him, their faces bright with the sheen of desperate hope.

The policeman began to speak. The sheen faded. His father's wife let out a howl. His father staggered and almost fell, unbalanced by the sudden, terrible weight of grief.

Now you're sorry. Now you know how it feels.

Rising to his feet, he walked away, head high and heartbeat steady.

And never once looking back.

* * *

Ronnie finished speaking. His eyes were still shining while, outside, fireworks continued to blaze against the cold night sky.

Susan told herself that it wasn't true. That it really was just a story, made up to shock and frighten her. Though why he would want to do that she couldn't say.

Then he took the faded newspaper from the drawer. 'Look,' he said.

And there it was. On the front page in black letters one inch high. 'Local Boy Drowns in Dreadful Tragedy'.

Her eyes focused on the accompanying photograph. A little boy with a lovely smile and trusting eyes stood in a garden posing with a cricket bat that a man with Ronnie's eyes was teaching him to hold.

Beneath the photograph it said 'Alan Frobisher with his father, Edward'.

Ronnie started speaking again. She tried to listen but the drawer pulled her like a magnet. It was still full of paper. She reached inside to find a drawing. One of a quarry with steep stone walls and brackish water and a little child floating like a twig on the surface.

She crouched down, opening the drawer wider, pulling out its entire contents. Not believing what she seeing.

Because there wasn't just one drawing. There were dozens. Some in pencil. Some in inks. Some from different angles. But all of the same scene.

Except one. A picture at the very bottom of the drawer that had been torn from a book. A reproduction of a painting she knew to be Ronnie's all-time favourite.

Millais' Ophelia, young, golden and beautiful, drowning herself in the lake.

Slowly she rose to her feet. A strange numbness was sweeping over her, just as it had when her father died. The protective balm of shock.

Ronnie wrapped his arms around her, tenderly stroking her neck. 'I learnt the lesson long ago,' he said softly, 'that if you really want to hurt someone then you hurt the person they most care about. For him it was his son. I knew it when I saw them together. You can feel the love people have for each other. They give it off like heat and his was stronger with his son than with anyone else. When I saw them together I wanted to die. I was fourteen years old, and for every day of those years I'd dreamed that one day I'd be that boy. That I'd have what he had. That my father would come and give it all to me. But I was nothing to him. He'd used my mother, then thrown her away. I couldn't let him get away with that. You see that, don't you?'

'Yes,' she whispered. 'I see it all.'

'I wish I could tell Mum. But she's not like us. She doesn't see things the way we do. She doesn't understand that people who hurt you have to be punished. We couldn't punish your stepfather that way. He was the one who had to die. But we can punish others. Anyone who ever hurts you . . .' He paused, kissing her cheek, '. . . will be made to pay. I've been waiting for you all my life and now I've found you I'll never let anyone hurt you again. My darling. My beloved. My soulmate.'

He continued to kiss her. She remained quite still, watching the fireworks explode but no longer hearing the sound they made. For the third time in her life she found herself in a silent movie. One with title cards that would act as prompts for how she should behave.

She waited and waited, feeling his arms around her and his lips against her skin.

But no prompts came.

One hour later Ronnie returned to his bedroom after walking Susan home.

This time he left the door unlocked. The newspaper and drawings were back in the drawer, hidden from those who did not see things the way he and Susan did.

She was gone now but yet still here. He could smell the residue of her presence. Lying down on his bed, he breathed slowly and deeply, sucking the last drops of her out of the air. Making them a part of himself.

Just as she was.

Nothing could part them now. They belonged to each other for ever. Bonded by love and their understanding of how the world really worked. Of how life was cold and cruel and that forgiveness was nothing but a placebo for the weak. Hatred was strength. Loathing was power. And vengeance was not the Lord's but theirs.

He stared up at the ceiling, half closing his eyes, picturing the faces of the people who had wronged him and those he loved. Vera. Peter. Susan's stepfather. His own father. Conjuring them up, one by one, all with faces lined by pain and shadowed by fear, while realizing that he had grown weak himself because he didn't hate them any more. At last he could forgive. Forget. Let go and look to the future.

Because he had Susan. His soulmate. His other half. The person who made him complete. The person who made the shabby, drab existence called life mean something in a way that even his beloved mother had never quite managed to do.

The person who had taught him what it was to feel totally and utterly happy.

His eyes remained focused on the ceiling. He smiled up at the faces of his victims, watching the dread fade from their faces as slowly, hesitantly, they began to smile back.

Midnight. As Ronnie exorcized the ghosts of vengeance past, Susan sat in her bath plastering her skin with soap.

The bath was deep, the water hot, but still she shivered. Shock was wearing off, its shields fading and leaving her to confront the full darkness of what the evening had revealed.

She rubbed soap into her neck, scrubbing hard at the flesh he had kissed. Still feeling the touch of his lips like an infection from which she would never be free. As with Lady Macbeth, it would take more than all the perfumes of Arabia to make her clean.

Her fingers were shaking. She dropped the soap. As she reached into the water she saw a face staring back at her. The face of a boy who had never hurt a soul and then been left to die in a cold, dark pit, terrified and alone. She shut her eyes, trying to escape from the image, but still it remained. Playing in the cinema of her mind where she sat with Ronnie, his arm around her shoulder and a smile upon his face, certain that she was enjoying the film as much as he was.

From somewhere in the house a floorboard creaked. For a moment she thought it was Uncle Andrew, back to pay her one of his secret visits. But that nightmare was over. Ronnie had helped her escape it before leading her into one that was even worse.

Is this my punishment? For what I've done? For what I am?

Downstairs her mother was sleeping. The woman who depended on her as the weak always depended on the strong. But she didn't feel strong now. Just filthy, frightened and alone with nothing but the flickering picture in her head for company.

She began to cry, sobbing into the water that cooled around her. Crying for her father to come and save her, just as a drowning boy had once cried, in vain, for his.

Half past eight the next morning. Dressed in her school uniform, she sat by the living-room window, watching for Ronnie.

He was due any minute. Coming to walk with her to school as he had every day since Uncle Andrew's death. Playing the role of protector as Uncle Andrew himself had once done thousands of midnights ago.

But she had no protector. To believe otherwise was to wish upon a star. Now, more than ever in her life, the only person she could depend on was herself.

Her mother hovered anxiously in the doorway. 'You look tired. Why not stay home today? No one will mind you taking a day off. Not after what you've been though.'

Oh, Mum, if you only knew what I've been through.

Hysterical laughter bubbled up inside her. She swallowed it down.

'Don't fuss. I didn't sleep well, that's all. I've missed enough school as it is. I really need to go in today.'

And that was true. She really did need to go. Keep up a façade of normality.

For if Ronnie even suspected a change in her feelings there was no telling what he might do.

Her stomach began to churn. She rubbed it with her hand while her mother looked suddenly embarrassed. 'Are you having your monthly visitor?'

She nodded, though in fact her period was two weeks late. Normally she was as regular as clockwork, but stress could cause delay. She had read that in a booklet her mother had given her, and she had certainly suffered a great deal of stress in the previous weeks.

That would be the reason. There could be no other.

Except one.

But she wouldn't even allow herself to think about that.

Ronnie appeared at the corner of the square, striding towards her house. 'Ronnie's coming,' she said, keeping her tone bright, feeling as if she was going to be sick.

You're strong, Susie. You can do this. It's just acting.

And you have to survive.

He rang the doorbell. She went to answer it, stopping in front of the mirror in the hallway to pinch colour into her cheeks. Preparing for her scene like one of the movie stars she had been told she resembled while the director and crew waited impatiently for her to hit her mark and say her lines.

Lights. Camera. Action.

The actress opened the door to find her leading man standing on the doorstep. He was smiling, his face a beautiful mask that gave no clue as to the ugliness that lay beneath. She smiled back, her expression as open and relaxed as his.

And when she spoke her tone was relaxed too.

'Hi, Ronnie. How are you?'

'Happy,' he told her. 'How else could I be when we're together?'

She rolled her eyes. 'My mother's warned me about boys like you.'

'And what sort of boy am I?'

'A charmer. The sort who'll say anything to get a girl's knickers off. But not me. I've got a reputation to keep.'

He laughed. She took his arm. Gave it a squeeze. He squeezed back. And heard a voice whisper inside his head.

She's different. Something's not right.

But her tone was animated. She looked happy. She looked just as she always did.

Except . . .

'I'm really glad you told me about Waltringham. I know it can't have been easy, just like it wasn't easy for me to tell you about what I wanted to do to Uncle Andrew. I was frightened you wouldn't understand. That you'd be shocked.' Another squeeze. 'I couldn't be sure you saw the world the same way I did.'

He felt himself relax. 'But I do.'

They crossed the square and entered Market Court. Women with baskets stood outside shops, waiting for them to open. 'It's always the same faces,' she remarked. 'You'd think they'd have learned to tell the time by now.'

He held up his arm, pointed to his wristwatch and raised his voice. 'The little hand is pointing to the eight and the big hand is pointing to the nine.'

She laughed. He kissed her cheek then waited for her to return the gesture.

'Aren't you going to kiss me back?' he asked.

'People are watching. I'm embarrassed.'

'Go on. I dare you.'

So she did. A peck, similar to dozens she had given him in the past, yet this one felt lighter. The effect of self-consciousness perhaps.

Though she had never displayed it before.

They entered the school lane, still arm in arm. She talked about the day ahead, complaining about teachers she didn't like and whose lessons she would have to sit through. 'I wish it was Saturday. I don't feel like another week of school.'

'Next Saturday let's spend the whole day together. We can do whatever you want.'

She nodded. Still smiling. Though he thought he felt her shiver.

But it was cold. Everyone shivered when it was cold.

They reached the gates and faced each other. 'I'll wait for you this afternoon,' he said. 'We can do something, perhaps.'

'I can't this afternoon. Mum's been feeling down. I should really be with her.'

He felt jealous. 'She takes up too much of your time. I want some of it too.'

'You get all of it. We're soulmates, remember, and soulmates are always together, even when they're apart. You mustn't be jealous of her. You're the one I want to be with. You know that, don't you?'

Then she kissed him. Properly this time, ignoring the others, who stopped and stared. He kissed her back and knew that it was true.

'Yes,' he said. 'I do.'

She headed through the gates. He watched her go, feeling reassured. Feeling happy.

And suddenly he saw it. What his brain had tried to tell him outside her front door. Her stride was as measured as always. Her shoulders back and head held high.

But her physical presence was diminished. Her aura of invulnerability reduced. Just as it had been around her stepfather.

The man of whom she had been afraid.

Two minutes later Charlotte saw Susan rush into the first-floor toilets. Concerned, she followed her in.

Susan stood at one of the sinks, vigorously scrubbing her face. 'What are you doing?' Charlotte asked her.

'Washing. What does it look like?'

'Then ease up on the elbow grease. Soap's supposed to clean your skin, not take it off. Anyway, you look spotless to me.'

Susan started to laugh. A shrill, edgy sound. Charlotte's concern increased. 'Is something the matter?'

The laughter stopped. Susan began to dry her face. The skin around her mouth looked raw. 'Susie, what's going on?'

'Nothing. I just feel grubby. The air always seems dirty this time of year, don't you think?'

Charlotte didn't but nodded anyway. A pretty third-year girl entered and began to comb her hair, checking her reflection in the mirror above the row of sinks.

Susan continued to dry her face. 'I enjoyed Saturday,' Charlotte told her, 'and so did Colin. He really liked Ronnie. He was saying that the four of us should go to the pictures. I'd like to see *Breakfast at Tiffany's* but Colin wants *The Magnificent Seven*.' She giggled. 'I said I didn't mind that either as I could drool over Steve McQueen and he got really jealous.'

Susan shook her head.

'Doesn't Ronnie like the pictures? We could do something else if you like. Colin's got a friend called Neville who's in a group. They're more jazz than rock'n'roll but Colin says they're quite good. Does Ronnie like jazz?'

'How the hell do I know? Ronnie and I aren't joined at the hip. Stop expecting me to know everything about him.' Susan marched out of the toilets.

'Is that Ronnie Sidney you're talking about?' asked the third-year girl. 'He's really gorgeous, isn't he?'

'Mind your own business,' a bewildered Charlotte told her before leaving herself.

Half past three. Susan walked out of the school gates to find Ronnie waiting for her.

She had expected him to be and had her smile ironed and ready to wear. It was only a short walk home. Ten minutes. Fifteen at the most. She could keep up the façade until then.

But for how much longer? Weeks? Months?

Years?

He walked towards her, looking just like the polite and charming boy everyone believed him to be. She felt like a rabbit caught in the headlights of an oncoming lorry. Cornered and helpless with no idea of what she was going to do.

But she would think of something. She had to.

For there was no one else who could help.

Once again the cameras were running. She kissed his cheek and restrained the urge to wipe her mouth. That gesture was not in the script and survival meant following the script to the letter.

'Hello, Ronnie. How was your day?'

*

Wednesday evening. Charles heard Ronnie talking on the telephone in the hall.

'Well, what about tomorrow evening? Surely she can spare you then.'

Guessing he was talking to Susan, Charles went to listen.

'I know it's difficult for her and I know how much she needs you, but what about me?'

The hiss of conversation from the receiver.

'I'm not being horrible. I just want to see you, that's all. We don't seem to have spent any time together. Not really. Not since . . .'

The hiss started up again.

'Friday, then. I'll look forward to it.' A pause. 'I love you.'

Again the hiss. Softer than before.

'Good. Because you'll always be that. No one else could ever take your place.'

Charles heard the receiver being replaced. He walked into the hall. 'All well, Ronnie?'

No answer. Ronnie kept his back to him, staring down at the phone.

'Ronnie?'

'What?'

'Is everything all right?'

'Susie's busy at the moment. She has to look after her mother. But that's all it is.' Ronnie's voice was calm but his body gave off tension like static. Charles was concerned. The last thing Ronnie's relationship with Susan needed was turbulence. If they were to fall out then who could tell what the consequences might be?

'Well, that's understandable,' he said soothingly. 'Her mother's been through a lot. They both have.'

'That's all it is,' said Ronnie again. 'There's no other reason.'

'Of course. What other reason could there be? Anyone can see how much she loves you, Ronnie. No one could take your place in her life.'

'The way you tried to take my place in my mother's, you mean?'

He was taken aback. 'I've never tried . . .' he began.

At last Ronnie turned, transfixing him with those eyes. But this time the barriers were gone, allowing the real Ronnie Sunshine to reveal himself.

Hate-driven. Savage. Murderous.

'You tried to buy her but it didn't work. She's still mine and always will be. Just like Susie. And no one, least of all you, is ever going to change that.'

They stared at each other. For a moment Ronnie's expression was almost bestial. As if he could attack at any minute.

And then, suddenly, the barriers were back in place. Ronnie began to laugh. 'Don't look so worried. I was only joking.' A pause. A dig. 'You should see your face.'

He nodded, swallowed and found his throat bone dry.

'I'm going upstairs to do my homework. See you at dinner. Mum's making lamb chops.' Another dig. 'One of my favourites.'

Ronnie walked upstairs. Charles remained where he was. His heart was racing. Afraid for Susan.

And, for the first time, himself.

Friday, late afternoon. Susan walked through Market Court with Ronnie.

They were on the way to his house. She was spending the evening there just as she had agreed. It was the last thing she wanted but she couldn't keep using her mother as an excuse to avoid him. The façade of normality had to be maintained. He must not guess that anything had changed.

Though she was beginning to suspect that he had done so already.

He was talking about Vera's accident. Describing it with relish and in detail while all the time studying her with eyes that seemed to be searching for something. 'One night,' he told her, 'soon after it happened, I crept into her room when she and Uncle Stan were sleeping and pulled back the blankets. I needed to see it. To see how bad it was. You understand that, don't you?'

'Of course.'

Are you testing me? Is that what this is about?

'I wanted to touch it but didn't in case I woke her up. I only ever touched it once. On the day I left. When I told her how much I hated her.'

She forced herself to smile. 'That must have felt good.'

'It did. I wish you'd been there so we could have shared the feeling.'

'We shared Uncle Andrew dying. I doubt anything could have felt as good as that.' She kept her voice steady and her smile in place. If this was a test then she had to pass. No matter what it cost her inside.

'Who knows what else we'll share?'

'Everything. That's what soulmates do.' She squeezed his arm. 'And that's what we are.'

His eyes roamed over the Court. Suddenly he began to smile. She followed his gaze and it led her to a little boy with curly blond hair, holding hands with a woman who was presumably his mother.

'Does he remind you of anyone?' Ronnie asked.

She nodded, not trusting herself to speak.

'It's incredible. They could be twins. All he needs is a pair of shorts and a beach ball.'

Her stomach was churning. The image of the body in the quarry forced its way into her mind like a drill in spite of all her attempts to keep it out. His eyes returned to her. Again they were appraising. They made her afraid.

But fear was for the weak and survival depended on remaining strong.

'I love you, Ronnie. You see what needs to be done and you do it. People say I'm strong but I've never met anyone as strong as you. You make everyone else look weak and me feel safe. And I love you for it.'

Then she leaned forward and kissed him full on the lips. For a moment they felt hard. Then they relaxed. He began to respond, probing her mouth with his tongue while the churning in her stomach increased.

She released him and stared into his face. At last it was warm and tender. The face of the boy she had fallen in love with, only to discover that it was a mask more concealing than any she had ever been forced to wear.

They were standing outside Cobhams. 'I need to use their Ladies,' she told him. 'I would have gone straight after school but I was too keen to see you.'

He smiled. 'Hurry, then. I'll be waiting.'

From her table by the window Alice watched Susan enter Cobhams.

Ronnie remained on the pavement outside. He looked handsome and happy, and the sight of him filled her with a mixture of aching desire and blinding hate.

But Susan didn't look happy. Her face was pale and strained and there was something odd about the way she moved. Slowly, but as if fighting the urge to run.

Susan entered the Ladies. Curious, Alice rose to her feet and followed her in.

Ronnie waited outside Cobhams.

Alice appeared and walked towards him. 'Who'd have thought it,' she said sweetly. 'Not me. I'd have thought you'd be rather good.'

'At what?'

'Kissing. I saw you and Susie kissing just now.'

'So?'

'So it looks like I've had a lucky escape.'

'From what?'

'A boy whose kiss makes girls vomit. Because that's what Susie's doing right now. I heard her in one of the cubicles.'

'That's a lie.'

'Ask her if you don't believe me. Or, if she tries to spare your feelings, then smell her breath.' Alice smiled. 'Poor Ronnie. You must be really terrible if even the town tart needs to be sick every time you touch her.' A soft giggle. 'Just wait until I tell people. If you take my advice you'll get the first bus back to that slum you came from, because you'll be a laughing stock in this town by the time I've finished with you.'

'And you won't have a face by the time I've finished with you.'

The smile faded. 'What do you mean?'

'That the skin on your face is very delicate. A single cup of acid could strip it bare.'

The blood drained from her cheeks.

'So please don't stick your pretty little nose into my business. Not unless you want to lose it altogether.'

She hurried away. He remained where he was, waiting for Susan.

A minute passed. Then another. What was going on? Why was she taking so long?

She appeared, looking relaxed. 'Sorry I was so long. There was a queue. You're lucky being a man. Being able to answer the call of nature without having to sit down.'

He nodded. It was plausible enough. He had spent enough time waiting for his mother in similar situations. Alice was lying. The way vicious bitches always did.

Susan gave a sniff. 'I think I'm getting a cold. Better not kiss you again in case I pass it on.'

And that was plausible enough too. He believed her. He wanted to believe her.

But he had to know for sure.

She opened her mouth to say something else. He put his hands around her face and pulled it towards him.

To smell the rotten, acidic stench on her breath.

She struggled free. 'What are you doing?'

He stared at her. The girl he had killed for. The girl he loved and believed to be his soulmate. The girl who knew him better than anybody. The girl to whom he had confided his greatest secret.

But she didn't love him. He frightened and repulsed her. Even more than her stepfather had.

He could see himself reflected in her eyes. Two magic mirrors that distorted his image, turning it into something ugly and monstrous. He gazed into them, seeing himself as she saw him.

Seeing himself as he really was.

And it hurt. More than anything or anyone had ever hurt him before.

'I've got a headache,' he told her. 'I should go home and lie down.'

'But . . .'

'You should go home yourself. Be with your mother while you can.'

He turned and walked away. She called out his name but he didn't look back.

*

Saturday, half past six in the morning. Susan sat at the kitchen table, cradling a mug of tea in her hands.

She had been there for hours. Unable to sleep. He knew. She was sure of it. All her years of drama training under Uncle Andrew had been for nothing. Less than a week of playing opposite Ronnie had exposed her for the pathetic amateur she still was.

Be with your mother while you can.

What did he mean? Was it a threat? Was her mother in danger? Was she?

From the garden came the first chirping of the birds. Soon light would come creeping through the window, banishing the shadows from the room but not from her head.

There were footsteps. Her mother appeared, wrapped in a dressing gown. 'Susie? What are you doing up so early?'

She didn't answer, just stared down at the stone-cold tea in the mug.

'Is something worrying you? You can tell me if there is.'

'Can I?'

'Of course. I'm your mother.'

She looked up at the pretty, fragile woman she had spent most of her life trying to protect. But now, more than anything else, she wanted some protection herself.

And there was one worry at least that it was safe to share.

'I think I'm pregnant.'

A look of absolute horror came into her mother's face. 'That's not possible.'

'I'm three weeks late, Mum. What else can it mean?'

'You can't be!' Her mother's tone was shrill. 'He hasn't been near you in months.'

She was taken aback. 'In months? What do you mean? I only met Ronnie two months ago and we didn't . . .'

She stopped. Understanding coming with the force of a bullet to the chest.

They stared at each other.

'You knew.'

A multitude of emotions darted across her mother's face. Alarm. Shock. Shame.

She rubbed her head, feeling as if it were about to explode. 'How long?'

'Susie, please . . .'

'How long? Not since it started. Don't tell me you've known since then. You can't have known since then!'

She waited for denial but none came. And in the face the shame remained.

'I was only eight years old! How could you stand by and let him do that to me?'

Her mother swallowed. 'Because I had no choice.'

'No choice? What do you mean? Did he threaten you?'

'We needed him. He gave us a home. He gave us security. If we . . .'

'We had a home! We may not have had much money but we would have managed. How can you say you had no choice?'

'I was alone. I was frightened. I . . .'

'Frightened?' She was almost screaming. 'How do you think I felt? I was eight years old! Just how frightened do you think I was?'

'He didn't hurt you. I wouldn't have let him hurt you. I used to hear him go up to you and I'd lie awake and listen. If I'd heard you cry out I would have gone up and stopped it. You have to believe that, Susie. I wouldn't have let him hurt you.'

'He gave me gonorrhoea, Mum! He infected me with a disease. You don't call that hurting me?'

Her mother shuddered.

'Well?'

'Susie, please . . .'

'Do you know what he said to me the first time? He told me it was my fault. He said that it was because I was wicked and because I wanted it to happen. But he said he was my friend and that he wouldn't tell and that I mustn't tell either because if I did and you found out you'd have another breakdown and you'd go away and I'd never see you again.' Suddenly she started to cry. 'And I couldn't let that happen because I promised Dad I'd always look after you. Every day I was terrified that someone was going to find out how wicked I was and tell you and that I'd lose you and all the time you knew too!'

By now her mother was also in tears. 'I'm sorry. You have to believe me.'

'Is that what you were going to say to Jennifer when she reached my age? Because he was going to do it to her too. She's only six and you were just going to sit there and let it happen!'

'No. I wouldn't have let him. I swear to you . . .'

'You're a liar!' She rose to her feet, hurling the mug against the wall. 'You're a bloody liar! You were going to let that bastard hurt her the way he did me. But I don't suppose she matters as much, does she? After all, it's not as if she's your daughter.'

'But it's over now. He's dead.'

'Because I killed him! I did it with Ronnie. I would have done it on my own but he wanted to help. We planned it for weeks. How to make it look like an accident.'

'I don't believe it.'

'What's the matter, Mum? Does the truth hurt? Then just pretend it's not happening, because that seems to be one of your specialities, doesn't it.'

Her mother began to whimper. Momentarily, years of conditioning kicked in. The urge to comfort. To shield. To protect. But the feelings were all based upon lies, and as long as she lived she would never surrender to them again.

'You're so weak, aren't you? You're the weakest person I've ever met and I despise you for it. You're no longer my mother. You're nothing. And I never want to see you again!'

Then she turned and ran from the room.

A quarter to eight. As she had done every day since he had come to live with her, Anna brought Ronnie an early-morning cup of tea.

The curtains were still drawn and the room in virtual darkness. She assumed he was still in bed. 'Are you awake?' she whispered.

'I'm here, Mum.'

She jumped. He was sitting at his desk. Quickly she put on the light. 'What are you doing there?'

'Thinking about you.'

'Me? What about me?'

'That you deserve better. You've always deserved better.'

There was another chair beside him. She sat down on it. 'Better than what?'

'Do you remember when I was little? When Vera used to say that you should have had me adopted?'

'Yes.'

'Maybe you should have listened.'

She was taken aback. 'How can you say that? You're the most wonderful thing that's ever happened to me. There's nothing and no one on this earth who could ever have made me give you up.'

'I know.' He took her hand and pressed it against his cheek, kissing it softly. 'I'm glad you married Charles. I wasn't when it happened. I hated him because I didn't want to share you. But I don't hate him any more. He's a good man. You were right about that. I'm glad he's going to be here for you when . . .'

His words petered out. She felt alarmed. 'Ronnie, what are you saying?'

'Only that I really love you. No matter what happens you must never, ever doubt that.'

A chill passed through her. 'You're frightening me. I don't know what you're saying.'

'Neither do I.'

'Ronnie . . .'

A faint Ronnie Sunshine smile. 'I'm sorry, Mum. I didn't mean to frighten you. I'm just tired and people always talk rubbish when they're tired.'

He leant across and hugged her, holding her so tight that it felt as if he would never let her go.

A quarter to nine. Charles was in his car, heading out of Kendleton towards Oxford, when he saw Susan walking by the side of the road.

The morning was cold but she had no coat. Her arms were wrapped around herself, her lips moving continually. Alarmed, he stopped the car and called out her name.

She didn't answer. Just kept walking. He climbed out of the car and hurried after her. 'Susie? What is it? What's happened?'

'She knew.'

'Who? Knew what?'

'My mother! She knew! All the time she knew!'

He could see her shivering. 'Come with me,' he said. 'Out of the cold . . .'

Ten minutes later Susan was sitting in Charles's car, his jacket wrapped around her while the engine rumbled and filled the car with warmth.

'So what does she know?' he asked her.

'I can't tell you.'

'Is it about your stepfather? What he did to you?'

She stared at him. 'How can you know about that?'

'Because once, two years ago, Henry Norris told me about a young girl patient of his whose father was hurting her. He didn't tell me who the girl was. Only that she looked like a film star. When I saw how nervous you were with Henry's widow I put the pieces together.'

She felt exposed. Vulnerable. Quickly she pulled the jacket tighter round herself.

'Does Ronnie know too?' he asked.

'Yes.'

'Was it his idea to kill him?'

Silence. Except for the hiss of the engine.

'I'm not trying to trap you, Susie. I'm not judging you either. I just want to help.'

'It was my idea. I would have done it even if I hadn't met Ronnie. He was going to start on Jennifer, you see, and I couldn't let that happen. I couldn't let her go through what I'd been through. I had to stop him and I didn't know what else to do. I knew no one would believe me if I told them, and if I did try to tell he might have hurt my mother and I didn't want her to know and . . .'

She couldn't go on. A lump in her throat blocked the words that would have followed. He moved closer, putting his arm around her. 'It's all right,' he said soothingly. 'You're safe.'

'Not from Ronnie. When he told me what he'd done he thought I'd be pleased but I wasn't. I was disgusted. And he hates me for that.'

'What had he done?'

She told him about Waltringham and Ronnie's father. About the body in the quarry and the pictures in the drawer.

'How many pictures were there?' he asked eventually.

'I don't know. Dozens at least.'

He whistled softly between his teeth. 'Jesus Christ.'

'I tried not to let him see how I really felt. But I couldn't fool him. He's too clever.' She swallowed. 'And anyway, who am I to judge him? I've killed too.'

'You can't compare yourself to him.'

'Yes I can.'

'No you can't.' Taking her chin in his hand, he stared into her eyes. 'Susie, listen to me. You killed because you were frightened. You wanted to protect Jennifer and didn't know how else to do it. Perhaps you were wrong. There are people who would say that you were wrong and that you did a bad thing. But that doesn't make you a bad person and it certainly doesn't make you like Ronnie. You are nothing like him. Nothing at all.'

'I'm still a murderess.'

'And Henry Norris was a murderer. But he was still a good man and one I was proud to call a friend.'

'Henry Norris?'

He nodded. 'Though we met as undergraduates he was a good dozen years older than me. He'd fought in the First World War in the trenches. He never liked to talk about it but one evening when we'd been drinking together he told me a story he'd never told anyone else. It was about a young private in his regiment called Collins. A decent enough man on the surface, so Henry said, but there was something missing in him. Some basic human empathy. The expression Henry used was 'dead behind the eyes'.

'One day a German regiment attacked them. They were repelled but one German became trapped in the trench. Henry said that he came across Collins torturing the German. Stabbing him again and again in the legs and arms with a bayonet. The German was little more than a boy. He was wounded and helpless and screaming for mercy but Collins just kept laughing, enjoying every second of it. Henry begged him to stop but he wouldn't. Just kept on and on laughing. So Henry shot him. A single bullet in the heart. And when he told me the story he said that though he knew it was wrong he's never regretted it.'

She leant against him, pulling the jacket ever tighter. Breathing in

338

its musty scent of old tobacco and remembering how her father's jackets had smelled the same way.

'Do you think that about Ronnie?' she asked. 'That he's dead behind the eyes?'

'I think there's something missing in him, yes. I sensed it as soon as I met him. That and the fact that he was hiding something. His mother senses it too. I think she always has. In fact, I think she knows about Waltringham. But she won't acknowledge it because Ronnie's been the whole joy of her life since she was just seventeen, and when you love someone like that you can't allow yourself to accept anything that could take that joy away. Love makes you blind. Wilfully, perhaps, but blind none the less.'

'My mother didn't love my stepfather. She was just weak.'

'But she loves you.'

'I don't love her, though. Not any more.'

'Yes you do. You can't just choose to stop loving someone. It doesn't work like that.'

'It does for Ronnie.'

His arm was still around her. She turned to stare into his damaged face and the eyes that were so like her father's. She wanted her father. She wanted to be a little child again. To escape back to the time when she had never been afraid.

'I think Ronnie's going to try and hurt my mother. He as good as said so the last time I saw him, and we both know he's capable of doing it. Waltringham is proof of that.'

'But that was aimed at a father who was never more to him than a dream. A fantasy. It's easy to hurt someone like that because it doesn't seem real. It's different with someone you truly love, and he still loves you, I'm sure of it. He can't stop caring about you because he wants to, and if he still cares then there's a chance he can be reasoned with.'

'There's something else I could do.'

'What?'

'Go to the police. Tell them what we did. They'd take me into custody but they'd take him in too, and that way he couldn't hurt anyone else.'

'But you can't do that. They'd send you to prison. You'd be ruining your own life.'

'I don't care about my life. Not any more.'

'But you care about Jennifer. You say you're her big sister but you're wrong. I've watched the two of you together and you're the closest thing that little girl has ever had to a mother. She's already lost her real one. Do you want to deprive her of another one too?'

She shook her head. 'That's not fair.'

'But it's true. Do you want to hurt her like that?'

'Of course not! I wouldn't let anyone hurt her ever. I love her more than anyone in the world and I'd rather . . .'

Then she stopped.

'Susie?'

'Oh my God.'

'What?'

'Jennifer. If Ronnie wants to hurt someone to get back at me, she's the one he'll pick.'

She saw him pale. Felt herself do the same.

'Where is she now?' he asked.

'At home.'

'Then she'll be all right.'

'Like the little boy in Waltringham was?'

He started his engine. 'She'll be all right. I'm sure of it.'

'Just drive. Please!'

Five minutes later Susan climbed out of Charles's car in front of Jennifer's house.

The door opened. Uncle George appeared, waving to her, looking surprised but relaxed. 'I was just coming to find you,' he said. 'I thought you'd be at home.' Reaching into the pocket of his jacket, he handed her a sealed envelope. 'This is for you.'

'What is it?'

He smiled. 'The first clue.'

'For what.'

'The treasure hunt Ronnie's organized. Jenjen's very excited about it.'

Her heart began to pound. 'Jenjen? Where is she?'

'With Ronnie. He phoned yesterday evening to say that you were still feeling down so he'd thought up a treasure hunt to cheer you up and asked if Jenjen could help him plant the clues. He came for her first thing this morning but asked me to wait for an hour before telling you. Like I said, Jenjen's very excited. She told me last week that Ronnie's one of her favourite people.'

The door of the house was still open. From inside came the sound of the telephone. Uncle George looked at his watch and frowned. 'I'd better take that. I'm expecting a call about work any minute.' Then he walked back into the house.

She tore open the envelope to find a note inside.

Come to the hut in the wood. For her sake come alone. And tell no one.

For a moment she thought she was going to scream. But she couldn't do that. She had to be calm. She had to think.

Charles took the note and read it. 'You can't go,' he told her.

'I have to go. What else can I do?'

'Call the police. I don't think we have any choice now.'

'He said tell no one.'

'Half an hour ago you were all for telling them.'

'Because I wanted to stop him doing something like this. But he *has* done it. He's got her and that means he's the one with the power. The note says for her sake come alone. If he sees the police, who knows what he might do.'

'And if you go alone, what will he do then?'

'At least she'll still be alive when I get there.'

'Then let me come with you. You can't go alone.'

'I'm not alone.' She touched her stomach. 'I'm pregnant, or at least I think I am. He doesn't know that. Maybe it'll make a difference if he does.'

'And maybe it won't.' He seized her arm. 'Susie . . .'

'I can't wait any longer!'

His hold remained firm. 'One hour. I'm waiting one hour then I call the police.'

She pulled free. 'Do what you want. I'm going now!'

Fifteen minutes later she ran through the woods. A cocktail of panic and adrenalin making her heart thump so hard that she feared it might explode.

She was deep in them now. The part where people rarely came and where fallen leaves lay in piles on the ground like unmarked graves. Once, centuries ago, a woman had searched these woods for a daughter she would never find. Or so the story went. Perhaps, in time, there would be another story told of a girl who had been lost for ever and of another who had searched in vain.

But the story was still being written. It could change. She had the power to change it. She just had to keep believing that she could.

She carried on running, on legs that felt as if they were made of lead, while the wind tugged at her hair like the spirit of a mischievous child.

Charles walked into his study and sat down at his desk.

His head was spinning. He didn't know what to do. Every instinct screamed for him to call the police, but what if Susan was right? What if Ronnie felt provoked? Threatened? What might he do? Who might he hurt?

And if he did call, what would he tell them? Attempted abduction? What was his evidence? Jennifer liked and trusted Ronnie and had gone with him willingly. How could anyone think that she was in danger? To the outside world, Ronnie was the perfect son. The perfect gentleman. To shatter the façade he would have to tell them other things that Ronnie had done. And who he had done them with.

But there was the note. That was evidence of threat. It was, wasn't it?

He drummed his fingers on the desk as the thoughts jostled in his brain.

And noticed something.

The bottom left-hand drawer of the desk wasn't closed properly. The drawer where he kept college papers and, buried beneath them, an old handgun.

He had never told Ronnie about the gun. But he had told Anna, and she could have passed the information on. Innocently. In conversation. While Ronnie gave her one of his angelic smiles and stored the knowledge away for a rainy day.

Opening the drawer, he searched for the weapon. And found it gone.

That decided him. He went to the telephone in the hall, picked up the receiver and dialled. 'Hello. Police. I need to report . . .'

'No!'

Anna stood behind him on the stairs. 'Don't. Please.'

He put down the receiver. 'I have to. He's taken Jennifer.'

Her eyes widened. He saw her swallow.

'You know what he's capable of, Anna.'

'He's not capable of hurting her. Not a child.'

'He's taken my gun.'

Again he saw her swallow. 'If he has, then it's only for a game. That's all.'

'And what about Waltringham? Was that a game too?'

'Nothing happened in Waltringham!' Her voice was shrill. 'Not that involved him. It was just coincidence, that's all.'

'Do you believe that, Anna? Do you really believe that?'

'He knew what his father looked like. I'd given him a picture. He must have seen his father in the paper and decided to keep it.'

'And what about the drawings?'

'They're just drawings. They don't mean he's guilty. He wouldn't hurt a child. He's not capable of it.'

'He told Susan that he did. And he was proud of it. He wanted her to be proud too.'

'She's lying! You know what she is. She's a . . .'

'Murderess? Is that what you're going to say? Because that's right. She is. And so is he, because they killed her stepfather together.'

She sank to her knees. 'She made him do it. She used him.'

'Nobody makes Ronnie do anything, Anna. He's not a puppet. He does what he wants to do, as he did in Waltringham.'

'He is not a monster!' It came out as a wail. 'He's not! He's just a baby. He's my baby and he's not capable of hurting anyone. He's good. He's perfect. I know he is. I know him better than anyone!'

She buried her head in her hands and began to howl, just as she must have done on the day when she was thirteen and returned home to find her house destroyed and her family lost for ever. The sight cut through him like a blade. He hated himself for what he was doing.

He didn't want to hurt her. All he had ever wanted was to protect her from pain.

But he couldn't protect her from the truth.

And there were others who needed protection too.

He crouched down beside her, pulling her to him, stroking her hair while she buried her head in his chest. 'I don't want to do this,' he said softly. 'But I have to. For Jennifer's sake. She really is only a baby. You see that, don't you?'

Silence. Her sobs were easing though her body continued to tremble.

'Don't you?'

Still no answer.

'Don't you?'

He heard her sigh. Then a faint whisper. 'Yes. Do it. Don't let him hurt Jennifer.'

He went to the phone. She came too, wrapping herself around him as he made the call, like a vine that could not stand without support.

Susan reached the hut.

She stopped just outside it, desperate to enter yet terrified of what she might find. Her lungs felt raw. She bent over, gasping, trying to slow her breathing.

And heard Jennifer laugh.

Straightening up, preparing herself to do whatever it took, she knocked on the door. 'It's me. Susie.'

More laughter. Jennifer's once again. She turned the handle and walked in.

They were sitting together on the floor in the far corner of the hut. An old box stood between them, covered with playing cards. A perfectly innocent scene, or so it would have been if it hadn't been for the gun that Ronnie was cradling in his lap.

Jennifer beamed at her. She smiled back, trying to act as normally as possible. Not wanting to frighten Jennifer. Remaining by the door. Not making any sudden moves that could provoke Ronnie, who watched her with eyes that seemed empty. Blank. Dead behind the eyes. Like the soldier in the trench who had tortured his prisoner. Was he going to torture Jennifer? Was he going to torture her?

'What are you two doing?' she asked. Struggling to keep her voice calm.

'Ronnie's showing me card tricks. I can do a new one.' Jennifer fanned the cards then held them out. 'You have to pick one.'

She hesitated. Not sure what to do. Through the window she could see the wind shuffling the leaves that covered the ground.

'Pick a card!' Jennifer insisted.

She took a step forward. Ronnie pointed the gun at her. 'Freeze!'

She did. As rigid as a statue. Once again Jennifer laughed. 'We're cowboys and you're an Indian,' she told Susan.

'That's right.' Ronnie stroked Jennifer's hair. 'She's a wicked squaw who wants to scalp you with a tomahawk. But she's not going to because I'm going to shoot her. Do you think I should shoot her, Jenjen?'

'Yes!'

The gun remained aimed at her. She stared down its barrel, wondering whether this was the moment when she was going to die. Not that she was afraid. If her life could save Jennifer's then she would give it gladly.

But she was afraid of Jennifer seeing it. Of what the sight might do to her. The effect it could have on the rest of her life.

However long that might be.

She took a deep breath, steadying herself. Determined to stay calm. The air in the hut was stale and rank. 'If you're going to shoot me then you need a sheriff present. One of you must ride back to town to fetch one. The other can stay and guard me.'

Jennifer frowned. 'Do we need a sheriff?' she asked Ronnie.

He shook his head.

'Yes you do. A real cowboy wouldn't shoot a squaw. Not without a sheriff present.'

Ronnie continued to stroke Jennifer's hair. 'A bad cowboy would.'

'I'm not a bad cowboy,' Jennifer told him.

'But I am,' he replied. 'There always has to be one bad cowboy in a film. The sort of cowboy who drinks too much and gets into fights and shoots people he thinks are cheating at cards. Have you been cheating, Jenjen?'

Susan felt herself grow cold all over. Once again Jennifer laughed. 'No!'

'I think you have.'

'No she hasn't.' She fought to keep her voice from growing shrill. 'She's too young to cheat or to do anything bad. Not like me. I've done a lot of bad things. I deserve to be shot, even without a sheriff. But she doesn't. Not even the baddest cowboy in the world could shoot her.'

'Couldn't he?' Ronnie turned to Jennifer. 'You've been cheating, partner. You have to pay the price.'

Then he aimed the gun at her face. She sat there, still laughing, still thinking it was a game.

And Susan couldn't stand it any more.

'No, Ronnie, please don't hurt her! Hurt me. I'm the one you hate. I'm the one who deserves it. Think of your mother. Think about how much you love her and of what she means to you. If you kill Jennifer she'll know about it. This isn't like Waltringham. It can't be kept secret. She may manage to forgive you if you kill me but she'll never forgive you if you kill Jennifer! You know she won't!'

Jennifer was staring at her. Her smile gone as she realized that this wasn't a game. She began to cry, suddenly terrified. Susan rubbed her face and found that she was crying too.

For a moment Ronnie continued to point the gun at Jennifer. His other hand covered her arm, holding her in place.

Then he put the gun back in his lap.

'Go and get the sheriff,' he told her.

Jennifer ran towards Susan, throwing her arms around her. Susan wanted to offer comfort but there wasn't time. This was her moment and she had to act. She shoved Jennifer towards the door. 'Run, Jenjen. You know the way home. Run as fast as you can and don't ever forget how much I love you.'

'But, Susie . . .'

'Go! Go now!' She thrust Jennifer outside then closed the door behind her. From the window she watched a little figure running into the distance.

I've done it. She's safe.

She turned to face Ronnie. He was still sitting on the floor, the gun in his lap.

'Thank you,' she said.

He didn't answer. Just stared at her with eyes that didn't seem dead any more. Warmth was creeping into their corners like the first rays of sunlight at dawn.

'Are you going to kill me?' she asked. 'I'm not afraid to die but there's something you need to know. I'm pregnant, Ronnie. I'm going to have a baby. Our baby.'

'Jennifer was our baby. That's what it felt like when we killed him. That we were protecting our child.'

She swallowed, wiping at tears that continued to fall. 'Did it?'

'Yes. I couldn't hurt her. I wanted to but I couldn't. I don't expect you to believe that but it's true.'

'I do believe it. You've just proved it, haven't you?'

They stared at each other. 'Would you really have died for her?' he asked.

'Yes.'

'I would have died for you. I still would. I want to hate you but I can't. You're not like my father. He was nothing but a face in a photograph. Just a dream I had that helped make life more bearable. I could walk out of his life and never look back because I'd never been a part of it anyway. But I was a part of yours and I want . . .' He stopped, rubbing his head. 'And I want . . .'

'What?'

'I want things to be like they were before I told you about Waltringham. I want it to go back to how it was the day before. In Cobhams with Jennifer and your friends. Kissing in public and shocking your neighbours. I've never been as happy as I was then and I want it back.'

She shook her head.

'We can pretend Waltringham never happened. I'll burn the stuff. We'll never talk about it again. We don't ever have to talk about it or even think about it again.'

He rose to his feet, looking suddenly like a frightened child. Feelings of protectiveness rose up in her. She didn't want to have them but they clung to her like leeches.

'We can do it,' he said, his tone a mixture of hope and desperation. 'I know we can. We have to do it. We're going to have a baby. We have to be together for that if for nothing else.'

He reached out to touch her face. His eyes were beseeching. For a moment she thought it was possible. She had loved him once. Perhaps she could again. He was smiling at her; his eyes those of the boy she had fallen in love with. She gazed into them.

And saw a dead child floating in the water.

She pulled away. 'I can't. Things can never be like that again. We can go back to town together. We can tell them that this was just a game. They don't have to know anything else. But it can never be like it was between us, Ronnie. Never.'

He sighed. The pleading look faded from his face, replaced by acceptance. 'I know.'

Silence. Except for the wind hammering against the window.

'So what happens now?' she whispered.

'This,' he replied, picking up the gun.

Her heart began to race. 'What are you doing?'

'What I have to.' He smiled. 'Don't be scared. Just tell my mother I couldn't have hurt Jenjen. Tell her that I love her. And that I'm sorry.'

Suddenly she understood. Horror swept through her. 'Don't, Ronnie. Please.'

Still smiling, he shook his head, put the gun to his temple and squeezed the trigger.

January. Two months later.

Saturday morning. Grey and cold. Susan lay in her bed, staring up at the ceiling.

It was her sixteenth birthday. By rights she should have been spending it in a cell. When, stunned and shaking, she had walked out of the hut, it had been to see two police officers hurrying towards her.

'Are you here to arrest me?' she had asked one of them.

'Arrest you? Why? You're no kidnapper. Where is he? Is he still armed . . .?'

And even in her dazed state she had realized that Charles had told them nothing of her own crimes. That they believed Ronnie's actions were those of an unstable, jilted lover and that she was as much a victim as Jennifer had been.

So she had got away with it. There would not be justice. Not for her. But there was still punishment.

Her mother was downstairs, cooking her the breakfast she would eat in silence, just as she ate every meal they shared. They existed together but that was all. Occasionally her mother would try to speak. Try to explain. But though she listened she never heard anything that could make her understand. And she could not forgive.

Just as Uncle George could not forgive her.

She hadn't seen Jennifer since that day in the woods. Uncle George had forbidden it. 'She could have died because of you!' he had screamed at her. 'You should have called the police at once. You never should have got involved with that lunatic! I could have lost her for ever and it would have been your fault and I can never forgive you for that.' She had sensed that somewhere in his words lay anger at himself and that he found it easier to blame her than deal with his own guilt. But the knowledge didn't change anything. He had taken Jennifer to stay with friends on the other side of the country, and she had heard through others that he did not plan to return.

Her mother and Jennifer. The two people she had loved most and had killed to protect. Now, for different reasons, both were lost to her for ever in the aftermath of that act.

The papers had had a field day. There were moments when she could smile at the irony. Where her stepfather's death had barely merited a paragraph, she was now the subject of a dozen articles. 'A teenage femme fatale,' was how one paper had described her, as it slavered over the story of young love gone so dreadfully wrong. On more than one occasion journalists had followed her in the street, calling out questions, wanting more. But she had remained silent, keeping all her stories to herself.

There were still some friends. Charlotte. Lizzie. Arthur, when he came home from school. The ones who didn't join in the gossip that people like Alice were spreading like wildfire. And most important of all there was Charles Pembroke. She saw him regularly and treasured the time they spent together. He was the one person from whom she need keep nothing secret. For hours at a time he would listen without judging, and often she would stare into his ruined face and wish he had been the man her mother had married all those years ago. A man she knew her father would have liked and would have wanted to take his place in her life.

'You have to go on fighting, Susie,' he had said to her over coffee during one of their meetings. 'You can't allow this to crush you.'

'I'm not.'

'Yes you are. The fire inside you is going out. You look defeated.'

'Maybe I am. Jenjen's gone. My mother might as well be. And Ronnie too. I miss him, you know. I miss being with him. I miss the way he used to make me laugh. The way he stuck up for me. The way he could make me feel brave when I was afraid.' She paused. Swallowed. 'I miss all of it before Waltringham.'

Her hand was on the table. He covered it with his own. 'But in time you won't. At least not in a way that hurts. The pain will ease.'

'For me, perhaps. But what about his mother?'

'For her too.' He sighed. 'I hope. I'm doing my best to help her. In a way it's pointless. No one will ever take Ronnie's place. But at least she's not alone. Unlike when she lost her family, this time she has me.' A rueful smile. 'For what it's worth.'

'It's worth a lot. She's lucky to have you as a husband, just as I am to have you as a friend.'

'You'll always have me as a friend. I'll always help you. I want you to have a good life, Susie. A happy life. You deserve it but you have to fight for it. For you and your baby. If all that's happened is to mean something, then you have to go on fighting.'

'Do you think I'll end up winning?'

'I know it. You're strong, Susie. Every bit as strong as your father once told you, and a bit more besides.'

Perhaps he was right. She wanted him to be right.

But she didn't believe it. Not inside. She was tired, and yet there was always more fighting to be done. Somehow one of the papers had found out that she was pregnant. There had been a story about it the previous day. There in black and white for everyone to see and pass judgement. And they would judge. People in Kendleton were masters at judging others.

And so, after lying awake half the night, she had finally decided what she must do.

Rising from her bed, she dressed and went downstairs. Her mother was waiting for her in the kitchen at a table laden with food and presents. 'Happy birthday, darling,' she said in a voice dripping with apprehension.

'I'm leaving, Mum. As soon as the baby's born. I'm going to have it adopted and then I'm moving away from here.'

'Move away?' Her mother looked horrified. 'But you can't. What about . . .'

'You? You'll just have to look after yourself. You're the parent, after all, and I think I've looked after you all I want to.'

'You can't just decide this, Susie. We have to talk about it. Sit down. Have something to eat. Open some of your presents.'

'You should have saved your money. I don't want presents. Not from you. See you later. I'm going for a walk.'

Turning, she made her way towards the door.

Noon. Charles, who had been working in his study, went to find his wife.

Both the living room and the kitchen were empty. His heart sinking, he realized where she would be.

She was sitting in what had once been Ronnie's room, at a chair in front of the window where his desk had once stood, staring out at the river.

'You shouldn't sit here,' he said gently. 'You know it upsets you.'

'I wanted to watch the water.'

'You can do that downstairs. There's no heating here. It's cold. Come downstairs where you'll be warm.'

Her eyes remained fixed upon the window. 'I'm fine.'

'Can I bring you anything?'

'No.' A pause. 'Thank you.'

He turned to go. She called out his name. He turned back. 'What?'

'Will you answer me something? Honestly. Even if you know the answer will hurt.'

'Of course.'

Silence. He heard her sigh.

'Ask me. I'll tell you the truth.'

'Was it my fault? That he did the things he did. That he . . . that he was what he was.'

'No.' His tone was forceful. Striding across the room, he crouched down beside her. 'None of it was your fault. You did everything a mother could for him and he loved you for it. That's what he was telling you at the end.'

She stared at him with red, swollen eyes. She cried often and her face looked tired and worn. But it was still the loveliest face he had ever seen.

'It's not your fault, Anna. You must never, ever blame yourself. Some people just don't see the world the way others do. It's to do with how they're made. It has nothing to do with how they were raised or how they were loved.'

'There's something else Ronnie told me at the end. Something I haven't told you.'

'What?'

'He said he was glad I'd married you. That you were a good man and he was glad you'd be here for me when . . .' She swallowed. 'When he wasn't. And he was right. I haven't had much luck in my life, but one thing I know is that I struck gold when I met you.'

'Do you really mean that?'

'Yes. I love you, Charles. It may not be the hearts-and-flowers love I felt for Ronnie's father, but it's real. More real, if anything. I'm proud that you're my husband.'

He took her hands in his and kissed them. 'I'm the proud one,' he whispered.

Silence. Outside, ducks and swans fought on the river.

'Did you see Susie yesterday?' she asked eventually.

'Yes.'

'How is she?'

'Struggling. But she'll cope. She's too strong not to.'

'Do you think the baby will be strong too?'

'I hope so. And I hope it has its grandmother's warmth.'

She leaned over and for the first time kissed the scarred side of his face.

'And its grandfather's heart,' she said.

He pulled up a chair. They sat together, her hands still in his, watching the water.

Lunchtime. Susan walked through Market Court.

She had been walking all morning. Through the woods and along the river bank. Two places she had always loved because of their association with her father, until other associations had come along to spoil them for ever.

But it didn't matter. Soon she would find other places to love. When finally she had left Kendleton behind.

She walked by Cobhams. Charlotte, who was sitting in the window with Colin, banged on the glass and gestured for her to come in.

The place was full, as it always was on Saturday. The air was thick with voices and the pounding beat of rock'n'roll from the jukebox. But as she entered it seemed to quieten.

She sat down beside Charlotte who smiled at her. 'Happy birthday. I've got a present for you at home. I was going to bring it round later.'

'Thanks.' She smiled back while feeling eyes creep over her from other tables.

'Colin and I thought we'd go to the pictures this evening. Why don't you come too?'

'I don't want to intrude.'

'You won't be. We want you to come.'

Colin nodded. 'My friend's band is playing later on. We can go and listen to them.'

She shook her head. He grinned. 'They're not that bad.'

'I'm sure they're not. It's just that I don't feel very sociable at the moment.'

'It doesn't matter what they say in the papers,' Charlotte told her. 'Getting pregnant isn't a sin. Only stupid, small-minded people think otherwise.'

'And if it was,' Colin added, 'the human race would die out.'

Again she smiled. But it was a weak gesture. She felt weak. Tired and defeated. Others continued to stare. Once she would have shrugged it off and laughed. But not now.

She wanted to be out of this. To escape. To hide.

And then someone called out, 'Murderess!'

Startled, she looked for the source. Alice Wetherby sat surrounded by friends, her expression both condemning and triumphant. She tried to think of a retort. The sort she would have tossed out so effortlessly two months earlier. But she had been a different person then.

And besides, it was true.

Charlotte rose to her feet. 'Shut up! You don't know what you're talking about.'

'Don't I? We all know why Ronnie really shot himself. Because that tart got herself pregnant and was trying to force him to marry her. I think he did the right thing too. No one but an idiot would want to saddle themselves with a slut like her for a wife.'

Charlotte looked furious. Colin did too. Momentarily she was touched by their concern. But it was her fight, not theirs, and she didn't feel up to climbing into the ring any more.

'I'm going,' she told them. 'Have fun tonight.' As she hurried for the door, Alice shouted, 'Good riddance!' and a few others laughed.

She made her way across Market Court, through the shoppers and strollers, not knowing where she was headed, just needing to get away, despising herself for her weakness but unable to find the strength inside herself. Sensing that it had been worn away into nothing.

And then she saw Jennifer.

She was standing on the other side of the Court, holding Uncle George's hand, scuffing her foot and looking bored as he stood talking to one of her neighbours.

Until she saw Susan and her face lit up like an electric bulb.

'Susie!'

Uncle George turned, saw her too and frowned. He tightened his hold on Jennifer's hand while she tried to pull away, eventually breaking free and charging across the Court. Susan crouched down, holding out her arms, and Jennifer threw herself into them. Susan was so overwhelmed with happiness at seeing her that she burst into tears, just as Jennifer did.

'Oh, Jenjen, I've missed you so much.'

'I've missed you too. It was horrid with Dad's friends. I hated them.'

They gazed at each other. Still crouching, she wiped Jennifer's cheeks. 'Jennifer, come back!' roared Uncle George. Others turned to look but Jennifer remained where she was.

'Why are you here?' Susan asked. 'I thought you were never coming back.'

'That's what Dad said but we stayed with Uncle Roger and Auntie Kate and I didn't like it at all. I told Dad I didn't like it but he said we had to stay so I was really bad. I kept singing all the songs that made you cross and Uncle Roger got cross too and Auntie Kate had some stupid china dolls and was always saying how lovely they were so I threw them out of the window and she went mad!'

In spite of her tears Susan began to laugh. 'I wish I'd seen that.'

'I kept telling Dad I wanted to come home, so after I broke the dolls he said we could and we came this morning and we saw your mum.' Suddenly Jennifer's expression became anxious. 'She said you were going away. Are you?'

She swallowed. 'I thought I might.'

'Don't. Please don't!' Once again Jennifer started to cry. 'You mustn't!'

Again she wiped Jennifer's cheeks. 'Does it matter that much to you, Jenjen?'

'Yes.'

'Then I'll stay. Always. I promise.'

Jennifer smiled. Once again Uncle George called out to her. His expression was still angry. Susan expected him to march over and drag Jennifer away but he didn't. Just remained where he was, watching. Allowing the two of them to have some precious moments together.

He wants to forgive me. He hasn't done yet. But he wants to.

But there was someone else she needed forgiveness from. The person from whom it mattered most of all.

'Jenjen, I want to tell you something and you must believe it. What happened with Ronnie in the woods. I never meant for it to happen but it was my fault that it did and I'm more sorry than you can know. I don't want anything bad to ever happen to you. I'd rather all the bad things in the world happened to me than even the smallest bad thing happened to you.'

Jennifer's expression became solemn. 'I know.'

'Do you forgive me?'

Once again Jennifer hugged her. She hugged back, feeling the tears welling up for the second time, but once again they were tears of happiness. Taking Jennifer's hand, she pressed it to her stomach. 'I'm going to have a baby, Jenjen. Did my mum tell you that?'

Jennifer's eyes widened. 'Really?'

'Yes. And when it's born I want you to be its big sister, just like I'm yours.'

The smile returned. As bright as the sun. 'What will it be called?'

'I don't know yet. We'll choose the name together. And when it's bigger we can take it to the river and the park and do all the things I used to do with you. Would you like that?'

'Yes!'

'I love you, Jenjen.'

'I love you too.'

Again they hugged each other. She stroked Jennifer's hair. 'Now go back to your dad,' she whispered. 'And I'll see you soon.'

Jennifer did as she was told. For a moment Susan remained crouching on the ground. Then she began to rise. But it felt as if she were being lifted. As if a pair of invisible hands were guiding her, pulling her shoulders back and straightening her spine.

Her father, perhaps.

And suddenly the weak, frightened person was gone, replaced by one who felt as if she could fight the world single handed. The Susan Ramsey who knew exactly who she was and was not going to allow anyone's narrow-minded morality make her feel ashamed.

Uncle George led Jennifer away. He turned and looked at her. She raised her hand in greeting. He didn't wave back but for a second his eyes looked warm and she knew that he would forgive her, just as eventually she would manage to forgive her mother. It would take time but it would happen. She would make it happen.

She stood in the middle of Market Court, watching the people who walked by, many of whom were casting glances in her direction.

The girl who had been in the papers. The girl who was notorious. She brushed their stares aside like insects. It didn't matter what they thought. It didn't matter at all.

Charlotte appeared beside her. 'I'm sorry, Susie. I shouldn't have called you in. I should have known Alice would say something spiteful.'

'It doesn't matter. It'll take a lot more than that to ruin my day.' She pointed at Alice, who was now walking across the Court with her shopping-laden mother, both of them giving her dirty looks. 'Watch this,' she said, and then, gesturing to Charlotte, raised her voice. 'Why are you staring at her, Mrs Wetherby? I know she's going to be a bastard's godmother and that's terrible but it's not as terrible, as being a self-satisfied, judgemental cow like you or a spiteful, vindictive bitch like your daughter, now, is it?'

Mrs Wetherby turned crimson, as did Alice. Both quickly turned. away. 'Bye-bye,' she called after them. 'See you soon. Missing you already.'

Charlotte let out a shriek. 'Susie!'

'Oh, Susie what?' She rolled her eyes. 'They asked for it.'

'And you certainly gave it to them.' Charlotte began to laugh. 'Pity there weren't any cowpats lying around you could have thrown Alice into.'

'It *is* a pity. I think I'll buy a pet cow so in future I'll always have some to hand.' She saw Alice looking back and gave a mooing sound. Once again Alice hurriedly looked away.

Charlotte took her arm. 'Can I tell you something?'

'What?'

'I've missed this Susie Ramsey. You don't know how much. I hope she doesn't go away again.'

'Not a chance. She's back and she's going to stay.'

Charlotte kissed her cheek. 'Good.'

Colin was striding towards them. 'Sorry,' he told Susan. 'I had to pay for our drinks.'

'Don't apologize. If the offer's still open I'd love to come to the pictures and to hear your friend's group.'

He looked delighted. As did Charlotte. 'Come back to my house. I can give you your present.'

'I can't now. I need to see my mother. There are things we need to talk about. But I'll see you both later.'

'Definitely.'

As she made her way home she remembered Charles's words when he had told her that she had to go on fighting.

You're strong, Susie. Every bit as strong as your father once told you, and a bit more besides.

She hadn't believed him then but she believed him now. She had strength. She had brains and looks. She had friends like Charles and Charlotte and she had Jenjen. She had everything she needed to make a good and happy life for herself and her child, and no one on earth was going to stop her doing it. If she had to go on fighting, then so be it. She was not afraid of what the future might hold. She would accept whatever battles came her way.

And she would win.